The $how

Lawrence H. Sola

BLACK ROSE
writing™

First printing

This is a work of fiction. Names, characters, businesses, places, events and incidents are either the products of the author's imagination or used in a fictitious manner. Any resemblance to actual persons, living or dead, or actual events is purely coincidental.

ISBN: 978-1-61296-669-4

PUBLISHED BY BLACK ROSE WRITING

www.blackrosewriting.com

Printed in the United States of America

Suggested retail price $19.95

The *$how* is printed in Palatino Linotype

To those of you who believe:
the second star to the right,
shines in the night for you,
to tell you that the dreams you have,
really can come true.

Author's Note

Early in my sales career, I became a firm believer that spiritual connections should be celebrated. Appealing to a person's heart over their brain was something that just became a way of life for me. From my first sales job I realized that human beings are drawn to emotion, which is rarely logical. I also quickly learned that consumers gravitate toward things that make them *feel good* and therefore are perceived to hold a higher value. The excitement derived from impulsive purchases overrides any feeling of regret when the consumer realizes the intangible benefits are not cost-justified. How, you ask? Well, think about it; what you're really buying is the spontaneous splendor, the "high" of the moment, if you will. This is very tangible and often extraordinary, therefore, giving it a perceived value that outweighs the actual value. The justification is simple: life is too short to pass up on those rare occasions of explicit emotion.

As a salesman I was extremely successful selling emotion. It's who I was. (Okay, it's who I am) It's what I do. I rarely, (and by that I mean *never*) sold logic. I'll confess now that this came naturally to me from my first sales gig. I don't believe in born salesmen, but I do believe that there are certain individuals who are born with a gift to produce extraordinary reactions to ordinary products and services from others, which enhance the sales process.

These people are able to showcase a rare but perceived value in whatever it is they are selling because they are selling themselves first. The reason I was so successful was not because of the company or the product I offered. I was successful because of the instant connections I made: selling myself first. Some who witnessed this extraordinary showcase of perceived value had a different explanation for it: sorcery. Seriously? That's just silly foolishness. A sale starts with that perceived value gaining a tangible foothold in your customer when you sell yourself first.

Interestingly, this rare human interaction heightens during the 'close of the sale' and became a constant necessity for me. This adrenaline rush provided such drive and focus, it laid the foundation of my career with endless potential and...well, let me just say it, for better and for worse.

The final result of this was the provocative tale of a promising career climb. Amidst an imaginary backdrop—finally culminating with a connection that encompassed such dark devotion—it was ultimately used to set-up my own destructive demise.

I am grateful to those of you who choose to read on.

This narrative is best enjoyed with a delightful glass of your favorite wine, with the bottle nearby.

PROLOGUE

THE DARKEST HOUR

DECEMBER 8, 2010

I frantically backed out of my parking space, raced through the security gate and onto the wrong side of the road. I was speeding away from the office that I had renamed *The Asylum*. The fatal blow? The company, who had promoted me four times in five years, had dealt me the big one, leaving me distraught and reeling. My wife's attempt to calm me was futile. The words from the twisted termination report— *"Lying about an affair"* – *"Not signing a relationship waiver"* — caused me to lash out furiously.

"What are you talking about?" she cried out. "Just come home."

"Three months of a bullshit investigation to end with this insanity?"

"Larry, enough," she pleaded. "Please calm down."

"I was warned." I rubbed the headache across my eyes. "Part of this is my pay. The other part—"

"Please stop and focus on the road!"

I ignored her. "The lies, corruption, and debauchery that goes on in this place, and they set me up for this?"

"You were just promoted again."

"And that was the other part," I said in a distressed tone. "I was warned. How could I not tell you? I'm so sorry—"

I couldn't utter another word. A knot had formed in my throat. I gasped for air and tossed the company BlackBerry on the passenger seat. A horn blared as I cut back into my lane nearly clipping a truck. I slammed my fist against the dashboard. My heart pounded. My shirt was drenched through with sweat.

My charmed life had abruptly expired. The fantasy crashed and burned. All of the promotions, the relocation, and one of those super-fucking-bright-future labels had turned to ash when the executive responsible for it all had moved on. I should've heeded the warnings about *The Wizard*.

I drifted into the other lane, again swerving back when a blaring horn caught my attention. I certainly was no angel, but this was very wrong. The fact that I had allowed myself to be taken out by these few individuals made me nauseated. Wiping tears from my cheeks, I realized it was more than my ego-driven impulses that had left me destitute. It was my feelings for "the girl." My thoughts turned darker.

They knew I would be consumed with saving my marriage. They were also very aware that she was getting married and would run and hide. It was a perfect setup. I was blamed for everything, including a guilty charge for the current state of her heart, which amazingly excluded her after one interview from all future proceedings. Apparently, it doesn't take two to tango when sorcery is involved. I was crucified for wielding my powers recklessly. This faux pas was only tossed on the pile of the other connections I had made over my career as if it was no different. But it was.

I struggled to breathe with cogitation of the girl.

I called her as I pulled off the exit ramp headed to the dream home I had just moved into with my family. Fury overrode any rational thoughts. I had a strong urge to drive back to *The Asylum* and stick someone's head through a wall. My BlackBerry dialed her number. I pulled it up to my ear and it slipped out of my hand. I wanted to throw the stupid thing out the window. I wanted to drive into a tree, but I did neither.

She nervously answered, "Hey—"

"They fired me."

"W-h-a-t?"

A tear rolled down my face. "I was fired for lying about having an affair with you."

She was speechless.

"I have to go."

"Larry, w-a-i-t—"

Click.

Driving through the gate of my Tampa neighborhood, I fought to regain my composure. If my life, up to this point, had had even a few speed bumps, I would have been better prepared for this. It hadn't. And I was not at all prepared. Reflection on my family's pain tore through me. I had taken so much for granted.

I treaded through the garage door into a dead calm. How

appropriate. I entered the kitchen and then had to look into my kid's teary eyes. I crumbled. My wife, at this point, was strong only because I was not. I reassured them everything would be okay; at least I tried to. I collapsed as the room seemingly spun, and wiped away my tears. With a deep breath, I leaned back in the chair. I scanned the room until my gaze met my wife's. My heart sank. This was just the beginning. I wanted to explain everything. I just didn't have an inkling of where to begin. She had warned me we were too close. Everyone had. But I kept racing along as if normal rules didn't apply to me. In my mind, for so long, they hadn't.

I wanted to just rip the scab off, but what if it wouldn't stop bleeding? It was unexplainable. I thought I had control. I didn't. My sacred Never Land turned dark.

CHAPTER ONE

LEFT FOR DEAD

TAMPA
JANUARY 2011

The reality that Florida is an "at will" state means you can be terminated for anything, at any time.

I was edgy and restless awaiting another recruiter call. The sun filtered through the majestic oaks as I jogged beneath their shade headed back into our desirable Tampa community. I stretched out before stepping in the house. With an eye on the clock and tension shooting up my back, I turned on ESPN to watch the highlights of Auburn beating Oregon in the BCS National Championship game. In an attempt to ease the anxiety, I blended a berry smoothie. It helped. And then I began reading an email from a paralegal, which provided a ray of hope.

After a lengthy review of my career, the law firm concluded the final termination report was a deliberate defamation of character, aimed at eliminating an inflated pay package after a state restructure. In summation, they were now eager to continue questioning me about it.

My optimism was short lived though. Before I even responded to the email I glanced back at the clock. The time for my scheduled call had passed and I panicked. It quickly became apparent that the news I feared would become my reality as thoughts of the prodigious position from the week before mysteriously disappearing, suddenly assaulted me.

Fretting about this was only deepening my distress so I

impetuously reached for my phone when it rang. I swallowed hard when I saw it was the recruiter and answered apprehensively. "Hello? This is Larry."

An awkward silence was broken by an exhale. "Hello, Larry? It's Tom. I'm sorry for the delay, but I wanted to speak with a trusted colleague before I called you."

His solemn voice caused me to collapse into my chair as my waning self-esteem crashed to the floor.

"Larry, everyone I've spoken to has confirmed that you have talent," he paused took a breath and added, "But realistically, you'll need to look outside of Florida for opportunities."

His words tore through me confirming my worst fear. My eye began twitching. I was at a loss for words.

"That's all I can say. I'm sorry." He sighed deeply. "And please watch who you trust."

This despicable act of blocking someone who was terminated from future employment within the wine and spirits industry was an unwritten rule amongst this organization, but one I never dreamed would affect me. My nauseated reality covered me like tar. I sat numb squeaking out questions he couldn't answer. He only wanted to end the call while again emphasizing how I watch who I trust. I thanked him and he hung up without even faking a follow-up. I spiraled deeper into this depressed state that was draining me.

I gazed out into the preserve behind our home. Bright sunshine cloaked the sawgrass and palm trees taunting me with its unaffected beauty, while my life turned to chaos. I wandered into the family room passing a stack of bills. I curled up on the couch, cold and tense, yet without feeling.

The monetary commitments to our excessive lifestyle only added to the misery. I felt paralyzed. I fell asleep for hours only waking up comatose to a call from "the girl"—Wendy Darlington; the leading lady in this titillating tale and the individual the company used to bury me. She was someone, at this point of the story that most assumed I was no longer in touch with.

The truth was that we were still intensely and deeply connected. In fact, we spoke often. Her name flashed on the screen. Lethargically, I answered, "Hey."

"Hey…what's wrong?"

I allowed her to rethink her choice of words hurrying for fresh air.

"What happened?" She hesitated, but then quickly added anxiously, "With the recruiter?"

I made it outside and took a deep breath. "My career is over." She was speechless so I continued. "He told me to look into other states…and to watch who I trust."

"How can they do this? How can a company ruin someone's career?"

"Wendy it's gone on in The Asylum forever."

She sighed, before pleading, "You can't give up, and there will be something."

I didn't respond. Thoughts invaded my mind still festering from our last conversation.

After a brief pause she changed the subject. "When anyone from the company calls you do you ever tell them we still talk?"

I rubbed my eyes furiously. It didn't help; I began pacing. "No. Wendy, I listen to people tell me you've disappeared since my termination blotting my bloody tongue as they ramble on clueless."

She sighed. "You don't have to be rude. I hate being there without you and you know that." Her tone suddenly changed. "S-h-i-t." Now flustered, she said, "Jessie's calling."

"You should take your fiancé's call."

She didn't. She took a deep breath. "Are you going to come to our wedding?"

I collapsed in a patio chair speechless staring above the tree line of the preserve.

She sputtered, "Marie wonders how I'm still getting married, doesn't she?"

My wife couldn't care less, actually, but I didn't tell that to Wendy. The clouds seemed to be suddenly moving in slow motion. I felt anxious and sad and then angry. "How can you even ask that after all of this?"

She sat quiet.

My eyes swept the preserve discomforted with how I was changing. I took a deep breath. "I'm sorry,' I said feeling indignant. "I have too much shit in my head, too many conversations with you…too many glances into my wife's eyes… I should go." My eyes were now blinking, dazed like the eyes of a newborn. I sat vulnerable.

She interrupted my internal chastisement and spoke just above a whisper. "You know very well what you mean to me."

Tears welled in my eyes. I couldn't speak. I began to tremble.

"I really hate this," she continued full of emotion. "And I'm sorry."

I took my own deep breath while mustering all the strength I had to end the call. "I know. So am I. I have to go."

Click.

It felt like needles were stuck in my back as the stress shot up it. I pushed up to head inside, but I stood there for a moment in a cold sweat before walking to the bathroom sink to splash cold water on my face. Leaning on the edge of the sink, tears mixed with water dripped from my chin. I lifted my eyes, ashamed to stare into the ones reflecting back at me. "You had it all," I cried out. "How could you have thrown it all away? You idiot!"

I wandered back in the family room doubting everything. The guilt bound me there amidst the ashes of my wrecked life clouding my judgment. I loathed the pain I caused my wife while sighing in resignation running from the fact that the severe discord in our marriage played heavily into all of this for too long. I was on an emotional rollercoaster. I wandered around the room thoroughly exasperated until the air conditioner kicked on infuriating me. "It's sixty-eight degrees outside. Open a fucking window." I barked into the empty house glancing at the exorbitant electric bill. Maddening thoughts cut into me. I sat down beating back the resentment bubbling up inside me as the dire message from a marriage counselor ten years before resonated in my head. Her analysis was nothing my wife Marie agreed with, although I thought she was dead on.

I was in quicksand.

I rubbed my bloodshot eyes redder.

Numb, I stared out the window suddenly having a skeptical deliberation that my feelings for Wendy caused painful debate. It was as if I was sinking fast, now up to my neck.

Certain conversations with her early on now confounded me. The many 'what if's' that I began questioning were now consuming me as the warnings of the dangers of this unique affinity burning out of control for too long now haunted me.

Those who had witnessed any part of it were amazed on so many levels that they could only shake their head, while whispering that we'd be better off if it was a typical "sexual" office fling. Disquieting to digest, I realized, but much more easily explained, and more importantly, easier to end.

But it certainly wasn't that.

Was I only pretending these unexplainable connections outside of my marriage were all part of the sales game? And if that were the case, and I did push it all searching for something that I thought my marriage was lacking, was I only kidding myself that after a career of selling play dates—Peter Pan playing with his Mermaids—that I wouldn't eventually meet my Wendy?

It was like a demented child's fable. One I couldn't escape. Aside from the information in the termination report constantly being thrown at me, I had to deal with hours of questioning this law firm's paralegal requested while then attempting to explain another two-hour conversation with Wendy on my new iPhone because the company had finally turned off my BlackBerry.

It became a schitzy slapstick comedy as my wife monitored my actions as if I was her third child. I began laughing deliriously, desperately in need of solace. My eyes rolled to pictures of our two beautiful children, Lauren and Jerry, before landing on a faded picture of Marie. I hoped for a spark, something deep inside me to ignite, actually anything.

I picked up the photograph.

Ironically, it was when Marie and I first met, so I reminisced full of penitence. The clear vision of when our eyes met in a bar was so obvious that her boyfriend's buddy leaned into me, while pointing to him. "That's her boyfriend…and she loves him."

Of course that really didn't matter to me because I had just stared into her soul and drew a very different conclusion.

The eyes never lie.

I exhaled thinking about it all, how I asked her on a date during a little downtime in their relationship…and the fact that she politely declined and hung up. No small talk with this one. *Click* and a dial tone.

As the annoying sound cut through my ear, I hung up and fell on my bed with a lifeless thud, completely dazed, as Chris Isaak's 'Wicked Games' video flashed up on MTV. My eyes grew wide. I became fixated on the black and white masterpiece. The haunting lyrics vibrated out of the small television speaker as I began to pout. I often did that when things didn't go my way. But then, to make matters worse, my roommates wandered in grinning mischievously. They couldn't wait to inform me that Marie just said yes to dinner with a banker. And before my eyes stopped rolling in my head they were gone.

I was left there, destitute, sprawled out on my lumpy mattress singing the words to the song:

What a wicked thing to do,
to make me dream of you.

It was at that point that my roommates screamed in unison, "Turn that shit down and get ready!"

But I couldn't. I found it necessary to console myself, so I sang on, "The world is on fire and no one can save me but you!"

Within minutes I heard banging on the wall along with hysterics. "Get in the car, we're leaving!" they shouted.

I had a clear understanding of the things desire can make foolish people do. I was consumed by her...and her cheeks. I realize that sounds a bit disturbing, but I promised to be completely truthful with this tale. And if you're wondering, that detail is important, along with the fact my buddies thought she played my sick ass perfectly, so much so, they couldn't stop laughing.

With the night rolling on, we ended up at Finnegan's, our favorite bar. I must confess though, I was sulking, full of enchantment, for a girl who I really didn't know, now hindered by the fact she was on a date...with a banker.

As time passed though, strange things began to happen. First, I noticed her best friend glancing over at me while I stewed, grinning uncontrollably. That was strange. She seemed to be making fun of a little boy who didn't get his way. Oh wait, that's exactly who I was: Peter Pan, pouting in a corner just waiting for someone to end his madness. And it was always "madness" if something didn't go my way.

I couldn't take it anymore. My buddy wore a sinister grin as he glanced over my shoulder. "Will you look at Marie's face?" he exclaimed. "And that poor bastard just bought her dinner."

I turned.

She was beaming; pushing her way through the crowd coming right at me. The eyes never lie; hers were sparkling. And with a clear visual of her staring at me with the greatest smile I'd ever seen...the garage door in my present day reality abruptly swung open.

It was Marie and the kids coming back from school.

"What's that smirk for?" she snapped bitingly.

"Nothing," I answered, abruptly crash landing back in the here and now.

I fell right back into the depressed state that held me captive. I couldn't move as her eyes burned into me while she walked into the kitchen. "When is your meeting with the lawyer?"

"Next Tuesday," I muttered apathetically.

"You need to get out of the house. Do you want to go to dinner? Something inexpensive?" I nodded appreciatively; however, the sound of a text hitting my new iPhone caused her to change her tune. She opened the patio door. "Never mind."

Pain vibrated in her voice.

She knew it was Wendy.

The door slammed shut as rage radiated in her eyes.

I slowly pushed myself up and made my way outside to talk to her, to thank her for her suggestion, but the conversation quickly veered off in another problematic direction. This time it was as if we were speaking two different languages without an interpolator. As I blinked at her furiously, the sensation that I was rapidly losing my equilibrium overwhelmed me. I broke free of it all and went to grab my 401k statement. By the time I made it back she was engrossed in another venting conversation with something I loathed, a lit cigarette.

I turned and walked away.

CHAPTER TWO

A MERMAID AND MR. WEINSTEIN

LEGAL OPTIONS
FEBRUARY 1, 2011

That following Monday, with my energy and creativity noticeably waning, I painstakingly muddled through the monotonous resume uploads to nowhere with one appointment on my calendar. Tuesday February 1st, 2011, glimmered beneath a yellow streak of highlighter, the date I had a scheduled meeting with a law firm eager to go over the options of my perplexing predicament.

With little sleep Monday night, I woke up Tuesday morning groggy, feeling embittered. My thoughts were consumed with the fast approaching two-month anniversary of my company execution: ultimately the death of my stellar career. I was desperate to relax my mind, free it from the panicked state that was draining me. I was also getting ready to head to the law firm and wanted to clear my mind for this meeting. As I put my coffee down, I could barely recall what it was like to experience a favorable outcome, something I used to expect. Stress again shot up my back as I noticed Marie putting a cigarette out and coming in from the patio.

"It's a little early for that, isn't it?" I said with a gesture to the lingering cigarette smoke she brought into the house.

She ignored me, tossing our iPhone bill on the kitchen counter, and pounced with sarcasm. "You keep telling me yours and Wendy's asinine amount of time on the phone is to see exactly how she can help us with the lawyer. I personally think it's just your latest excuse to continue something neither one of you can stop." She took a sip of coffee as my hand slowly reached for the folder I needed, ignoring the fact she was right.

She turned back to me now concerned I was contemplating jumping. "Think positive." she said. "That was your motto...remember?"

I nodded, swallowed hard, and walked out.

Upon my arrival, I checked in and sat in a lineup of misery, which worsened my bleak outlook. Anguish settled over me. I noticed I was changing.

That said, I have always been open to and have received signs throughout my life that have given me hope when I'd thought there was none. And just like that I noticed a lady down and across from me smiling as she nodded to my left.

I turned and there she was: the cutest little girl, with big cheeks and curly blond hair. She was just staring at me, smiling, while gripping a magazine with her tiny hands. Her big blue eyes instantly energized my darkened spirit as she walked up and placed the magazine on my lap. I melted. Then, after thanking her, she came back with another one lunging into me and pushing the magazine up to my chest, laughing. She was adorable.

Her mother who just couldn't get over her actions moved to the vacated seat across from me. "She's never done anything like this before."

The irritated guy next to me changed seats after my little princess kept nailing him with her foot as she was now trying to climb up on my knee.

Since her mother was somehow giddy to this little encounter, while now, amazingly, holding up her phone for a picture, I thought it best that I help her up on my lap.

"I have to take a picture," the mother gushed. "Emily, turn and smile."

Emily placed her adorable head against my chest. As her mother took the picture, my long lost smile crept back across my face. I needed that, especially as I then heard my name called. I turned to the open door to the law offices.

"Mr. Sola?" Susan, the paralegal was calling me in. As I got up, she was staring at Emily, smiling oddly. As if I didn't have enough problems. "Right this way, please."

After saying goodbye, I realized I could not allow this situation to destroy me.

Susan led me down a long hall to an open door.

During her introductions the lead attorney, Allan Weinstein, Esq., was on the phone. He had an unsettling look of intrigue, which incredibly, didn't affect me in the least. After that maladroit moment, the burly austere man pointed to an oversized chair where I quickly sat. Continuing to gawk at me he finally hung up his phone. He must have been checking his voicemail because he never said a word.

Glancing at the page Susan pointed to, he pushed a long wisp of white hair off his domed forehead and slammed the paper down with his chubby hand, scaring the shit out of me. "You were a top performer right to the end!"

I felt like a little boy who had wandered into the wrong class on the first day of school. And to make matters worse, his short stubby hands were now freaking me out. It was as if he had a difficult time placing them down as he slammed another page to the desk. I became fixated on the way his little stubs shuffled the pages as I sank further in his big chair.

"Your old boss is praising you in these emails." He held one up before adding, "And this executive went on record warning you not to talk to or trust anyone in this office." He sat erect in his chair rereading the email in disbelief as I nodded.

He squinted to read the top of the page. "This email was sent to you after you were terminated and he's admitting these people are not trustworthy," he snapped, smirking devilishly.

"Yes."

He grabbed a pen and wrote feverishly on a pad. "I'm sorry, this is...good. I'm just shocked a general manager sent this." He continued to take notes while reading, until he said, "This is very good." Then he confirmed a sizable investment the company had made in order to move me to Tampa in the summer of 2009. He held up the company's relocation paperwork and looked up. "This was less than two years ago?"

"Correct." I watched him grab another page with an inquisitive eye.

"So you were one of those chosen for the bright future?" He seemed like he was on to something as I confirmed there was a bigger plan for me than the director's position. "And you didn't think that by itself could present a problem?" He flashed a mocking smile.

"The executive whose email you just read moved on. He runs another division for the state out of the Miami office. He had the vision for my future and was responsible for my relocation and the corporate apartment. Basically everything."

Mr. Weinstein's eyes grew wide. "Well, now that's interesting." He studied each promotion letter, holding his head, breathing heavily. "And you were promoted four times in the last five years with the last promotion just five months prior to you being terminated...shortly after this same executive...Geno Franc moved on?" He spread the promotion letters out in disbelief to double check the dates, anxious for my answer.

I shrug. "Yes."

"That's unheard of. Did you think that was normal?"

I adjusted in the big chair and babbled, "Yes...no, not normal, but yes...my track record for motivating sales teams over the years was rare."

He nodded, and as the reality of my situation came into focus he read on with sneering sarcasm. "And you really didn't think that you would become someone's target?"

"I never thought that way. That was my mistake. I worked hard for that position."

"And you clearly played hard too. Then your rapid career advancement made someone nervous." He reached for the next folder.

"Apparently."

"And besides your excessive partying, you also continued your close relations with your manager. Susan is bringing me that folder, although it appears to be our problem."

"How do you mean?"

His head rose slowly and his eyes narrowed at me eerily before he continued reading.

At this point, the little voice inside my head mentioned it would be wise to conserve my energy and just nod. Within the minute, he shook his head gravely before glancing over at me. "You have to understand my concern." I nodded but honestly wasn't exactly sure what he was referring too until he added, "This relationship with your manager, Wendy Darlington, is…rather incredible." He tossed the pages on his desk and swiftly got up to grab a folder from his secretary's office. "Catlin, did Susan leave notes on the first folder?"

Catlin was his secretary. I glanced over at her and our eyes connected briefly before she handed the folder to him and peered my way once more. Mr. Weinstein was too preoccupied to notice. In fact, he hit the folder against his hand coming back in. "I'll be honest," he said, "I've never seen anything like this. This is the good, the bad, and the really ugly!" He opened the folder. "How can all three of these people report you had trouble getting Miss Darlington's bra off?" he took a deep breath and snorted, "Did something like that come up in story time?"

"No. But many rumors were spread."

"And many truths…" He paused, grabbed another page, and added, "But it seems as if these same three individuals compared notes throughout all of this."

"Because two of them did."

He reached for his glass of water in silence rereading the original complaint. "Was another complaint filed?"

"No. As I mentioned, the investigator moved away from the original complaint quickly while shifting the focus to Wendy Darlington."

"Did this investigator explain the fact that this manager tied this complaint to a night out that happened three months prior, that wasn't a company event and had no incident reported?"

"No."

"And you didn't know who was saying what until you were handed the final report?"

"For the most part, that is correct."

He tapped his pen on the page until he took his glasses off and rubbed his eyes. "And how was this disgruntled manager…what's his name?" He searched the page. "Bud Fox. How was he in a position to warn you to end the relationship with your manager Wendy Darlington?" Mr. Weinstein was now fully absorbed leaning in for my response.

"We were extremely close."

His jaw dropped. "You were close with the guy who filed the original complaint too?"

"Close would be an understatement—"

His hand shot up to stop me. "The original complaint is absurd...we need move to this." He reached for a page that had a heading "RELATIONSHIP QUESTIONS" at the top.

His secretary's door opened just a crack. His head again jerked up, as if thinking I had said something, but he didn't notice her. "Hold on a second, son," he said.

Referring to me as "son" at forty-three added nicely to the mysticism of it all. After what felt like too many minutes I said, "I realize this sounds crazy—"

He cut me off stupefied, and in a raised, chaffed tone bellowed, "Son, it sounds like reality TV and truthfully, I've been looking for hidden cameras ever since Susan made me run to the monitor to watch your interaction with the baby in the lobby. But I saw that with my own two eyes." A discourteous guffaw from his young secretary's office caused him to stop in mid-sentence. "Catlin?" he snapped. "Are you okay?"

After an awkward pause she cried out, "Yes, sir. I'm sorry."

Mr. Weinstein's eyes slowly closed before his hands shifted to his forehead. He lowered to study the pages in front of him, but glanced up after the soft knock on the door to the secretary's office, which now stood ajar. Susan entered to hand him a folder that had a big number three written across it. "Thanks," he uttered, and with a curt cutoff, she left, leaving the door open as her office was next to Catlin's. "Did this investigator not like you?" he asked abrasively.

"He did not," I replied, catching him off guard. "At the end of our first interview, he stated I was full of 'bravado' and that he would have no problem 'taking me out.'"

His eyes narrowed at me as he collected the pages. "I've seen a lot, but this is just amazing. Okay, so they used this to open an investigation on you and begin to dig for anything of substance, which we all feel this original complaint completely lacked." He scribbled another note on the pad before continuing. "So what we do know is that you had a very successful thirteen year career full of promotions, the relocation, and a clean company file, to this point. That is important." With a fresh smile he added, "You were not only well-liked, but also respected. Crushes aside, these will be good." He flipped back to another page. "And you had a clean driving record, while trending over seventy thousand dollars more than the other sales directors in the new restructure when...Geno Franc the executive who relocated you moved on...correct?"

"Correct."

Falling back in his chair he said softly, "Let's continue."

Aside from his sarcastic jabs, I thought everything was moving along swimmingly. But then he picked up folder number three and the lights seemed to dim. I swallowed hard as he read pages from it; his face seemed to contort. Each second felt like a minute as I watched, helpless to the look of trepidation exploding across his face.

With noticeable ambiguity he held his hand over his mouth. I wanted him to say something. But he didn't. He only read on, shaking his head gravely as his eyes blinked erratically at the content. Finally, he slammed the last page to his desk as he anguished over texts Wendy had sent me that another manager read in a bar on her birthday the year before. "How did this guy read these?" he asked softly as his hand held his head baffled.

"I'm not sure—"

"It's documented...confirmed by the company."

"I realize that...and I never denied it."

"So you knew she texted you this a year ago?" he paused, rubbed his eyes and muttered, "When did she get engaged?"

"Two months after that."

He let out a gentle laugh staring off at the wall. "Wow." With a deep breath, he shook his head and added, "Her fiancé didn't know anything about this investigation, did he?"

"Only that she was questioned."

He spun his chair without saying a word and shuffled to the last page in the folder while dialing Susan.

"I'm coming in."

Click.

He came back minutes later.

"This is our problem." He wrote a note and asked, "When did they bring up the company relationship waiver not being signed?"

"Right before they escorted me out of the building."

He placed his pen down staring in disbelief. "Never before that?"

"No."

He grabbed another page. "As Susan checks on something let me get into these emails—" He stopped in mid-sentence while reading intently. "What is this daily "Wine Time" ritual that you had with Wendy? It stated that you would secretly meet her to partake in this."

"It wasn't a secret and it was often, but not daily."

"But she attempted to hide it? It says she lied on numerous occasions to her colleagues." I stared at him in silence as he exhaled. "Listen, Larry, I'm not judging anyone here but there is sensitive subject matter that was passed forward and backed by her own words to you—"

"Mr. Weinstein, we were admittedly too close. And, yes, she never wanted them knowing she was with me, because so many people were talking."

"Larry, do you see why? I've never seen so much documented on two people? And now I see her fiancé knows nothing."

"I didn't say that."

"And you weren't going to. I've done this for a long time but this is unlike anything…"

I leaned forward in anticipation of him finishing his statement.

"She would now have to sit this guy down, right before their wedding and tell him. Larry, with due respect, there is no way she can help." He waved the folder in the air jumping up again to go into his secretary's office. I stared out his window before my eyes slowly closed. "Larry, you were done wrong by this company, but this is not your typical office affair and they knew it." He grabbed another page now seemingly talking to himself. "They knew she would never cause a problem. She couldn't." He looked up at me. "You told Susan you two still speak, which only makes this more obvious."

"How do you mean?"

"I'm sorry, that's not relevant."

I sat up in the big chair and leaned in toward him.

"When Susan reached back to me, I thought maybe there would be a way around her?"

He let out a long exhale, shaking his head. "The problem is they tied it all to her, and it will be rehashed and more." He lunged for my emails. "And there is an issue with these—" He held up my team emails. "Because of your relationship with her." He was immersed, reading on with a touch of sarcasm. "Tell me about these code names you had for the days of the week you would meet her."

"That was all just for fun."

"It's stated that you referred to them as your Never Land holidays with your princess?" He paused, peering at me again, as if I was a fucking alien. "Please do explain."

"Much of what I did was to entertain them. It was all done to build the team camaraderie. And she enjoyed that. They all did."

"And then these three spun it all against you? Oh, I found it. It's in this email with your team goals: Super Tuesday – Wine Wednesday – Thirsty Thursday – and Fun Friday and your admin states that it was all tied to Wendy in this world of make-believe."

"My team worked very hard and I always felt strongly that a little nonsense went a long way to relieve that stress."

His eyes narrowed at me before bellowing, "So did Dr. Seuss, but he wasn't a sales director over two of the largest cities in the state for one of the most powerful wine and spirit distributors in the nation." His eyes suddenly began to twitch again. "You certainly pushed your team's buttons; this is brilliant. A motivator you are, but dangerous it is, and easily spun. You continually take unhealthy risks email after email." He flipped another page, engrossed. "This could almost be considered self-destructive."

I fidgeted in the big chair.

"How about these references to Mermaids, are they code for something?"

A guffaw echoed out of his secretary's office as I witnessed her duck below her desk.

"Catlin," Mr. Weinstein snapped. "Why is your door open? Please, close it."

An eerie silence settled over us like a diseased blanket as the young secretary, Catlin, slowly sat back with her hands over her face.

"This is beginning to seduce me," he confessed in a soft inquisitive tone. "Is this in reference to Peter Pan's Never Land?" His eyebrow froze in that raised position as he waited for my incredulous answer.

"Why, yes," I said, not to disappoint. "Is there any other Never Land?"

Catlin stood up silently clapping her hands as Mr. Weinstein's arm fell limp. With worry that I was disrespecting him, I leaned forward and said, "You can see it was all for entertainment purposes. The Never Land bit had started back when my career began, in a bar, when a girl who bought me a shot—" I stopped abruptly as his mouth dropped open in awe with his hand up.

He immediately grabbed another page. "In this email you refer to Wendy as Pepper." He frowned. "I'm scared to ask."

"You should be. Please, just move on."

It was at this point I had hopes that the ceiling fan above his head would fall on him so I could just haul ass. He took his glasses off while painfully rubbing his eyes again before reading on. I struggled to contain my composure as Catlin then held her arms out as if she were flying, completely waggish, before she feverishly hit her keyboard wearing a broad smile. She absolutely loved this. I now couldn't contain the smile spreading across my face watching her eyes display that light.

This was the high.

It was never about any sexual addictions or end results, but the wondrous world of these spiritual connections, which infused my career rise, while fueling its demise. Mr. Weinstein was correct. The irony of it all came into sharp focus causing me to fade in the big chair, until my eyes caught Catlin holding up a picture, hot off her printer, of Peter Pan and Wendy flying off to Never Land. I did a double take.

That pretty much summed it all up.

I struggled to contain my composure and the expression on her face made it all worse. She seemed suddenly even younger, while beaming brightly.

Mr. Weinstein flipped to another email and blurted out, "Your imagination is as hypnotizing as your ego, Mr. Sola. And every one of these emails has your administrative assistant, who I see you renamed Mama Bear, thoroughly engaged."

I sat there suddenly wondering if Mr. Weinstein's fascination for my emails was now due to the fact that he thought I was borderline certifiable, while stalling for the proper authorities to come and take me away. But that concern quickly faded as my eyes were drawn back into Catlin's office as the imaginary pixie dust, I'd grown accustomed to, flew around her gleeful grin.

I was captivated…until he recaptured my attention. "Larry?"

"I'm sorry." I twisted my body back to him as he received the call from Susan he'd been waiting for. It was literally seconds. He then only exhaled and hung up. "Larry, the truth is that this woman is linked to you in ways that neither of you could have explained. This rare experience that you create is what they've used to bury you. It's clear to me that you've been playing by a different set of rules for a long time." He paused for effect. "And by playing by your own set of rules, you allowed your relationship with this young lady to ultimately become your demise. That is the ugly reality of this."

I felt sad yet deliriously energized as my new Mermaid entered. Maybe this was a self-destructive period of my life, but this couldn't have been scripted better, and that's all that I thought. It was fucking incredible. He intently followed her, as she walked over to me with a glass of water, one that no one asked for.

She leaned in and whispered, "I have to tell you that I would've loved working for you too. And your shit show would make an amazing book. If anyone can pull it off, it's you." She gently squeezed my arm. "Good luck, Larry."

I thanked her, thinking she smelled delightful, while noticing Mr. Weinstein had that odd smirk raked across his face again. And as she closed the door, he let out a chuckle before his demeanor changed. He sat back down with a look of an "off the record" plea shooting across his forehead, probably to make sure I didn't blow my head off in his parking lot. "Larry, I'll be very blunt. I believe there is a reason that this has happened. It might be impossible to see now, but please don't lose sight of that for the big picture. I do believe this company can destroy lives. I just don't believe they can destroy yours. Understand?"

"Yes. Thank you, Mr. Weinstein." Suddenly, I was met with a recurring vision of a book cover. It had red curtains opened to a stage where a table sat with two chairs, two wine glasses. In the background, pixie dust bathed the scene in magic with the second star to the right shining bright.

***

The knot that had tightened around me was seemingly intractable. I collapsed in my car and couldn't move. After reading a text from Wendy I placed my iPhone in the cup holder and opened my window for fresh air. I then noticed my new Mermaid come out in a Green Bay Packers jersey. She was being picked up by a big guy in a pickup truck. She waved over at me, excitedly took a step forward, and yelled, "Larry, I get it...and I believe! And the reason I know you can pull it off is because Susan let me read your emails. I loved them!"

Emotion overwhelmed me. I waved as she hopped in the truck. A tear traced down my face and into my smile. They drove right by and she lowered her window. She had the enthusiasm of a little girl as she feverishly threw her arms out, smiling wide.

Softly, I said, "Second star to the right and straight on til morning."

CHAPTER THREE

A FATHERLY CONCERN RESONATES

FEBRUARY 2011
DRIVEWAY INTROSPECTION

On the ride home my eye began twitching uncontrollably. I had just begun experiencing this and I couldn't escape the discomfort as I struggled to read a text from a friend. He informed me he liked the Packers over the Steelers in the upcoming Super Bowl while wanting to meet up for drinks. Right after I read it I dropped the iPhone to rub my eye.

Desperate dark thoughts raced through my head. My chest hurt. My eye twitched rapidly again as the leading edge of anger snapped out. "How the fuck could I allow this to happen?" I was deep breathing to calm myself. And then my iPhone rang. I lunged for it as it sat in the cup holder. All my actions were exaggerated, almost uncontrollable. Holding it up I noticed it was Wendy. I hadn't replied to her text.

This lawsuit scenario was her worst nightmare and one that had her on edge, although—at least for her—the end result of today's meeting would provide her relief. Her thoughts exactly mirrored what Mr. Weinstein had stated; there was just no way to rehash this relationship and have her still get married. My impetuous thought process, as stated, was that maybe there was a way around her. Only now did I see the absurdity. That said, she had no idea how much of this I kept from her because of her upcoming wedding. The truth was that she had little idea how brutally detailed any of this was while admitting to blocking it out.

That wasn't the case for Marie. She wanted to know everything.

With each passing day, the painful details of this salty saga became increasingly intolerable as it continued to put emotional bullet holes in our walls.

Earlier that week, with emotions running too high, she hopped in our bed with drawn battle lines and threatened me that she was going to take the final report to Wendy's fiancé, Jessie. This was more of a dig at me than an actual action plan by her, although she couldn't believe it was humanly possible for anyone to block out as much as he did.

The next day it flared up again out on the patio as all explanations unavoidably circled back to the obvious, after I deliriously said, "You know I love you...and Wendy does Jessie—"

Marie's eyes popped forward so far in her head I thought I was going to have to chase them down, as they rolled off the patio and into the grass. "Only you two could utter those words while your actions continually scream otherwise. You and your female equivalent should work on your actions before you open your mouths again because nothing has changed. That new phone bill has her number looking like a fucking typo."

I took another wrong turn while wondering how the hell I was going to explain why I couldn't move forward legally. I was fully aware any wrong words would've had Marie literally running me over in the driveway as I went to stop her from driving to their house....with a loaded gun.

Twenty minutes later, I finally made it home. I pulled back into our driveway (the one I just had visions of being run over in) weary and overcome. I fought the depression, anger, and this reflective state, which for some reason, insisted to haunt me. They were messages that professedly scared the shit out of me from the beginning of my career. And it was this introspective period I was running from that finally knocked the wind out of me right there in my driveway. I felt paralyzed, captive to a twenty-year-old message from my father, Jerry.

It all began when I shared the stories of my first sales job selling the housewives of New York moving and storage services. At first, the entertaining sales tales would ease the pain during his fight with colon cancer, one he lost in March of 1991. He would become so amused by them, his laughter would bellow throughout our comforting East Williston, Long Island home.

As time went on though, that changed. He couldn't continue to pass my unopened sales books, while ignoring the disturbing pattern to my inconceivable success. I could see it in his eyes. He knew this was pushing me far from the real world, a mindset that would entice me to believe that I was the exception to long standing rules. And worse, he knew the longer I played there, successfully, the less chance there would be that I'd ever even think about booking a return flight back.

This aberration was best summed up by one of the young and outspoken secretaries at the moving company. It was shortly after the company hired another "old school" sales manager who just refused to understand my triumphant start. Our friction escalated rapidly. And the fact that I found his sales trainings outdated and irrelevant didn't help. But it was right after he received a call from another confused husband that sent him over the edge.

"Larry, you tell me how someone signs a contract with us but knows nothing about our moving service."

But he wasn't done. He started into this rambling tirade about my hair growing beyond my collar and stubble on my face and not wearing suits and on and on, until I noticed his beady little eyes bulging out of his head, just as my Mermaid's—I mean our secretary's—finger came slicing through the air like a switchblade over my shoulder.

"Hey," her sassiness shouted. "His appearance is a big reason he's so successful. It's called *fuckability*, so thank your lucky stars he's here and lighten up!"

She was a badass.

And I was recruited to sell solely based on the female follies the company owner had witnessed me partake in. This sounds insane because it was. I was his son's longtime friend and roommate during our freshman year of college, and as the story goes, he became so enamored with these hijinks he would continue to visit me after his son transferred to another school. He simply loved life...and these girlie antics.

It was back in November of 1987 when we were at a bar with his friend. They intently watched me play my egg crack game, (I'll explain this later) with one girl, while playing my "eyelash" game, (I'll explain this one later too) with her best friend. His wheels were spinning, but it was a chance meeting in New York City over our spring break when he became convinced I could be an asset selling corporate executives wives' his company's moving services.

This was paramount because this lady was ten years older than the typical twenty-year-olds I was playing with back at college and closer to who I would be selling in his position. We were walking back from lunch during a Citibank move when he noticed an attractive well-dressed woman waving like a teenager from across the street. Full of intrigue, he grabbed my arm. I turned. It was one of my older Mermaids darting between cabs, with that whimsical look in her eyes, one that I had become addicted to.

I had hit it off with her during an open casting call that was ironically held at a hotel I was asked to check out for his son's birthday party back in the summer of 1985. I was never a model, but did, even at twenty one, possess a strange teen-idol type look that she fancied, one which she thought was worthy of a few auditions. But that was a few years back.

"Oh my God, Larry, I thought it was you." She skipped onto the sidewalk. "You look great. You're really growing up. We have to take some new pictures. I'll call Leonard for the shoot."

The owner of the company stood there clueless as to what she was even talking about. But as she gleefully rambled on, his fascination piqued. That's when he leaned in to introduce himself. "It's nice to meet you, dear. I'm Charlie and the Prince is like a second son to me. We're heading back to finish the Citibank move."

She appeared to have a difficult time believing I was actually moving furniture as she let out this guffaw, while putting her hair up in a ponytail. (I love ponytails.) "The Prince is such a perfect nickname for Larry. Hi, I'm Theresa. It's nice to meet you, Charlie, and I'm sure Larry is supervising your job in style." She shook his hand while bringing up two more auditions she knew I would blow off before reprimanding me about the one I actually showed up to, landed, and then blew off.

Just then my iPhone rang, thankfully shaking me out of this disquieting introspective. Realizing it was Marie, I hesitated. I hadn't even opened our garage door. I had been sitting in our driveway rehashing all of this. "Hey, I'll explain the lawyer's meeting at dinner."

I could tell her wheels were spinning and thankfully heard Lauren and Jerry in the background. She said, "Hold on Jerry. Larry, take a shower. We'll be home soon."

Click.

I wanted to call my mother.

I exhaled and jumped out, walked through the garage, and Wendy called again. "Hey." I hit the alarm on my car.

"You're not going to believe who I ran into today."

Wendy often opened our conversations with nonsense to make sure I was alone. But on this day, I had no patience for it. "You realize I just got home from the lawyer," I said. "Let me call you back."

"Will you stop? I know, so you're alone?" she said with apprehension adding, "You sound down."

"I sound down?" I murmured. "I guess you could say that. I mean, how would you feel if you spent the day with a lawyer who now thinks you're an alien, with no end to this nightmare in sight?"

"Larry, I told you that would be impossible," she cried out. "What were you thinking? I told you." I was now furious listening to her rant while staring at a new stack of bills that Marie opened from both houses and time shares with a post-it-note: "We still need $8,350!"

My eyes squeezed shut fearing impending doom. I struggled to get air into my lungs. "Wendy, I am done. My life is in fucking shambles. Our savings is gone; my 401k will be by the end of the year." I took two short breaths. "I really don't know what I'm going to do." I pushed the stack of bills to the side and as she was silent I added, "And strange shit is coming back to me like this was all a test…that I failed. It actually began right before they fired me. It's too much."

Finally she softly said, "I know the feeling." Her voice sounded increasingly strained, "Not like that but I'm dreaming again during the few hours I actually sleep."

Preoccupied, opening a bottle from my wine collection, I said, "What about?" Right after those words left my mouth I wanted to reel them back in.

"You know what about and I can't deal with that this close to the wedding."

I had her on speaker frantically tearing the cork out of our favorite Napa Meritage, *Franciscan Magnifacat*. And as I marveled at the lust red hue, her voice rose, "LARRY?"

I lunged for my iPhone. "I'm sorry. I was opening one of our favorite bottles."

She exhaled deeply. "Let me guess, Magnifacat?"

"Yup." I took a sip of wine. Everything I had with her had to be buried and it had been taking its toll. With my emotions again all over the place I brought up my vision. "I'm having visions of a book cover for our shit show. It had a red curtain and a table with our two wine glasses. And our second star to the right." This was the first time I brought this up to her. It would be nearly a year before I would again.

At this point she let out a nervous laugh. "A star-crossed love story about two fools who can't stay away from each other and a fucked up company who used their amorous disposition to get rid of one of them? Great…should be a best seller." She thought I was kidding until she took a deep breath and exhaled. "Are you being serious?"

"I don't know." I had to say that because she was now scaring me. I then had to say something else because it was eerily quiet, so I said, "I've been having crazy thoughts and I'm not sleeping at all."

She quickly replied, "You need sleep."

"You're right. Anyway, I have to shower before Marie gets home."

"Okay…well, I'll call you tomorrow."

"Bye."

Click.

I took another sip, unable to shake this vision while thinking back to that euphoric juncture in my life that had me embarking on this adventure. I dozed off with fragments of my career flashing in front of me. I raced forward from the beginning, through all the warnings and achievements, until I heard Marie's voice.

"Larry...Larry?"

My eyes opened.

"The kids are washing up." Marie peered back at me. "You were dreaming. Are you okay?"

I rubbed my face. I wasn't at all, but I softly lied. "Yes."

"You look really tired...are you sure?"

I looked away. "I should probably just go to sleep."

CHAPTER FOUR

LIVING THE DREAM

AUGUST 13, 2009
DREAM STATE

I'm dreaming.

It's August 13th, 2009, the big promotion/relocation celebration! With the first bottle of Dom Perignon settling into the bucket of melting ice, I fixate on the ascent of tiny bubbles as I slowly raise the elegant champagne flute. The remarkably rich bouquet reveals itself with intense fruit as I thought life is grand! So here I am, forty-two years old, with a career as hot as the Florida sun. The feeling is surreal as I continue my climb up the corporate ladder in an industry which I adore. I am awarded my third promotion in four years along with the keys to a corporate apartment and an office in Tampa to run my new sales division. Euphoria! I am living the dream as the cork of another bottle of Dom shoots across a backyard sunset exquisite as a painting.

The news of this latest promotion, my most noteworthy to date, is exhilarating. I feel like a frat boy on spring break as I race past my beautiful wife and two adorable kids with a couple of bottles of my cellar's finest. Our grateful guests enjoy the selections as their warm expressions of achievement fill the space surrounding our fire pit entertainment area.

"Congratulations, Larry!"

"Another promotion, huh?"

"I'll have what you're drinking."

After everyone raises their glasses for a quick toast, the wine induced jubilation kicks up a few notches with Pitbull's "I Know You

Want Me" echoing through the moist tropical air. Word of this exaltation spreads, like a flame on a hillside doused with gasoline, as I take one last call although my battery's dying. "Hello?"

"Larry?" the man answers; the music drowns me out.

"Yes. I got your message. Can you hear me?"

"Sounds like you're at a concert!"

"Sorry, hold on a second…"

"Hello?…Larry?"

"YES!"

"My point from earlier was to make sure you are aware of the politics in that Tampa office. This is a huge step and all eyes will be on you and…well, you have to be careful. There are often two very different agendas."

"How do you mean?" I ask, as an awkward silence follows.

"I'll call you Monday. Enjoy yourself tonight and just trust who put you there. It's very important you understand—"

My phone dies.

The statement forebodes evil, yet I sprint past this blatant stop sign with flashing red lights without hesitation. After splashing some cold water on my face, I tuck the warning shots in my back pocket and race back out to the merriment and tomfoolery.

Flames lick the sky from the fire pit, as festivity fills the air. My awe-inspiring wine vault makes it seem my dear well-wishers are still boasting in my honor even though they are really just yearning for the next outlandishly expensive bottle to be corked. Enjoying a powerful cabernet is a ritual at "The Pit" which many wine lovers have relished over the years.

The revelry concludes as only a few survivors are left to enjoy the traditional big red: on this night, a celebratory bottle of 94 Opus. The high end Napa blend of Cabernet Sauvignon, Cabernet Franc, Merlot, Malbec, and Petit Verdot is the one bottle I have with all of my promotions. It is a selection, my boy, and protégé, Bud Fox always remains for. On this night he throws the cork of that particular bottle in the flames. It is then I jokingly shout at him that it is bad luck to burn a celebratory cork just to watch him dig it out of the fire.

After he flips it out we laugh all the way back to the house. We put our Montecristos out before gravitating to my new ostentatious, super spectacular sports memorabilia room to catch some late scores. Surrounded by dashing autographed jerseys, helmets, hats, bats, balls, and pictures, I settle into my favorite chair. Many nights encompass tipping back a flute of Laurent Perrier while celebrating, as we do on this night, the most special of them all. POP! After the Opus we can only take a few sips, but it doesn't matter.

Excess? You bet! The industry winery suppliers have long gifted me their best wines with an undivided trust in my program. They display observable appreciation for the accomplishments of the team effort, while some have already voiced congratulations and a duly noted displeasure for my move to the new position as I will no longer be responsible for their brands.

But my sights are already on my new team. I have a vision of an ambitious group that I will be constantly fine tuning their competitive fires. Not only for the good of their careers, but to ensure the company's sustained success. This unique experience inspires a team philosophy that is passionate about making a difference every day, while maintaining an outrageous sense of fun.

This triumphant formula has such strong team camaraderie that many refer to us as a cult. I know I will continue that. Winning is everything and any excuses are your own. It is infectious. It is paramount. We work hard to win, and play just as hard as we carouse after an illustrious victory. POP...WE CELEBRATE LIKE ROCK STARS.

CHAPTER FIVE

HEADING WEST

AUGUST 14, 2009
TAMPA BOUND

I sat up in bed the next morning hung over, yet ecstatic. My life was playing out like a movie with nothing but scripted bliss. Everything was perfect. I had even received a congratulatory email from the dark Sith Lord. Although his nickname suggests a wrathful disposition, he was an executive that played a profound role in my career rise with the company and someone who I was grateful to be under. As I finished reading his uncharacteristically sentimental and prideful message I received another. It was one that finally had both of our top two executives—our general manager, Geno Franc, the man responsible for this relocation and rare plan for my future, and The Wizard, an executive who seemed to have disparaging thoughts—at least pretending to be on the same page with this move, something that hadn't happened to this point. I felt euphoric.

I leaped out of bed with a hop in my step, following the delightful scent of coffee into the kitchen. Marie stood off to the side brushing our adorable eleven-year-old daughter's hair. "Lauren, please hold still," she pleaded as our handsome ten-year-old son Jerry--much taller than his age suggested--sat off to the side of them.

"Hi, Daddy-o," they bellowed in unison.

"Good morning, family," I said with enthusiasm.

Marie didn't respond, although her inquiring eyes followed me, authoritatively. "Make yourself useful and brush Jerry's hair," she barked. It was an attempt to take some wind out of my sail as I took the brush from him to fix what he had messed up.

As I completed the task, Marie continued asking questions about the relocation. The only topic we had actually agreed upon was the kids' school year. Since it had already begun, we felt it best not to make any changes until we were in the new house with a full summer for them to acclimate.

She leaned over the counter studying the relocation paperwork. "Was the increased amount approved?"

"Yes. I should have the confirmation this morning."

Her hand went to her forehead. "It all just seems too good to be true."

I turned to her.

"What?"

I sighed.

"Don't take this the wrong way," she said, "but it scares me that you think this is normal. It is not."

I filled my Tinkerbell mug with coffee and snapped. "Why do you keep saying that?"

She gawked at me. "Oh, I don't know, Larry. Maybe it's because you live in Never Land. You're a forty-two-year old man who drinks coffee out of a Tinkerbell mug. You've had three promotions in four years and you're beginning this new position in a ridiculous bachelor's pad on Harbour Island."

"It's a corporate apartment!"

"I saw the brochure, Larry. Stop! Everything about this has the makings of a Hollywood movie." Her raised voice reeked of sarcasm.

Lauren's cute little smile spun across her face. I crossed my arms and stared back at Marie with annoyance.

"Oh, stop pouting, little boy. I'm just amazed by you, okay? And we will celebrate your greatness again tonight, but now I have to get the kids to school. Besides, you don't need any more cheerleaders in your life."

She walked over and kissed me goodbye before whispering, "And if you can't deal with the shit I give you, how are you going to deal with the haters that are cursing you behind your back full of envy?"

"Everyone loves me."

"To your face, but you have more daggers in your back than

anyone I know."

Her eyes peered into mine. It was a little scary.

She yelled for Jerry and Lauren to get in the car. "Don't be naïve to that, and do not divulge the details of Geno Franc's career plan to anyone." She grabbed her purse. "Not to mention the fact that The Wizard does not seem to be on the same page as him. You should tell Franc about his call to you while he was on vacation. How does that guy not know what Franc is grooming you for...or is that the problem?" She lowered her voice to a whisper. "This company scares me."

"What did you say?"

"Nothing."

"Please, stop."

She opened the door to leave, but turned. "No, I won't. You're too trusting and someone has to bring you back to the real world." With that, she walked out.

I meandered over to the couch and collapsed to read another congratulatory email. This one was from one of my first bosses with the company, a handsome man named Johnny Promise. A smile spread across my face as I read it. I couldn't help but think of the first time I was called to his office. It was for a covert meeting that the dark Sith Lord orchestrated having me take over the east coast off-premise sales team.

The ostentatious introductions instantaneously exceeded the legal limit of fluff, smoke-and-mirror bullshit one office should ever have had behind a single closed door. There was a brief moment where I was concerned that some of the pictures on the wall would spontaneously combust as the hot air became a bit overwhelming. And if you think it's impossible to display pageantry while sitting in an office chair, think again.

After batting delusions of grandeur back and forth, we spent the first ten minutes critiquing each other's wardrobes. Looking back at this, it would have made a good SNL skit. The only things missing were a bottle of chardonnay and a fucking picnic blanket and maybe one of those tiny little dogs that you can stick in a purse.

As I shook my head smirking I couldn't deny it was a critical time early in my career. I sent my gratitude before turning on ESPN, waiting for the Yankee highlights. I glanced back and forth between the television and emails, reminded that I had bumped up the times for my two interviews. After confirming that my favorite baseball team now had a six game lead in the American League East, I jumped into the shower with an overwhelming feeling of joy, one I had become accustomed to.

Thirty minutes later I left the house for the Melbourne office. I wanted to give myself time to pack up everything before the interviews that were set for nine and eleven. As I hopped in my navi (Navigator) I received a text from my boy, Bud Fox. I didn't read it until I came to a stop a few minutes later on Front Street.

The sun climbed over the river in front of me. I turned up Lady Gaga's "Poker Face" while I read it: "You're taking me with you. I'm serious. I'm not working for anyone else." I laughed and waited for a stream of cars to pass. Three emails flashed up. The first was a hotel confirmation for the downtown Hilton on that Sunday, August 16th because my corporate apartment wasn't ready. The second asked for updated information needed for my promotion letter, and the third was the approval for the adjusted relocation package. That made it official.

Feeling pretty fucking pumped, I took a left and raced up the river. Two dolphins appeared to be celebrating alongside me. Twenty minutes later, I took the left into the office parking lot. For some reason I cruised by my normal spot. I wasn't sure why. But just as I slowed to a stop, I realized I forgot the boxes I set aside to pack up my stuff. At that very moment, I noticed one of the company merchandisers grab a broom from his van and jokingly sweep the parking lot in front of me. He motioned to me that it was clean and to pull forward.

As I passed, he shouted, "Congratulations, and thank you for the wine."

I smiled at him. "You're welcome." I cleared his van and pulled into the spot. Two wine boxes sat at the end of the space. I pointed to them. "Are you using those?"

"Using what?"

"Those boxes."

He ran around the van and stood speechless for a moment.

"Larry, those weren't there five minutes ago when I pulled in."

I smiled. "Perfect." Unfazed by his reaction, I hopped out and replied to a text from Marie, grabbed the boxes, and thanked him. I walked into the office with a grin I couldn't seem to conceal while flipping the lights on realizing it would be for the last time. I felt nostalgic as I recalled the day I first checked out the space. Ironically, it was another situation that had Geno Franc and The Wizard on two separate pages. I then recalled the extremely awkward call where The Wizard had no clue that Franc had put our company realtor in touch with me personally for the space after just telling my on premise counterpart we were not getting an east coast office for a couple of months.

Two more texts hit my BlackBerry and moved me along. It was clear many individuals were looking to go with me. I filled one of the boxes with my sales plaques, a stack of printed emails full of accolades, and some nifty winery letters that stated my future was bright.

I then noticed three new emails in my inbox. One was from a member of the other Tampa team's selling division, someone I had always liked. The subject line read *Confidential Inquiry*. The email read: "Larry, I was very happy when I heard (TJ) Faggalo (his division's sales manager) tell the guys that you were getting the big promotion. Congratulations! Well deserved. I'm sending this to express my desire to work for you. You have always found ways to motivate sales teams in positive ways during challenging times. The success you've had is unparalleled and you are respected because of it. I look forward to speaking with you about an opportunity in your new sales division. My goal is to grow with this company under you."

After I read the email, I printed it and jotted a note on it to call him, placed it in the box with the rest of my emails, and my office line rang. It was TJ Faggalo. The other division's off-premise sales manager, and he was panicked.

"Hey, T."

"Larry, listen to me. The Wizard is not going to stand for you recruiting my people for your new division. And it's bullshit that I'm hearing this already."

Stunned, I collapsed back in my chair. "T, hold on. You're

misinformed."

"These guys are all telling me you are."

As I went to answer he cut me off informing me that our winery suppliers were upset I was gone. I asked him if he was going to allow the people that reached out to me to interview.

"The Wizard's not going to allow you to recruit my people," he whined.

"So we tell Cosmopolitan Wines...," (CWUS the company linked to my new division) "...what? The Wizard wants me to hire everyone new?"

"Larry I'm not saying that. I have some people for you."

I laughed. "Oh, I'm sure you do. No thanks, T."

There was a gaping pause. It was obvious he was being fed information as he reiterated that certain people were not going with me. My eyes rolled as I listened. It was then that Bud Fox stuck his head inside my doorway. "T, I have an interview. I'll call you back." I motioned for Fox to wait outside my office.

"God dammit, Larry, I'm going to see The Wizard right now."

Click.

I rubbed my eyes and noticed an attractive brunette staring at me before quickly turning away. I went to my file cabinet to grab an interview form as Bud Fox ran in. "Hey, Lisa's with me."

Both my office line and BlackBerry were ringing.

"Who?" I was distracted by this idiocy.

He took another step toward me. "The girl I asked you to interview." He held up his head.

"Oh yeah, I know. I'm sorry. I think I just saw her. I'm looking for the form now." I thought I had found the form as he left. I pulled the sheet out but realized it wasn't it. What I found were the cozy pictures of me with a female winery supplier and wine tasting girl with a post-it-note that read, "Wouldn't want Marie to see these."

This was a note that Bud Fox had denied writing. It had mysteriously been placed on the pictures right after I warned him that he had to change his ways because he wasn't cutting it as a salesman in his territory. The fact that I never resolved this with him, after being warned about his deceptive ways, was difficult to fathom, as was the fact that I kept these pictures in the first place. And it didn't matter that the times depicted in the pictures were harmless fun. No one knew that. It was that I was warned numerous times about his character flaws while thinking I was the one person who could change his ways that caused the harm.

That said I was now being given a second chance to correct this, like many other little things that were resurfacing before this move. It was quite strange. And if I had handled it all differently, it would've changed the path I took, but I didn't. I only fucked it up again, as a female's voice filled my head.

"Hey, he's off the phone. I'm not waiting for you. I'm going to introduce myself."

And that was the end of that.

Miraculously, my ego allowed me to block it all out a second time as that young, attractive, brunette sashayed into my office with a smile. "Hi, you must be Larry. I'm Lisa Fenna."

Bud Fox raced in breathless as her hand extended to shake mine.

"It's nice to meet you, Lisa." Her fingers lingered briefly on the take away before her arm slowly dropped to her side eloquently.

Fox stood behind her anxiously.

Her eyes displayed an interest that went beyond simply landing a job from this interview. Incredibly, I didn't think that was odd at all as she took a seat. It was at that moment I threw the post-it-note out, while placing the damn pictures back in the folder. This never came up again, and as I closed the file cabinet it was old news. Lisa needed me. As she walked me through her resume, The Darkness stood next to her and celebrated my vanity.

So, after the thirty-minute chat, I felt she was intelligent, aggressive, and a good fit. I immediately set her up to meet with Bobby Blue. He was another close friend and the guy who would be her immediate boss—so I thought.

I left him a message. "Blue, I have someone I want you to interview. Call me."

Click.

Thirty minutes later, I received a text from Fox: "I had to give Lisa your number. She is going to call you from a 7-7-2 area code and wants you to program her in your phone."

Ten minutes after that Fox called. "Jesus, this girl thinks she's reporting to you."

"Will you stop? I have a call out to Blue."

"Are you listening to me? Lisa thinks she's reporting to you."

Bobby Blue called on the office line.

"Fox, I have to call you back. It's Blue."

Click.

"Blue, I have someone I want you to interview."

"Do you realize how fucked up this is?"

I thought Fox briefed him on my new Mermaid, Lisa Fenna, and panicked. "Huh?" I held my breath.

"I'm not going anywhere. That fucking cocksucker Danny Koppelli (a sales manager under TJ Faggalo) submitted a list of names that (TJ) Faggalo took to The Wizard!"

"What?"

"Yup. And mine was one. They are not letting me go with you. This is the typical bullshit I knew Koppelli would pull."

TJ Faggalo was calling back.

"Blue, I have to take this."

Click.

"T, what the hell is going on?"

"Larry, listen to me. You know I've always looked out for you."

My eyes rolled in my head with the bullshit that spewed forth out of his mouth.

"So I'm going to tell you that The Wizard just had Tricheto Winery call him pissed off that you're gone, and won't let you take these people."

"What?"

"Larry, they aren't going to fucking allow it."

"Wait a minute, T. You're telling me a winery supplier just randomly called The Wizard and told him this? Do you realize how insane this sounds?"

"God dammit, Larry, this isn't a joke."

"It's hilarious. Is Koppelli sitting across from you?"

Irate, he continued rambling.

I noticed a number calling that I didn't have programmed in. And then my eyes grew wide as I realized it was Lisa Fenna. I hung up on Faggalo, but it was too late. She went to voicemail. Then he called back fired up.

"Larry, God dammit. Why did you fucking hang up on me?"

"T, I have to call you back. This is very important."

Click.

After I listened to her sweet message, which was about as ridiculous as Faggalo's idiotic exhortation, I called her back. But on the second ring I had to hang up because now The Wizard was calling. It was clear the baton of lunacy was passed to him as both TJ Faggalo and Danny Koppelli stood in the background shaking their pompoms. Sitting back, The Wizard cautiously confirmed that I would be checking into the Hilton on Sunday and be ready to go for the Cosmopolitan Wine U.S. (CWUS) meeting on Monday morning. Then he got to the real point of the call.

"Listen, Coach, (he called everyone Coach) this is a unique situation that I can't have getting out of hand. I realize you have some friends that like you and want to go with you."

I bit my tongue, incensed by his choice of words. "We need to be realistic with this." I glanced at my screen. Lisa was calling back. My eyes closed as this charade continued.

"You have to understand what I'm dealing with. These winery suppliers are not happy you're gone. I need you and TJ to work this out on Wednesday when the conference room is available. I'll have Lori Wells, (his assistant), set up a grid that you guys can use, like a draft sheet."

I shook my head in disbelief. "Okay. If you feel that is best."

"Thanks, Coach. So you're checking into the Hilton on Sunday, correct?"

"Yes."

"Okay. See you Monday."

Click.

CHAPTER SIX

THE DRAFT

AUGUST 19, 2009
EXECUTIVE CONFERENCE ROOM

The promotion letter went out at eleven o'clock in the morning on Wednesday, August 19th, and made it official. More toasts were made, drinks were drunk, and the Monday meeting with the Cosmopolitan Wines U.S. Florida team was a success. So after two meetings in Miami, I flew back to Tampa on Tuesday for a side-bar briefing on the talent chart for the Wednesday "draft" which would ultimately fill my new sales division's roster.

The new sales division I was relocated to run was tied exclusively to a group of wineries that were owned by one company: Cosmopolitan Wines U.S., or CWUS. It was only their brands that my new sales division would be responsible for, selling their portfolio in a very transparent relationship. In summation, we would be their exclusive sales force working as one team under two different companies, both in need of a sales and management staff under me...hence this idiotic draft.

The rest of the state had a similar draft that wasn't referred to as "idiotic" because they used this session to select talent, such as sales and management, in a fair and reasonable manner that made sense for all parties involved. Regrettably, since I was in Tampa that would not be the case. What I prepared for was an hour of mind boggling antics and senseless justifications to the sham I was warned it would be, one solely aimed at blocking the truly talented who desired to join my program in earnest, in exchange for the terribly troubled that one could argue should never have been hired to begin with. The festivities were set to commence with the host of this aberration named as TJ Faggalo, at two o'clock sharp, in the executive conference room.

At five minutes to two, I threw back a glass of one of my favorite New Zealand wines, Nobilo Sauvignon Blanc, which was just gifted to me and opened before I made my way up. With the pungently aromatic, fresh and frisky flavors arousing my senses, I gleefully swiped my security card to gain access to this afternoon's main event. I ran the last few strides to slide to a stop on the swank marble floor in front of the opulent space's open door.

A considerable portion of the mahogany table was covered with team rosters and pages with boxes. My eyebrow rose when I noticed many of the boxes already had names in them. As I leaned over this plot thickening puzzlement, a voice whispered my name from behind me.

I turned to see the affable Operations Manager, Robert Boyd. "Did I take care of you or what?" he said in a jovial tone. He took a step forward with a wide grin.

"Oh, yes. Thank you, Robert. It's perfect." I was extremely appreciative of the nifty tucked away L-shaped office that he specifically singled out for me on the first floor.

"Good. And your office furniture is here, so I'll have them bring it in."

"Thanks very much, Robert." I spun back to the scattered sheets in front of me.

His presence lingered. I twisted back and his eyes shifted erratically from the clutter.

"You're very welcome, Larry. You just seemed to be the type of guy who likes to live in his own little world."

He strolled out and I said, "You have no idea."

Seconds later, TJ Faggalo lumbered in. I picked up the punch line to his party.

"Larry, hold on," he snarled. "Those are the people that already had a meeting with The Wizard."

I winced, scrambling for the smelling salts I didn't think I would require this quickly. "What?" I gripped both sides of the chair and braced myself for his infamous prattle.

"These people have requested to go to your new division, so you don't have to draft them. That should make this easy."

I sighed and spun my chair. "T, you know that's a total contradiction to what you said on Friday."

He looked up. "Larry, I'm saying they want to go with you."

"These are the wrong people."

He dropped the paper with theatric flare and sneered. "I'm not going there again."

"What? You know these aren't the names that reached out to me on Friday."

"Larry, I already told you. The Wizard's not allowing that shit and no one cares if they want to go with you."

My head shot up. "What? You just said these other names are going because they want to go."

There was a knock on the door and then it opened. It was The Wizard's good-hearted assistant, Lori Wells. Wide eyed, she held the doorknob and sputtered, "I'll...I'll come back." She closed the door.

I took a deep breath and exhaled. "Let's back up a second. So what you're really saying is that everyone you want to get rid of met with The Wizard and is now in a box, but anyone with talent who reached out to me can't come. I'll just call the Sith Lord!"

"Goddammit, Larry. You're not calling the Sith Lord. The Wizard already signed off on this."

"This is crazy."

"Larry, listen to me." He glanced at the ceiling, face full of frustration. "One thing you have to understand now that you're in Tampa is that The Wizard wants everyone to like him so he yes's everyone. It's fucked up, but it's what I fucking have to deal with."

I had no idea what he was saying. I titled in the chair and blinked at him fiercely, holding onto the sides with only a clear visual of that dancing bear that goes back and forth on the ball at the circus in the tutu. I struggled mightily to gather enough strength to move this along, but as I raised the paper again, the pain only worsened.

The next name I read was Tony Trappelleti, also known as TNT, as in dynamite that goes BOOM! Frantically, I scanned the rest of the list. I didn't recognize one name that I wasn't warned about in my covert meeting to prepare for this insanity. I hit the bottom of the page. "Talk to me about Tony Trappelleti."

"Tony's a good one." He taunted lifting his face to me.

My eyes rolled to his. He raised the sheet to cover his face, to mask his smile.

"Tony Trappelleti? T, I've been warned by everyone in Tampa about this guy."

He didn't answer right away because he was regaining his composure. "The Wizard happens to think Tony is one of the best managers we have. They play racquetball together."

Both of my hands went to my head. "T, you told me last month The Wizard was a poor judge of talent."

"Larry, I never said that. What I said was that sometimes he makes poor choices because of friendships and family ties."

I began seeing little stars and the room went dark. As light hit the page again, I said, "I thought we were using pencils for this round. Why are all of these names written in permanent ink?" I lunged for my water pretending it was my crisp New Zealand Sauvignon Blanc.

"Because they already spoke to The Wizard, so it's final." He held the paper up over his bright red face again.

"Right. Silly me." It was my turn to pick. I wrote Bobby Blue's name in the next box and passed it to him.

"Goddammit, Larry, this isn't a fucking joke." He fell back in his chair. "We spoke about him already."

"T, seriously, who would you like me to have run that area?"

He stabbed at the draft roster, which was also rigged as names were mysteriously missing, and pulled it up to his face. "Larry I'm going to help you out here," he said astonishingly with a straight face. I couldn't help but like this guy, watching him breathless with anticipation. He turned the paper to me and pointed his finger at a name. "Bud Fox, isn't that your boy? Shit, I know he'll do a great job."

The comic relief expired. "That is not happening!"

He peeked at me with one eye from behind the sheet of paper. "Larry, are you saying you don't like Fox now?"

My jaw dropped. "What?" I sighed. "No, T. That's not at all what I'm saying. I'm saying that I'm not setting him up to fail. He is not ready for that position."

"Larry, listen to me. We do this shit all the time in Tampa. If they work great, if not—"

I finished his sentence. "They become disgruntled cancers who cause riots. I've seen it for years. No."

"Larry, this isn't going to be perfect. Look at what I'm left to deal with. I'm screwed."

"You're screwed? T, what Fidel Castro did to us in the early eighties pales in comparison to what you've done here today." I got up and walked downstairs and collapsed in my chair. Rubbing my eyes I noticed an email from Mike Fritton, our CWUS District Manager. He informed me he was stopping by the office at five o'clock.

I realized CWUS wanted to keep a close eye on how the team roster was taking shape and that was the sole purpose for Mike Fritton's visit. He wanted to check out the draft sheet to see how badly we got screwed. And he too was aware of how things operated in this Tampa office and knew it would be a fiasco. I started to reply to him when my phone rang. It was the Sith Lord. "Hey, John." I sat up in my chair.

"Hey, Larry, have you found an administrative assistant yet?"

"I have a couple in mind, but no."

"Listen, can you interview my son's baseball coach's wife? She speaks broken English, but I think she'll work out well."

I knew I should've grabbed the bottle of Nobilo. "What?"

"I only met her a few times, and she didn't really speak at all, but when she did, it wasn't too bad."

"Oh...and is that what she does now, admin work?"

"I'm not sure, but I really think she'll be fine."

"Oh, okay. Sure. I mean I'll interview her."

"I'm going to email you her information to set it up, but I want to be there for it."

"Okay, yes. I'll look for it."

"Thanks, Larry."

"Sure."

Click.

I glanced at my watch. It was just after three, time to see The Wizard. This meeting was a planned get-together that was set after the Monday CWUS meeting. I grabbed my pad and walked out. As I passed through the main part of my office I was stopped by the warehouse handyman.

"Hey, Larry. I have a request for a four-by-six picture board for your office. I've never had that request before. What do you mean?" he asked with a priceless look of puzzlement.

"I envisioned a large picture board. I think pictures and achievements are important. They build camaraderie and display team unity." I stopped abruptly when I noticed his eyes blinking rapidly. I thought I should just show him where I wanted it, so I put my hands out against the wall. "I want it hung right here."

After an awkward moment of silence, he realized I was serious and muttered, "Robert wants me to take care of you, so that I will do. It could be a couple days before I find this, but I will."

I nodded. "Thank you, very much."

He peered at me, and then at the wall, and then back at me. "You're welcome."

I shook his hand and merrily continued on my way as I was off to see The Wizard. I stopped at his open door. He was on the phone, but still waved me inside. After he hung up, he seemed worn down, yet hurried to provide a bright spot to this draft day delirium. His emphasis was on the managers I was getting that were CWUS recruits. In other words, individuals that CWUS recruited out of college who would work for a distributor before going to work for them as a winery supplier.

It was an ominous sign early on that suggested The Wizard realized that his buddy, TJ Faggalo, had abused this draft by dumping the troubled on me and my new division, and now felt the need to shine a light on anything bright. So he did with these recruits.

"Coach, I know these two are exactly what you are looking for," he said boastingly. "Their names are Matt McMullen and Wendy Darlington. They're young, sharp, and aggressive." He grabbed his BlackBerry awkwardly and felt the need to wave his wand one more time. "And I'm close to landing Dan Schultz." My blank stare caused him to add, "I thought you knew him."

"No."

He reached for a folder. "He's a guy who has solid relationships in

North Tampa. I should know tomorrow."

He spun his chair around to grab a paper and asked me when I was meeting with everyone. I told him I wanted to meet before the appointment with TJ Faggalo's division, which was set for the following Tuesday. The premise of that get-together was to have the district managers mirror each other's territories as best as possible.

After that, I casually slipped in Andrew Rawley's name as someone I had to have. Andrew was someone who I hired and mentored, and was now a close friend who I had planned on running my old area on the Space Coast. The Wizard took a breath, and after a long exhale said, "I didn't think this would turn into a negotiation."

I didn't utter a word.

"Okay, take him. But let me inform TJ." He stopped suddenly and read his computer screen. He threw his hands up, exasperated. "Here's another one. This gets worse by the day." He didn't elaborate. "They're all complaining about this shit now."

"I'm sorry. I'm not following?"

"You moving over to run the Cosmopolitan division and the fact it's a dedicated sales force selling against their winery brands has become a nightmare to deal with." His phone rang. "Let me take this, Coach."

I nodded and took off to my new office.

Before I made it there, the infamous Tampa office charm abruptly stung me for the first time. The text: "Watch your back. You and your new team are being targeted and they're talking shit to your old supplier buddies so they stop complaining that you're now gone. It's pretty fucked up. Welcome to Tampa!"

As I rubbed my eyes rereading it in the hall he sent a follow-up text: "I'm not even allowed to talk to you. Forget my email—I'm stuck in hell."

I shook my head but also realized how fickle the industry was and knew that the backlash of not being tied to them anymore would cause a natural separation. I didn't dwell on it. I moved on to my new world issues.

The daunting challenge I had in front of me was that I was moving forward with this team of castaways while having to find a way through, where no one else could. And that was my eureka moment. The lightbulb went on as the keywords "in ways no one else could" resonated in my tiny little head. I reached out to two of my newly drafted managers. Tony Trappelleti was one of them.

After brief calls, they were both thrilled. Within an hour they had entered the office together to meet me. They were extraordinarily curious as they explored the tucked away, windowless, bomb-shelter type, L-shaped offices, while grinning mischievously. They opened the conversation by stating that they enjoyed being forwarded my emails. Strangely I didn't think that was odd or even inquire by whom. I was only focused on connecting with these two with the goal to bring this sideshow together to win.

That was it.

The six-foot-four Tony Trappelleti paraded around the space polluting it with prattle and insisting he refer to me as 'Sir Sola.'

"Sir Sola, I told The Wizard I had to be on your team. I've got to tell you, sir, I'm fucking pumped." He seemed to be totally full of shit, just like I was warned, yet sincerely fascinated and quite ecstatic to be a part of my new division.

"How about a crisp glass of Nobilo Sauvignon Blanc boys?" I though it made perfect sense to finish that bottle and Tony agreed.

"Yes, sir," Tony bellowed. "Now you're talking!"

The other manager stood off to the side with a boyish grin. I couldn't help but notice that his intrigued gaze followed me. "We're going to drink wine...in the afternoon...at the office?" he asked curiously as his breathing quickened.

Tony belched loudly as I cringed discreetly. "This is what Sir Sola does." He paused and grinned as if he knew me, and added obnoxiously, "He works hard and he plays hard. Take notes."

As my eyes slowly closed listening to him ramble on I couldn't help but think this other guy was an anomaly too. He was a genuinely nice person who couldn't seem to answer many of my questions about his territory, but showed pride in his computer spreadsheets. His appearance confused me, as well. He had this young-looking face with a conservative haircut and this pear-shaped, fatherly figure that threw it all off. But then his phone rang, with a *Journey* ring tone.

He had the Bluetooth ear piece wrapped around his cute little ear and as he held his wine glass in a very feminine way the song played

on until he answered. "I'm with Larry Sola. I have to call you back."
He paused waving his free hand in the air listening before he cut the
person off excitedly. "Yes, right now. We're in our new office drinking
wine." He nodded. "Yes, he does, it's true." His arm went up and
down, hitting his side. "Yes, I have to call you back!"

Click.

Twenty minutes later, as they were both leaving rather upbeat,
Tony dramatically turned to me with a pressing point. "Sir Sola, I
must tell you we have one problem."

I smiled. "What's that, Tony?"

"One of the CWUS recruits is looking to stay with her old
distributor."

"Where did you hear that?"

"I hear everything, sir. Her name is Wendy Darlington. She took
some time off after the announcement when we won the CWUS
brands. She was very upset and went to the Keys and no one has seen
her since."

It then dawned on me that she was one of the two names The
Wizard passed on.

Tony added, "She also has our number one area, and it is being
raped by Koppelli."

I nodded. "Thanks, Tony. I'll reach out to her...and Koppelli."

"Don't believe a word he says, sir. I fucking hate that guy."

I winced, feeling I'd endured enough. "Stay positive, Tony."

I took a downward peek at my wristwatch expecting Mike Fritton.
Within literally seconds, he strolled in. Tension cut across his face. I
had only met him once before, and have to say he too wasn't at all
thrilled that our company—one known as the *evil empire*—won the
rights to his company's brands either. He seemed guarded with his
walls way up high and wasted no time asking for the draft sheet,
which I knew was his sole purpose for this visit. He was also aware
that the company culture of this time was one that many just
accepted, but did not enjoy. Although I realized I would change many
things in and around me in accordance with my desires to lead a
productive program, he did not. He grabbed the sheet and
shuddered.

Within seconds his serious demeanor turned to frustrated anger as he vented passionately. "No way. How can the company blatantly dump these individuals on our new division?"

I was impressed by his zeal, but concerned he was going to have a heart attack.

"Mike, give me a chance to work with them. I plan on separating the new team from—"

"Larry, this is so wrong."

"Mike--"

He rambled on. "I cannot believe this—"

"Mike," I snapped. He turned to me reluctantly and froze. With his undivided attention I added, "We will win. Regardless of whom they dump on us, we will win."

Leery of my words and stunned by my ego he checked his watch. "I have to call Doyle (his boss) by six; he wants to know how we made out."

"Stay positive, Mike. It's all going to be great."

A smirk formed on his face as he made his way out with plans to speak the next day.

During the drive back to my ostentatious suite at the top of the Hilton, I took a call from Bobby Blue. He too was upset at how everything turned out, but was now more concerned that the company was pushing Bud Fox as a viable plan B to him being blocked. There was no doubt he had my best interests and was close enough to me to voice them.

"Larry, you cannot promote Bud Fox. This is fucking crazy."

I tried to calm him down. "Blue, nothing is finalized yet."

"Larry, what worries me is that you plug into these challenges, but with all due respect, not even you can save that guy."

It was at that moment that my ego overrode any rational thought. I knew with those words I was going to promote Bud Fox, while thinking only I could fix him.

"Blue, I hired Fox as a promotable piece to our company's future."

"He is failing as a sales rep, but worse, he lies all the time. And Faggalo would love to see you two go up in flames. They planned that draft, Larry. Don't kid yourself. They're all pissed and full of envy about the rumors that Franc has you set for glory. Regardless of how close Faggalo is to The Wizard, they all know Franc has the final word, and they want nothing more than to see you fail."

I laughed. "I can't control that negative bullshit, but I will demand separation from it." The valet at the hotel motioned me forward. "Listen I'm pulling into the valet at the hotel. I'll call you tomorrow."

"I know you're going to give Fox a chance he doesn't deserve. I know it."

"Positive thoughts, Blue."

"It's called reality. Fox is not qualified and he worships you. It's a recipe for disaster."

I laughed.

"Just remember what happened to Gekko the Great when he gave his Bud Fox a chance."

I laughed louder. "You've been watching too many movies. Talk to you soon, Blue."

"Goodbye, sir."

Click.

CHAPTER SEVEN

MOLLY THE MERMAID

SEPTEMBER 2009
THE CORPORATE APARTMENT

After two weeks at the Hilton, I moved into the corporate apartment off Channelside Walk Way on Harbour Island. On the second night, I was still moving some of my suits and shirts up. I approached the security gate by the elevator and frantically checked my pockets for the damn key I had left on the counter.

"Shit." I hung my dry cleaner, plastic clad attire on the gate and searched in all directions for a sign of life to rescue me. Discomforted, I exhaled with no one in sight. This was a bit odd in a complex of this size, which left me frustrated. My suits fell from the gate to the ground. As I went to pick them up, my company BlackBerry rang. It was the Sith Lord.

"Hey, John."

"Hey, Larry. I'm at the ball field." He paused as someone on his end spoke. "Listen, can you hire Katrina?"

"Who?"

"My son's baseball coach's wife. To be your administrative assistant."

"John...um...she didn't speak English. Remember the interview?"

"Okay. I'll call you back. Hey, great job on that email."

Click.

I rubbed my eyes in disbelief and unknowingly turned up the volume on the ringer. I bent over to pick everything up, and was spooked by a black cat. My BlackBerry rang again, only much louder. Startled, I shot straight up against the wall as it flew out of my hand and onto the bag echoing obnoxiously into the quietude of the night. I hastily lunged for it, to stop the annoying ringing more than anything else. I noticed the cat was gone.

"Hey." It was Bud Fox.

Twenty seconds into his puzzling prattle, I thankfully heard a sign of life. It was Taylor Swift's, "Love Song" reverberating out of a car headed up Dockview Way. I had dropped the BlackBerry from my ear to listen and then brought it back to my face. "Fox, I have to call you back." The music grew louder.

"No, wait," he shouted, "Did you tell Lisa Fenna she's reporting to me?"

I didn't respond. The scary black cat came back with its luminous eyes staring at me from across the street. My sight shifted to the vehicle that drove in front of the spooky creature. It was a yellow Jeep with its top down. An attractive young lady peered my way as she sang the song and slowed to a stop.

"Larry, did you tell her?"

The driver backed up.

"Yes."

Our eye's locked, and she smirked blissfully.

"Fox, I did. And I gotta go."

Click.

I hung up; she pulled away.

"Shit," I said even louder than before.

I stepped toward the street. She looked back and erratically spun around. She held her iPhone while turning her steering wheel. Her fingers kept slipping but eventually she came to a stop in front of the parking garage. Head down, she seemed to be texting someone. She turned the music off and stared right at me before she drove back down Dockview. A little freaked out, I took a cautionary step backward. The Jeep swung onto the wrong side of the street in front of me.

When she stopped, her hands shot up over her pretty pale face and landed beneath her glistening, blue eyes. She wore a Georgia Bulldogs tee-shirt; her strawberry blonde hair was pulled back in a high ponytail. "Something tells me you're not breaking in," she said with attempted swagger. Her face was now the same color as her hair.

"No," I smirked. I'm moving in and I left the key on—"

She sped off and made an abrupt U-turn.

I stood there in bewilderment, slightly humiliated, as she raced into the parking garage, leaving the rest of my explanation on the curb with the trash for pickup.

How embarrassing was that?

I casually spun around and prayed no one was behind me. I schlepped my lavish load in plastic wrap back to the fucking gate I couldn't' open, leaned against the familiar wall, and searched for the number to the Hilton. Bud Fox called to resume the conversation I had just hung up on. I intended to send him to voicemail, but accidentally answered.

"Don't hang up," he pleaded. "I have to talk to you about this."
"Fox, I can't talk right now. I'm locked out of my new place and I'm being taunted by a scary black cat and a nutty girl who has the key."

The cat appeared on the sidewalk mere feet from me. I panicked in silence and took a step back. I shooed the thing back while I held Fox's infamous hissing cackle away from my ear. He began to babble. I couldn't understand him because he laughed uncontrollably.

"Fox, hold on. Hold on." I heard voices coming from inside the gate and another voice directly behind me.

"You owe me a drink for this you know." I turned to see it was the crazy Jeep girl.

"Fox, I have to go."

"Who the fuck was that?"

Click.

"I saw you looking all sad and lost from the parking garage. That's when I drove around."

My back was against the gate. I nervously nodded. If she didn't look like she was thirteen, I would've been terrified. But since she did, I was suddenly enthralled.

"You had such a pathetic look on your face." She smiled mischievously. I stood abashed, but she didn't stop. She waved her handful of iPhone at me. "I was going to workout, but you just looked so lost...sorry, but it was pathetic." She reached out her hand to shake mine.

"Oh, huh…okay. Well, thanks. I'm Larry."

She bent over to pick up a tie that had dropped from my dry cleaner bag. "Hi, Larry, and welcome. I'm Molly."

Obviously, that immediately translated to Molly the Mermaid, in my imaginary world, as she walked by me to unlock the gate. As she pushed it open I held it for her to walk through. She placed my tie around her neck. Three tenants strolled in right behind her. I shook my head and chuckled as two more people walked out. As they passed, I noticed the black cat was back under the light. A silly smirk spread across my face as Molly the Mermaid gazed and tied my tie around her neck.

"Oh my God, your helpless stare." She sighed. "It's really ridiculous. You need to stop."

I must admit, she wasn't shy and had an overabundance of the kittenish bliss I used to be addicted to before I became the sophisticated leader of this new sales division. Just kidding, I was still addicted. In fact, the high raced through my veins as she attempted to tie my tie. We walked through the courtyard under the stars. She asked me where we were going.

Having a hunch she would get it, I glanced up and said, "Second star to the right, and straight on till morning."

And she did get it.

She froze, as childish delight bloomed on her face, and stomped her little Nike on the pavers. "I can't believe you just said that." She swung my tie at me. "I just watched *Peter Pan* with my niece. She loves Wendy. Oh my God, that is so fucking weird."

Let's face it, this was more than weird. Although we'll tap into the origin of this Peter Pan stuff much later in the story, at this moment, it worked…again. So much so that she paused, and glanced over at me with her starry eyes. "What girl doesn't want to be Wendy?"

I nodded and smiled. "None I know."

She merrily strolled along. I waited for her to ask where my apartment was, but she didn't. We approached the corner where we needed to turn, and I finally had to say, "Hold on. Take a right. Third floor."

She shrugged. "What?" She seemed confused and blurted out,

"Oh, yeah. I still can't believe you said that second star to the right thing. I love it...cause I really don't want to grow up, ya know?"

"Yeah, I figured so. Somehow your kind gravitates to me."

"What?"

"Nothing."

I could tell her mind was wandering as we took the right. Within a few strides of the back elevator, she said softly, "I still want to go Never Land though."

I smirked. "I can arrange that."

She laughed. "I'm sure you can."

It turned out she lived there with two other University of Georgia graduates, who were as sweet and helpful as she. Shortly after that, I took them out for a pineapple pizza, (their favorite) a few bottles of wine, and a round of some orange shot (they requested) and renamed them the Dawg Pound.

All three raised their shot glasses.

"To the Dawg Pound and lost guys with puppy dog eyes," Molly the Mermaid chirped.

They tapped each other's glasses as we shouted, "Cheers."

Three young men swaggered past me, heads held high, eyes focused on Molly. As one of them circled, I meandered over to the window to watch a large sailboat cruise up the channel. I felt hypnotically drawn into the mesmerizing scene, as the water danced playfully in the moonlight. I had this repeated premonition that this would be a special time in my life. That said, I had no idea that this intriguing encounter with this fun, inquisitive young lady would turn out to be a meant-to-be moment for the story.

More on that shortly.

At this moment though, as the Dawg Pound barked, Molly the Mermaid called me back to the table craving I crack another egg on her head, which brings us to the "egg crack" game, mentioned earlier. I would put my hand on the girl's head in a fist and come over the top of it, lightly hitting my fist with my other flat palm down, and it would cause a loud pop, if done correctly. Then, it would be the girl's turn and the loudest pop would win the game, the "egg crack" game. The fact that I first cracked an egg on a girl's head in college and was still playing this game at forty-two (with three, twenty-four-year-olds) was a bit unexplainable, but also somehow, just worked.

"Larry, my pop was louder...I won!" Molly the Mermaid shouted with glee.

Five minutes later, they finished a bad sing-a-long to Lady Gaga's "Bad Romance," and Molly the Mermaid cried out, "Larry, I can't find you on Facebook!"

She had my business card on the table making this weird, yet adorable face. I couldn't help but laugh as I told her that at the time, I wasn't on the social network. Right then Bud Fox called back.

I answered, "Fox, let me step outside."

They transitioned into a Taylor Swift time-out, which they sang into spoons, something that made me realize I should've sent him to voicemail.

"Where the fuck are you?" he gasped. "Who was barking? Jesus, I love it. I'm coming over next week for the meeting and staying with you."

Molly the Mermaid stuck her head out the door. "Larry, are you leaving?"

I shook my head. "I'll be in to finish my wine and say goodbye."

Fox blurted, "Jesus, it fucking never ends. Who was that?"

Molly hit me from behind.

"Fox, I have to go."

Click.

CHAPTER EIGHT

A SOUTHERN PEACH AND AN ENCHANTING APPLE

SEPTEMBER 2009
THE DISTRICT MANAGER'S MEETING

The next morning, I awoke to the sun, just a tad bit too high in the sky, creeping in through the blinds. I sat up, panicked that I'd overslept, and clutched my chest as I noticed two missed calls from Marie. I wasn't having any chest pains; it just made me feel better to do that in this situation. Explaining my pizza party on the second night at the apartment was not an option.

What I did have though, was hangover pains. I frantically searched for my water and realized I had fallen asleep with my laptop open on the bed, half a glass of wine on the coffee table, and no alarm set. I typically didn't need it. I glanced at the clock. It was just after seven. My BlackBerry rang. I pulled it off the charger and noticed it was my new friend, Tony Trappalleti. "Hey Tony." I found my bottle of Evian, which had fallen on the floor.

"Good morning, Sir Sola. How was the party last night?"

I took a gulp and almost spit it out. "What?"

He laughed. "That was a joke, sir. I heard you're a party guy."

Uncomfortable, I stumbled to the giant picture window and peeked through the curtains thinking this nut job was outside with binoculars.

"Are you at the office?"

"No. Are you?"

There was silence before he said, "Not yet, sir, but I'd like to talk to you at the office."

My back was to the front door. I surveyed the street for this giant loon as the door opened. I fell over backward and flipped the tiny table by the window. I spun around and held the curtain around my waist. I stood in my underwear and stared at a lady I'd never met.

"Oh, oh, I'm so sorry. I clean your apartment. You were gone by this time yesterday. I'm so sorry."

I held up my hand and told her it was okay. As the door closed, I heard Tony laughing.

"Sir Sola, getting a little action in early, huh?" He snickered.

"What? That was my maid."

I tore the curtain as Tony babbled on. "I love it. I heard you're always playing with the ladies."

He was probing. "It's not like that." I banged my toe. "Fuck."

"Sir, did she come back?"

"What? No. I told you I don't do that. I nailed my toe on the coffee table."

"Sir, your secrets are safe with me. Just know that now."

"Tony, please, stop. Wrong guy." The room began to spin. "What do you need to speak to me about?" I muttered as my eyes fluttered.

"Some issues in South Tampa. Danny Koppelli is screwing us badly."

I hopped in the bedroom and fell on the bed.

"Sir Sola, did I lose you? He's—"

"He's my friend, Tony. I know how he gets. I'll call him." I took another swig of Evian.

"You're friends? I wouldn't call him a friend, sir. I'm hearing a lot of shit."

I sat up slowly and limped to the bathroom. Although at this point I liked Tony, I loathed the negative energy he emitted. "Well, Tony, I hear rumors about a lot of people that aren't always true, so don't jump to conclusions."

He changed the subject while I brushed my teeth. By the time I wiped the crescents of toothpaste from the corners of my mouth I was unable to digest his relentless ramblings.

"Sir, did you find Wendy Darlington? Your South Tampa district manager?"

"No." I took a deep breath, "I will. Tony, I'll be at the office at eight."

"You haven't met her yet?"

I slammed the toothbrush down. "No, Tony. The plan was that if I'm not delayed in Miami, I'd meet her at the meeting tomorrow in Tampa."

He sighed dramatically. "Well, sir, I realize we haven't officially started, but as I told you in the office, no one has seen her. I hope she shows. Anyway, I'm interested to see what you think of her. I hear you're an excellent judge of talent."

I felt nausea coming on. "Tony, I'll see you soon."

Click.

Forty minutes later, I pulled into my spot at the office. Rachael Howe, our un-stereotypical Human Resources manager, waved from the steps like a school girl. She waited in the lobby to pull me aside. A call from Lisa Fenna came in. I sent her to voicemail because Rachael wanted to make sure everything was going well. I assured her it was and thanked her again for all that she had done for me.

"It's my pleasure. Geno wants you happy. We all do. So let me know if you need anything."

I nodded graciously and thanked her again. "Oh, Rachael, is there a maid for the apartment?"

She turned and laughed. "Yes, she is supposed to come every day. Have you seen her?"

"Yes. I met her today. Just wanted to make sure. Thanks."

I made my way down the hall to my office. There was no message from Lisa. She had found out the day before that Bud Fox was going to be her boss and was taken aback with the news. I sat down at my desk and received a text from Fox that he was going to meet with her. I figured I'd call her back after that.

I began to read an email, when my other CWUS recruit, Matt McMullen, walked in. Matt was my Sarasota district manager and a guy in his mid-twenties. We had hit it off the week before. He had wide eyes brimming with enthusiasm and full of information. It was clear that he too had heard a few stories and wanted to create some new ones of his own. My first assessment of him was that he was a young, ambitious guy who was excited to be a part of my program, and one of the few coming over who was actually pleased that our distributor landed the CWUS brands. After some small talk, he deliberately made a point of telling me that he agreed with my work hard, play hard mentality. He exaggerated the joy he had for the play hard part.

"You don't seem like you're in your forties." He smiled, glanced at a picture, and referred to me as "Mayor" while checking out my pose with an old friend from another winery. "Mayor, this is a great picture. I didn't know you knew Jayme."

"Yes, I've known him for years. He's a great guy."

He continued to pick up the framed pictures. "We need to hit Ybor, smoke some cigars, and drink some wine. I heard your corporate apartment is right there in Harbour Island. It'll be perfect."

He carried on. I read another email about the South Tampa issues.

He repeated himself and snapped sarcastically, "Mayor? Are we partying or what?"

I glanced up at him. "Sorry, Matt. Yes, of course. Just let me know when. We'll tear it up."

He noticed I was preoccupied and quickly got to the point of his visit. He wanted to remind me that he had vacation time, with the move from the other distributor, and was taking it before we officially kicked off. I thanked him for reminding me as he got up to leave. But as he walked out, I remembered I'd wanted to ask him about Wendy Darlington before I had any more conversations with Tony Trappalleti.

"Matt, was it you who mentioned Wendy Darlington was thinking of staying at her old distributor?"

"She'll be at the meeting tomorrow, but she's not happy with the outcome of this."

"Is anyone from Cosmopolitan?"

He laughed. "I am. I mean I feel this is going to be a great experience. You're fucking awesome and how often do you get the chance to work for one of the largest wine and spirit distributors in the nation?"

I nodded and thanked him. One of the ladies interested in my administrative assistant position checked in, again. Her name was Lori Ersatz and she seemed to be the sweetest southern peach from

Georgia. A real Mary Poppins type; professional, competent, and someone I envisioned being a perfect Mama Bear for my new young cubs and me, even though she was actually a few months younger than I was. With each visit, she turned up her southern charm and walked me through more of her attributes. It was obvious she had a strong desire to join me for this new adventure.

The irony was that what really sold me was the very reason I should've politely taken a pass on her. She slipped in the fact that she had an intricate issue with her current boss. What the problem was, no one knew but her, him, and apparently the all-knowing Wizard behind the curtain.

I should've at the very least asked for a little bit more information about her problem, but I didn't. Truthfully, at the time I really didn't want to know. I trusted her and felt if she needed a fresh start it probably stemmed from something negative, which to my detriment, was nothing I wanted to deal with. It was bizarre how I thought this way. Yet another significant side-note to the storyline. So ultimately, when she mentioned she had to move on from him, I felt I had to help her. And that's what got me. In my mind, she needed to be rescued, and of course being a superhero, I could do just that. Did she play me perfectly? Yes, she did.

So with my fucking imaginary cape flowing behind me, I put my hands on my sides, and flashed my patented smirk that screamed, "If you need to be rescued, rest assured. I'm the idiot egomaniac that will do it. Welcome to Never Land."

We discussed finalizing everything the following week, and she left ecstatic.

I sat down to an email from the Sith Lord. He requested that I send the information for a spreadsheet to my new counterparts because he didn't think the ones they used were effective. The direction at this time was still foggy at best. Our state leader wasn't in place yet, so we were dealing with multiple voices and mixed messages, along with Mike Fritton and the CWUS team. I refreshed that list and sent it out. My good friend and the company's trainer, Jerry Lakers, was my eyes and ears in the office, and texted me a warning shot that Tony Trappalleti was headed my way.

I gripped both sides of my chair as Tony made his way through the front part of the office back to mine. I counted down: five, four, three, two...

"Well, good morning, Sir Sola. I have a plan to fix our South Tampa issues."

I took a deep breath and blew it out as he spewed on. "I know back in the day, before your manicures and three hour lunches, you were a ruthless street warrior who would cut your opponents--."

"Tony, stop." With both my hands high in the air I pleaded, "Please. I appreciate your concern with the situation, but let me assure you, it is being handled." Nausea hit me again like a train. My eyes felt like they were bleeding as I watched him peer inside my garbage can.

"Are you sure you weren't partying last night, sir? That's a lot of Evian empties. It seems as if you're nursing a hangover."

I shook my head. This guy was amazing.

"It's a good thing we sell Evian." He sat there with this devious grin.

"Tony, I thought you knew me." I sneered. "Water and wine, my friend."

He laughed and shrugged. "I didn't say I knew everything, sir. I'm learning though, as fast I can. But you keep throwing me for a loop. So fascinating. No soda, huh?"

I shook my head. "Never. Let's get back to business."

He again brought up Wendy Darlington, and how enough people were aware that she was seriously exploring other options and definitely not engaged like everyone else. The reason this was so crucial was once again, she was slated to run my most important territory: South Tampa. This was an issue TJ Faggola's team was aware of and targeting tenaciously.

Later that evening, on my way back to the apartment, I was getting off the Crosstown Expressway when Bobby Blue called inquiring about this situation as well, but not before he had to bring up the fact that Bud Fox's entire team already loathed him.

"Lisa's so over him she's ready to kill him and the fucking idiot spent his first four paychecks buying new suits for a position he won't last a month in." With my silence he changed the subject. "So, what am I hearing about that one manager not wanting to join the new division?"

"What?" I turned down the radio. "Who are you talking about?"

"The district manager that has South Tampa."

"Oh, yes it might be a problem."

"What has she said to you?"

"I haven't met her yet. I will tomorrow at the meeting. Will you be there?"

"Oh yeah. I have to drive over for that bullshit. Hey, it's your boy, Fox, calling. I'll see you tomorrow."

"Okay, Blue."

Click.

I bumped the district manager meeting in Tampa back to five o'clock. I felt I had to meet this girl face to face and figure out what was going on with her. At just after nine that night, I received an email from Mike Fritton. He too was now very concerned about the situation. He had heard that Faggalo and Koppelli were trashing Wendy before we officially kicked the division off. So with my cape again flowing behind me, I assured him that I would save the day. I ended the email informing him I planned on meeting her when I flew back from Miami the next day.

Twenty hours later, I sat anxiously on the tarmac. The plane landed in Tampa on time, but was parked just off the gate. The pilot said that something was wrong with the plane in front of us. I checked my watch twenty minutes later and sent an email to the team that I wanted to meet in my office afterwards. Ten minutes after that, we were finally cleared. When we exited, I raced around the pack, through the airport to my car, and sped to the office. While in route, the sunset began to fill the sky setting the clouds ablaze. I pulled on the exit ramp and Marie called. She asked me how the meeting in Miami went and filled me in on how Lauren and Jerry were doing in school.

"Are you heading back to your apartment?" she asked.

"No, I have a district manager meeting at the Tampa office."

"This late?"

"Yes. I had to push it back to make sure I'd get there."

"Oh, was the issue with the South Tampa guy's territory resolved?"

"I'm meeting her now."

"Her?"

"What?"

"I wasn't aware that you had any direct female reports?"

"Yes. I'm pulling in."

"You didn't tell me he was a she."

"Yes, I told you that. She's a CWUS recruit. The meeting already started. I'm an hour late. I'll talk to you later."

"Oh, I can't wait to hear." She turned up her sarcasm. "We love you."

"Okay Marie, enough...I love you. Tell the kids I love them too." *Click.*

I closed my car door as the second star to the right was burning bright. I flew up the steps, into the office, and to the executive conference room. Both divisions' district managers were jammed around the giant mahogany table and going around the room in an attempt to mirror each other's territory. I certainly couldn't admit this then, but this exercise in futility was only important to me to see how my new managers were engaged and how well they actually knew their territories.

As I stood there, a couple of Faggalo's managers whispered in my ear. "Congrats, Larry."

"Thank you," I replied softly, inching around them. I really wanted to take mental notes on this so I moved on. I still didn't see two of my people. I leaned forward to a manager in front of me and whispered, "Is Wendy Darlington here?"

"Oh, shit. Hey, Larry. I didn't see you come in. Yeah, she's over there." He pointed behind two other district managers.

"Thanks." I squeezed around the two of them and watched her sit with her head down. For two minutes, she never even looked up. This fucking girl's taking a nap, I thought. I could only see the back of her from where I stood. As I squeezed more to the right, I noticed her grab her phone. She pushed back from one of the managers she sat next to, wearing a look of disgust. It was the same three or four managers who began to take over the meeting.

I interjected. Every head turned as I suggested they team up, exchange numbers, and went down the customer lists together.

One of Faggalo's managers shot up proud; however, his pride didn't extend to his appearance. His shirt was stained and his belly hung over his belt, as he rambled on with an answer that had nothing to do with what I stated. I peered at him thinking it was time for me to leave.

After a moment of silence, the animated chatter instantly amplified much to my chagrin.

At that point, I caught a waft of body odor that stung my nostrils and buckled my knees. It was definitely time to go. I had the information that I came for. I pushed through the crowd to the door as the idiocy carried on. I quietly shut it and walked back to my office concerned. I had two managers disconnected, and one of them, Wendy Darlington, had my number one area.

Fifteen minutes later, I sat at my desk as they all filed in. I was tickled by the devilish roar of glee not just from my new team, but my old team, and some of the other managers joining the gathering as well. Inquiring minds seemed to want to know. Naturally Tony lumbered in directly in front of me and stood like a giant oak tree with managers flanking him.

Bobby Blue squeezed in on the far wall as another one of my old managers, and favorite guys I referred to as The Cowboy, shouted out, "Mr. Sola, it's too crowded in here. I can't breathe. I'll see you next week for dinner." He had visible sweat beads on his forehead.

"Okay, Cowboy," I yelled back. "Loosen that tie."

It was great to see everyone, but my objective was to meet with my new team and address this major problem with Wendy Darlington.

I waved at one of my new guys. "Hey, Jeff, let all our people know I need to meet with them, please."

He nodded and abruptly shifted against the wall. My eyes rolled to the bodies being tossed to the side as if a tornado had touched down. Little Wendy Darlington rushed through the crowd.

Tony fell awkwardly off to the side. "Damn, Wendy."

She stopped for a fleeting moment with one of the most magical, whimsical glances I could ever remember seeing. She placed an apple on my desk without uttering a word then went out, pushing bodies to the side before stopping suddenly to turn back to me. She had this wicked little smile, but it was the look in her eyes that captured me.

And then she was gone.

I sat spellbound. My eyes shifted to the apple. I smiled. The ceiling light shadowed the emergence of Tony who grinned from ear to ear.

"Sir, Sola," he said. "It looks as if one of your problems is solved." His laugh was foreboding. "I am extremely excited to be a part of your show, sir." He shook my hand, glanced down at the apple, and let out a guffaw. "Sir, Sola. I'm assuming it's not necessary to meet now?"

"We're good, Tony. Kickoff is Wednesday."

"I love it, Sir Sola. Can't wait."

Bobby Blue remained. "Well, sir, I must say I've never seen a room exit so quickly. All on their phones." His comment had bite. An awkward smile spread across his face as he began walking out. But then he stopped and turned to me. "Oh, this is just going to be fantastic," he said. "Just fantastic!"

CHAPTER NINE

KICKOFF MEETING

SEPTEMBER 23, 2009 (MORNING)
THE MEETING ROOM

The sun rose to the east glistening down on the water over which I drove, as my life continued playing out blissfully. But as I moved off Harbour Island to our division's long awaited kickoff, I had more than a sense of a career achievement. To this point in my life, I had never pondered the possibility of fate or destiny bringing me to a certain place at a certain time, although this moment simply felt right; I was there. I embraced the feeling.

Fifteen minutes later, with a sanguine disposition, I took a left into the office parking lot and let out a gentle laugh. It was the first time I had seen the new sales force. They were jittery heading in. I cruised past the office security gate and had to lift a bottle of Evian to my lips just to conceal my smile. I abruptly stopped as one of them wandered right in front of me. He squinted blankly at what he dropped and then proceeded to fidget with his stained tie instead of picking it up before he fell back in line.

I went over, in my mind, how I wanted this meeting to play out, suddenly distracted by a sales rep that got out of his car and wandered the wrong way against the masses. It was then I decided it was not the best forum to open this up to much feedback; the goal of keeping it simple while setting a positive tone before scooting off for a jovial night at the trop—Tropicana Field for a Ray's game—made the most sense.

My plan was to quickly shake each hand, grant them the fresh start they craved, and let the CWUS boys read their script that would rock them to sleep, before I woke them up to hand them a ticket to the game. Pulling into my spot I heard my name yelled loudly. I looked up to a group walking in. The buzz already was building.

I sat there for a few seconds, again hit with this wonderfully strange sensation. With an uncontrollable smile I opened my door. The sun continued to climb high, full and golden, shining brightly against the azure sky. I turned down "I got a feeling" by the Black Eyed Peas as our operations manager walked up.

"Your day is finally here, huh, Larry?" Robert Boyd said with enthusiasm.

"That it is, Robert." I grinned and hopped out of my Navigator.

"It's quite an accomplishment. You should be proud."

"Thank you. It's only now sinking in."

"I'll bet. You've had a busy couple of months." He smiled walking up the steps to the office. "Let me know if you need anything at all."

I thanked him and it hit me that I had achieved one of my long-held ambitions: to run my own sales division. I raced up the steps in the lobby like a hyperactive teenager and stopped at the top to read a text when a hand reached for my shoulder from behind. It was the Sith Lord. He was reading an email on his BlackBerry. His eyes then shifted to mine. They displayed that eerie reddish glow again as he said, "Geno and I have looked forward to this day for some time. Congratulations, Larry."

I had a sudden flashback to the first time I'd met him at an odd covert meet and greet at the old Orlando office just weeks after I was hired, something that never happened back then, and the Sith Lord's first step in his recruitment phase to bring me to the Dark Side, like Anakin Skywalker in the movie. It's important to note that there was a Dark Side and an even Darker Side to the company hierarchy at this time. The Sith held out his hand to shake mine.

"You've always been my guy. No one deserves this more than you, Larry," he said earnestly as I thanked him graciously. He checked another email. "Everyone in there is excited and it's because of you. You should be very proud of that." His BlackBerry rang. "I have to take this. Good luck with the kickoff." He answered as I made my way to the meeting room.

A moment later, I approached the double doors it. Two young sales reps I hadn't yet met lurched in front of me to open the doors as two others patted me on the back.

"Good morning, sir. Tony speaks very highly of you," he sputtered.

"Thank you." I turned to a hand stuck in front of me.

"It's really nice to meet you, sir!"

I shook two more hands.

One of them held his tie next to mine and grinned. A voice behind him muttered, "Your management style is refreshing, sir." I looked him over as he continued with an odd smirk. "Well we've heard stories, and we're just really pumped to be here."

I thanked him kindly.

I swung widely between being overwhelmed with emotion and actually at peace with the attention. The whirlwind, two-month process to get here was now in my rearview mirror. The first class ticket to the pot of gold at the end of the rainbow was finally stamped. This enabled the first step in Geno Franc's grand plan for my career. A scenario that only he, I, and The Wizard, were aware of. It was an early blueprint that had ultimately been passed on by the dark Sith Lord back in 2005, when Franc was appointed the general manager title of Tampa.

I made my way around the room. It was clear this would be the most emotional and rewarding meeting I'd ever been a part of. I guess it should've. It dawned on me that much of this positive energy was spread through the team I had managed for the five years prior to this promotion. I felt honored and grateful, which was something I rarely did during this time. It was nothing deliberate; it was just that I constantly had my sights on the next challenge fueled by those highs. I was extremely motivated to build on them.

After a successful kickoff, I gave out the tickets for the baseball game that night. The Rays against the Seattle Mariners, was one of Ken Griffey Jr's last games before he retired.

As I tore the first tickets off the thick pad, I was tapped on the arm by Bud Fox. "Is this for the party suite?"

"Yes."

"That's awesome." He paused, leaning into me. "I think she needs to speak to you."

I glanced up and noticed Lisa Fenna. She smiled and pointed at the door. I thought she was leaving so I smiled and waved. Fox walked behind her. My gaze shifted to him as he rolled his eyes shaking his head. Within seconds Wendy Darlington walked in front of him and stopped. I stood fascinated watching her read something. I didn't know why, I just was. She looked over quizzically at Lisa and then back to the paper before she glanced over at me. I smiled and she quickly turned away.

After tearing through the ticket pad, Andrew Rawley walked over. "Can you believe everyone's reaction?" he said. "Word has spread my friend. Congrats."

I nodded. "I'm blown away."

He smiled wide. "You deserve it. And it's obvious there are bigger plans for you. Just make sure you keep taking me with you."

I laughed and leaned into him. "You're a talented manager, not just a friend. I wouldn't have it any other way."

The plan was that Andrew was going to drive a small group over to check out the corporate pad and then we would all head to the game. I shook his hand and brought him in for a quick hug. I glanced over his shoulder as Lisa came right around him.

"Hey, you." She walked right up to me with her chin just off my tie. Her eyes were dark and alluring as she gazed into mine. "Is it all right that I go with you?"

I paused for an instant when I noticed that The Wizard was staring solemnly from across the room. He had the same discomforting scowl throughout the entire meeting. After a moment's consideration, he meandered toward the center of the room.

I looked back at her. "Weren't you suppose to drive with us?"

"Oh, I guess I was." She held up the text verifying it. "I'm really excited. This is going to be such a fun night." She hugged me and walked out.

Within seconds, Bud Fox pulled me aside. "Listen to me. This girl is something else—"

"Fox, you have to learn how to manage her. She's attractive, aggressive, and a great asset for you. Earn her respect, her trust."

He was frustrated. "Larry, this fucking girl doesn't want to report to me. She wants to report to you and that's the only reason why she's not happy with me."

I could tell he was deflecting. There had been tension between them from the onset. "No, it's not Bud."

"What? Bullshit, it is."

"It's not, and you're getting defensive. Listen, we need people who we can promote. Not the slobs wandering into traffic with stains on their ties."

I glanced over his shoulder to see The Wizard trudging over.

"Larry, she had your number programmed in her fucking phone right after you interviewed her and probably calls you more than you're admitting to. But you think that's normal."

He stopped mid-sentence when The Wizard tapped me on the shoulder. After his eyes went back and forth from Fox to me curiously, he walked me off to the side to question me about a pay issue we had with one of the managers. Then he walked out.

I turned to Fox. "Enough. Get your shit together because we're tearing it up tonight."

His head turned as his infamous cackle kicked in. "Jesus, forget this sales division, you'd be running the country if you didn't have demons constantly driving you off a cliff. I fucking love it—"

"Stop it," I barked, unable to resist another opportunity to have some fun with him.

His eyes grew wide. I stared at him intently.

"Fox, do you know what time it is?" I paused as his eyes closed and head slumped. "It's Showtime!" I grabbed his hand and pulled him in while whispering, "And that, my dear friend, is always our best time."

He lit up like a dried out Christmas tree ablaze. His silly smirk settled across his young, attractive face.

I took a few steps to the door and turned to him. "Work hard, play hard, Fox. I need to know if you're in."

His demeanor changed as he snatched his laptop bag off the chair. "Don't ask me that shit anymore. There is no one in here more fucking in."

I gave him my Gordon Gekko the Great smirk. "See you at the pad, Fox. The launching pad."

I let the door go and all I heard was his infamous cackle as it shut. He tried to contain it, but he couldn't. As I made my way down the steps, the door opened.

"The pad," Fox repeated. "The fucking launching pad. I love it."

CHAPTER TEN

TIMEOUT AT THE TROP

SEPTEMBER 23, 2009 (EVENING)
TROPICANA FIELD

Two hours later, after responding to fresh emails, I texted Andrew Rawley to tell him I was heading out. I tore off my tie, hopped in my giant SUV, and sped off. As I pulled onto the Crosstown Expressway, I cranked the Kings of Leon's, "Use Somebody." I opened the windows and took it all in. It was just after four when I pulled into the parking garage at the corporate apartment, walked across the street, and leaped up the steps to the raised sidewalk. That's when I heard a female's voice scream out. "Laarry!"

I spun around startled to see it was Molly the Mermaid. She waved. Her hair was pulled back in a pink headband as she zipped up the street in a convertible BMW. I raised my hand with a curious smile, but the car sped up. It was driven by a handsome young man with a scowl. They pulled into the parking garage, and in a fleeting moment they were gone. The bastard, I thought, as I turned to go up.

The first thing I did when I got up to the apartment in honor of this momentous day and the fact it was also "Wine Wednesday" was to tear the cork out of a Simi Landside Cabernet. Lisa Fenna texted me (again) how excited she was as this intensely seductive selection was apropos for the evening that was about to unfold. I then picked it up and stared at myself in the giant wall mirror and said, "To step one in the journey." I took a healthy swig and placed the goblet down on the black dining room table and turned on the stereo. I hit scan and Bud Fox's favorite artist, Lady Gaga was on three different stations. I settled on her song "Paparazzi" and walked into the bedroom to change.

Within the minute the group made it in with beers.

"Gaga," Fox shouted.

I checked my emails while the iron heated up. I noticed a message from Geno Franc congratulating me on the kickoff. He heard it was a great success and wanted to meet me for lunch the following week.

After making everyone comfortable, I went back to my oversized diva-licious closet to change into my baby blue long sleeve Tommy Bahama. I was worse than a teenage girl.

As I pulled my arm through Lisa ran back. "Oh my God. I love this closet." She playfully ran around me and my wardrobe. "Do you think you have enough suits and shoes and shirts?"

I buttoned my shirt and held my arms out as I said, "Good?"

"Fucking handsome."

"You ready?"

"Oh, fuck yeah."

"Let's move out boys, and girlie."

Forty-five minutes later, we gleefully strolled into the giant party suite at the Trop with a full understanding that baseball is much like a great opera. The systematic build up keeps you occupied all the time, preparing you for that ultimate crushing climax. On this particular night The Wizard seemed to be concerned our climax would eclipse the one played out on the field. He peered at us upon arrival. His hands clutched his chest uneasily. The first thing we did was take a group picture with the CWUS team. They seemed to have hit happy hour before they got there. At this point, everyone had smiles tearing across their faces, except The Wizard. He didn't even smile for the picture. After it, he retreated off to the side. The palms of his hands rubbed the top of his light orange Tommy Bahama.

As great a day as this was, every time I looked at him I became increasingly unsettled. I would think of the call he'd made to me the Friday before as I drove back east for the weekend. It was right after Lori Ersatz (who will later become Mama Bear) and I finalized her move to become my administrative assistant when he literally lit me up for stealing her. I'd never heard him so irate, but the fact that I was being accused of something so far from the truth baffled me. I kept repeating myself. "She approached me." But he spoke through me. "She came to me. She wanted to work for me. She told me she had an issue with her current boss and said you were aware of it." He never acknowledged knowing anything. I mean nothing. He just ended the call.

After I spoke with Lori again, she told me that The Wizard did in fact know what the issue was. She acted like she couldn't believe his reaction, but I had difficulty digesting any of it at this point. Shortly after, he told me he was going to call her. She called me back to inform me he never did. I left him a message about it, but The Wizard never responded. I informed Geno Franc I was moving forward with her and that's when she became my administrative assistant, just days before this.

I pushed my thoughts away from it all. The party kicked up a few notches as the state director for CWUS gave me an inebriated high-five walking to the bar. It was then Lisa pulled me aside to tell me she was going to help me by "working the room." The gorgeous twenty-six-year-old brunette mingled with the mildly intoxicated CWUS boys while wearing this cute little short outfit with a tight white shirt that accented her assets up high. And they loved it.

While that played out, I walked over to the bar. Mike Fritton meandered over to chat. By this point, he and I were in a better place. After the company tension lessened, he realized his brands were in good hands, and that was the important part. That aside, we sincerely liked each other. During some small talk my old counterpart, Jimmy Johns, walked over. Jimmy was passed a ticket because he was now an account manager for our brands. We laughed for a bit reminiscing about some classic incentive trips before he was interrupted by a call. My gaze shifted over his shoulder and right into Wendy Darlington's as she walked in.

It seemed as everything was moving in slow motion. And I couldn't look away. She wore her sunglasses on her head approaching her team's table. Within seconds her head cocked back to me. A smile spun on her lips. I heard my racing heart, pounding in my chest, and then noticed Lisa sashaying right into my sight line.

She came right up to me. Her head rose as she stood on her tip toes and whispered in my ear again. That's when The Wizard's eyes locked on us. Fox, who wasn't getting along with Lisa, ran over and grabbed me.

"Listen to me. You have a problem. I have people asking me if Lisa is your wife," he said.

Wendy glanced back over.

"What?"

"Larry, are you listening? There people think Lisa's your fucking wife."

Jimmy Johns ended his call and walked off with a curious smirk.

"Who? Stop. You're overreacting and you just scared my friend Sweet Cheeks away."

Anger crept into his voice. "Who the fuck is Sweet Cheeks?"

"Jimmy Johns."

"Larry, The Wizard's been watching you like a hawk and this girl is a problem."

I then noticed The Wizard was heading towards the door. He motioned us to follow him.

Within seconds, we were off to see The Wizard. He stopped at a time-out area twenty feet outside the suite. He was tense. "Guys, are you both aware of how this looks?" he said.

I didn't want to disrespect him, but I was miffed. I turned back to the suite and everyone was having a grand time. We both remained speechless.

The Wizard continued with a sharply interrogatory, hard gaze. "Who is this girl?"

"She's my sales rep," Fox muttered.

The Wizard turned to me. "Larry, she's been hanging on you. How do you know her?"

I cleared my throat. "I interviewed her before I left Melbourne."

He just peered at me. "Who did she come here with?"

"She came with us." I held my breath and awaited his response.

"Guys, you can't be doing this shit. How old is she?" He didn't want an answer. "I need you both to stay away from her." He glanced back in the suite. She ran by and I almost lost it. He drew in a breath and said, "Can she get a ride back to the hotel from anyone but you two?"

We both nodded.

"All right. Get back inside. And behave."

Within a few strides of the door Fox whispered, "You're a fucking forty-two-year-old leader of a sales division who just got put in time-out because of a twenty-six-year-old girl wanting to fuck your brains out. I fucking love you!"

I felt it was time to have some fun with him. "Fox, do you know what time it is?"

He staggered. "Stop. No...get away from me."

"Sheep get slaughtered and the weak make me ill, buddy boy—"

"You're fucking—" He began laughing so hard he was unable to finish his sentence.

I pulled him into me. "It's Showtime, my dear friend..."

"...and that is always our best time!" he said completing the sentence with glee.

We marched back in and once again, my gaze caught Wendy's. I then went to say hello and after a brief conversation, Fox waved me to the side. He was now panicked because Lisa was telling people she was going back to Harbour Island with me to party at a bar by my apartment. Of course, that didn't stop Lisa from circling. I mean, why would it? She had no idea we were in time-out. I calmed Fox down. Then I attempted to avoid her by talking to one of the CWUS boys. Within the minute she snuck up behind me. Frantic, Fox took off.

I turned to him and noticed Wendy peeking over. Even amidst this drama it was difficult to ignore the feeling this girl gifted me. I pretended it was the damn "Mermaid" high as Lisa seductively whispered, "Let's go sit down."

Just then Fox scooted back to me with a disturbing look of intrigue. "Lisa give us a second," he said waiting for her walk on before adding, "I just found out Wendy's the girl who dropped the fucking apple on your desk after that DM meeting."

I nodded.

Fox slumped over nearly lifeless. "How many Mermaids does your ego need?"

I shook my head slowly. "She's different..."

"What the fuck is different about her?" Fox fell against the bar.

I thought he was actually having a heart attack. He extended his arm to it, as if holding himself up while gasping for air. "I fucking—"

He started cackling so uncontrollably he had trouble spitting out the rest. "Love it."

"Hey, hey." I hit Fox on the arm. "The Wizard's leaving."

I grabbed my drink and shot to the seats overlooking the field. Fox stared at The Wizard as he walked out. By the time he turned around, I was in a seat watching Ken Griffey Jr's last at bat, but that too came with added drama. Lisa landed next to me with a full beer. As a flash went off, she dumped the thing on my crouch and started patting it dry. I jumped up as the chill of it stung me. "Whooa, s-h-i-t."

I've never seen hands move that quickly. This girl had talent.

"Larry, I'm so sorry let me dry it."

"Lisa those napkins aren't going to help. I need a towel— mop— and bucket."

"Larry, stop. Move your hands…"

Fox, who was still bright red from the apple inquiry, wandered over.

When he made it to the seats his mouth dropped open. "Jesus Christ." He turned around slowly annunciating another of his trademark lines, "I f-u-c-k-i-n-g l-o-v-e it!"

Two of the CWUS boys made their way over with goofy grins. They held their beers and gazed out to the field. I turned to face them.

"Larry, what a great night," the one said as the other chuckled. "Helluva show."

I held my wine over the wet spot as they walked on.

Then Lisa continued to pat me down as the camera flash brightened the dimly lit area. It was clear someone was playing paparazzi. Within seconds, another flash went off.

"Lisa…stop." I grabbed the napkins away from her. I had to. I felt I was black and blue. She threw herself back in the chair like a child and then tore off to the bathroom.

It was then The Darkness taunted me. "Pssst! She needs you. Get up and take a look."

I casually stood up and turned around. Directly behind me, staring right at me was Wendy Darlington. Her eyes were open to her soul and she wasn't looking away.

My arm unconsciously shot out with this ridiculous "You're up" finger point. But it didn't matter. It worked. She gracefully sprang from the bar stool like a jack-in-the-box, and that alone was exhilarating. Her team sat in awe. Two were staring at me, and the other two stared at her. Their heads switched. She took a step forward and motioned she was going to the bar to grab another glass of wine. Thirty seconds later, she was next to me in Lisa's seat.

It simply felt right.

Her hair was up in that damn adorable ponytail (which I love) and her eyes still had that alluring sparkle. I realize I've touched on that, but it was now outwardly evident, and unlike anything I could remember, therefore important to note.

This was a magical moment.

I figured I would build some camaraderie by actually having a real conversation with her, along with whispering some frivolous shit in her ear because I had to believe she was a Mermaid.

But that wasn't easy. The Darkness outwardly mocked me. "Gotcha now, you smug little fucker. That's no Mermaid, Peter Pan Man. That's your Wendy. Hahaha."

I empathize with the magnitude of this development and naturally had to block it out. Pretending I did, I then decided to sit back and play it cool overwhelmed by the chill that hit me and every goose bump I got sitting next to her. As the pixie dust began to swirl, not even Sweet Cheeks peering at us from behind a pole could hinder my racing heart, and pounding of my chest. With each breath, my eyes were being pulled toward the silly smile on her face; she was incapable of controlling it and didn't even bother to try. The buzz behind us grew. Lisa stormed back in, red hot, for that ultimate crushing climax.

Bud Fox bellowed, "I fucking love it!"

His words echoed over us. Lisa flew by, grabbed her purse, and tagged Wendy in the arm hard as she stormed out. She barely flinched and didn't miss a beat in the conversation either. Her eyes continued to shine as they poured into mine.

Twenty minutes later a voice interrupted us from behind.

"Larry, sorry to bother you, Andrew said he texted you...we're leaving."

CHAPTER ELEVEN

THE WIZARD WAVES HIS WAND

OCTOBER 2009
THE FIRST WINE AUDITS

Not surprisingly, Bud Fox called to recap the antics at the Trop early on that last Thursday in September. Like all of his ritualistic rehashes, he vehemently highlighted the night with his typical mirth. After ridiculing Lisa Fenna's hijinks, the basic thrust of this silly summation focused on Wendy Darlington. His tone changed after a light probe of how Wendy ended up sitting next to me.

"The two of you looked like you were in your own little world." He paused as his dog barked. "Hey, hold on a second."

I opened my laptop bag to grab my note pad. He came back. "So, why haven't you mentioned her?"

I read my notes. "I just met her."

At that moment, he let loose his infamous cackle. "That's not true...she had already dropped an apple on your desk."

"Yes, but we weren't formally introduced."

He began cackling again, only louder. "You fucking told me she was different..."

My eyes shifted to the clock on the living room wall. "Hey, I'll call you back."

"You okay?"

"Yes, but I have to do something before this call."

"Listen to me. I'm staying with you after the meeting next week."

"I know."

"We're going to that cigar bar—"

Click.

I hung up and anxiously opened my laptop, checked my inbox, and noticed another email about the incessant issues in South Tampa, which now required immediate attention because of the upcoming CWUS audits. These audits were when the winery suppliers would tour a specific area with a checklist of their brands and overall business plans.

With that, there was a sudden urgency to explain the whereabouts of display pieces that mysteriously had disappeared when the new division was announced back in August. I held my head as I read it, until I received a text from Wendy Darlington on the matter. She requested I ride her territory with her. Right after that I received a call from Tony Trappalletti volunteering to do just that. I thought that was slightly strange, but as he continued on with more than I had patience for, I agreed.

"Yes. Sure, Tony. Just call her and let her know we spoke. Oh, and did you study for the tests?" (We had our new wine portfolio modules to learn as well.)

"Yes, sir. I have that handled. It's this issue with Koppelli that has me concerned."

It was quite obvious Tony had an issue with Danny Koppelli and wanted him to burn.

"Sir, I told you he is deliberately targeting us, and certain people are allowing it. You might have to go to Geno before the audits."

"Tony, do you realize what happens if I do that?"

"Yes, sir."

"You'd like that." I laughed. "Okay, listen I have to finish something and hop on a call. I'll call you later."

"Okay, sir. I know you're busy. I'll call Wendy and take care of her."

"Thanks, Tony."

Click.

The next day, Tony came into the office with an odd smirk. He let me know Wendy blew him off the day before. As he filled me in on the details, she called on my office line. I had her on speakerphone, because I thought it would be a brief conversation to coordinate a meeting time for Tony to get with her, but it wasn't. She only repeatedly brought up her need for me to come out sooner.

"Wendy, I can't get out there until after the Miami meeting and the CWUS state kickoff."

"Larry, I need you before that. The audits are right after it. I have your number one territory—"

"Wendy."

"I have a list of stores that I have to have you see before—"

"Wendy."

There was finally silence.

"I'm impressed by your passion to resolve this, and I certainly will. But in the meantime, Tony has volunteered to help you."

"Larry, No!"

I snatched the phone up off the speaker. I didn't even want to look at him. I thought he'd be upset, but he wasn't. He was actually smirking deviously, thoroughly relishing the moment, as she snapped, "I'm not dealing with Tony...am I on speaker?"

He still heard her and lost it.

"Not anymore."

It was as if he was testing her, while he knew she would say exactly what she said.

"I have to go, Larry. I'll call you later."

Click.

Later that afternoon, we spoke again. She informed me that she lived in South Tampa, which was not far from my corporate apartment, and suggested we get together as study partners over the weekend. I informed her that I went back to the east coast each weekend to be with my family. She quickly transitioned the conversation to ask me how far I had gotten with the modules for each wine category and seemed to be totally plugged in to everything we were doing. I was impressed.

After a few more texts back and forth, I received a distressful call from The Wizard. He realized that the South Tampa situation was about to get ugly, and called me into his office. Just as I sat down he attempted to tell me that his buddy, TJ Faggallo, had nothing to do with it.

"Coach, we have to be careful here. There are too many questions to be pointing fingers. This is going to cause a major problem on this audit if we do."

"I agree that it will cause a major problem."

"Why didn't I know about this?"

"I don't know. We had this discussion twice before—"

"I didn't know anything about this. How did your people allow this to happen?"

I listened quietly, and then said, "They didn't. These issues began before any of my people were in place. Before I even checked into the Hilton."

"Larry, I had no knowledge of any of this."

"As we discussed, this began in a store you told me you shop in. You were going to get with Faggalo." He didn't respond, so I continued. "It's the account that had the giant Woodbridge end cap that was mysteriously replaced with a Yellow Tail end cap."

One brand we sold; the other Faggalo's division did.

He sighed deeply as this unsettling back and forth persisted. The bottom line was that he couldn't explain that individuals in another division, under his leadership--the same company--deliberately removed our display pieces for any reason, never mind one targeting a new division before it even had sales reps.

I informed him that I had spoken to my counterparts throughout the state, who all confirmed this was only happening in Tampa. That's when he questioned me about Wendy. He asked what I thought of her, insinuating she was over her head managing a high pressure territory.

He craved a scapegoat. I envisioned him behind the curtain waving his wand. It was a vision many had of him over the years, but one I wished not to have.

"Coach, I'm just looking out for you here."

I bit my tongue and forced myself to believe he had my best interests as he would repeatedly state. Ironically, he shifted gears by asking me if I had gone to lunch with Geno. Translation: he was only concerned that I informed him about this madness as he continued to work damage control.

That following Monday, I left the office to meet my realtor to continue searching for our dream home. It was just after six o'clock when we pulled into another neighborhood, with no idea where we were, I received a call from Mike Fritton. He had a serious overtone and got right to the point. He had heard through the grapevine that Wendy was viewed as a liability and that the issues in South Tampa would soon be blamed on her.

"Larry, I know what's going to happen and I just want you to be aware of it. There is no way they can blame her for this situation when it's the other side who continues to play these games."

"Who is blaming her?" I asked. "Who is saying that?"

"All I can say is I hear things. I just want to make sure you're aware of them, and that nothing happens to her."

"Mike, nothing is going to happen to her."

At that point, I thought of the conversation I had had with The Wizard. One I did not convey.

"Wendy is comfortable with you. She trusts you, so please keep a close eye on this."

"Sure. And relax; I'll be in South Tampa next week." My cape flowed behind me again.

"I plan on coming out as well."

"Good. Hey, I'm house hunting so I'll call you tomorrow."

"Okay. Thanks, Larry."

Click.

I was pleasantly surprised by Mike's sincere concern. He seemed to have a genuine interest in her well-being. Much of that had to do with her being a CWUS recruit, but I was still impressed. Looking back, this call turned out to be a real turning point as he began to develop a trust in me. Being astute, he recognized the role I played with Wendy's comfort level and planted the seed to ensure that I diffused this potential disaster quickly, which I did.

The next day, The Wizard casually called me back in his office and then shifted gears in an attempt to pass the blame on Wendy for everything. I could tell this wasn't his script, but one he was passed, and exactly what Mike had heard. The Wizard first stated he went through one of her accounts that didn't look up to our standards.

"I'm not at all impressed." He glanced over at me. "And it certainly wasn't up to your standards."

"When were you in there?"

"Just yesterday."

"You didn't see Woodbridge (wine)…I was just there and it was out front and center."

He hesitated before answering, and only vaguely stated he saw some, but not enough. He then asked what I thought of Wendy, as if we didn't have this same conversation the day before.

"You really think she's the right person for this territory?" He leaned back in his chair.

"A month ago you thought so. And now, I agree with you."

He took a deep breath. "So you think it's her team. You picked them."

"No, I didn't. I'm making the best of that situation as well."

He completely ignored my response and squinted at his computer monitor. "You can't tell me this is all Faggalo and Koppelli."

"Yes, I can. You know that I know them well. They're friends, not to mention Koppelli's own people have said it's him. Like I said, this is not happening anywhere else in the state."

The Wizard paused and glowered at me. He was uncomfortable. He nodded and picked up his BlackBerry. His glasses were down his nose. Clearly frustrated, he realized I was not going to allow them to just rewrite this. And it was then, as he stared at the ceiling, that he incredibly changed his stance on Wendy. After leaning forward he casually proceeded to share a much lighter story of when she first interviewed with him. "I thought Wendy was interviewing for a sales position during her first interview. She nearly came across my desk when I mentioned sales. I'm a district manager she shouted. She's got fight."

I took a deep breath and exhaled. "Yes, she just needs a chance."

"You told me you didn't know her a month ago."

"I didn't."

He paused and awkwardly gazed at me. "And you think you know her now?"

"Yes. I can assure you I do."

He fell back in his chair and wiped his forehead. "All right, Coach, I have to take this."

"Sure, let me know if you have any other questions."

As I walked back to my office, I thought I should reach out to Wendy. She beat me to it when she called first. Without informing her of Mike's warning or of the conversation with The Wizard, I casually questioned her about the latest issues. She was anxious. It was clear she had heard the rumors too.

"Larry, I just really need you to ride with me. I know you're busy, but I need you."

"I will, right after the big meeting. I promise. We will fix this. Okay?"

"Fine."

Click.

CHAPTER TWELVE

TO INDULGING OUR SENSE
OF AMUSEMENT

OCTOBER 2009
AFTER HOURS

The next day, smoke settled while another fire caught on the east coast. As I walked in the office, Lori Erstaz informed me that Bud Fox had called looking for me. I thought that was strange because I had no missed call from him. I checked my BlackBerry again. She mentioned how wonderful a job he was doing and how happy she was for him.

I glanced at her with a raised eyebrow as I realized it was he who had told her that. Not wanting to say anything negative, I changed the subject. I asked if she had booked my hotel for the east coast holiday show then strolled into my office. It was clear Lori had a genuine liking for Fox and that he had begun using her as a crutch for support. With that to mull over, I exhaled as I picked up the phone to call him. But just then Lisa was calling me again.

"Hey, Lisa."

"Oh my God, Larry. I seriously am going to lose it."

I took another deep breath and exhaled. "What's wrong?"

"Larry, this guy thinks he is you. It's scary. He tries to sound like you, but everything is wrong. He doesn't have a clue how to manage people. Everyone on the team wants to file a complaint."

"Okay, hold on. That is not going to happen. Just breathe and relax. What is he doing?"

"Oh my God. He holds these meetings…he screams at us. He uses phrases I've heard you use, but he just fucks them all up. We have no direction, and then he curses at us. I won't be spoken to like this."

"No, of course not. I can't believe he's doing that."

"Why? He's not who you think he is and he does nothing but lie."

"Okay. Let me handle this. He's staying with me after the meeting. Stay strong until I have a chance to speak with him in person."

"Wait, what? He's staying with you?"

"Yes, after the meeting."

"That's all he cares about. He wants to party with you. He idolizes you. Don't do it, Larry."

"I didn't say 'party'; I said staying with me."

"Oh my God. Really, Larry? Okay, let me know how that works out. I have to go. Bye."

Click.

The big CWUS state meeting was just days after that call with Lisa. After it ended, we gathered at the hotel bar. The long day of wine classes had everyone dragging a bit. Well, everyone but Fox and I. We had plans to have dinner and a cigar. I had another early meeting at the office planned the next day with Mike Fritton.

Interestingly, I had spoken to Fox briefly about how everything was going with his team. I expected him to give me an earful, but he said very little. Since I would have the opportunity to get into his head at dinner, I ended the conversation. I noticed one of Fox's other sales reps, the one who drove them over, was clearly antsy to hit the road. So I gave him the "lets wrap it up" sign to head out. But then Lisa pulled me aside to chat. She put her hair up in a ponytail and with her blithe spirit beaming, suggested a change of plans.

"Larry, I think I'll stay." She leaned in with a smile. "I can go to dinner and then do the paperwork I need for Lori in the morning."

My gaze shifted across the room.

Annoyed, Fox threw his arms out. He was clearly mumbling something under his breath as he called me over to tell me Lisa's ride was leaving. Aside from the fact I was totally in the wrong for even entertaining her request, I could tell these two loathed each other.

As I made my way to Fox, he turned so our backs faced Lisa. "Did she just ask to stay?"

"Yes. But why do you two seem to be on such separate pages?"

He ignored me. "Listen to me. If it wasn't for Wendy pissing her off at the baseball game she would've jumped on your back and rode you home. You can't let her stay."

"Fox, calm down."

"You fucking already told her she could stay, didn't you?"

"No. Well, not exactly."

He displayed the traits of a jealous girlfriend. "I'm sending her home now." He stormed over to her as I went on to the bathroom.

When I got to the door I glanced back. She exhibited a look of disdain for him. By the time I walked back, they were all headed out. We went straight to dinner.

Since my corporate apartment was next to Channel Side—a bar and restaurant area where the cigar bar was—Fox talked me into eating at the Hooters right next door. As we pulled in, I said he would have to change his ways as a manager, dancing around his own delusions of grandeur. He became defensive as he digested the complaints and went off on them. I let him vent and then asked why he waited to tell me all of these negative things. He had no answer and interestingly, seemed more confused than angry.

After an awkward moment, he asked for my advice without actually admitting any wrongdoing. I spoke about building their trust, which would lead to gaining their respect. He nodded to everything I said, but then incredibly swore everything they reported to me was a lie. He seemed sincere, something I was also warned about. I remained calm and asked him why they would do that.

He leaned across the table. "They're fucking targeting me because I'm young and the boss."

I stared at him, pointing out that Lisa was his age and she was saying the same thing.

He had no response.

Shifting to a more positive slant, I emphasized how much I needed him. To have my confidence, seemed to be gratifying. He relaxed as I went through a list of things he had to do to get back on track with them. After that he leaned into me and informed me that the waitress thought he was hot.

"I'm sure she does," I said. "So do you have any questions?"

"No," he replied. "She's staring over here again."

"Fox, work hard comes before play hard. Any questions?"

He laughed. "Sorry...no this is perfect...thank you...I got this."

I wanted to keep it positive, but looking in his eyes I realized he would need to be micromanaged. As planned, we finished dinner and walked next door to the cigar bar. I felt a boost of energy because he really seemed appreciative of the talk and embraced the line that I needed him. We ordered a couple of beers and toured the cigar vault. The attractive bartender came in and facilitated our selections as we kicked back and lit up. Lady Gaga's "Love Game" blasted over the speakers. Fox's mood drastically improved

"Gaga." He began a little dance in his seat that I had to abruptly put a stop to.

"Stop. We don't dance, Bud. I'm getting another; do you want the same?"

Still dancing, he shouted, "I love it."

I walked up to the bar and glanced back. He was still dancing. I asked the bartender for two more. One of the waitresses from the Italian restaurant by my apartment noticed me.

"Hey, Larry. Working late, huh?" She gave me a once up and down in my suit.

"Oh, hey. How are you?"

"Great." I could feel her eyes burning into me before she said, "And I cannot believe you forgot my name."

I was upset that I went blank, but then noticed the bartender's eyes screaming she wanted to save me so I said, "Being the best waitress on the planet doesn't give you the right to insult me." I casually turned to the bartender. I raised my credit card up as she mouthed her name: "C-L-A-U-D-I-A." She was barely able to contain herself.

Claudia said, "Well, I'm waiting."

"It's Claudia. I'll see you next week, and I really do like the table overlooking the water. If that can be arranged it would be greatly appreciated."

"Oh, you did remember," she said with a warm smile. "Cool."

I felt great relief walking back to the table with the beers as two very young ladies (girls, really) came in. They walked up to the bar for drinks as two young guys cruised up behind them seemingly annoyed. My guess was that they were their boyfriends. The conversation became heated. Within seconds, they all walked outside. One of the girls glanced over at us. Minutes later, they came back in alone.

"GG, (Gordon Gekko)" (an old nick name of mine) "it's Showtime," Fox yelled as Claudia strolled over to chat.

"Bud Fox, this is my friend, Claudia."

Fox turned to me and rolled his eyes. He leaned in to shake her hand. "It's nice to meet you," he said.

I raised my glass to theirs. "To indulging our sense of amusement."

Fox's head slumped. "Jesus Christ, it fucking never ends."

Now bright red, Claudia shrugged and hit my glass. She repeated my toast and smiled.

It was after ten and the music seemed to be getting louder with each beer and shot. Fox was dancing again, now to "Circus" by Britney Spears. I grabbed another cigar. Fox rudely interrupted a conversation Claudia and I were immersed in.

"Listen to me," he whispered in my ear. "Those girls were our waitresses from tonight."

I looked over at them. "That's not them."

Fox grabbed his beer and leaned back to me. "It's them."

And it was. They had changed and let their hair down. He was hell-bent to convince me of this and extremely excited.

"Larry, the one kept asking where we were going tonight, remember?"

I nodded, but I really didn't. I told Fox to go in for the kill. The night suddenly had lift-off.

"You better lock that shit up, buddy boy," I laughed as he made his move.

"Shut up."

I was humored by his smitten reaction to them.

He wore his suit well and was looking handsome as I playfully continued. "Is Showtime your best time, buddy boy?"

He turned toward me. "Larry, I'm serious. Stop. Grow up."

I turned to tell Claudia that Fox was in love again. Just at that moment the very young waitress jumped up and ran over. She had that look in her eyes and landed right next to me as Fox stopped suddenly, turned in slow motion. He squinted at us and shook his head, then proceeded to the other one. Without wasting a second, she asked if I'd enjoyed dinner, so I lied and said yes. She asked if I enjoy Hooters, but that's where I had to draw the line, and say no. Claudia introduced herself to the girl, who completely shut her down. I sat back humored as she went to the bathroom. Through small talk came the fact that she knew my name. I realized I needed to be briefed.

"Can you give me one second?" I jumped up and pulled Fox aside. "Hey, what's this girl's name?"

He walked me further to the far wall and spewed, "Jesus Christ, Her name is Brittany. Did she ask about me?"

I hesitated for a brief moment. "Yes, she did. That's what I'm handling now for you." Fox lit up so I added, "But see if you can get her friend too, you fucking stud." I patted him on the back and said, "Showtime is your best time, my friend," while hauling ass and praying the other girl would grab his dick.

"Of course it is," he replied cockily.

The smell of perfume invaded my nostrils as I approached Brittany. She must have freshened up or something. I asked if she liked champagne. (She did.) I turned back to Fox, who now looked like he had just unwrapped his favorite gift on Christmas morning. His confidence seemed to be growing. I thought this was perfect. I was pumped.

I ordered a couple bottles of Moet to celebrate. "To magical moments," I said.

Brittany seductively replied, "And magical men."

I placed the bottle back in the bucket of ice. The Darkness blew cigar smoke in my eyes to cloud the fact they were alarmingly young. The music seemed even louder after the first bottle of Moet was upside down in the bucket of rapidly melting ice. Every other song caused the girls to dance with flashes going off to the merriment. Brittany pulled my suit jacket off while striking a stunning pose with her cigar for a memorable shot that Fox pleaded me not to hang on our new picture board at the office.

"Fox, life is a celebration, and tonight is the night you've seen the light, my boy."

"How are you going explain partying with your daughter's friends?"

Ten minutes later I went to the bartender to see if she'd even carded them.

She laughed, "Yes, they are good."

I felt better now wanting to let my handsome protégé know that he had clearance for lift-off. In the few minutes I stood with the bartender, my back to Fox, everything seemed to go awry. When I turned around to head to him I noticed the girl he was hitting on was now on her iPhone alone in the corner. Fox was just awkwardly standing there, seeming defeated. Shit, I thought. He walked toward the bathroom. I asked him what happened.

"She's not interested," he huffed.

I asked him if he wanted any champagne and that's when he completely lost it.

"It's fucking midnight. Will you look at the table? Listen to me. Jesus, don't even talk to me. Just give me your key. I want to go to bed."

"Money never sleeps, pal."

"This is so fucked up." He leaned to me and whispered. "This fucking child is giving you the fuck me eyes."

"Will you stop? This night is for you, buddy boy."

"Yeah, that's how they all start. I'm done. Give me your key."

"Weak people make me ill, buddy boy, and sheep..." I paused and pointed to him.

"Get slaughtered," Fox said. His cackle kicked back in.

Brittany rolled up my suit jacket sleeves and suggested we go into South Tampa.

"That's a great idea." I patted Fox on the ass and he closed his eyes.

"Come on, boys." Brittany tried to grab my hand in route to the parking garage. We looked at each other as Fox pushed me away. He mumbled under his breath, something about Lucifer again, and then chuckled uncontrollably.

After a brief ride through the pitch-black streets of South Tampa, Brittany turned down Eminem's "Crack a Bottle" and we pulled into the Green Iguana.

"You boys ready to paaartaaay?" she shouted.

I turned to Fox. He stared at me and let out a sudden guffaw. "The fucking guy sitting next to you is older than your father. He's just a freak of nature. Jesus, does anyone care?"

I took his rant as him having a second wind, but the reality of the situation was not that. Within an hour he was by himself on his phone.

"Fox, turn that frown upside down," I said. "Go get another round."

He squinted at me. "And pay with what?"

"Use your card! I'm gonna make you rich, Bud Fox. Rich enough to own this dump."

On occasion I've been known to provide bad information. This was one of those of times.

I found out a week later he had rung up so much nonsense on his brand new corporate card he had blown half his budget before his second full month on the job. But that didn't matter, at least not on this night, because as I walked back from the bathroom Brittany had another round of shots, beers, and something in a giant pink cup with ice cubes, all lined up and ready go.

"Laaarrrry, shots. Yup, yup." She proceeded to sing some rap song I'd never heard in its entirety while grinding her bar stool.

But it was at that point I couldn't even joke about them being

Mermaids. I mean they were minnows, clearly years away from Mermaid status. The reality was that with Fox now out of the picture this was all so fucking remarkably wrong.

Suddenly unsettled, I turned to Fox and whispered, "We need a cab."

"Get the fuck away from me!" he snipped.

It was then Brittany's seductive voice whispered in my ear. "You're the reason I came out tonight, and I'm keeping this jacket, ya know."

My eyes grew wide as Fox's head dropped back between his knees when the two girls jumped up to grind each other. That's when the lights went off and then on and the music turned off, and a mean voice shouted. "We should've been closed an hour ago...everyone out!"

We stumbled into the street. He stated they called us a cab, but that was bad information. Since no cab came and no one could drive, we left the car there and wandered through the streets of South Tampa to their house.

"You guys can call a cab and give them our address," she said, now with hiccups.

Fox had an exaggerated smile, reminiscent of the Joker in Batman, etched across his face. "You okay?" I asked as he staggered on.

No answer.

By the time we made it to their house, I realized my morning meeting was only a few hours away and we still were in our suits from the big CWUS meeting the day before.

Brittany again tried to hold my hand. I had visions of her father coming at us with a bat. That's when I stopped, pulled my hand away and motioned for Fox.

"Fox, find out if they live with their parents," I said softly.

"I would give my right arm for a bucket of Holy water to throw on you," he replied deliriously. "Get away from me. I hope the guy has a gun and shoots me first." It was seconds later that his infamous hissing cackle kicked in before he muttered, "I fucking love you."

He was clearly torn.

Two hours later, with my tie wrapped around my head and sunlight seeping through the blinds, Fox pulled me out of bed. It was actually a mattress on the floor.

"Listen to me, the cab is out front. You need to get up," he said.

My eyes opened slowly. "What time is it?"

"It's after six."

I pulled my tie off and sat up. "F-u-c-k...Okay."

The cab dropped us off in the empty parking lot at Chanelside to pick up Fox's car. We were both dragging, although Fox giggled deliriously driving the mile back to my apartment. Even though this night didn't go as planned, Fox's take away was another party night he cherished. This was something, at the time, I thought was a positive. It was not. We went up to get thirty minutes of shut-eye before showering and running back out the door. I tore my suit off and jumped into bed.

CHAPTER THIRTEEN

THE PAJAMA PARTY THAT WASN'T

OCTOBER 2009
THE EAST COAST WINE SHOW

Thirty minutes later, the sun was up. I rolled over in the bed to plug my BlackBerry in. Just as I did, it rang. It was The Wizard. He inquired about the itinerary and who was going to be on the South Tampa audit for CWUS. I regained my composure and informed him that both the state director and east coast VP was on the run.

"When you get to the office I need the list," he said in a curt tone, and ended the call.

After I showered I ran into my closet, tripped over the suit I had just ripped off, and flew into my hanging shirts with the sensation I was going to puke. I got up slowly, proceeded to pick out a spectacular ensemble, and shouted across the apartment at Fox. I realized he was still unconscious, left him there, and ran out the door.

Within five minutes my BlackBerry rang again. It was Fox.

"Fox, I have no time for recaps today. Lock the door, get back to the coast, and fix your shit."

"Listen to me, my Goddamn good man. That was the greatest night—"

Click.

I pulled through the security gate, and raced into my parking spot. I hopped out, flew up the steps, swiped my security card, and dashed down the hall toward our office. I ran right into Tony Trappelleti.

"Sir Sola, looks like you've been entertaining again, sir," he said.

"Another late night?"

I shook my head and continued on my way. I passed my friend Jerry Laker's office and couldn't help but notice the inquisitive look on his face. It was one that I would soon expect. Not in the mood for entertaining, I strolled past Lori without my normal humorous one-liner. She noticed my sunglasses were still on and decided to check on me.

"You all right?" She was clearly looking for a scoop.

I nodded my head. All was good. I noticed Tony right behind her. He came back to the office after we passed in the hall, as if he were the Paparazzi looking for a story and picture. He stopped at the edge of my desk, shading it from the dim yellow light as if he were a giant oak tree.

"What's up Tony?" I asked as he sat down.

He gazed at me and reiterated how special this experience had been and how happy he was to be a part of it. Unfortunately, he didn't stop there. He bared his teeth with a smile. "I've noticed you have a special way with women, sir. I enjoy watching you in action."

I scrambled for my water. "I enjoy connecting with people, Tony."

He smirked. "Yes, I can see that, sir, and they enjoy connecting with you. It's a gift."

I looked at him. "Not like that, Tony."

He raised his hand to his mouth to wipe the smile off. "When am I going to be blessed to have a night out with you?"

I ripped the cap off my Evian. "Soon, after we have a successful audit." I took a giant gulp.

"I wanted you to know that Wendy still doesn't seem to want my help, sir."

She was calling me.

"Who is that, sir?" He smiled wide, as if he knew.

At that point I had had enough. I sent her call to voicemail and informed him I needed to prepare for a meeting. I made my way up to the meeting with Mike Fritton and the new Tampa wine director, John McFallon. I had only recently met John, but could sincerely say he was someone I had hit it off with. He was definitely one of the good guys.

He congratulated me upon arrival. "Larry, I'm really impressed, man. Pulling that off in a transition month is nothing I thought possible."

I shrugged, feeling queasy.

He read the final September numbers with a smile. "I've heard many good things. I'm really looking forward to you being in Tampa, man."

I thanked him as Mike added, "It was a great first month, especially with all of the games being played in South Tampa."

John casually kept it positive while avoiding that controversial lead in. We went over the audit itinerary. Mike handed us CWUS's audit expectations. New nausea came on when he hit the lights to begin his presentation. I took a quick nap. Minutes later, he questioned me and I had no idea what he was asking. I sat up and spewed some bullshit.

They nodded and John said, "Good stuff."

With each new slide, I held on for dear life. Finally the meeting ended. The battery on my BlackBerry had died halfway through. When I plugged it in back in my office, I noticed one missed call from Fox, two from Lisa, two from Wendy, and a text from her stating to call her. It appeared that Tony was still testing her by pushing his helping hand in her face, knowing she would continue to refuse it. Everything I had heard about this guy was now coming into focus as the truth.

The fact that I was still as supportive as I was with him spoke volumes to the success of our fast start. The reality was I shouldn't have been. Days before he'd attempted to throw Danny Koppelli under the bus for foul play in another account. There was definitely bad blood between them and this was Tony's way of attempting to get even.

It was a lie that was not only blatant, but gave them reason to cast doubt on everything that was true. To make matters worse, it was one of our sales reps who stated that even though Koppelli was responsible for a lot, he wasn't guilty of Tony's accusations. This was something that baffled me and another important side-note to the storyline.

When Tony came back into the office I asked him why he would do such a thing. He stated that the sales rep backed Koppelli because he was scared of him. He went on to say he shouldn't have said anything, but never admitted to lying. Later that day, I confirmed it with another conversation with the same sales rep. I shook my head and thanked him as another email came in, one which made this disturbance fade into the background.

The Sith Lord, who was now in charge of all North Florida, reached out to personally thank me for producing the highest increase in the state for the new division. Right after that, I received another email from John McFallon reiterating his appreciation while copying in the Sith Lord and The Wizard: The Sith was the only one who replied to the email.

By early October, we had our first successful month on the books along with a stellar recap of the first audits. I received an email thanking me for our efforts from the new State Director who'd been just announced, yet someone I would only be temporarily reporting to. He ran the entire CWUS business plan for our company.

Moving into the second week of the month, I had one major event left: the east coast holiday show. After receiving another text from Wendy I let her know my calendar finally cleared in time to assist her. I spoke about meeting the following Tuesday while I made my way back to the apartment to pack for the East Coast Holiday Wine Show. She called me to discuss a few things on my ride east, relieved that we had a date set for Tuesday to meet.

Two hours later I checked into the hotel and noticed Lisa stroll by with a smile and her thumb pointed behind. Fox followed, looking to talk. A long time winery supplier walked up to say hello. Fox kept going. After the conversation, Fox was nowhere in sight, so I went to my room and showered. Within the hour, I made my way down to the wine tasting without ever speaking with him.

Wine tasting is not just like art, it *is* an art. While wine tasting can be subjective in nature, wine connoisseurs follow some general "guidelines" when evaluating a wine. This was not that. No, this particular tasting was a debacle. Within three hours the upstairs "party" (tasting) came to a close, as the downstairs "party" at the bar had begun. As I walked in, I was handed a shot and a sarcastic remark I didn't catch. It was loud and a glass shattered on the floor. I turned to it and noticed Lisa approaching. She quickly made a table for four into one for two.

"Larry, we can sit here," she cried out with a broad smile.

Fox walked in.

He was upset. Lisa informed me she was going up to her room to change and again pointed to the table she reserved to make sure I didn't lose it. People continued to stumble in. When she skipped out, Fox grabbed my arm. He wanted to talk.

"Listen to me, this fucking girl has to go. She is bad news for both of us," he said.

I motioned him to the side. As he continued, I let him know that we would speak in the morning, but that sent him into a paranoid tailspin.

"She's using all this complaint bullshit as an excuse to talk to you. Believe me, I hear things, and all of these suppliers talk."

My eyes grew wide at him as I pulled him further off to the side. "I'm serious," he said looking behind him. "They no longer have your back. And now that you're not handling their brands, they don't give a shit about you."

"Calm down. This is about your issues managing your team."

He ignored my statement. "I'm talking about having your back. I don't care how many of them hug you and tell you you're great. Some of these guys want to see you go off a cliff."

TJ Faggallo walked in.

"Who?" I asked.

"I don't trust Faggallo at all. Lori Erstaz told me the other admin in Tampa hate him. He's a lying prick, and The Wizard is best friends with him. They don't like you, Larry."

"Fox, we will talk about this in the morning."

I turned and he grabbed my arm. "There are people in this room that are envious of you and want to see you fail. You've climbed too fast. That is what I'm talking about."

I looked him in the eyes. "Success always brings envy, and enemies, Fox, but you can't stop being successful because of them."

"Yes, but these fucked up people will burn you, even with something this ridiculous. You are too trusting. These people are not your friends."

Out of the corner of my eye, I noticed a random taster wave at him with a salty smile. Fascinated, I allowed this little wine induced fling to be the diversion to what I knew was more truth than I could digest. "Who's that?" I asked.

Fox's mood changed rapidly. "This chick wants me bad, would you mind...?"

"No, go ahead."

He took a step and turned to me. "There are fucked up people in this company."

I raised my hand like a proud father. "Go."

To further help me along in this matter, The Darkness tapped me on the shoulder. "She's back."

I turned to see Lisa wearing her pajamas with her hair up in a cute ponytail. I couldn't believe it. I tried not to stare, but I had to confirm that she came back in her pajamas. She pulled my chair out for me. I smiled awkwardly. Glancing out, I quickly realized Fox had definitely heard some nasty shit because I turned to my right and noticed TJ Faggalo and three suppliers staring at us. Fox's words continued to resonate in my head.

I kept going back and forth attempting to play it off. I looked back over to see TJ Faggalo quickly look at his phone. And he was not at all smooth. Lisa asked me what was wrong. Faggalo looked back over at us and abruptly turned away. Was I paranoid? At the moment I thought I was, but that changed within five minutes.

The Wizard appeared at our table and tapped me on the arm. He sternly stated he needed to talk with me outside, briskly escorted me through the double doors and into the parking lot, refusing to stop in the lobby.

He informed me that he'd received a few calls, during his card game, about a girl getting way too close to me. I stood in shock while calmly giving him the benefit of the doubt. I then explained emphatically that I had it under control. He only pressed on as I became increasingly irritated.

Should I have been more discrete? Absolutely, but I had no idea the girl was changing into her pajamas. Even with that, pulling me out of there as if she were carrying a deadly disease was ludicrous.

"Larry, how many of these am I going to have to pull you out of? Do you realize how this looks? She's sharing your drink, leaning over to whisper in your ear, in her pajamas."

"She wasn't sharing my drink."

He glanced at his BlackBerry. "I heard she was drinking from your glass."

"She wasn't. But I understand what you're saying. Once again, I have this under control," I said as he continued to ignore me.

He carried on, seemingly targeting me. My eyes grew wide as I then wondered why he didn't stop of one of the guys who passed us with a prostitute. But what happened next actually had this second time-out, in as many weeks, seem somewhat justified to an outsider looking in.

Just as his lecture was wrapping up we heard a female's voice scream out. "Laaaarrrry." The Wizard winced as if he just took an electric shock.

Lisa sashayed down the long hall, in her pajamas. She gleefully waved, with her ponytail now in the attack position. The reality simply was that nothing I could've explained would've been believable at this point.

Nothing.

She gave it a few minutes and came right out the front door of the hotel with both guns blazing and her ponytail saluting. Her passion and lascivious moxie was unstoppable. My hands wiped the smile off my face, as the disbelief etched across The Wizard's. His eyes bulged forward as he pushed me behind him. "Go straight to your room and don't come out. Now!" His reaction caused me to turn and haul ass.

Minutes later I shook my head to it all opening the door to my room. I tossed my tie on the dresser and collapsed on the bed with an unyielding desire to speak to Wendy Darlington. My head turned to the clock on the nightstand. I should've realized it was too late. But since I still felt like a sixteen-year-old, (in another time-out) I didn't. So I called her.

Wendy answered. She sounded delighted.

CHAPTER FOURTEEN

WENDY'S INAUGURAL FLIGHT

OCTOBER 2009
SOUTH TAMPA

I pulled into the driveway at our east coast home that Friday night preoccupied with the new team. The successful start was encouraging, and from a business standpoint all was well, but from a personal one this abbreviated family time and how I handled it began to take its toll.

After sharing a few laughs with the kids, I would then brace myself for the mounting tension that became the elephant in the room. This was when Marie would peer at me cockeyed after I trivialized her latest inquiry as my mind amazingly wandered with a fresh focus to ensure October's success.

It was all incredible. I was able to motivate a sales division in ways few could, yet was unable to properly answer my wife's Friday query sessions. I wanted her to show some form of confidence. But I was a fool not realizing these unfathomable indiscretions weren't making it all worse. This particular night's interrogation focused on Lisa Fenna after Marie noticed her name flash up on my BlackBerry.

"Oh, it's that Lisa girl again." She hovered like jealous teenager.

I took a deep breath and attempted to change the subject. "Where do you want to eat tomorrow?" I lunged for the bottle of Wild Horse Pinot Noir, yearning for its flavors of cherry, pomegranate, cola, and Asian spices.

Her head tilted to me as her eyes grew wider. "Are you going to answer me?"

I took a sip and then another. "It seems that the only time we speak is when you have a question about a female."

Her eyes blinked erratically and she knew it was true. But she said, "That's not true."

I nodded. "It absolutely is."

She ignored me; focused on one thing. "What happened at the tasting with Lisa?" She paused. I could only shake my head as she quickly added, "You never told me how you handled her issue."

Now pissed off and anxious and overwhelmed by the absurdity of it all, I ignored her. "I still have to talk to her." It became a slap-stick comedy with serious overtones.

She grabbed the wine bottle for a bit more. "I thought you did." She took a sip.

"Not to resolve it," I said, chafed as she impatiently shrugged her shoulders.

It was during this moment of trepidation that I went over how the truth would sound in my head: "The reason I didn't get to resolve her problem was because I was pulled out of a bar after an idiot with ulterior motives called a vice president to "warn" him that she "appeared" to be too close to me, again—but this time wearing her pajamas with her hair up in a cute ponytail." And that's when I made an executive decision to babble on while racing to the wine vault for another bottle.

But therein lies my point. See, I knew I was going somewhere with this.

The magnificent mystery of how destiny grants us encounters that are so compelling, we can't stay away. And before you get all judgmental on me, just think about it.

See, I knew you could relate.

And as Marie continued to question me about Lisa these mystical forces that be, had my mind zeroing in on Wendy. I didn't know why. Ten minutes later Marie took a call out on the pool patio as I began flipping through the channels. Then a text hit my BlackBerry. I grabbed it to see it was Wendy: "I sent you my update for tomorrow's team email. I'm going to win the incentive!"

I smiled and glanced back to the television. I had landed on a program explaining that destiny is a fixed sequence of events that is inevitable. I sat fascinated as the narrator detailed the conditions and experiences attracted in life, as new material hit me for my team emails.

But let me back up a second.

It was at this moment of the story that these team emails became a platform to entertain as much as they were a catalyst to drive the team to achieve the attached goals, (now even more so than with my previous teams) and much to their delight. So much so, that my administrative assistant, Lori Erstaz, insisted on being copied on them. In fact, the week before, Andrew Rawley, the district manager who ran my old Space Coast territory, had called me tickled, curious to know how many admin start their Saturdays enthusiastically chiming in on work emails with subject lines that read: Team Sales Goals.

In essence, what it boiled down to was that my new crew was excited to be a part of a productive program that instilled outrageous fun; one that seemingly had everyone's undivided attention, specifically, young Wendy Darlington.

The next day, shortly after sending my Saturday email out, two members of the team were quite amused at how Wendy had excitedly joined the team email retorts. On Sunday she texted me: "I love reading your emails! *Smiley face* Do you head back to Tampa early Monday? We have a busy week ahead."

I informed her I did and looked forward to finally helping her.

She called early Monday morning as I drove back to Tampa. It was almost exactly the same time she had the Monday before. So as I merrily rode along, I turned down Kelly Clarkson's "My Life Would Suck Without You," and answered, "Hi Wendy."

"Hey, did you get my email?"

"No. I'm driving. When did you send it?"

"Oh, ten minutes ago. I sent the list of accounts we're hitting tomorrow."

"Right, and I'm actually going to have to move that to Wednesday."

"Larry, really, really?"

"I'm sorry, but Wednesday for sure. Are you not available Wednesday?"

"I'm available, but you know I need your help. Are you going to the office?"

"Yes. It's going to be a long day of meetings." There was a pause in the conversation. "Wendy?"

"Fine. Bye."

I couldn't help but smile. "Goodbye, Wendy."

Click.

After a long day of meetings, chocked full of grey area, an email flashed up with the subject line that read: Holiday Budget. It was from Mike Fritton, who copied Dan Schultz, my new North Tampa district manager. In time, Schultz became my dear French friend, who really wasn't French. I actually made him French when he called me after we had one too many bottles of wine while stumbling through France at EPCOT center. Too much information? You're probably right. Let me try that again.

Schultz was a seasoned veteran who The Wizard had brought up to me after he realized I wasn't happy with Faggalo's "draft." But it was Mike who was ultimately responsible for bringing him on board, a special talent who utilized a large portion of that budget for his team's holiday tables. That's the reason he was copied. As I finished reading the details of the budget, Lori stuck her cheerful face in to say goodnight. I wished her the same as I was leaving.

But just as I reached for my laptop bag to pack up, I received an email I was expecting the next day. As odd as that was, it came with urgency that required a prompt response. So I sat back down and read it before I made my way to the bathroom. I couldn't help but notice there seemed to be an eerie calm throughout the building. Even stranger was the fact that I didn't see anyone. Not even the cleaning crew.

That was really weird.

I received a text from Bud Fox. He wanted to know what brand of shoes I wore at the last tasting. I laughed and headed back to my desk to respond to the email.

In another case of seemingly scripted magical meant to be moments, I didn't end up leaving the office for twenty minutes. Why is that important? Well, if I left when I was supposed to, I would've missed a surprise guest, one that bestowed an enchanting evening on me that transcended the storyline.

It was as if I was on a movie set and the director yelled, "Quiet on the set." I finished my response to the email and the director shouted, "And action."

My finger hit send as in strolled Wendy Darlington. "Hey," she said casually, perfectly on cue as a small smile broke from her lips.

"Oh, hi, Wendy." My eyebrow rose, and froze, to the director's delight.

With her lips slightly parted, she took a step back, hit her mark, and peeked into the main part of the office. She glanced back at me. Her appealing eyes twinkled with mirth. I sat there enthralled—the casting director would've marveled at our chemistry—and exuded glee.

Wendy had the same look in her eyes that she had when she placed the apple on my desk, and at the baseball game, just more guarded.

"Is everything okay?" I asked, increasingly intrigued.

She nodded and walked back into my office nonchalantly. "Yes, I have to..." She paused pretending to read something before spouting, "Fill out something for Lori. Is she gone?"

I peered at Wendy, captivated. "Yes, she leaves at five. Can I help you with something?"

She continued on into my office and calmly replied, "No, I'll wait."

I refused to ruin this magical moment by asking her what it was. I placed my laptop in its bag. "Oh, okay." I paused, at a loss for words, until she took another step toward me.

Her eyes glistened as she turned away. I felt this indescribable rush of euphoria.

"Would you like to grab something to eat?" I said.

She turned back to me and said rather collectively, "Sure."

I nodded smiling.

"I'll take you by 611 (one of her accounts) first."

"Okay. Lead the way."

Clearly I didn't have a clue. What I did know was that something very odd was settling in around us, something dark and mysterious, and oh-so alluring.

"I'm right over there," she said.

It was perfect weather, a gift with all the promise of an evening of enchantment. The second star to the right was burning bright. I turned to the empty parking lot and grinned as I told her I'd drive around to follow. We drove into South Tampa and quickly toured her account, 611, for shits and giggles before spinning around the block to Cork, a trendy wine bar.

The owner greeted us. "Hi, folks. Have a seat. I'll be right with you guys." He smiled warmly and walked to the bar. The conversation flowed as if our mindsets were synced, before the owner came back over. After we responded to two of his questions with the same answers, he smirked oddly and asked us what our selection was.

Our heads turned in unison to him. "Kim Crawford Sauvignon Blanc," we said congruently.

His eyebrows arched trying to figure us out before realizing he didn't want to go down that road. Nodding, he then rushed off to grab our favorite New Zealand white, quite humored.

Rushing back, his eyes shifted to Wendy, then to me, as he poured our first glass. And it was just as the complex nose evoked floral and fruity notes that I realized Wendy planned on booking return flights to my sacred Never Land without ever using a runway. She was coming in hot, arms out, soaring high through the bewitching moonlit sky, and her dress was black, not light blue, with her hair up in an adorable ponytail to conceal her delightfully dark aura.

With time absconding as rapidly as the delicious wine was flowing, I was drawn to her eyes. They reflected the same enraptured state I felt. As if I was looking in the mirror. It's impossible for me to put it in words, so I won't even try. I just felt we should celebrate it.

"Kind sir, please bring us another bottle of Kim."

With each delightful glass, my palms inexplicably began to sweat. I found myself held captive, defenseless to the absolute clarity that she exhibited the same irresistible traits of Peter's Wendy. It was something that I had pushed my thoughts away from since the baseball game, but no longer could deny, so I dreamt for a diversion…and poof! A flurry of pixie dust landed on her phone and it rang. It was her mother.

"Mom, I'm with my new boss, Larry," she said excitedly. "Wait, you have to say hi to him, hold on."

It was thirty minutes after that amusing conversation when we returned to the real world. I glanced at a bunch of missed texts as Wendy received another call. It was her boyfriend, Jessie Reese. Just as it rang, I hopped up to go to the bathroom, and spun around with my own dilemma: Marie called.

"Hey." I stood outside the bathroom wondering why I answered.

"You haven't responded to my texts? I thought you were calling me when you got back to your apartment." She huffed.

"I know. I will…but I'm not back."

"Do you realize what time it is?"

"No."

"It's really late, who are you with?"

"Oh…I'm sorry. I didn't realize. But I was finally able to spend some time with Wendy Darlington."

There was an awkward pause as I heard something slam shut. "Call me when you get back to your dorm room." *Bang.*

Click.

Oh, that went well, I thought.

I began to walk back to the table and Bud Fox called.

"Hey," I said.

"Why aren't you answering my texts? Where are you?"

"A wine bar in South Tampa called Cork."

His infamous hissing cackle pierced my ear. "I fucking love it. Listen to me, my Goddamn good man, don't even attempt to tell me you're with (Tony) Trappelleti."

"What? No, I'm in a team—bonding—meeting with another manager."

"Jesus, you're with Wendy Darlington. I fucking love you."

"Fox, I'll call you tomorrow."

Click.

I walked back to the table. Wendy smiled and we held each other's gaze before she mentioned a new pressing issue in her territory. I stood thoroughly impressed that she still had such a sharp focus to her work priorities after consuming that much wine, so I pretended.

I glanced at my schedule and said, "I already have you on my calendar for Wednesday."

"You had me down for Tuesday before you changed it…Larry, this is important."

"I'll make time for you tomorrow—late in the afternoon…okay?"

"Okay. I'll call you in the morning," she replied.

My chest was out and my hands were on my waist when the owner walked around my flowing cape to drop the bill off.

"It was a pleasure, Wendy and Larry. I hope to see you both again soon." He smiled curiously.

We strolled out to the parking lot under the enchanting moonlit sky where we chatted some more before another text hit my BlackBerry. Smiling brightly, she reached up to hug me goodnight. I thought that was sweet. I walked over to my navi and knocked the inch of pixie dust off my door handle to get inside. I began to back out, when she quickly pulled her little white car up to mine.

"I'll see you tomorrow," she confirmed.

"Yes, Wendy. Goodnight."

"Goodnight."

CHAPTER FIFTEEN

THE SLEEPOVER

NOVEMBER 2009
HARBOUR ISLAND

The team's camaraderie, more so than its talent, fueled our triumphant October. The buzz in the office air had members of other divisions wandering in, wide-eyed and curious. This was more than a sales function; this was a winning culture that drove us. And it was infectious. The images of our weekly conquests hung on our illustrious picture board, leaving many mystified.

By early November, I had a folder of (confidential) emails from individuals inquiring about opportunities in the new division. Word was spreading that we won, and had fun doing it. It was a team that understood the benefits of making a difference each and every day. There was no doubt we had to work smarter, with fewer home run hitters in our lineup, but it was a healthier business plan that the young team embraced.

With our sights set on November. I packed up, yet again, to head back to Tampa after another short weekend. By this point, Marie and I seemed to be using the excitement of shopping for our dream home as a distraction from the tension between us. It wasn't an ideal situation, but it lessened the stress to have an ultimate goal of the family being together in Tampa that following summer. I made my way into the kitchen to pour my last cup of coffee and caught the World Series recap on ESPN. My Yankees closed in on their twenty-seventh World Series Championship, which they would win that Wednesday. With all in my world seemingly splendid, I placed my Tinkerbell coffee mug down, kissed the family goodbye, and raced off.

The further west I drove, the more apparent it became that I was living more of a separate life with each passing week than I wanted to acknowledge. So I didn't. I only merrily drove past the red flags that were rising, while I hopped onto I-4, gleefully taking Wendy Darlington's early "drive back" call as if the ever increasing time we spent together was normal.

Wendy had actually begun rearranging her workout and team meeting schedules for earlier in the morning so that her late afternoons were free for our alluring "Wine Time" ritual. This is a tradition I'll expand on as the concerns about how close we were getting began to circulate. The first of these warnings came from Matt McMullen. By this point, we were close as well, and since he knew Wendy from their previous distributor, we all began hanging out.

Our favorite place was the Greek restaurant "Acropolis" in Ybor City. We would call it the "Greeks." "Meet ya at the Greeks," we would say. Once there, I would sit in the same chair against the wall of wine and place my wallet and BlackBerry next to me as the hilarity commenced. Even with the entire team tight, there was no doubt Matt and Wendy were two of my favorites.

We shared some great times, until one night Matt turned to me when Wendy went to the bathroom hissing, "Mayor, really? Really?"

"What's wrong?" I smiled while texting Bud Fox.

"She's completing your fucking sentences, and you think it's all normal?"

I read a reply from Fox before I turned back to Matt and winked. "It's all good."

"Mayor, when you both say the word "what?" you say "whaa?" Then you smile at each other as if the joke's on everyone else."

I smiled. "It is."

He awkwardly peered at me as I explained that I just had a strong connection to her. Although he seemed unconformable I thought he was done, but he wasn't. His message suddenly came with urgency. "Our waiter, Chops, thinks you two are married."

"Matt, the team is being recognized by everyone for doing some great things and it starts with our camaraderie. Plug into the positive energy."

"Mayor, no doubt this experience has been great, and that's awesome for the team, but the way she acts with you is not normal, and people are talking."

"You're overreacting."

"Do you think her boyfriend would think so? And I know him." He paused and stared at me as I sent my reply to Fox. "Mayor, I know him."

"I do too." I took a sip of wine. "I met him. He was fine." I placed my BlackBerry down. "We all went to dinner. It's all good." I raised my glass to his.

Wendy came back to the table with lusty eyes. I ordered another bottle. Matt then texted me that he couldn't believe I'd met her boyfriend, Jessie Reece. I didn't say why we met because it was an eye-opening phone conversation that would only back his concern. So I focused on the dinner afterwards, which was pleasant. Although one that Wendy frantically set.

You see, Jessie's rather agitated call came when Wendy was driving me back to my corporate apartment, again later than expected. During that conversation—which I heard crystal clear—he became incensed that she was with me again. And although he was livid, it was actually her reaction that fascinated me. She compartmentalized it all safely away before the call even ended. I was amazed. This was a side of her I hadn't seen yet. Now I was dying to know what was going through her mind. It was clear her wheels were spinning.

After she dropped me off, she sped to his house and called me back with her plan. "You have to meet us across the street from your apartment to have dinner."

My hand fell against the kitchen counter to hold myself up. "Wait. Meet who?"

"Jessie and I will be there in twenty minutes."

"What are you talking about?"

"Larry, you have to meet him…and just do what you do."

"Are you fucking kidding me right now?"

"No."

"Wendy, I heard the conversation in the car. He was losing it and you said nothing."

At first, she didn't respond, but within seconds she shouted, "That's why you have to meet us!"

That's when I didn't respond.

"Larry, I swear I will come up there and carry you down if you don't come meet us."

"Okay. Calm down. You're starting to turn me on."

"Larry, twenty minutes," she snapped.

"Okay—"

Click.

I walked down, twenty-five minutes later, and they were already at a sidewalk table with cocktails. Mind you, we already partook in our "Wine Time." That was why we were late, again. So with both of us throwing back a bottle of Kim each, I did my best to come across as if we weren't in Never Land all afternoon celebrating the fact that Cupid shot us in the ass with his arrows. It wasn't easy, but I smiled at them and as I crossed the street this little skit she concocted commenced.

My first thought was that she appeared anxious and older. I didn't like it. My second, which should've been my first, was that I didn't want to sit across from him in fear he had a gun. After an awkward introduction, I quickly realized he was nothing like I envisioned. He was attractive, short in stature, normally dressed, and actually one of the nicest people I'd ever met. He was a sincere and caring individual who loved her. It figured. I mean, to go from the conversation I heard in the car to an evening that ended up flowing nicely with light laughter and libations, floored me. And he was a fellow Leo. It was funny because Wendy had guessed that about me during our first date; I mean that first time we went to Cork…our first date.

Aside from her being a completely different person than what I'd grown accustomed to, the night as a whole was a success, one which interestingly included a conversation where Jessie took business trips to Connecticut a few days a month. His next trip was a couple weeks away, which brings us to where we are presently in the story. It was another enchanting evening when Wendy reminded me that she had a key to the cloud door above my sacred Never Land and was never giving it back. But let's back up to that afternoon first. I was at a lunch meeting with Geno Franc when Wendy texted me about meeting up.

Just as I noticed her first text, she sent another. I casually pulled my BlackBerry under the table to read them during Franc's sermon—one I marveled at how different each conversation with he and The Wizard was. When Franc went to the bathroom I sent Wendy a reply: "I can't meet today. I have a late conference call."

As the lunch concluded, Franc again reiterated his appreciation for our early accomplishments while informing me that he was going to be on the next market audit. He went on to say that one of the CWUS big wigs would be on it as well, and wanted to make sure everything would impress him. I assured him it would as we were going through Dan Schultz's territory in North Tampa, an area that always looked good because of his long-standing relationships there.

Back at the office, before my conference call, Wendy and I continued to communicate while deciding to meet up much later, around seven.

We met at Jackson's, a bar on Harbour Island, not far from my apartment. By this point we had moved our play dates out to Westchase, a suburb of Tampa. But with Jessie out of town, we decided to begin at Jackson's. And since it was just around the corner from my apartment, I walked over. While sitting at the back bar—which was outside with views of the water—waiting for Wendy, Bud Fox called.

"Hey, hold on," I answered.

"Did Lisa call you?" He paused before he shouted, "Where are you now?"

I pulled the BlackBerry up to my ear. "Hey, I told you to hold on." I waved to an old supplier friend who had been mysteriously banished from the industry. He looked different. I was taken aback. "Fox, I'm out. I'll call you tomorrow morning. I need to say hello to someone."

"Jesus. Are you with Wendy again? It's every fucking day...I love you—"

"I'll call you tomorrow."

"Listen to me. I'm staying with you again next week and we're going to tear it up—"

Click.

I walked over to him and realized it had been a of couple years since I'd seen him. He briefly explained that it was the company politics that ultimately did him in. I felt badly, because he seemed to be struggling with the entire story. He had to get back to work and said he would catch up with me later. I told him we would be around the bar.

After he disappeared with a tray of glasses, I glanced out over the water. The moon was shining down on it beautifully. I walked back to the bar. The warm autumn night had an enchanting tropical feel to it. I sat back down and Wendy texted me: "I'm here."

Minutes later, I noticed her coming around the bar. I didn't see her walk through the door so I assumed she came in stealth: arms out soaring through the moonlit sky with pixie dust all around her. As she turned to me, her irresistible youthful glow was beaming bright.

I caught her gaze before she looked away. It was clear she was scanning the faces and praying she wouldn't recognize any of them. I laughed gently.

She casually approached me acting like this was some fortuitous encounter. "Hey," Wendy said softly as she hopped up on the bar stool. Her eyes continued to search the space.

I peered at her, astonished. "Oh hi," I replied, "What a coincidence seeing you here."

A smile curled on her adorable face.

I stared at her for a moment, and then said, "Seriously though," I paused and chuckled. "We've spent a ton of time together and —"

She interrupted. "Um, hello, I have your number one territory...we better." Her green eyes glistened as she added, "Besides I had a dream about you. It was so weird...but good."

I sat enthralled.

We were such similar creatures who both naturally — and masterfully, I might add — overrode reality, while fueling the fire that allowed this dark affinity we shared to continue to grow. And our unique chemistry seemed to be noticed by everyone.

So with the emergence of my old supplier friend and his newly formed raised eyebrow to our special friendship, we decided to leave. We went down the block to Chanelside. Back to LIT. We were laughing giddily as we pulled into the valet.

The guy grabbed my cash and her keys. "Have a great night

folks," he said.

"He thinks we're a couple," she gushed, tickled.

I smiled and made a head gesture to the second star to the right, as our Never Land jesting, once again, took flight. "Wendy," I whispered. "That's the star that will always lead you to me...in Never Land...where those dreams of yours really can come true."

Her eyes were ablaze. "Um, I know. That's why I plan on keeping the key. And don't think I'll ever forget what cloud the door (to my sacred land) is in—it was a really good dream."

I stood captivated.

So again, with a smile I couldn't wipe off my face, and in no rush to grow up, we soared off like two kids, (even though I nearly sixteen years older) far away from any adult reasoning or rational thought. And this is when she gave me her little patented head nod, full of verve, while reminding me again that she had the key for her uninterrupted access to my sacred land.

This key bit was something that started in our office when I found an old key in my desk. I left it on her laptop with a note: *Your key to the cloud door to my sacred Never Land, Milady.* She walked back in, lit up, and skipped out sportively. But then she came right back in standing proud. "And don't think I'm giving this key back," she cried out, riling the eavesdroppers that were eating this connection up.

So back to the story: it was now roughly eleven o'clock and Wendy was well on her way to being wasted. We were at a bar just down the sidewalk from LIT and actually had to grab the car keys from the valet before they shut down. We went back, and after a couple of more jello shots, which put Wendy over the edge, we closed that bar and headed out.

Within twenty yards of the parking lot, she leaned into me. We had our sights on that second star to the right. She grabbed my hand. I turned to her. She glanced up at me and smiled. Then, we started running. I shit you not. Like two teenagers who snuck off to kiss behind the bleachers at school. Hand in hand we raced through the empty parking lot as if we were in a John Hughes movie and I was twenty-five years younger. When we got to the car we hopped in like two kids and drove out really slowly. Thankfully, my apartment was just a mile away.

We pulled into the parking garage. She got out of the car and crumbled on the sidewalk. "I can't drive home," she mumbled as her head bobbed at me.

"No, no. Of course not." I then ran off to grab a bottle of wine from my navi. What I was thinking, I have no idea. But as I walked back I must have had that idiotic boyish grin going. She stared at me for a moment, and then screamed, "Larry, get me up!"

I jumped back as she scared the shit out of me.

After helping her up we went up to my apartment. I noticed Molly the Mermaid's curtains close. I smiled as Wendy began to moan. Upon entry to the apartment I showed her to the guest bathroom where she went off to puke. Even though she couldn't hold a wine glass I still opened the bottle anyway. I placed the cork down and heard her moan my name.

My BlackBerry rang.

It was Marie.

"Oh fuck," I said softly. I picked it up and then put it down as Wendy continued to hurl. It was like a scene made for yet another teen movie. My eyes grew wide to the time. It was one o'clock in the morning. I answered right before it went to voicemail. "Hey," I said.

Wendy moaned my name softly.

My eyes shot open as I ran into the hallway outside the apartment. The conversation continued and Wendy groaned loudly. I then ran back in with my hand over the phone. "Sshh. It's Marie!" I ran back out as she moaned even louder.

I shot down the hall, all the way, took a deep breath, exhaled, and within minutes somehow I pulled off a small miracle. I held it together long enough to appease her and say goodnight. My breathing was erratic as I walked back in. I wiped beads of sweat off my forehead. I was exhausted. It all hit me as I went to check on Wendy. But just as I turned, I saw her crawling across the thick plush carpet.

"Are you okay?"

She shook her head. The carpet was so thick she left a trail through it as if it were snow.

"You can crash in the guest room," I said but she continued coming at me.

The room began to spin.

She didn't respond. She kept crawling. I froze with a vision of her throwing up on my shoes, so I quickly kicked them off. Once she got to my feet, she looked up at me with lusty eyes, but she was so far gone it was comical. She smiled oddly, grabbed my hand, and pulled me to the floor. Now we both lay on the plush carpet. I thought about doing a snow angel. Do you remember doing those as a kid? Sorry, never mind that.

So we were on our backs and it was actually comfy. Within the minute she grabbed my arm and rolled over as if I was her blanket. She pulled my hand over her breast and held it there tightly. I was impressed by the strength she had in the state she was in. That was the last thing I remember.

I woke up a couple of hours later. My hand was still over her chest—held there by hers, just not as tightly—and my other was between her legs. Up high. I'm not sure how that happened. My eyes fluttered as I noticed our clothes were still on. I sighed and carefully pulled my hands away from those sensitive areas and got up. She moved, but didn't wake. My neck was stiff. My head ached. But I was relieved. I viewed this as a victory. Okay, strike that. I stumbled into my bedroom and crashed on the bed. I immediately passed out...

I saw her naked body walk toward me. She slid under the covers and called my name softy. "Larry..."

My eyes opened slowly. I realized I was dreaming. But wait, she was actually standing off to the side of the bed, fully clothed.

She whispered, "Larry."

I blinked as the sun came up through the blinds. She had this curious grin spread across her face, one I hadn't yet seen, it was difficult to describe. I squinted because I couldn't decide if it was disturbing or delightful. But she snapped me out of that spell.

"Larry, you have to get me out of here. It's after seven."

"Oh yeah. Sure. Are you okay?" I threw the covers off me and hopped out of bed.

She smirked mischievously, turned to walk out, but then stopped and turned back to me. I threw my pants on and we walked to the elevator. She told me she had a dream I was holding her romantically. I informed her that it wasn't a dream. She gave me her patented little head nod. It was something I had begun to expect. I chuckled as the elevator door opened.

We walked across the street to the parking garage, the early morning sun bearing down on my hangover, a reminder I needed water, desperately. I said goodbye and crossed the street when I heard a car door shut. I turned and noticed Molly the Mermaid's Jeep light was on. As I peered into the shadows of the garage Wendy took a right instead of a left. She raced down the wrong side of the street and zipped right up to me.

I stood spellbound.

We gifted each other a ridiculous love-stricken stare, (which I find out about later in the story) before I walked back to her open window. Her eyes again said it all. I felt a mixture of euphoria and wonderment and I knew I had to have more. At this point we decided that it was best we pass on "Wine Time" for that particular day, which was really the same day, but that was only temporary, anyway. Our plans miraculously changed by eleven that morning as this dark devotion we shared pushed this wooing to an even more precarious place.

Nothing could stop this. Not even this being the week Marie was coming over to view the house we finally selected. It was just two days later and after she approved it, we drove back to the apartment. We planned to go out for a celebratory drink, when she mentioned Wendy.

"Well, since you're so close to Wendy why don't you invite her and her boyfriend? Don't they both live in South Tampa?"

I nodded while frantically texting her. It was something that we discussed as a possibility, but nothing Jessie knew about until Wendy told him that night. But he refused my invite.

"Give me a few minutes. I'll talk to him again," Wendy texted.

Just then, I winced as the light bulb went on in my head. It brightened a dark memory that I blocked out. The last time I'd seen Jessie.

I'll sum it up by saying he got fucking hammered at a wine tasting that was a mess.

In short, everyone had consumed way too much for a tasting, but Jessie was the worst. One of the kill-joys believed it had to do with our dark devotion, singling out Wendy's private parties with me, just down the hall from the open door event. But even Mike Fritton, who attended, had a raised eyebrow to our actions. And even though Wendy noticed, she wondered why. "This feels so weird. Mike keeps staring at us," she said, while glowing amorously.

I wasn't going to enlighten her. "I love him…that fucking guy," I said with a slight slur, "and you're a big reason we're getting along so well lately."

"I know…how crazy is that. He's beginning to like you…and it is because of me."

I smiled. "Dammit…"

"Whaa?!"

"Your cheeks are calling to me…again. I want to tilt your head and suck on those things…right here…and right now," I paused as her eyes glistened and added, "Oh…and how's Jessie? He seems pretty plowed."

Her expression turned serious. "He's fine. Did you get my text?" I pulled my BlackBerry up to check. "We'll go out with you after. But do not bring up Cork. I'm serious."

Minutes later, we walked back in the tasting and one of the buzzed sales reps pulled me aside. "Her boyfriend has been watching you two. He's not happy. That could be the reason he's here tonight…and why he's hammered."

Obviously, I chose to go with Wendy's recap—"he's fine"—and blocked out everything else. How sick was I? Rhetorical question; let's just move on.

Wendy texted me back: "I don't know what's wrong with him. He refuses to go and he seems to be in a really bad mood. I think it's his job."

I shook my head while quickly having to move on to a much more pressing issue.

We were back at the corporate apartment and Marie walked up to me as I sat on the couch deleting Wendy's text. Her face began to harden as her eyes narrowed at me. "Whose little feet are these going into your bed?" she asked sternly.

My eyes popped forward in my head painfully. "What?" I reached for my wine as she stormed back into the bedroom. I tipped the glass back now wishing I was besotted with wine.

She called me in and pointed to the far side of the bed. The side I never get in or out on, next to the window. It was where Wendy walked up to and the one area in the entire apartment the damn cleaning lady hadn't vacuumed.

I panicked. Reflecting on this with a frown, I observed Marie examine the prints as if she were a fucking detective. Oh wait, she was. My heart began to race. Where is my fucking wine? I could not believe what was transpiring at this very moment. My eyes closed in disbelief.

"Are you fucking kidding me?" she shouted as the entire room began to spin.

"It's the maid," I blurted out as I fell back on the couch.

"The maid sleeps with you?"

"What?"

"These little feet came from here." She pointed to a spot, which was vacuumed. "And then go alongside your bed, which hasn't been vacuumed, and head right into your bed on the side you don't use."

"What? What do mean? She just missed that side."

"I can see she missed it, Larry. You need to look at this and tell me these little bare feet heading right into your bed are the maid's."

"Yes, I see. She missed it. That's all I know. So let's go. You're scaring me."

"I'm scaring you? I will kick your little ass into Tampa Bay…from here!" she began breathing erratically.

"Marie, stop. Just breathe normal. You're putting me in a fragile state."

Her eyes popped forward, which was scarier than her crazy breathing, so I walked over to finally peek at the crime scene. I mean they were perfect footprints as if they were in the snow and it was very clear to see they went right up to the bed. I walked back into the living room, took a deep breath, and exhaled. That's when I insisted she calm down and agreed that it was strange. But that only made it worse. Her interrogation continued. She knew those feet belonged to Wendy. And then she asked if they were meeting us. I told her they couldn't. She nodded with conviction. "Shocking, her boyfriend has probably seen all he can possibly stomach."

"Marie, it's late. Let's have a couple of drinks and celebrate the house. Okay?"

We finally headed out and salvaged the night, but not before I had another panic attack. "Larry, let's go there." She pointed to Cork as I almost clipped another car passing it.

"What?"

"The wine bar."

"Oh. Yeah, no...negative ghost rider."

"Stop being a freak. Grow up and speak English. Why can't we go there?"

"They stopped carrying our wine."

We then pulled into another bar and after a few laughs everything seemed better. She left first thing in the morning to head back east. I would join her a day later.

The following Monday I headed back to Tampa. I received Wendy's early call, but right after it, I received an interesting call from Bud Fox. He stated that Matt had mentioned Wendy was on Facebook and posted a couple of comments that she couldn't wait for Monday.

There's more to his concerns than I wish to deal with, however. I was aware that she had stopped calling and texting me over the weekend and at night, but I turned a blind eye to the reason why.

Although I didn't need Inspector Clouseau to figure this out, there was something else. Our communication during the week had become borderline batty. This obvious pattern to her calls and texts to me exposed the fact that she had begun hiding them. Yet despite this being a critical side-note to the story, it doesn't surface until much later. The important take away, at this moment, was that this thing between us was about to catch fire. And since we avoided acknowledging the spark, we refused to believe there could be any flame. My call to her about this proved it. She sold me that everything was peachy. I felt better. And then ecstatic, as she ended the call with an exclamation.

"I have to go. I'm late for the spin class I had to switch to so I can meet you at two! (o'clock)"

"Ah...yes. Well done."

"I know."

Click

Later that afternoon when we met up, she seemed so happy. It was a genuine joy that showed in her eyes each time we sat across from each other. When she gifted me her little head nod I ignored my soul which was now whispering, "Yes. You are the one. I've been waiting." She possessed an intangible appeal as if I knew her from another time. And it was apparent from the day she placed the "magical apple" on my desk—without even uttering a word.

I sat thoroughly mesmerized and slightly unnerved. Our electricity and chemistry were constantly zapping and bubbling in and around us. After we finished the first bottle, I desperately needed a diversion to this feeling that my heart was irrevocably gone, so I ordered another. "Yes, we need another bottle…and please hurry," I sputtered.

Two hours later, Wendy took a long sip and fell back in the booth. Her eyes moistened, with their unguarded glow. The rush of emotion was undeniably arresting. "I can't sleep through the night anymore," she said. Her eyes closed slowly, and then opened, wide to her soul. "Larry, I've never felt this way before. I'll do whatever you want. I will."

Wendy's eyes produced the most amazing chemical cocktail, making me feel as if I were floating atop a cloud. I blinked back to recent conversations where she had questioned me about my marriage. I scrambled through it all searching for words. I should've been mindful this was fast approaching, but I chose to block that out as well. Her eyes overwhelmed me, and mine provided her answer.

She drew herself up and went to the bathroom. When she returned she actually opened her laptop, as if this was a working lunch. "What are we doing about GreenWise (an account in her territory)?" she said curtly.

I stared at her for a moment, and babbled, "I…um…I'm sorry…I can't even describe what I feel…for you." I paused as her eyes dulled. "Are you okay?"

"I'm fine. I need an answer to this." Her voice was impatient.

"Oh…I thought we…aren't we going to GreenWise tomorrow?"

She took in a slow deep breath. "Yes. I need you…we…need you there—tomorrow."

"Okay." I signed the check.

She abruptly closed her laptop and put it in its bag.

Minutes later, we walked out into the alluring autumn night. We hugged each other tight, under the second star to the right, as our little fairy tale caught fire.

CHAPTER SIXTEEN

THE TUNNEL OF LOVE

EARLY DECEMBER 2009
THE TAMPA OFFICE

I woke up the next day anxious. An hour later, at just after seven Wendy called. She acted as if that conversation never took place. When I questioned her about it she only, very convincingly, responded by saying, "Don't worry, I'm not the girl who will stalk you."

I drew in a deep and steadying breath before informing her I never thought she was. I forced my thoughts away from it all. After a shower I wanted to plan something fun with the family for that weekend. Adjusting my tie in the mirror, I called Marie. It went to voicemail. Three minutes later she texted: "I just got out of the shower!" I glanced at my watch and exhaled realizing they should've left. Ten minutes later, on my way to the office, I called her back.

"I'm running late and can't talk," she snapped.

"Okay...I'll call you later."

She was preoccupied with the kids. "Lauren, stop talking that way to Jerry...enough!"

Click.

It was the first weekend in December and I arrived home late that Friday. I spent that night and Saturday morning writing my team emails. On Sunday I strolled out onto our patio to see if Marie wanted me to start the fire pit.

"Yes," she said. "So has your friend, Wendy, ever been to the corporate apartment?"

I lied and said, "No," with the audacity of adding, "why do you keep asking?"

The conversation that followed was arduous and brief. I walked away annoyed that she was consumed with it. At this point of the story, I still amazingly didn't think I did anything wrong. Later on, at ten that night, she was back out there so I went to see if she wanted to go to bed. In fifteen years of marriage, she rarely ever went to bed the same time I did. She also refused to believe that was odd, or an issue. But it was. And now I was desperate to connect in any way before I left the next morning to go back to Tampa. I opened the door but she was on the phone.

She pulled away from the conversation and said, "I'll be there in a couple of hours."

Three hours later I jumped out of bed for a glass of water and went back out on the patio. As the door swung open the cigarette smoke—which I loathed—overwhelmed me. I quickly retreated as she spoke to her cousin on the west coast, because everyone on the east coast was sleeping, while holding up five fingers. I assumed that meant she would be done in five minutes. I was wrong.

I left our home earlier that Monday and received my "clockwork" call from Wendy. I suddenly felt better, much better. I then received a call from another manager of the team. He passed on his appreciation for what he expressed was the best experience in his career.

It was clear the team had a burning desire to win and that the outflow of positive energy had everyone engaged. I pulled into the office parking lot appeased, but craving more. After receiving a text from Wendy I stood just down the hall from our office reading it. A young sales rep approached me from another division as I was responding to her. I thought he was just passing me, but he stopped as my eyes shifted from the text to him curiously.

"Hello, sir." He reached out his hand to shake mine and introduced himself. "I'll get shot for saying it, but I've heard amazing things about your division and how you run it…I would love to talk to about any future opportunities."

I paused shaking my head thinking the first part of his statement, one I had heard too many times, was troubling, before smiling. "Thank you and we can talk any time."

He thanked me graciously. As I nodded I noticed our office door was shut. I walked on and heard laughter. When I got to it I stopped and heard Lori, Tony, and Matt's voices. By this point I also realized these three loved to gossip. What I hadn't realized, at that moment, was that they would become a destructive triangle. I opened the door to sudden silence.

"Good morning, team. Special closed door meeting?"

Lori smiled wide to the side of the blue glow of her computer monitor. "Well, good morning, Larry, and don't you look handsome in your suit." Her southern accent was turned up as the boys both remained silent high-fiving me as I headed on to my office. As I sat down my mind raced toward the busy day ahead. Today completed our holiday audits and was an early yet important test that I was focused to win, and did.

We scored high marks at our review meeting and to continue the momentum, as this particular day's festive wonderment included accolades from Cosmopolitan Wine's (CWUS's) hierarchy. This latest victory was deemed triumphant by a senior vice president who boasted earnestly, "Every account showcased what we strive for. The attention to detail was outstanding. I was most impressed with the positive energy this team possesses. It is a tight group and it was refreshing to see." He paused and turned to me before adding, "Please, keep doing what you're doing, Mr. Sola. It's working."

Two days later, my realtor, Ryan, bestowed more nifty news on me as he confirmed December 20th as the date we would close on our handsome home in Tampa Palms, a spiffy suburb of North Tampa. This "officially" marked the six-month countdown for the family to be together again, something that relieved the increasing anxiety levels that accompanied each weekend trip back east.

On the surface everything seemed to be coming together rather remarkably. So much so that even my inquisitive dry cleaner congratulated me before asking if I would like her to pinch me.

I only shrugged with a clumsy smile as I was ironically responding to a text from Wendy.

This caused her to glance back at me adding, "Well, my friend lives in your new community, and it's exquisite."

My gaze shot over to her and met her peering eyes. I shrugged.

"I'm sorry. My mind was on business. We love it too."

She took my credit card. "You should slow down and enjoy your charmed life a little more, Larry. You never know how long it will last."

I thanked her and only wondered why she would say such a thing. She handed me a lollipop. I threw it in the garbage can outside the store and strolled along the gorgeous waterway that wrapped around the corporate apartment to its elevator. Perhaps I should've taken a long look in the mirror at this point, but I didn't. I only laughed out loud at Wendy's response, thinking all was grand.

Part of the ease with which I rationalized this came from the success that we achieved. Masked by the celebrations that followed and, unbeknownst to me, I was setting the stage for some very dark times. Aside from compartmentalizing this separate life that I only thought I had control over, there were things that began happening behind the scenes that were in some way related to my actions, or perceived actions, almost unimaginably.

Just two days later, the team was enjoying some wine in the office after a meeting that focused on the recap of a program we had won. The main part of our office beamed with the typical mirth and tomfoolery you would find in a frat house.

Roughly twenty minutes later, some of the boys were still finishing the wine we corked for our celebratory toasts. They perused the newly posted pictures of an outing to a Lightning game on our illustrious picture board. I passed them as I headed to the bathroom and tossed a couple of our coasters at their backs.

They turned around.

"That was a great night, boys," I said.

Without hesitation they shouted back in unison, "Yes, it was."

I walked up to open the door and my mind began to race to another place. The coasters came back at me. I ducked.

"And who's the best team in the state?" I sang.

They yelled in unison, "We are."

I opened the door and naturally Tony couldn't leave it at that. "Without a doubt, Sir Sola. You have led us to the Promised Land and we are most grateful—"

Bang.

I slammed the door behind me, and proceeded down the hall to get this thought out of my head. It turned out to be a little poem inspired by words the district manager, who was on the other side of that picture board wall, had spoken. I stood there and texted it to her.

Five minutes later, I came back and Tony whispered, "I went to get the bottle and I noticed she's got that look in her eyes again, sir. I asked her a question, but she seemed to be off in your fantasy land—"

I put my hand up to cut him off. "We have to be out of here soon. Let's finish up."

"I have to tell you again how happy I am to be a part of your show, sir. All of it. Our success and how entertaining it's been." He pointed to my office. "It's all amazing, sir."

At first, I thought he meant the camaraderie displayed on the picture board, but later I found out he meant more the drama surrounding the young lady sitting in my office.

Wendy Darlington sat where I left her, across from me with her laptop up on my desk. It was her favorite spot. She had just placed her empty glass down but held her BlackBerry.

"It must've been good." I gestured to the empty wine glass.

Her glistening eyes rolled up to meet my gaze, beckoned to me; a pull of attraction, and desire. She exhaled deeply before answering the question my poem presented by whispering, "Enchanting, it is."

Our "dark devotion" was ever present. Her head angled to a picture on the wall as if she was concealing her apparent enthusiasm.

"Um, you look ridiculous in that picture by the way; your face looks way too young. And you should've shaved your head back then. (I actually looked like a Chia Pet) Were you in your twenties?"

"Please don't make fun of me. I was thirty four."

"Oh god, that's right I forgot how old you really are—"

I pouted.

After I straightened that picture I glanced back at her. No words were necessary. Certitude filled her soul. Her eyes spoke volumes and inspired me to carry on the fun. I jumped into my chair like a little boy on a mission. With my hands poised to hit my laptop, she knew something was coming her way. At the time I never thought about my creative energy as anything but fun. If it made someone, especially Wendy, smile or laugh I was in for more. It was just how I was wired;

there was no filter and by this point the material she inspired was coming in waves. She loved it.

She lunged for the empty wine glass. Her eyes peered back over at me. "I need more," she said in a dire tone.

I leaned in with an accommodating smile. "Poems, songs, or cryptic team emails?"

She gave up on subtlety. "Wine...wine. Larry!"

I smirked. "But of course. Perhaps a delightful bottle of Magnificaaaatee."

That was our slang for our favorite red, Franciscan Magnificat.

"Fine. Do not send me anything else until my glass is full. I can't handle any more of it."

"You always enjoy my...creative energy. And it seemed as if you liked my little poem."

"Larry, I didn't say I didn't enjoy it. Just get me more wine so I can handle it."

I swirled my glass of wine and stared in her eyes. Her lips compressed to conceal her growing grin. She looked away again. When she turned back to me her eyes slowly closed. She seemed to be bracing herself for what she knew was next.

Not wanting to let her down, I said softly, "I love it when your cheeks exude that rosy glow."

Wendy held up her pen as if she was going to stab me with it. "Larry, open another bottle before I will hurt you."

"With your pen?" I put my finger up to my lips. "Sssh, Tony's on the other side of the wall with a glass against it. He's fascinated by you."

"He's fascinated by us, you freak...they all are."

I smiled as Tony loomed in my doorway with his sinister smirk.

"Sir Sola, we're taking off. You two have a good night."

Wendy's hands went over her face. "Get the fucking Magnificaaaateeee."

I spun the chair to my wine cabinet to grab the bottle as all was disturbingly divine. But then our eyes grew wide as the magical moment was stained with Tony's obnoxiously loud and vexing voice.

"You just noticed?" he bellowed. He was talking to one of the managers that rarely ever came into the office as they were leaving.

"Their shit show's been on nonstop since she dropped an apple on Sir Sola's desk on the first day of class back in September."

The door slammed.

It took a ton of jerky justifications to continue to deny this wasn't a smoking white hot mess, but aside from the fact that I deluded myself I had control of it, there was something else.

You see, even though there were rampant rumors flying that it had been a "sexual" affair from the onset, the truth was that it wasn't, which made it all worse for the long haul. That, curiously provided us the essential excuse to justify it much more easily, while only pretending it wasn't what it was, and that it wouldn't go up in an even larger blaze later. It is extremely difficult to reconstruct how inconceivable it truly was.

By December, it seemed that our tickets were mysteriously stamped for this ride we couldn't seem to get off. It was a dark ride into the enchanting tunnel of love. Yes, the one that's full of spooky shadows and those maddening mirrors that often show you in 5D.

It was during the third "Wine Time" in a row we'd partaken in, right after the audits, when a waitress we had had before delivered a message with our second bottle. She smiled eerily at me and said softly, "I must say you two certainly have some dangerous chemicals between you." Her statement was quite unforgettable and caught me off guard. I nervously nodded as she placed the cork on the table and added, "Don't beat yourself up; I believe a bad thing has something good hidden inside it,"—She knew we weren't married—"and with you two it's obvious that good thing isn't so hidden."

I nodded again. "That's interesting."

She smiled sharply. "It's true; I was fascinated the last time I served you two."

As she walked away Wendy jumped back into the booth, beaming. With her little head nod that I loved and the clink of our glasses, it was as if this understanding passed between us, one that had us ready to cope with the scary shadows coming out of the flickering light as the ride would no doubt get a little rough.

It was at this point I pulled the six-month time table that my family would be in Tampa out of my excuse bag, pretending I would slowly transition this "special friendship" into a more normal one. I acted as if I knew what one was.

I was in route to meet Wendy again when she sent me a text: "You're not going to believe it, but I got our booth in the far back!"

She was referring to a "Wine Time" episode from one of our, now earlier, classic shit shows. But as it all came back to me, I drifted into another lane recalling the conversations. But then my BlackBerry rang.

It was Wendy.

I answered. "I realize you need me. I'm almost there."

She ignored me. "Can you believe we got that booth again?" She was full of enchantment. "The message from that waitress last week and now this, it's so weird. I wonder if it's all a sign."

I pulled off the exit ramp just as Colbie Caillat's "Fallin for You" instantly provided another magical moment I couldn't resist. "Whaa...a sign?" I turned the music up and paused for the lyrics to fill in the dead air properly before adding, "Whaa did you say?"

"Are you done? Grow up! And hurry up. You drive that navi so slow. I have to go by six. Jessie thinks I'm in a team meeting."

We used to make this abbreviated yet slightly disturbing sound, like an elephant, when an unbelievable statement or situation would arise, such as her last line *"Jessie thinks I'm in a meeting."*

I made the sound and slowed to a stop at a light.

"He does think that," she shouted.

I made the sound again.

"Whaa?" she said.

Just in case you forgot, when the moment warranted it, we would change "what" to "whaa." This was one of those times. The traffic began moving again as I answered her with a deep sigh.

"Shut up. We're not in the real world right now, remember?"

"Oh, right. How's that view of Mermaid Lagoon?"

I heard a muffled guffaw as she hung up and texted me faster than I ever thought was humanly possible: "Hurry up. I cannot have a repeat of yesterday."

By this point, to no one's surprise—except our own because we had to pretend this really wasn't happening—I met Wendy for a spontaneous "Wine Wednesday" episode of our beloved "Wine Time." We had neat names for every day of the week to enhance the experience and added the "spontaneous" part when we pinky swore we wouldn't meet so she could sleep after the "Super Tuesday" edition of our beloved "Wine Time" went up in flames. That was what she was referring to in her last text: *"Hurry up I cannot have a repeat of yesterday."*

So as our dark devotion propelled us to meet on a day we weren't going to—again, the whispers in the office halls spread swiftly about a torrid affair.

CHAPTER SEVENTEEN

A MYSTERY CALL AND RESIGNATION

DECEMBER 15, 2009
THE TAMPA OFFICE

With the romance part of this tale screaming on through the dark tunnel, and off to my sacred land, another intriguing layer of the story peeled back, exposed. It was one that, again, had The Wizard waving his wand. This mysterious conference call he hosted took place the second week of November and included me, Fox, and his team. This turned out to be a call that detailed verbally abusive behavior by Fox that I assumed The Wizard would have to have documented to our Human Resources department. But he didn't. I was shocked but relieved. Unbeknownst to me, he only called for a follow-up at the end of November that never happened. The only reason I found that out was because two of Fox's people called me.

On December 15th, where we are now in the story, Lisa Fenna abruptly resigned. She ultimately had lost all hope that the issues with Bud Fox would ever be resolved. Her last text to me on the matter came the week before: "Larry, I wanted to let you know that The Wizard hasn't reached out to any of us like he said he would. I also realize Bud told you it is fixed, but it's not. He is a liar. Please call me when you can. I know you're busy, but this is important."

There were no answers to how The Wizard became involved in this. His team had sworn that it was Fox who was in touch with him after a heated conversation I had with him just before the conference call was scheduled.

Fuming, as Fox denied it, I sat at my desk agitated with how I let

Lisa down. I couldn't escape the truth and it stung. I was with Wendy on that afternoon when Lisa texted me. I had all intentions to get back to her, but I didn't. Wendy never liked her (for obvious reasons) and I didn't bring up Lisa's text in front of Wendy because she had gone on record saying it wasn't normal for a sales rep to reach out directly to the leader of the sales division.

I know. Please relax; it's all fucking amazing.

Anyhow, since Wendy and I were out much later than I anticipated, I was preoccupied with emails when I landed back in the real world and never called Lisa back. The next day Fox's people told me he deliberately kept this news from me.

He swore differently.

But that would only be the beginning. After that, I spoke to the rest of Fox's team in detail. They all said the same thing. Nothing had changed and they now wanted to know what The Wizard was going to do because he made a promise to all of them on that call, how he had their best interests and would make sure the problem was rectified.

But The Wizard already called for a follow-up that never happened.

When I spoke to The Wizard in his office, I had to refresh his memory that the call even took place. After that moment of puzzlement he only asked how I could put Bud Fox in this position. I fidgeted in the chair stunned. This was something from the day of that idiotic draft with TJ Faggalo that I was adamant about not wanting to happen. I, once again, reminded him that my selection for that position was Bobby Blue and it was he who TJ Faggalo said blocked him.

In a defensive high-strung tone he snipped, "Larry, I didn't know anything about this. I don't know why TJ told you that. If Blue wanted to work for you I wouldn't have stopped him."

I sat there speechless before he had to take an urgent call about a termination.

That night I was back at the corporate apartment. I continued conversations for the best move forward. I had the television on as President Barack Obama announced that the U.S., China, India, Brazil, and South Africa had reached an agreement to combat global warming. I changed the channel to watch the same report on another network as I realized I would have to micromanage Bud Fox...again.

In the coming weeks it worked, but was only a temporary fix because the new division didn't have a mid-level manager who could hold him accountable in the field. Tony volunteered to assist by driving across the state to work with him.

As I spoke to Tony about this at the office, I received a congratulatory email from the Sith Lord on a program that we led the state on. With everything else going so well, I allowed Tony one day with Fox. At the time, I thought it could help. In the coming weeks, they became closer, and although Fox would tell me Tony was totally full of shit, he manipulated his way into my inner circle, all with an ulterior motive to keep tabs on me.

CHAPTER EIGHTEEN

THE RABBI

MID - DECEMBER 2009
FLASHBACK TO 2006

Despite the federal stimulus package, much of the U.S. economy sputtered through the end of the year. This had a trickle-down effect on everything. The company continued its cutbacks and itched to end the lease for the corporate apartment and my exorbitant expenses attached to it. With the closing of our house complete, I gave them a move out date of January 11th.

Looking back at the month of December there was no doubt it was a turning point in the storyline, which also brought some important changes to our new state roster. The most noteworthy was a replacement at the top. It was my new boss, our division's general manager, vice president Gary Rabinski, aka The Rabbi.

I had met The Rabbi in 2006 on an incentive trip to a Universal Studios resort in Orlando, Florida, and had run into him again on a similar trip a year later. At this (flashback) moment in the story (going back briefly to 2006), we were not only in different divisions—he was in Miami/South and I was in Tampa/Central—as he held a higher title than I; yet he seemed to be aware of the "rising star" tag that I wore proudly. It seemed as if he knew back then that our paths would one day cross.

This first entertaining encounter was by chance. A bunch of us ran into him while he gleefully held court under the stars. We stumbled off the boat that brought us back to the resort from the theme parks. I adjusted the torn bag of souvenirs in my hand while approaching a bar with outdoor seating. He was at the table littered with empty wine bottles. He turned to us curiously.

"So." He paused for a brief instant. "So why don't you guys join us?" he said in his thick New York accent with a notable twinkle in his bulging eyeballs.

I was taken aback by this impromptu invite and certainly felt honored. I mean, this was The Rabbi. The fucking Rabbi! A man of his stature and protruding peepers fascinated me. So we nodded nervously and joyfully strolled over to this mishmash of "Goodfellas" look-a-likes. We were like a bunch of kids who were just gifted a pass to sit at the big boy table. I caught The Rabbi's bulging beauties following me eerily.

Now, I was slightly uncomfortable. I continued to take sneak peeks at him while I searched for an empty chair. To make matters worse, I felt like I was suddenly playing musical chairs when a couple of his cronies came back from the bathroom and took the seats we were targeting. One of the guys pulled a chair over and nodded at me. I gripped my souvenir bag tight and made a beeline to it.

I sat down, placed my kid's shit on the ground and The Rabbi said, "So." He paused for a brief instant. "So, this is fucking Sola?" A devious smirk curled up on his pudgy puss. "Larry fucking Sola."

I smiled apprehensively. I realized they quite possibly had had even a tad bit more to drink than we had, which was quite impressive.

After he gifted me my first shot, I nodded to thank him. I thought he was done, but he wasn't.

"So." He paused. "This next shot goes to fucking Sola," he bellowed as he raised his glass.

I grimaced and threw it back. Now all I saw was Marty Feldman. I rubbed my eyes. He leaned back, but his eyeballs remained over the table. I had the sensation they were actually getting closer while exuding glee.

I checked to make sure I wasn't still wearing the 3D glasses I stole from the Spiderman ride and contemplated my options. That only took a couple of seconds. I have to go...immediately. See, it was that quick. The Rabbi's eyes were now scaring the shit of me, and even though I realize I scare easily, I was too fucked up to consume anything else without having any Mermaids to play with. There were none. Strike two. All this water, but not one Mermaid. What kind of lagoon was this? It certainly wasn't my Mermaid Lagoon. Where was I? I was about to strike out, and the guy next to me belched emitting an odd odor. Strike three. I'm outta there.

But how?

I had the damn bag of Spiderman and Grinch toys to haul ass with and The Rabbi seemed to be eating this shit up. I began to pout. I needed a classic diversion, like an explosion or a dancing bear. Then it hit me. TJ Faggalo. He was missing from this table of tomfoolery. "You guys didn't invite TJ?" I said.

Everyone's eyes shot open followed by a deluge of drivel.

"Where the fuck is Faggalo? That fucking pussy."

"What room is Faggalo in? Wake that giant pussy up."

Through the inebriated shout outs, The Rabbi ordered everyone to call Faggalo. But not only call him, they all had to leave a brutal voice mail berating him. I let out a gentle laugh and thought maybe I would stay. But then I took half a breath and almost blacked out.

One of the "Goodfellas" yelled, "Faggalo's not answering."

I had a vision of Faggalo, I don't know why, as he leapt out of bed and stepped on one of those king-size bags of Ruffles potato chips, while desperately lunging for his phone. He wore one of those night masks over his eyes and some fucked up nightie. He screamed at his wife to double bolt the door.

I knew I had to stay focused on the goal of vanishing into thin air. I regrouped and thought I had it. My arms crossed, full of frustration. The bathroom was on the wrong side of us. In other words, I couldn't just say I was going to take a piss and not come back, unless I planned on swimming across the fucking Mermaid-less lagoon. Now I had to get serious.

With my game face on, I inched my chair back and waited for the moment. With this backdrop, I knew it wouldn't be long. Literally thirty seconds later, a group of intoxicated Brits rushed the bar. One of them tripped and caused a scene. The green light flashed in front of me and I said, "I think that's Faggalo at the bar."

I squinted as if I wasn't sure; you know, to make it more authentic. All of the "Goodfellas" looked at me and then turned to the bar and squinted. I pushed my chair back even further, swung my feet around, and grabbed my bag.

"It is Faggalo." Amidst the chaos, I took off like a bat out of hell.

Within seconds, I was forty yards down the cobblestone walkway and about to leap in the elevator to my room. I envisioned The Rabbi saying, "So,"—he would pause— "so fucking Sola just disappeared?"

But that was some three years ago.

Fast-forward to when I picked The Rabbi up at the airport in Tampa on a foggy December morn. He had his new title in tow, a serious demeanor, and he was craving coffee, not booze. Shortly after driving off with him, he got right to it: no briefing necessary. He was aware of my abilities and without any pats on the back, he now expected me to take on more responsibilities. His message was cut and dry, and his expectations were high.

Interestingly, his outlook was not the same for all of my counterparts throughout the state. As the conversation persisted, he seemed preoccupied with emails of issues arising in north Florida. He didn't go into much detail on this trip, but he would soon vent about certain areas missing goals while relying on me to pick up their slack. Much of this was due to the different plan the Northern division had for my position, along with much lower pay packages for it. With many complicated disparities it was the pay part that was the critical side-note to this story which we will revisit shortly.

So after we toured an account, with some more small talk, I couldn't help but think about the consensus that this move appointing The Rabbi was rushed as many others vented that our last leader was axed too quickly. I liked the guy, but disagreed.

Pulling out of that accounts parking lot, The Rabbi's eyeballs fixated on a Starbucks.

"So." He paused. "So Larry, do you drink coffee?"

"What," I swerved almost clipping a truck and as his protruding peepers were now over my dashboard, I said, "Yes, would you like to stop?"

"So." He paused. "So, yeah, why don't we pull into that Starbucks?"

I wiped my forehead and spun us around. Five minutes later, he received a call. He was frustrated. And his eyeballs were still freaking me out, but I couldn't dwell on that, because he came back reiterating his high expectations for me, which naturally I plugged into, while expanding on issues he wouldn't tolerate. He singled out another area of the state and told me he had to tend to them.

He quickly walked me through a plan to be more involved with the on–premise team. The division as a whole was struggling during this time which made it all a more pressing matter.

"So, Larry." He paused, "So, I'm also going to send our new on premise director, Mindy Amour, up to work with our key account managers and I want you involved in everything."

I nodded as I received a text from Wendy: "Do you know Mindy Amour?"

I went to reply and she sent another text: "I heard she's our new on premise director."

As we were leaving Starbucks I received a text from Mindy informing me she wished to have lunch on the day she flew into Tampa.

CHAPTER NINETEEN

THE CONCERT

LATE DECEMBER
THE HARD ROCK

That next day I found out Lori Ersatz knew of Mindy. Later that afternoon, I spoke to her to confirm the plans to meet for lunch when she flew in. Since she was friendly with my buddy Jerry Lakers, we planned on him picking her up from the airport and going to The Columbia Restaurant in Ybor City.

After that was finalized, I sat at my desk to break out our goals. One of the office lines rang. Lori, who by this point in the story was more commonly referred to as Mama Bear, went to grab it, but abruptly stopped. "It's your little girl, Wendy," she said. "I'll let you pick her up."

I winced and took a deep breath.

Three other managers, including Tony, sat at the district manager table in the main part of the office. Tony had a devious smirk on his face. As I answered he hollered, "Does she really think calling the office line is going to erase the fifty calls she places to your BlackBerry?"

I felt it best that I call Wendy back.

Tony stood up in my doorway. "Sir, even Dan Schultz has chimed in on your...*friendship* with Wendy. He's amazed. He used a classic line observing it all after last week's meeting." He laughed. "He said, 'where there's smoke, there's most certainly fire.'"

They all began to crack up. As I answered an email from The Rabbi merriment filled our cozy space. The revelry made it seem more like a high school cafeteria than our division's corporate office. I was plugged into the energy of it all. But as the room roared with glee Mama Bear cranked up her southern slant to add her, by now, usual, "Mmm, mm, mmm, mm, mmm."

Although this seemed to be harmless fun and games, it was at this time that foreboding winds began to blow storm clouds across my distant horizon. For the past month or so, Mama Bear had not only joined the allegiance against our *magical moments covered in darkness tour*, but now spearheaded a more vocal movement against it, and none done in jest.

Her first "warning" on this matter was a painstaking call, which hit me between the eyes at around seven at night just before Thanksgiving. I thought she meant well, but I also realized she had had conversations on the subject with Matt and Tony. Anyway, I'll sum it up by saying she carried on and on while proceeding to down too much of a Blackbox of Merlot.

Aside from the overt hostility towards our unique chemistry, the other issue was that Mama Bear wanted to come out and play too. She was a divorced mother who wanted to have fun just like Wendy. She also wanted to be a part of literally everything I had control over, which at the time I viewed as her having a passion for her job, not ever thinking about envy or ulterior motives. If I had, I certainly would not have allowed her to hold the keys to the division's expense account summaries and pay packages, especially Wendy's. Can you smell the smoke? Well, this smoldering animosity festered over the month and became combustible at this point of the story.

It was late December. Just before New Year's when Marie and I took Mama Bear to a concert at the Hard Rock in Tampa.

The signs that this night would turn to ash came toward the end of the concert when Marie went to get another drink. Mama Bear was wasted and babbled on about how happy she was that I was her boss. She thanked me for her Christmas presents, the hotel room, and the ticket to the concert, while she inched closer and closer to me. A new song began and she was up against my side. She put her arm around my back and slid her hand into my back pocket. I froze. She swayed harmlessly back and forth to the music and rambled on with some very interesting dialogue which I chalked up to her having a grand ole drunken time. In my mind it wasn't a big deal.

Unfortunately though, Marie thought differently. I noticed her jaw drop with the sight of this lady swaying back and forth against me with her hand tucked in my back pocket. Could I blame her? Well, I did. I quickly held my hand up to her, motioning it was fine.

"Relax, she's wasted," I whispered.

Marie staggered up to me and hissed that I was unbelievable. Of course, this was my fault. Believe it or not, I knew this would only be the calm before the storm when her eyeballs popped forward in her head, reminiscent of The Rabbi's.

"It's interesting how you stopped drinking, though," she said. "You knew she was going do something ridiculous, didn't you?"

I shrugged and she shook her head in amazement.

Thirty minutes later, Marie was now wasted too as we strolled out. She asked me if I was sleeping with Mama Bear and Wendy. She realized the truth without a word spoken, and dropped her phone. I picked it up. We were now off to the side of the path back to the hotel.

Her stare pierced me as she seemed to be contemplating stuffing me in the giant rose bush. I moved her back up, into the light from the path, as she grabbed her phone gritting her teeth. "Here is the picture. Her hand on your ass."

Suddenly upended by grief staring back at this nonsense, I exhaled.

"Marie, enough already, this is ridiculous."

She continued to sway and took a deep breath and then blew it out. She nodded, more relaxed.

"I want to like her and I do realize you're not sleeping with her, but there is something very wrong here. With her. She has issues and she speaks as if you two are closer than anything you've ever told me. Like she wants it that way. And she hates Wendy. I hope you realize that much, because that's what really scares me."

"Marie, everyone hates Wendy...except me—"

Her eyes narrowed at me angrily. "It's because of you! How can you not see this is a recipe for disaster? I have a feeling you're going to end up with a target on your head because of it. It never ends."

She pulled her hair back. I could tell she was digesting her entire life with me and was preparing for lift-off, so I asked her if she wanted ice cream. Unfortunately, she wasn't ready for her swirl cone with sprinkles.

"Please learn." She implored, "You are a male who cannot allow females in. Period. You're a freak of nature. Unexplainable shit happens when you do."

I think she was referring to my pixie dust, but I wasn't in any position to clarify that at this point. "What was this company thinking giving you women? Don't they know you?"

I had to look away. I couldn't contain the nervous smile that spread across my face. I only wanted to believe her statement was completely absurd, but in strange way, it really wasn't. It all hit me like a train.

I held my hands over my face to mask the hilarity. It didn't help; she stormed off. I had to sit down. I felt like a special needs child who wandered into a lion's den during feeding time, with no idea how to get out. I wished I hadn't stopped drinking. It became a slap-stick comedy. Within the minute Marie was coming back down the path as Mama Bear shouted my name coming out of the bathroom. We all met back up. After that, I left them for two minutes and fourteen seconds to take a piss. That's when the real fun began. Mama Bear's after hour's pool party. She pulled Marie poolside.

I came back out and swallowed hard. My eyes grew wide as I frantically searched the vacated area where I left them. I panicked and continued on. It wasn't until I got onto the path to the outdoor bar that I noticed them on chaise lounges at the pool.

"No," I shouted into my hands. I stomped my foot on the ground like a little boy. I left them for threeeeeeeee flipping minutes. This is not happening right now, I thought. But it certainly was. I took a deep breath, exhaled, and then almost blacked out.

When I saw the look on Marie's face, I realized this drunken deliberation was all about my special friendship with Wendy. I took steps forward and Marie turned to me. Her penetrating gaze was haunting. She turned back to Mama Bear. Her mouth was spewing as her arms were flailing in the air. I could see it all flashing up in lights on the scoreboard over the hotel pool. Obviously Marie knew that Wendy and I were close; but it was certain details that scrolled across Mama Bear's pool party PowerPoint presentation, I had reserved as "special bonus material," that seemed to be rushed for release without proper editing which caused concern.

Okay, I was completely panicked.

In short, obviously, Wendy and I didn't need our stories of affection for one another spun by anyone; they were quite magnificent on their own. So after I was cursed out, the dust settled. Since I was unaware of the many issues that were festering in Mama Bear's head, I only played this off as her simply getting wasted.

The sun crept up the next morning and an uneasy feeling settled over me. Like I was driving along in a dense fog not knowing if I was going to hit a wall. Mama Bear reached out for the damage report with little recollection of anything. I sat amazed. But since I had already spoken with Marie, who had little recollection of the night and no interest in rehashing any of it, I suggested that Mama Bear reach out to her.

And she did.

Minutes later, Mama Bear called me back to inform me all was well. The truth was that Marie really didn't want to deal with her and told her it was all fine. The slate was wiped clean. She thanked me again for the night and stated she would see me the following week. I felt better and said goodbye.

But then Bud Fox called in.

I answered softly, "Hey," and took a big gulp of Evian.

"Tony just told me you called Mama Bear at three o'clock in the morning wasted last week looking for her to take you home? They not only think your fucking Wendy...they think your partying all night and fucking everyone!" Fox laughed.

"You know the truth, so please stop. I had a brutal night and I'm not in the mood."

"I know but I think there is some truth to something else."

He seemed to be probing.

"What?"

"She said that Wendy met you last week before she drove to Atlanta for Christmas."

I exhaled, "Okay..." I rubbed my eyes, "Yes...but the rest is bullshit."

At this very instant I should've seen the red lights and heard the warnings bells. But I chose to doubt the source because the first part was outlandish. Even after hearing all the crazy shit she told Marie, I just couldn't believe this. I simply refused to. It had to be Tony. After seconds of silence, Fox asked if I was okay.

"I don't trust Tony. I want to like the guy...but I've now seen too much."

"I know that," Fox exclaimed. "Larry, I told you he's is full of shit. But I have your back. And just so that you know, she's said similar shit to me. She's envious of Wendy, but I know she really likes you." He paused. "Well, I had to let you know."

I had conflicting thoughts.

Fox interrupted them. "Hey, seriously are you okay? Did something else happen?"

My eyes blinked. "No. No, everything is great. I'll call you later." *Click.*

CHAPTER TWENTY

A MORDANT MESSAGE FROM MOLLY

JANUARY 2010
THE CORPORATE APARTMENT

The bleakness of Bud Fox's call was relieved by a showering of cool kudos on the business front, the coolest of which for being recognized as the top team in the country for an incentive from a winery in Washington's Columbia Valley. The owner called me personally to hail us "heroes" for our accomplishment. This pattern of praise kept me focused even more on the ambitious goals, which were naturally good for the continued success of the division.

Ironically, they also made it easier to avoid Bud Fox's contentious managerial issues and the perception problem that my trusted administrative assistant had with me. Both played a paramount part in the rest of the story, and if handled differently, would've drastically changed the outcome of it.

As far as Mama Bear went, the night at the Hard Rock was now a distant memory and she felt even more comfortable with me, rolling into the new year. The only problem was that she had this warped image of me that she didn't seem to mind, behavior she thought was appropriate for the career path I was on. This was quite evident the day I had to finish packing up the corporate apartment.

Regardless of the debacle at the Hard Rock, none of the colorful conversations had her shying away from Wendy. One had her restating her opinion that Wendy was uncomfortable with Mindy Amour becoming the on premise director. Mama Bear was fully convinced that Wendy was nervous that my reputation as a bad boy would have me focusing on Mindy next. She drew this conclusion when Wendy came to the office back in December knowing Mindy was flying in. At the time it was nothing I paid any attention too.

The next instance came at this point in the story during a conversation she overheard that I had with Mindy. The fact that Tony also chimed in only further salted the wound, as I hung up.

"I love you, Sir Sola. Your show is amazing and never ending."

Since the conversation was admittedly sprightly and Mindy was attractive, and personable, Mama Bear decided she was correct as she again did her, "Mmm, mm, mmm, mmm, mmm." Despite there being no truth to this, she was, in fact, as warned, fully convinced that I was sleeping with everyone: married women, engaged women, single girls, hookers, obviously Wendy; and apparently Mindy, who was married with kids, would be next.

Of course, at the time, I only laughed at it all briefly with more of an interest in the congratulatory shout-out from The Rabbi. I rode that high right out the door. But it's important to note that this disturbing slant Mama Bear had of me was camouflaged in revelry that literally boomed out of our office and could be heard in the breakroom down the hall.

So thinking all was still grand, without giving any of this nonsense a second thought, I hopped in my navi, and drove off to the corporate apartment to pack up the rest of my clothes. As I pulled out of my spot, Wendy texted me to remind me about her birthday the following week. I turned out of the office parking lot and received a call from Mike Fritton.

He congratulated us on selling the most (Hogue Winery) cases in the country and passed on more praise from the CWUS team. The conversation persisted and I couldn't help but feel more comfortable with him as the transparency issues of the new division were not as dramatic. As the call concluded, I pulled off the exit ramp to Harbour Island. I thanked him and hung up. I crossed the Garrison Channel onto the island, as a car raced up from behind me.

Within seconds, I noticed it was Molly the Mermaid in her Jeep with the top down. She drove up to the side of my car and honked as I lowered my window to say hello.

She waved singing along to a song, just inches from scraping the paint off the side of my Navigator.

She sped around me as we pulled into the parking garage together. We parked in side-by-side spots. The song echoed throughout the garage:

"I'm just a little girl lost in the moment
I'm so scared but I don't show it
I can't figure it out. It's bringing me down
I know, I've got to let it go
And just enjoy the show"

I sat mesmerized by the words of the catchy tune. The name of it was "The Show" by an artist named Lenka and it actually began to spook me as it played on. I couldn't help but visualize Wendy singing it. Actually, it was as if she wrote it. My racing thoughts were interrupted.

"Larry, it looks like you just saw a ghost," Molly shouted.

I couldn't find my voice as I turned back to her and forced a smile.

She lifted her sunglasses. "Oh, you did."

She giggled and covered her mouth before hopping out of her Jeep, on a mission. Ever since I met this little firecracker, I marveled at how inquisitive she was. At that very moment I received a call. I opened my door and grabbed my BlackBerry. Wendy's name flashed up. Molly stood on the sideboard and pointed at it excitedly informing me that it was the girl who freaked me out when I heard the song.

I sent Wendy to voicemail and glanced over at her. "What?" I said slightly panicked.

"You just smiled when you saw her name flash up."

"I didn't smile," I said unconvincingly as a headache spiked behind my eyes.

She searched them. "Larry, stop, I see it in your eyes. You were freaked out by the song."

My demeanor flashed culpability. I frantically grabbed my Evian bottle to counter my dry mouth. "What are you talking about?"

Her prying eyes peered at me as she said, "So, let me see here."

I pouted. "Molly, let me get out."

Increasingly discomforted I stepped out as she said, "Oh my God you're getting so defensive because she's the girl I saw you with! Now it's all making sense."

I slammed my door.

She smiled curiously and took a step forward. "So she works for you and fell for you, and your Little Larry Show. And is the girl who I also saw coming out of your apartment at seven in the morning a couple of months back literally glowing because she just got fucked by you."

"I didn't fuck her."

She slapped a book she was holding with her free hand. "Oh bullshit! I saw her face. You fucked her and gooood."

My eyes rolled. "Where were you?"

"Don't get pissy. I was jogging and went to my Jeep. I didn't want to bring it up when I saw you with that guy, (Bud Fox) but you two looked the same as when I saw you two in South Tampa the month before. I told you about that—"

I held up my hand. "Yup."

She laughed. "Well, both sightings made it pretty fucking obvious love was in the air. You two were in your own little world." She hesitated and opened the book she was holding before adding, "I love this. You two have to be the talk of your office."

"What. No. What?"

I began babbling while averting her eyes until she literally screamed out my name, "Larry," and waved the book she was holding inches from me. She took a deep breath and continued, "I saw her face up close that morning," her voice low and sultry, "and I watched her go to take a left and stare back at you and then turn the wrong way just to say goodbye to you again."

I stood there in disbelief and it continued to show on my face.

"Oh my god, I love this; look at your face." She walked right up to me. "I can't blame her and it's the reason this is so burned in my memory." Molly smirked inquisitively. "You have this way about you, and that look. It's actually quite pathetic." She paused as I winced, "But it works, I don't know why." Her head angled slightly as her eyes squinted up eerily. "You exude this fucking unexplainable boyish appeal."

My eyes closed. Her choice of words were needling. This all was only getting worse. If she had an off switch I would've paid money to flip it. I felt like curling up in the fetal position as her onslaught continued.

"You're ridiculous…in a good way. I like it. Anyway, "The Show" would be my theme song if I was with you." She threw that out deliberately and waited, drawing great satisfaction from my discomfort and then threw a piece of gum in her mouth and smiled amorously. I continued to fade before she added in a nonchalant way, "But I would be able to handle you."

I fell for the line she baited me with. "Oh, she does fine." Just as those words flew out of my mouth, I had the sensation the wind was knocked out of me.

"I knew it. It's so obvious. Anyway, life's too short. I would just keep singing it. *Life is a maze and love is a riddle. I know, I just have to let it go and just enjoy the show.*"

My BlackBerry rang again. It was again Wendy. "I'll bet you a bottle of wine that's her."

Hating to admit she was right, I frowned and answered, "Wendy let me call you back."

Molly smiled and handed me the book. It was a romance novel.

"No! I have to talk to you," Wendy bellowed as a gust of wind startled us. I hadn't felt a hint of a breeze on my skin before that.

With wide eyes Molly shouted, "What was that? Is your bitch a witch?"

I waved Molly back. "Wendy, hold on a second."

Molly was cracking up.

Wendy cried out, "HELLO?!"

"I have to call you back, ya ding!"

Click.

Molly stood thoroughly engrossed. "You call her ya ding? How cute. Oh my god you're going to really relate to that story. It's about two star-crossed lovers who can't stay away from each other. I'm actually a little jealous…weird, huh?"

I had to lie down. I smiled, waved Molly's book at her, and walked into the apartment. Molly's message and the fact she put all of this together along with that song had my mind zeroing in on everything that just hit me.

Later that night, my second to last in the corporate apartment, I tried to read the romance novel Molly had handed me, but the story of my own life kept inserting itself in the pages. I placed the book on the nightstand and turned the lights off.

At two o'clock in the morning, my eyes shot open, awoken by an odd dream about Wendy. I stared into the darkness before flipping the nightstand light back on. Within seconds I lunged for the book and opened it to the middle with disturbing intrigue. I began to read.

"I need you; I miss you like crazy," he said as Jennifer fought back tears. She knew she couldn't admit she had fallen in love with him, but was desperate for his plan anyway.

"We fucking can't stay away from each other and everyone is talking. Now what?"

His ego and love for her overrode all rational thought as he shouted, "Let them talk, I need you…and you need me. I'll deal with them!"

I closed the book hastily while convincing myself my eyes were too heavy to read on and turned off the light.

CHAPTER TWENTY-ONE

WENDY'S BIRTHDAY PARTY

JANUARY 2010
THE GREEKS/LIT

A week later, the day before her birthday, Wendy was full of fervor. She was about to turn twenty-seven years old, nearly sixteen years younger than I. Her celebration plan consisted of her boyfriend, Jessie, her best friend Lisa Lively...and me. Of course, she manipulated much to continue this. Ironically, her course of action plan included Matt at a time when she really didn't want to, but had to because it would look too strange to have me there alone.

The next day, her birthday, she called me to confirm.

I changed the subject, which only postponed the inevitable. We had a late meeting in the office when she had begun texting me to finalize the plans that I was dragging my feet on. My head was screaming no, while my heart was aching yes, and Matt knew it.

He ran into my office before the meeting with a grave look of concern. "Mayor, you can't be anywhere near her tonight. Let's just celebrate separately on another night." He paused hoping I would see the light, but The Darkness was in the way.

"It'll all be fine," I besought before taking a call.

After the meeting, he continued that conversation until Dan Schultz wandered in. Overhearing part of it, he suddenly found himself caught in the crossfire and said, "I see nothing, I hear nothing, and I know nothing."

My gaze narrowed at him.

Matt laughed, but was still determined to persuade me. "Mayor, do you remember the last time we were at the Greeks? We should not be going."

I loosened my tie. "Matt, we have to go."

Wendy sent another text: "Where are you?" She was still upstairs in the meeting room and Matt knew it was her. He shook his head. I amazingly said, "We'll go to dinner at the Greeks and have one drink at LIT and take off."

"Mayor, that's not going to happen. You know she can't control her actions with you."

Matt stopped abruptly as Wendy ran in. Her eyes frantically scanned the space. Then they shifted to mine. She had that look on her face that I couldn't resist. "Hey," she said. "So we'll meet you at the Greeks. Okay?"

Matt turned away from me without uttering a word as I nodded eagerly. "Of course."

Two minutes, later she texted me: "I can't stand how weird Matt has become. I really don't want him there."

I texted her back: "I can't go alone."

"No. Bring him. I just hate how weird he has gotten."

"See you there."

We got to the Greeks and I gave our waiter, Chops, the signal for two. He nodded and opened two bottles at once. Her best friend Lisa strolled in. Everyone was in good spirits, although Jessie downed his wine quickly. Noticing that, I signaled for two more. A light bulb went on in Chops' head and he realized Wendy's "real" boyfriend was in attendance. He shot me a sinister smirk and nodded over Jessie's shoulder. A minute later I caught him just staring at us before giving me a quick wink as the Greek dancers passed him screaming "OPA!" while throwing napkins all over the room.

Matt shifted in his chair awkwardly bracing himself for our imminent liftoff. I made plans for him to stay with me so that he wouldn't have to drive back to Sarasota that night. I felt that would relieve some of his stress about the situation, but it didn't. His eyes flashed with panic. There was little doubt he was having a discomforting recollection of our nights out that fall. At any rate, regardless of our apparent closeness, Jessie seemed completely unfazed, though removed from the core of the conversations. Wendy didn't notice and Matt let me know walking out.

"Mayor, she doesn't even realize her own boyfriend doesn't want to be here."

"Matt, he just laughed."

"He doesn't like you and is tense…and you know it's going to get worse."

After dinner we went over to the infamous LIT. I was recently there with two buddies from my old team, Bobby Blue and The Cowboy. Wendy and I had also been there, not once, but twice, and I had gotten to know the bartender enough for her to smile mischievously at me as we walked in. Little did I know at the time it was because of the dark affinity I shared with Wendy.

I did my best to use Matt as a buffer. He engaged in some talk with Jessie, but that didn't last. I was sitting on the other side of them when Wendy shouted out to me and shot her whimsical stare. The music seemed to stop.

Matt leaned into me and softly said, "Here we go."

I jumped up to get a cigar without even looking back. "You guys want anything?"

"I'll have one!" Wendy chirped enthusiastically, as Matt and Jessie sat in silence. Walking on I wasn't sure if she meant a cigar or a drink.

Minutes later, I was in the cigar vault with the bartender to pick out a selection. She laughed at something I said and then somehow we got on the topic of my "egg crack game." Well, she needed one. I placed my hand on her head and came across the top with the other for a perfect pop. That was when I received a text from Wendy: "You are making me jealous."

The atmosphere changed instantly. My head turned to the bartender who let out this sinister snicker. She seemed to know the text was from Wendy, and softly said, "Being in love is easily recognizable."

I froze before my eyes rolled to her silently nodding to Wendy. After a moment of restless quiet I replied, "No, that's her boyfriend." I made a gesture to Jessie.

"I know and I can't believe she brought him here…with you. She's been staring at you the entire time. You don't remember the conversation we had the last time you were in?"

It took a few seconds to register, but finally did. Dammit. The bartender was relentless and determined to decipher this dark devotion we shared. Astonishingly, at the time, I only took it as her flirting with me. She wasn't. I nodded, now abashed, as she continued, "You seriously don't realize how obvious it is." She paused as I just shook my head unconvincingly as Molly's message was flashing in front of my eyes.

She laughed. "When it shows in your eyes that clearly, it's not easily forgotten."

That sounds like one of my lines.

"Anyway, what I said then was when you're in love, reality doesn't always line up with your version of it." She handed me a cigar. "I also see you're married." She placed her hand on my back to console me.

I took a sharp and shuddering breath as she walked to the door.

Just then Wendy texted me again: "Hello? This is my b-day, not hers. How rude."

I bit my lip so I wouldn't display a ridiculous smile. My eyes then fixated on a box of cigars as the bartender grabbed the door and opened it whispering, "Good luck...you'll need it."

The door closed.

I sighed in relief just to have that end, but then as she passed in front of the glass, my eyes shifted to Wendy who was staring right at me. Her pouty cheeks grabbed at my loins. I wanted to just say fuck it all and gallantly march up to her, grab her, and kiss her. I then realized my thoughts continued to race across all lines, so I looked away. I could only imagine what my eyes were screaming out at this point, but I didn't care; hers were ablaze. The eyes never lie.

I went to walk out but stopped. Jessie was staring at Wendy. He didn't seem happy. But she didn't even notice. I resisted the urge to sit down on a box of cigars as he was off to the side gripping his cell phone. My eyes shifted to Matt next to Jessie.

He was awkward and nervous, so I felt it best to just avoid him, especially after the bartender's message. But then he texted me: "Mayor, she was staring at you with the bartender. You had to crack a fucking egg on her head? This girl is about to blow!"

I walked out and went to the bar to grab a drink without responding to him, but as I turned back to them I noticed Jessie walking out. He paced on his phone outside the bar. Matt walked over to sit next to Wendy as Lisa came up to me to order shots for the group. It was during another conversation with the bartender that I received a text from Wendy that proved the bartender right. And somehow it was one that Matt read as he sat next to her. When I turned to walk back to them, he glared at me. His face displayed utter shock. My heart sank. I went back to the bar and reread her line as my heart now raced through my shirt. My head turned; my eyes rolled into hers. This confident and capable young lady had her light of love burning brighter than I'd ever seen one burn, in anyone, and that's saying something.

Minutes later, she wanted our picture. We took one together when Jessie wandered back in with a forced smile that didn't belong below his frowning eyes. A couple minutes later we stood with our backs to the bar in a line for a group shot. Wendy was on the opposite end from me. I turned to the bartender who asked me if I needed a shot. Suddenly she shook her head with a smirk and nodded to my right. I turned back and Wendy was by my side, smiling wide. The flash went off.

Matt, at this point, was so mortified it was clear he couldn't take any more. He passed me. "Mayor, are you fucking me? I saw her text to you." His hands went to his head as he walked out. When he came back I found out he was waiting to hear back from a friend.

Within five minutes he got the word he was waiting for and said, "Mayor, I'm leaving." He looked at the girls who looked right through him.

"Where are you going?"

Even in the dark bar the tension was evident on his face, but he then began to laugh. "Mayor, this is seriously the most fucked up shit I've ever seen. I warned you she fell for you."

I couldn't believe he read that. I leaned in and said, "What are you talking about?"

His eyes blinked distressfully gathering his thoughts.

"Mayor, I knew before I read it. Everyone knows. I warned you about this shit months ago; it's fucking obvious. And you don't think he knows?" He motioned back to Jessie before staring back at me, "And I know you do. You just don't want to admit it." He turned away and then back to me. "It's your deal, but I'm staying with a friend."

I stood there speechless as I noticed Wendy behind him, leaning forward holding her hand up to me with her palm facing the ceiling. I couldn't help but smile as Matt was gone. He would end up the first CWUS recruit to get placed by Cosmopolitan Wine. The position would be working alongside Mike Fritton in a supplier role that would be dealing directly with us, and play into the end of the story, as this night would be duly noted and come back to haunt me. In the weeks that followed he distanced himself from us before being offered the position.

Incredibly, I still downplayed it all while interestingly, Wendy thought it was best. She knew he was aware of too much, but only thought he'd become a storyteller twisting the truth. Although she was correct that certain stories were exaggerated, and even lied about, he had seen way too much that was true and she knew it.

The day after her birthday, I received an early call from Bud Fox. It came to me as I was reading a long string of Wendy's affectionate texts she sent me after an awkward ride back to my car. I was distracted by them when I answered. "Hey man." My voice was horse and raspy from the cigars and alcohol.

"Jesus, you sound like shit." I lunged for water to clear my throat as he continued. "What did she do last night?" He laughed as I groaned with a mouth full of water. He continued as I swallowed. "I know she texted you that she fell in love with you."

I took a deep breath. "Matt called you?"

He ignored me. "Larry. Everyone knew, and now they're all talking."

I noticed Dan Schultz calling. "Matt gets nervous. Schultz is calling, I have to take this."

"Larry, wait. She lies about anything having to do with you. I've told you. The other day she actually told Tony that she was meeting me for lunch before racing off to you. But it was after that meeting you wouldn't answer my calls, so I called Tony…"

My eyes closed in disbelief.

"Well, that's the reason I'm calling now. Tony told me that if I can't find you to just call Wendy and tell her to roll over and tap you on the back."

I stood in front of our new bathroom mirror, numb. "It's all fine," I muttered glumly, feeling nauseas.

"Coming from the guy who married the president of his fan club," he teased.

I set the BlackBerry down and rubbed my bloodshot eyes.

"Hey, seriously, Wendy knows you're not leaving Marie. And because of that, she's panicking. No girl wants to be that person."

"No one is panicking...no one is running off together...just relax. This is all ridiculous." I said as my statement fell into an eerie silence.

I wanted him to say something. He didn't. I became overwhelmed by a spectacular visual of Wendy's eyes. For some reason they affected me even more than her words, which said too much. And when Fox repeated, "Larry, you know no girl wants to be that person," I panicked.

"What fucking person? Will you stop? This is crazy." I barked defensively.

"Larry, it's not crazy if you only admit what happened. This girl fell in love with you. And this guy she's dating is probably going to haul ass or throw a fucking ring on her finger. But when this shit blows up, and it will, you will see nothing but taillights from this girl."

"Settle down, Fox. You have too many birds chirping in your ear."

"Larry, I've hung out with both of you. What's your fucking line? The eyes never lie?"

"Okay, enough drama. We have to win that Franciscan (wine) incentive."

Click.

CHAPTER TWENTY-TWO

STARS AND STRIPES

FEBRUARY, 2010
WORLD OF BEER

The following Friday, I received an update that had us leading the Franciscan incentive. That Monday, I left our east coast home early to make the trek back to Tampa. As I drove, I found myself hardwired for the call that I had grown accustomed to receiving by this point in my journey. I glanced at the clock impatiently wondering why I was being kept waiting. She must be running late today. Just as I began to pout, she rang. I turned down the radio. "Hey, Wendy."

"Oh, my God I had another dream," she gushed.

A smile raced across my face. "Two weeks in a row, huh? WDD." (That was an acronym for her other nick name: Wendy Darlington Drama.)

"I know. You're beginning to haunt me."

The amusement level of the bantering rose as rapidly as the sun behind me, and always seemed to relieve the stress for the week ahead. Of course, she never brought up her words texted to me on her birthday night. I asked her if she was aware that it had been six months since the first "Monday call" she made to me.

"Um, yeah," she said. "It was my last good night sleep."

Another call beeped in. I expected to see The Rabbi's name on the caller ID, so my eyes grew wide when I saw it was Marie.

"Wendy, I'll call you back," I said.

"Stop pouting. I agree and they were happy haunts."

"It's Marie, ya ding!" (I used to call her "ya ding" and texted

UDING whenever she missed my point.) I then anxiously bawled, "Wendy, just hold on." I took a deep breath, exhaled, clicked over, and calmly said, "Hey, what's up?"

No one was there. I clicked back and said, "Hello?"

But it was Wendy, who giddily replied, "Um, ya ding…it's me."

Jokingly-jittery, I shouted, "Hold on. Damn you woman; I'm in a fragile state."

"Shut your mouth. You put people in a fragile state."

I was about to blackout. The BlackBerry beeped again and Marie's name flashed up. I clicked over, once again, and in a soft tone I said, "Marie, are you okay?"

She wasn't there, again. I clicked back over to Wendy and shouted, "I'm back, WDD!"

But it wasn't Wendy; it was Marie, who was seething.

"No. This is not WDD. It's your wife."

Click.

My eyes popped forward in my head. I drifted into the wrong lane and stared at the damn thing wondering how that had just happened. I heard. "Hello? It's me, WDD."

Aflutter, I hollered. "Wendy, hang up. I have to call you back."

"Whaa? Wait, whaa is going on? Do you want me to hold on?"

"No! I just called out your name like a love-struck sixteen-year-old boy thinking it was you, but it was Marie. Hang the fucking phone up, ya ding," I demanded, now thoroughly distraught with Wendy hysterically laughing.

Click.

I rubbed my eyes and exhaled deeply. I called Marie back. It rang once and went to her voice mail. I tried to remain calm, but it didn't work. A lady in an Escalade to my left began cracking up. I changed lanes to get away from her rudeness and called again. But now I heard her on the other line.

Beep, beep, beep.

I had the audacity to actually shout out, what kind of games is she playing? And then, incredibly, I turned up Taylor Swift's "Love Story" only to have Wendy text me: "I need to talk to you. Can you talk?" She called before I could even respond.

This particular call was a drastic contrast to the last one. She brought up her recent trip to Mexico and a conversation we had that she'd become uncomfortable with and was now resolved to rewrite. The trip was a short stay that I had approved her to take with her mother and one we didn't plan on speaking through because it was an international call. Forty-eight hours into the stay and actually on her last night, Wendy changed her mind, and reached out to me.

She went to the hotel business center to send me an email. In short she emphasized how much she missed me, which was now the cusp of her meltdown, or at least part of it. During the first conversation I ended up having to read her the email. After a rather stressful five minutes of her ramblings she became determined to rewrite it. But that obviously was impossible.

"Wendy, I read you the email that you wrote to me."

She bawled distressfully, "Permanently delete that now!"

I did.

She released her breath in a long, shaky sigh.

I sat stunned. She paused and her voice rose. "I think Jessie is going to propose."

My heart sank when she ended the call. "I have to go."

Click.

Behind the puissant princess she played so well, was a little girl lost in love, and so scared she refused to show it. It was at this time she began to rewrite what she couldn't rise above, because she realized she couldn't stop it.

The very next day, our "Wine Time" afternoon, full of frivolity, was abruptly interrupted when she received a text from Jessie. She glanced over to me and with a sharpened voice said, "Did you realize the time?"

I only shrugged. "No, I'll get the waiter."

She sighed. I texted her a quick poem to cheer her up as I walked to the bathroom.

When I came back to the table she held up the poem. "How do you come up with this shit?" She gave me her little head nod as her eyes flickered with my favorite light.

I smirked. "You inspire me."

She attempted to conceal her emotions but couldn't. She was back and wasn't leaving.

Thirty minutes later, Jessie called irate. This sent her into a tailspin and heading home. During that ride, after some troubling texts, she called me emotionally distraught. Obviously the two bottles (and some glasses) of wine didn't help this situation as words were flying that hadn't before.

After a heated back and forth she snapped, "Your marriage is troubled."

I took a deep breath and exhaled calmly. "I need to fix that, but what's your excuse?"

Her mind was in overdrive as she only answered my question with another question. "How many of these have you had?"

"Nothing like this one—"

She drew a sharp breath, "How many?"

"I've never met anyone like you, so never."

My choice of words and what happens from this point of the story on are pure irony.

I heard her sigh; my voice was quiet. "I didn't plan for this to happen, but it's difficult to deny that something else isn't going on here—with us."

She took in a slow breath and blew it out. "I know." Then nearly out of breath she said, "And in another life we live happily ever after, maybe in your fucking fantasy land."

"It's Never Land, Wendy."

"I can't deal with this fairy tale right now. I'm back home, where you don't belong...in the real world." She took in a shuddering breath.

"Wendy, I am real. And so is the key I left on your laptop to the secret cloud door to my sacred land—" I heard a strange sound; one I couldn't identify. "Wendy..."

"Please stop...because I'm starting to believe this—"

"Wendy—"

"Enough! Do not send me anything tonight. I can't handle it."

"But I had a special poem for you."

"Larry. Please...I need sleep. I'll call you tomorrow."

"Goodbye Wendy."

"Bye."

Click.

The next day she called me on the office line. She only commented on how much wine we consumed before suggesting we meet at a deli that was next to an account she had an issue at. I rubbed my eyes, responded to an email from The Rabbi, and raced off to meet her.

Two days after that I had a late conference call with The Rabbi and Mindy Amour. Wendy had a dinner planned at her grandparents' house, which was just down the street from my new neighborhood, in North Tampa. We had been in touch after the call, which ended earlier than I had anticipated. On my drive home she called again. She told me that Jessie had flown out on business again and that she was leaving South Tampa for the dinner, which included other family members who were visiting her grandparents. We ended the call with no further plans to speak that evening.

I pulled into my house and walked in through the garage on a call with Lauren and Jerry about their school day. I threw my tie on the bed and kicked off my shoes while heading to my wine collection to grab a bottle of Mondavi Napa Cabernet. I opened it and the aroma of blackberries, dried herbs, and floral hit me as I poured a glass and took it all in anticipating the dark chocolate lingering on the finish. "Oh that's good," I said placing it on my coffee table in my memorabilia room. It was the only room complete in the new house as I felt I needed it set-up first for my games. Tonight I had a New York Rangers game. I pulled my laptop out and set it up next to it. Everything was just right and ready to go as I went in to take a shower.

Twenty minutes later, my BlackBerry rang on the vanity. I wiped the steam off the glass to see it was Wendy. It went to voicemail, but then I immediately received a text from her: "I just pulled into the World of Beer across from your house. Meet me for a quick drink. I only have thirty minutes." I dried off and responded: "Give me ten minutes." She shot back: "No, five."

Just to drive her crazy, I texted: "See ya in 7:32:17. Ya Silly Goose!"

I glanced at my watch and chuckled. She was supposed to be at her grandparent's house in five minutes. I texted her back: "Do you realize what time it is?"

She replied: "HURRY UP!" I strolled into my closet to get dressed. For some reason, I wasn't in the mood to pick out a shirt though and just stood there staring at them.

I turned to check out the other side. As I did one dropped behind me off the hanger and onto to the carpet. Slightly taken aback by this, I stared at the shirt. I became even more intrigued because I had no recollection of even buying it. It was a short-sleeved polo with blue and red stripes. I walked over, picked it up, and snickered. I was hit with another text from Wendy, threw the shirt on, and realized the irresistible indulgence I corked in my memorabilia room was calling my name. I walked back to my Mondavi Napa Cabernet and softly said, "To the second star to the right." I tipped the glass back giggling giddily about the shirt, and this unstoppable star-crossed-lovefest, and ran out the door.

I walked into the World of Beer minutes later. Wendy sat in the corner of the bar. She was wearing the same stripped shirt and she was glowing. We gawked at each other for a moment and gleefully freaked out. It was unimaginable. But then we couldn't help but acknowledge how many times these mystical signs made this very wrong thing between us feel so right. Laughing and looking ridiculous, I hopped on the bar stool next to her and said, "And the shirt just fell off the hanger." Her smile exuded immaculate elation.

The young night had this enchanting magical feel to it. It was something we had grown accustomed to while preparing to leave the wicked world behind.

An hour later Wendy called her grandparents to tell them she couldn't make the dinner. She meant to call sooner, but we both had lost track of the time. It was then I realized I had a missed call from Bud Fox. Wendy noticed she had two missed calls.

"Shit." Her demeanor changed as she scurried out.

When she returned I said, "I don't know how we missed these calls?"

She grabbed her glass, took a healthy swig and replied, "It's the stripes."

We grinned and clinked glasses.

Twenty minutes later, she received a call that caused her smile to run from her face. "What is he doing?" she hissed heading out yet again. She seemed bothered, but hung up after a brief conversation that she didn't elaborate on. She only strolled back in, glanced at my shirt, pointed to hers, and gave me her head nod. She smiled wide again before she headed to the bathroom. I would say it was all incredible, but by now you get that.

By this point the place was packed. There was a trivia club in one corner and a large table of odd engineer types in the other. A softball team lined the far end of the bar and bunch of thirty-somethings that you would typically see jogging in my new neighborhood filled in the rest.

I went to check my emails and noticed a text from Fox: "You didn't take my calls so I guess I'll just call Wendy and have her roll over and tap you on the back."

I started to reply when the bartender scared the shit out me. "I have to say you and your wife are adorable together. I hope I find that someday. You guys want another bottle?"

I looked up at her speechless and nodded. She turned back to me and added, "And not many couples can make that work." She chuckled at my comical shirt and shouted back to me, "But you guys do. Very cute."

I shrugged and smiled awkwardly. Just another indelible impression we made. I was hit with the number of times this has happened. Thankfully Wendy came through the crowd of people. She had that look in her eyes. She jumped on her stool and leaned into me. "They think we're married," she whispered, amorously.

"What makes you say that? The fact that they're enamored by our matching shirts, constant glow, secret language, or—"

Her hand shot up to my mouth. "Shut your mouth. Shut it, Larry, shut it."

I then wondered how many of these poor people were my new neighbors. I had to purge that thought because I was about to blackout. I grabbed my glass and threw the rest of the wine back. It seemed the bar had caught fire.

Within the hour, (since the space seemed to be completely engulfed in flames) I felt it would be an opportune time to play my "eyelash game." Like two starry-eyed teens in heat, we did. It wasn't bad enough that all eyes stared at us while we were entranced in our giddiness, listened to our lingo, and wore our matching silly striped shirts. No, no, now just envision us playing this idiotic game, which I made up in college (like my egg-crack game) and was still playing at nearly forty-three-years-old with a girl sixteen years younger. I thought about explaining the game but then realized that part really doesn't matter. So we flicked each other's eyelashes until we saw stars.

See, I told you.

Wendy fell off her barstool and, full of mirth, hopped backed on it. "I won the last game because you pulled back first and then came back in for seconds. That's not fair."

"Wendy, it states in the rule book you cannot hold or touch your opponent in any way."

"Larry, I cannot stay on the stool and I'm allowed to touch you."

"You cannot hold my stripes, pat my stripes, or touch my stripes in any way."

"Shut your mouth." She reached her hand over and I fell off my stool as I pulled away from her. The good news was that I won the game because she began hysterically laughing and couldn't speak. "Wendy rule 674-A states that if you are unable to continue the game in a timely manner it is an instant forfeit."

She was purple at this moment. Not to mention she actually almost ended up with whiplash. By ten-thirty the pixie dust was falling at a rate of three inches an hour. Yet, it was like a blizzard of the shit and we had successfully, again, landed in my sacred land, which was far from anything remotely real. Phone calls, texts, and dinners were missed as time stood still. But the wine continued to flow and all eyes were literally glued to our antics.

Within five minutes of a detailed conversation about being soulmates, Wendy screamed out and fell into me with her hand up to my mouth...again.

"I'm sorry I brought this up. New subject, this is a fairy tale. It is not real. That's the only reason it feels so good."

"Wendy, my fairy tales are real."

We happily clinked our glasses, laughing while pretending we didn't notice that the lights go out and it was suddenly the three of us; her, me, and all that stuff we were so scared of.

When we finally did land back in the real world, we realized we were the last people in the bar. We walked out into a starry night, but the second star to the right was burning too bright. We flew back to Never Land. I gave her a piggyback ride through the empty parking lot. Her head rested on my back before she hopped in my navi. No words were spoken; it just happened. We drove off to the new house.

By this time, the intense sexual desire we shared had hit a boiling point. We had typically run from it after a couple of bottles each afternoon, but this was different. It was now very late, we had no curfews, and the new empty house was a couple miles away.

Feeling like a mischievous boy playing with fire, I hit two buttons on the car stereo and sat back as the lyrics to the song I selected played. It was "Jessie's Girl" from my idol, Rick Springfield. It would be safe to say this was another magical moment...

"But lately something changed that ain't hard to define," I sang. "Jessie's got himself a girl and I want to make her mine."

Wendy took an enormous breath and blew it out into her hands, which shot over her bright red face as the song played on.

I play along with the charade
There doesn't seem to be a reason to change
You know, I feel so dirty when they start talking cute
I wanna tell her that I love her, but the point is probably mute

As she displayed this euphoric glow I had another song hit me, it was a song called "Miss That Someday" and was also by my idol. Without missing a beat, I hit it.

You throw me out into the rain then you comfort me with pain
How can our love ever last? You're just a big pain in the ass
Ask of me, can we survive this stormy sea? Two worlds collide
You and I will love when love's invisible
Take the time to say I'll miss that someday

The look on her face was priceless, so much so that I had thoughts of just tearing her stripes off in the car behind the fucking Lowes that we were passing. Thankfully, I noticed her entranced in the lyrics and drove on reaching for my Evian. I took a gulp as we cruised under the stars to the gate of my community. The music blared as we waited for the gate to open. A shooting star flew by.

My head fell forward in disbelief. "I hope that wasn't our second star to the right?" I said into the blaring music. I turned to Wendy and her head was still down studying the words of the song. "Wendy?" I hit her arm as she glanced over at me.

"Did you write this shit?" she blurted out.

I smiled as her stare suddenly had that other damn song playing in my head. I cursed Molly the Mermaid while envisioning Wendy singing it.

I can't figure it out
It's just bringing me down I know
I've got to let it go
And just enjoy the show

But there was more. Her eyes rolled back to me, and a recent conversation hit. It was the one during which those same eyes pleaded with me that we must avoid this moment at all costs. It was a month before. She had this frantic fear that if we did have sex we'd be running off at ten o'clock in the morning every day instead of three in the afternoon.

She might've had that part right, but in all reality, it was a joke because of how emotionally attached we already were. And that thought didn't just creep into my mind; it was shot with cupid's arrow at this very moment.

I pulled into the driveway. She turned the song off, full of emotion. We both turned away to open our doors at the same time. As we walked into the house our voices echoed through the empty space. I strolled into the kitchen. I thought she was behind me and asked her if she wanted a bottle of Evian, but she wasn't there.

"Wendy?" I shouted.

She ran through the bedrooms upstairs. "I'm up here," her voice excitedly echoed down. "Oh my God, it's beautiful."

I turned to the window in the family room. She came back down as the moonlit sky was bright. It was an enchanting evening that highlighted the emotions that were consuming us. She collapsed on an air mattress that was in the family room. She gazed at me impassionedly as I walked over to scoop her up. With her in my arms she asked, "When does our fairy tale end?"

Carrying her into the bedroom I whispered, "Ours doesn't."

I placed her down beside the bed. Our lips touched softly. Her stripes hit the floor effortlessly. Her tongue tasted like wine, naturally, and candy, I don't why. Within seconds, she was half naked and we were lying down. My fingers inched farther along the smoothness of her skin. Deeper. Lower. She gasped in anticipation. She shivered intensely as my lips tickled the hollow of her neck before moving down over her nipples. And she was correct: this felt all too right. Minutes later, I got the sign. I pulled at the string on her pants and it knotted. I breathed in her ear, "Who wears pants with a fucking string?"

She moaned pleasurably.

I pulled the string again and made it worse, amongst other things that made it better, her body trembled. The heat was sudden. My eyes rolled to hers and they displayed extreme pleasure. Her climax achieved. I pushed up off her. My voice was practically inaudible. "Are you kidding me?"

She beamed. "Nope." She exhaled deeply. "Thank you."

She hopped up off the bed smiling blissfully.

I threw her bra at her flushed face and fell back sprawled out.

She walked into the master bathroom.

My eyes closed. "I'm already dreaming of your stripes," I moaned, adjusting my blue balls.

And then Wendy decided that although it wasn't nearly sunrise yet, it was time to go. "Larry, you can't explain me at the office; there is no way you will be able to explain me to your new neighbors."

My eyes shot open.

She came back out pulling her striped shirt over her head. "We have to go back to my car."

I sat up, nodded, grabbed my clothes and we snuck back out into the enchanting moonlit night. We hopped in my car. As the doors shut at the same time we turned to each other.

I could feel the heat still emanating off her precious cheeks. "Larry, I cannot take your stare right now. Start the car before I jump out and scream fuck it all and head back in."

I slowly backed out of the driveway with an undeniable feeling that I now had to beat back. I hit "Miss That Someday" again and drove off with her....

Ask of me, can we survive this stormy sea? Two worlds collide
You and I will love when love's invisible
Take the time to say I'll miss that someday.

CHAPTER TWENTY-THREE

MARCH MADNESS

MARCH 3, 2010 (MORNING)
THE TAMPA OFFICE

By March, I had six solid months on the books leading the new division. Regrettably, I was now using this business success as a blindfold to the flames burning out of control in my personal life. Two weeks later I took a sip of my coffee reading Wendy's morning text. I rubbed my eyes. It was another day of her spinning an emotional episode from the day before. Before I responded I plugged into two business emails praising our achievements. That gifted me the strength to readjust that blindfold to call her. An hour later, I pretended all was good and then straightened my tie just right to leave for the office. It was a day I was to meet with Geno Franc.

Everything he had envisioned for my career was playing out according to his plan, as he requested that we "catch up" the first week of March. This meeting did not include The Wizard.

Three hours later I approached him in route to this get-together. He shot me a quick hello and then stopped and asked intrusively, "Are you going to see Geno?"

"Yes." I replied.

He let out a frustrated breath and slowly turned to Franc's office at the end of the hall and then back to me. His eyes turned angry. "I have a meeting with TJ (Faggalo). I had no idea you were meeting."

His voice went through my spine as I said, "I believe he just wants to catch up."

That didn't comfort him. He glanced back down the hall with the same look of antipathy he had had at our recent general sales meeting. But I had been only kidding myself. He had had that same look since the day I first sat down with Franc in a covert meeting to bring me to Tampa, and it was quite apparent the success I had scored since was making my situation with him worsen. This is something I was warned about, but refused to believe. My discomfort level with him escalated.

I walked out of the meeting with Franc focused on the positive: his reassuring words of my bright future and what I meant to the company. So with a hop in my step, I took heed in the warnings to stay close to him descending down the steps to our office with glee.

For a moment, I thought, *this blindfold is awesome*, but then I was stopped by a manager of another division. After some small talk he whispered, "I wanted to let you know you were spotted at the Mexican restaurant by the mall," he paused peering over my shoulder.

My glare intensified. "...And?"

He became anxious. "Sorry, I have to hop on this call...but you were with your girl," he stuttered, "your manager...the girl." He paused awkwardly. I could only imagine what my facial expression was because he nervously added, "It was no biggie. I don't think...I don't know...but I thought you should know. It was a supplier who said so."

"Hey, come on...it started," a voice yelled out to him.

He was called into the office we were standing outside of. His boss caught my eye and smiled wanly. I popped my head in to say hi to the rest of them. They were on a conference call that had already begun. The room was cold and everyone seemed to be dreading the moment. I closed the door, readjusted my blindfold, and was hit with a text. It was from Wendy.

She had reached out to confirm meeting at our favorite new spot: The GrillSmith at the Westfield Mall in Brandon. I smiled rereading the text: "I'm wearing the stripes for Wine Wednesday. Can you do 2:30 at our GS?"

I strolled back in our office and the jovial space was alive and kicking. My chest was out full of Franc's commendation as Tony high-fived me. "Sir Sola, I noticed you haven't put all the pictures on the board." He held two of them up. They were a couple of pictures he actually took of Wendy and I after another impromptu celebratory toast we had after we won the Franciscan incentive. Another manager questioned me on his new goals. I motioned him into my office.

I turned back to Tony. "Don't quit your day job. They're a little blurry."

"But sir, she looks so alive. So happy."

Another manager blurted out, "That's why he can't hang them up!"

I cringed at his insinuation.

After I grabbed the pictures out of Tony's hand, I answered the manager's inquiry. He left and Mama Bear entered, right on cue. She leaned across my desk and asked if I was going to meet Wendy. I nodded yes, and buried the pictures in the back of my desk drawer.

"Larry, I've warned you," she whispered. "People are talking and it's getting worse. Were you two in South Tampa recently?" Her expression of concern was unconvincing.

I shook my head, forced a smile hoping to hide my impatience, grabbed a folder and threw a report into it. "Yes. I did meet her at the account we're hitting on the survey." The sarcastic energy in my voice made her grin although it was short lived.

She lowered her voice to an overly dramatic purr as she said, "Did you go for wine?"

I laughed uneasily. "Sounds like Tony's at it again."

She shot me a superfluous stare. "It wasn't Tony."

The warning I received in the hall on the way back from Franc's office was unrelated to this one, which now had me mildly miffed as another manager walked in.

Our eyes remained engaged for a few moments. Mama Bear's manner left a strange impression on me, and I tried to ignore it without success. But then a conversation hit me.

It was one with Tony on that same afternoon. It was an odd conversation about nothing, although it then dawned on me that he did confirm I was in South Tampa.

I put my laptop in my bag and marched out.

"Tell Wendy we all say hello, sir," Tony said snickering.

I glanced back at him and nodded as I walked out heading down the hall. I then turned back, questioning if I put the folder in my bag. I found it just feet from our office. Voices whispered.

"You would lie, too, if you were about to get engaged and were having an affair with the boss," Tony said. "Fox told me Sola's not leaving his wife, and Wendy knows it."

I struggled to draw a breath. On my way out I dialed Fox. He answered on the second ring. "Hey, what's up?"

"Please, don't add fuel to the fire with this thing with Wendy."

"Yeah, what happened?"

"Tony. I just heard something and I don't want to lose my temper with him."

"Jesus, they all love to talk...especially about you two—"

"Has she told you she's getting engaged?" My thoughts were racing.

He hesitated. "Yeah she waited for you to go the bathroom. I couldn't even look at her—"

"Where? When?" I was frantic.

"Calm down. It was when we were at the GrillSmith, and listen." He paused awkwardly. "Since she texted you that love note on her birthday everything's blown up."

"You haven't told anyone about that have you?"

He hesitated and sighed, "Larry no, I didn't have too...are you kidding me? Everyone knows. And I'll bet my paycheck you're in route to her now."

I sighed consumed with racing thoughts.

"Even my guys over here (on the east coast) are hearing shit about you two..."

I only again asked for his help. "I'm fixing it all. In the meantime, help me."

"Jesus, I'll help with Tony, but you can't just fix this. It's not a struggling sales team—"

"Fox I'll call you back later." I didn't need his reality check.

Fox got his dig in. "Jesus...tell her I say hi."

Click.

CHAPTER TWENTY-FOUR

ALTERNATING EMOTIONS

MARCH 3, 2010 (LATE AFTERNOON)
THE GRILLSMITH

Twenty minutes later, we pulled into the parking lot together. Wendy was wearing the stripes and gave me her little head nod before we walked in. We stood in the lobby waiting for the hostess. The television in the bar showed news updates on the January earthquake that had decimated Haiti. With no one there to seat us, the bartender waved as we watched the news report. The staff realized we weren't married and would smile spasmodically at us while enjoying their tidy tips with zipped lips.

As we were escorted to our booth I felt I had to address what I'd heard in the office. I waited for our wine and after some small talk I leaned in and said, "Have you told the team you're getting engaged?"

Her lips parted as she took in a slow deep breath while looking away. She turned back to me. Her eyes were distant. "Well, I am."

In that moment I changed my mind. "You know what, never mind."

She leaned in tense. "What?"

My emotions were tugging at me. I struggled to breathe but played it off and only said, "When you're at the office, why do you say you're going to meet someone else when they know your meeting me?"

She hesitated for an instant. "I never say I'm meeting you. And I'm not going too."

Frustrated, I exhaled deeply. "Wendy, it makes this look worse."

She took a long sip and swallowed hard. "Worse? It can't look any worse."

"When they know you're lying it does look worse."

"Really, in that place? They all lie." She looked intently at the menu she had memorized, "What's your point?"

"Oh I don't know Wendy, you panic and tell these people shit they know isn't true, your rewriting more and more of...us, you took a picture of Bud Fox and deliberately left it on your phone so your fiancé would see it in a ludicrous attempt to hide the reality of...us and you—"

"Enough!" she barked, blowing out a breath adding, "And that picture worked."

"If that worked, Jessie's craving for a diversion to the truth worse than you."

She wanted to pretend that too wasn't true but had no strength left for pretense.

"Maybe you need a spoon full of sugar to help the medicine go down." (She loved Mary Poppins and as a recent conversation came to mind I was unable to resist.)

She turned away attempting to conceal her smile. I then informed her someone spotted us in South Tampa, and also at our Mexican restaurant. Her head turned away, now deep in thought.

Her eyes rolled back into mine. "Now were being spotted in Brandon? Really..."

A sigh was my answer as her eyes suddenly displayed distress.

"And we stopped going to any place in South Tampa months ago, that was stupid."

She filled her glass erratically. The wine almost spilled over the side as she continued, "There are always too many people who see us there."

I watched her in disbelief. "You never fill your glass like that."

"Shut up. You're upsetting me." She tipped the glass back and took another long sip.

"By April we'll be having "Wine Time" in Lakeland." I paused as I received a text. "It's Mama Bear—"

She interrupted excitedly. "Really...these people need lives!"

The waitress quickly filled our waters and took off.

Wendy's eyes displayed pain. I could tell she was going to blow. She turned to me and went into a defensive tirade. "You're the only reason I left my old distributor. This type of bullshit doesn't happen there." She paused just to take a breath. "And that lady (Mama Bear) has no idea who you really are. It makes me sick. Why the hell do you continue to trust her? And your idiot Fox lies as much as Tony. Why you back that guy is the question I should be asking you. And I'm not even going to bring up Matt's storytelling. That guy can't keep track of his embellishments."

I smiled. "Okay." Her eyes were alive and even amidst her running tirade a silly smile spread across my face. Our eyes locked. The look between us was heavy with emotion.

She lit up. "Don't look at me like that." She exhaled deeply, "Grow up! You're a child."

I sat up in the booth. "And whaa are you?"

We both were instantly transcended to our world of make-believe far away from it all.

Her broad smile barely could relax long enough to take a sip of wine. Even amidst a troublesome conversation we couldn't help but enjoy each other's company. She then told me that she had a dream about the World of Beer night.

I smirked, "The PG-13 version at the bar...or the R version back at my house—"

She laughed. "The R version didn't happen...actually neither did, I went to my grandparents' house." She paused, distracted in thought, before adding, "How did we show up at that place in the same matching stripped shirts? How is that at all possible?!"

I laughed. "It's not. I think we've been over how crazy this all has been...and I still swear that I never bought that shirt."

She chuckled whimsically. "Why is this happening?" Her head titled to me but her gaze went off to the side as she blurted, "And you wonder why I'm so freaked out?!"

I couldn't contain the smile spreading across my face watching her. But then she was hit with a text. Her demeanor instantly changed reading it.

Her eyes turned sad as she redirected her gaze across the restaurant. Within seconds she replied to the text. "Jessie's taking me to dinner," she said now with something between a frown and a scowl, "when is Marie going to be in Tampa?"

I sat motionless as she took a long sip of wine. "What? You know exactly when Marie will be in Tampa. Are you okay?"

"I'm fine. And no I don't," she paused averting my eyes. "Jessie just asked me, we both want to know. I told him I had no idea."

I could not speak because suddenly it seemed that I might so easily, unwittingly say the wrong thing. I motioned for the check.

Two weeks later, Jessie proposed.

CHAPTER TWENTY-FIVE

WENDY'S RING ENDS UP ON THE CEILING

MARCH 2010
THE TAMPA OFFICE

The Monday after he proposed was the first day she didn't reach out to me with her "Monday morning call." Instead, she went to the office and hung a picture of her wedding ring up on our picture board. Minutes after she left, I was in a meeting with Dan Schultz in North Tampa when one of my managers sent me a text: "I can't believe she got engaged. She hung her ring on the (picture) board. It was taken down right after she left." I didn't respond and took a call from The Rabbi.

The next day the same manager called me on the matter while in route to the office. After questioning me on his goals he informed me that Wendy called the office to confirm I wasn't there before she came in with her picture. His voice rose, "Mama Bear swears she didn't want to do it in front of you."

"No," I huffed. "Please send your updated tracker and I'll adjust the goal."

"Yeah. I'm sorry Larry, I will."

Click.

Thirty minutes later, I walked in to a crowded office with a strange buzz in the air. I squeezed by Tony, who was standing at the district manager table. I was preoccupied with a project I had to complete for a meeting in Miami. I sat at my desk to send two emails back to The Rabbi and realized the room had gone quite. Everyone was gone.

I unscrewed the cap of an Evian bottle, while glancing across the space. In the corner of the main part of our office, was a picture stabbed to the ceiling with a pencil. I walked over for a closer look. It was a black and white, 8 x 10 picture of the ring on her finger. I was now pissed. There was little doubt it was put in an area of the office that I would notice from my desk.

"Fucking, Tony." I said softly.

With a feeling of guilt ridden umbrage, I went to call him. It went to voicemail. I grabbed a chair to get the photo down. My office line rang. It was The Rabbi. I grabbed it from Mama Bear's desk. "Hey, Gary." (The Rabbi)

"So." He paused for an instant. "So, Larry, I like this. Walk me through it."

I put him on hold and ran back in my office for the spreadsheet and notes. As I picked him up, I heard Wendy's voice.

"Are you fucking kidding?" Livid, she turned into my office.

The suspense of the moment had me holding my hand up and pointing to the phone. She ran back out and grabbed a chair to pull the picture off the ceiling. I couldn't concentrate as she let out a jagged exhale struggling to reach it.

"So." The Rabbi paused for a brief instant. "So Larry...is everything okay?"

I rubbed my eyes. "Yes, I'm sorry..."

"Okay, so how often do you have your managers update this?"

I had to spin my chair. "Every day, Gary. (The Rabbi) It has to be daily."

Within minutes, I hung up and Wendy was gone. I sent an email to The Rabbi to follow up on the conversation.

She shot back in, her face flooded with anger. "What is wrong with these people?!"

I was at a loss for words. I thought I heard Mama Bear in the background briefly. I never saw her though. Wendy raged on ignoring the fact that our entire office had witnessed her own actions for far too long. As wrong as this act was, I told her to come into my office because she sounded certifiable ranting about it right at the door. Finally she stopped. She took a deep breath. Her skin flushed with a light mist of nervous perspiration.

"Who stabbed my ring to the ceiling?"

I told her I didn't know and had just noticed it before the call. Her eyes were distant.

And then she blew all over again. Her fragile veneer cracked. All of the emotion of the past six months poured out. There was no way to ease her back either; she was gone, now wearing his ring.

As she continued, the pulse of adrenaline in my blood began to boil. "Wendy, you need to calm down."

The expression on her face wasn't hard to parse. Overwhelming anxiety, raging anger, and sincere worriment were flashing overtly. Beads of sweat erupted on my forehead.

She wasn't hearing a word I said either. She pointed to the spot the picture hung and shouted, "Why didn't you pull the picture down?"

"You're not listening. I told you I just noticed it and went to take it down when The Rabbi called." My voice rose rapidly as my emotions swung wildly. "I just got here and you know damn well I wasn't here when you hung it up."

The rueful excitement had her taking tiny quick breaths while refusing to look at me. After an awkward moment of silence, I realized everyone was aware that this was going to happen and had cleared out. It was like a Chinese fire drill.

I stood there not knowing what to do while still amazed she would hang that up in the first place. There was tightness in my throat and this susceptible feeling to my beating heart, which now ached. I was vulnerable and I didn't like it. She stormed out. I struggled to catch my breath. I sat back down breathing in and out rapidly.

Within the minute one of my managers wandered into my office. I pretended to act all together, but I was a wreck. He abruptly left. I had no idea what he even asked me.

Guilt overwhelmed me. The forbidden feelings I had and only pretended I kept in check deep inside of me were bubbling out. I swallowed hard and lunged for my BlackBerry. I called my wife just to say hi. It rang and rang as my heart raced. It was rare she wouldn't answer. But she didn't. I thought here is just another sign. I hung up without leaving a voicemail.

CHAPTER TWENTY-SIX

SHE'LL ALWAYS FIND A WAY
TO JUST ENJOY THE SHOW

LATE MARCH 2010
YBOR CITY

In the coming days, Wendy and I had no contact. It was evident how much a part of my life she had become. The troubling thoughts held me captive at my desk replying to an email from The Rabbi, and were only interrupted by a call from Matt McMullen. By this point, he had been working for Cosmopolitan Wines U.S. alongside Mike Fritton.

The next morning, he came into my office to go over a winery program. He mentioned taking me to the Greeks for dinner and then a drink in Ybor. He emphasized "just us."

Seven hours later, we sat at our table. Even though it had been months since we were all there together—Me, Matt, and Wendy— there was a maladroit moment when he glanced at her empty chair. I sat uncomfortably as the vision of her sitting next to me laughing, vexed me.

Matt raised his glass and clinked mine. "Mayor, what a shit show." He made a head gesture to her empty chair. "It should be interesting to see how she handles life without you." It was clear he was gauging my reaction.

I leaned in on my elbows, awkwardly nodded, and changed the subject.

After dinner we went down the street to an open air bar. As we sat down Matt stated, again, that he only had time for a drink and a cigar, and it was apparent he was nervous that the night would spontaneously combust. I think he had it worked out to have the check dropped off without being asked if we wanted anything else.

Forty-five minutes later, we were on our way out. We walked between the tables and approached the bar. I heard my name screamed out. I turn to see it was Molly the Mermaid and her group of friends from the corporate apartment I affectionately referred to as the Dawg Pound. I smiled curiously as Matt raced on out the far side of the bar as if it was on fire.

I couldn't dwell on that though because my little Mermaid energetically sprung from her stool as the stink of burnt rubber from Matt's tires peeling out of the parking lot settled over us.

After greeting the Dawg Pound, I received a text from him: "Mayor, I had to get on the road. We'll do it again soon."

I shook my head.

Molly came around to give me a hearty hug. She seemed buzzed. After some small talk, she pushed me off to the side full of curiosity. "So how's the show?"

I chuckled. "It's been cancelled."

Her hands dramatically shot to her sides. "Um, I doubt that...what happened?"

I shrugged, "It is best."

Her eyes shone brilliantly as she bawled, "Stop pouting, little boy."

I laughed, "Little boy? I'm probably your father's age."

"Um, it doesn't matter; you're different. Just accept it." She paused, beaming brightly.

I pouted.

She tightened her ponytail. "You're seriously the only forty-year-old who still pouts and I just love it. I have no idea why, but I do."

Embarrassed, I hushed her up. "Almost forty-three-year-old."

She made the weird (yet adorable) face she had made a few times before and scarcely above a whisper uttered, "Really?" She paused and peered at me eerily, "You have no lines around your eyes...and I know you party like a rock star..."

I nodded. "Aloe."

Her breathing quickened. "Oh. My. God. I can't. Get back to the girl."

I smiled and explained, "My family will be in Tampa in four months and she just got engaged, okay?"

Molly threw her hands up, as if surrendering. "Wait, are we talking about the same girl? The Show song girl—right?"

I nodded reluctantly.

She pushed me further away from her group. "She just got engaged?!" Her hands rose to her head with an intense look of intrigue. "Wow…really…holy…fuck."

I could feel my pulse rising.

She stood there alarmingly engrossed by this news. "Um, okay," she said, "I told you I saw you two, lost in love, in South Tampa. And her eyes the morning she went the wrong way just to say goodbye to you again." She paused smiling fervently, "You remember, after you fucked her…and good—"

"I told you I didn't," I exclaimed.

Staring in my eyes, quite possibly to see if I blinked, she inched closer to me. "If you truly didn't," she said spookily, "this is an even shittier shit show…and you need my insight."

I saw a flash of sincere concern. "Something tells me I'll need a glass of wine for this."

She let out a guffaw and took steps towards the bar, mock-fanning herself dramatically. "Uh huh…I know the bartender. Hold on," she said spinning back to me. "I was just thinking about you," her eyes intensified, "and your shit show."

My breathing became erratic.

I noticed the bartender catering to her and craved the weird (yet adorable) face she made, again. Seconds later, just as he handed her a giant glass of warm Cabernet Sauvignon, I yelled, "What the hell is that?"

It worked.

Racing back she whispered, "This isn't Napa…its Ybor, just drink it." She passed it off to me anxious for more. "Seriously, you made my night," she gushed, "and now I know why you couldn't get through the book I gave you…it's you and her."

I took a sip. "That certainly was weird."

"No. I figured this out months ago…its fate," she said soothingly, deep in thought.

With a nervous chuckle I said, "Huh, I might need the bottle."

"Seriously, the looks, the book, the song...fate relocated you to meet her...like the guy in the book—the similarities are freaky—"

I interrupted her. "But I'm married and my family will be here in July."

"So was he. And you didn't finish the book...so you're missing my point—"

"What is it?" I choked out.

"This shit show love story isn't over. You two have a love that has stained your souls."

I took a long sip. "Is this a permanent stain?"

A sharp breath escaped her. "Yes! You finally met your match...the one...your Wendy, Peter Pan Man."

I could feel a goofy grin sprout on my face. "You just called me Peter Pan Man."

"Um, yeah, that can't be the first time you heard that shit."

"It's not, but it's always funny when I do." I felt like an idiot but was tickled.

Her blue eyes shot open like saucers. "You were meant to run into me tonight..."

I took an even longer sip. "Mm, I'm so glad I did."

Her arms crossed. "Stop, this is serious shit. I'm fascinated by you two."

She coaxed a reluctant laugh out of me. "Yup, many people are."

"But I know best, I'm obsessed with great love stories. I study people that are in them—"

I shook my head disapprovingly. "That's...too much information."

She swung her hand at me. "Shut up, I'm really good at reading this shit and I even had a dream after I saw you the day you were spooked by the song...and in that dream you had a baby together...but I was there...and it was years from now."

I went to take another sip and spilled some. "Shit. Hold on, I'm still on the stained souls...and I need a napkin."

She handed me one from a table. "Here," she took a jagged breath, "it was so strange. You two are definitely soulmates as well."

I blotted my shirt. "Well...Wendy...the girl—"

"I know her name Larry, I just don't like saying it..." she rolled

198

her eyes, "go on."

I stood silent for an instant. "She recently changed her tune on the soulmate thing. She now claims to have two. Right before she got engaged she actually denied saying what she originally said."

She frowned, "Um, you can have two soulmates. And she did exactly what I would've done."

I rubbed my eyes, and refocused. "You rewrite the truth as well?"

"All females do when the shit gets too hot."

To conceal my smile I took another sip. "Mm, because of fate?"

"Fine, keep laughing. The reality is that you two are meant for each other...fate brought you together...you fell in love...and now she's marrying him because you're still pretending you can fix your marriage."

I spilled more wine. "Shit...Molly, I love my wife...and she loves her fiancé."

"Don't get testy," she scoffed, "if you can't handle the reality of this I'll stop now."

"Molly—" she cut me off with her finger up to my mouth.

"What you refuse to admit is that you were both meant to meet...you did...and you fucking fell *in love*. That *sick shit love*, which I witnessed, is what romance novels are made of. What did you grow up in a bubble...or are you really from Never Land?"

"I'm really from Never Land...ya silly goose." I couldn't resist.

She looked away wiping the smile off her face. "Stop, I strongly advise you take this seriously," she insisted impassionedly. "Fate brought you two together and your destiny is now driven by the mutual *sick shit love* you share for each other that can't be stopped."

I blinked at her, the slow blink that gave me time to think, because I was about to blackout.

She motioned her fingers to her eyes. "Stay focused." Her eyes again narrowed to mine and she said, "For a guy who has a unique appeal to females, you're clueless when it comes to them."

"Please stop making fun of me, it's not nice."

"Oh, my God! Why do I want to hug you, and kick the shit out you, and fuck you all at the same time?"

"I'm sorry, it's my pixie dust," I whispered.

"Cut the shit, I'm still getting over the aloe."

"Well, I'm still getting over the stained soul…so we're even."

"Stop hiding behind your humor. You're afraid!"

"Afraid of what?" I asked, suspicious yet curious and increasingly unsettled.

"Afraid of your true feelings for her, still kinda makes me jealous, but true."

I had nothing.

Her eyes again caught mine as they tried to run and hide. "Well, this is NOT over—" she said, and then I cut her off.

"This conversation?"

"No—your shit show love story. This is gonna produce drama that will haunt you both for a long time."

I smirked. "How long are we talking?"

"Okay, you smug fucker, tell me she hasn't initiated the baby name conversation?"

My head jerked back. "Did you just call me a smug fucker?"

She gritted her teeth in exasperation. "Look me in the eyes and tell me she hasn't snuck in a baby name conversation?"

"I'm not answering you, until you answer me first."

Her expression became stubborn. "I am trying to help you. I know females…and she seems to be just like me."

I leaned in and whispered, "That explains why I like you so much."

"Larry, stop. You need to listen to me."

"I'm trying to…" I paused as her eyes begged me to continue. So I did. "But…" I then hesitated hoping she would make the weird (yet adorable) face…yet again.

She did, while shouting, "But…WHAT?!"

"But…your ponytail has been a distraction that I'm struggling with…okay?"

Her eyes shut tight. But then burst open with delight. "Are you Lucifer…just tell me."

I narrowed my gaze. "Not so loud," I said softly as I turned to the Dawg Pound. "I don't go by that name anymore. And saying it might make your boyfriend even more unsettled. I'll let you get back to him. This has been…unnerving."

"No," she bawled, "you need me. Do you want my help…yes or

no?"

I placed the wine glass down. "That depends. You're scaring me."

"I'm scaring you because you know it's true!"

"Yes, that's it. Like your dream, where you were Wendy's...babysitter?"

"Larry, grow up! I didn't say I was the bitch's fucking babysitter— I said I was there. I'm not even sure why...it was a dream. And it takes two to make a baby...it was both of yours. I was there for you." She shook her head and continued, "I'm talking about the rest of your life. It can go one of two ways. The first is that you'll both be divorced—"

"What's the second?"

"I'm not done with the first."

"I knew that. I was testing you...to make sure you were listening to me. Carry on."

"She'll be this jaded thirty something bitch...and you'll be...shit, like fifty...but still jogging shirtless...rubbing the aloe all over your narcissistic ass..." she smiled wide, "while poisoning yet another twenty-six-year-old with your pocket full of pixie dust..."

I refocused on her face to meet her widening eyes. "Wait, back up."

Her eyes were glistening. "No, I really don't think I can...stop...what?!"

"Did you say narcissistic ass?"

Smiling wickedly, she said, "You're a text book narcissist. But for you, it works...well."

There was a moment of awkward silence. "Agreed, are we done?"

"No." She began laughing. "Oh my God...I love this!"

I nodded, and flicked a glance towards the guy staring at us sitting with the Dawg Pound. "Hold on. Seriously, is that guy who keeps staring over here with you?"

She turned and sighed, "He thinks he is...um, no, stay focused."

I stood enthralled.

She rubbed her hands excitedly and said, "Okay, the second part is the destiny part."

I sat overwrought.

"This is the part where you both realize this shit show for what it is, quite possibly the greatest love story ever, and end up together—"

"Can this happen before my wife kicks the shit out of me upon her arrival in Tampa?"

She shook her head. "No...this is years from now. Like my dream...and the book. Wendy will reach back out to you now—"

My head fell forward. "Engaged..."

"Yes. She can't stay away from you," Molly paused deep in thought before adding, "that's when this shitty shit show gets so hot something tragic happens...and then it all suddenly ends..."

"Can you please rewrite that part? My fairy tale doesn't end like that—think happy thoughts."

"Larry, grow up—it doesn't...because in my dream...and like the book...something amazing happens years from now when—"

I interrupted. "Years from now?"

"Yes! You reach out to her after you realize your love for her—"

"And we're both divorced?"

"I think. But what I witnessed...with you two, it doesn't matter?"

I took in shuddering breath. "Huh..."

"You fuck her up so bad...but in a good way. She needed you to prove your love for her." She flashed that wicked smile, "And you do...like only you can."

"That sounds about right. Is it a love letter that causes her to cry me a river...before she races along it...on a horse...to me?"

Her hands shot to her waist. "What fucking horse?"

I shrugged. "I'm sorry. Never mind the horse...and river...of tears. But was it a love letter?"

Her eyes narrowed. "My dream was so weird. That part I don't know...but I do remember you blow her away...and you're missing my point. You do end up together...and like I said, you have a baby...with your eyes—fucking adorable—and you name her, MOLLY! The name was in my second dream..."

All of sudden I felt a tightness in my throat and struggled to continue. "Okay, stop dreaming," I pleaded, "and reading so many romance novels." My mind raced on.

"Well, the look on her face that morning...and in South Tampa was that of a female right out of one of those romance novels." She waved her finger at me. "That fucking girl is in love with you. And you sir, had an expression after hearing that song, I will not soon forget. I'm sorry, but your life is a romance novel and this shit show is your best yet—GLSE!"

I lifted my gaze. "Wait...what is that, the GLSE part?"

She craned her neck. "Greatest...Love...Story...Ever....duh?"

I drew a deep breath. The acronym burned in my mind.

"What? No quick one-liner?" she quipped.

I felt vulnerable. "No, I'm all out," I said. The serious note in my voice had her turn to me as I added, "But I really have to go." I stood confounded. I didn't like the feeling.

Molly stopped laughing, watching me, and after a moment, she hugged me, tight. The embrace came with another message. Her head tilted up and she softly breathed in my ear, "She'll always find a way to just enjoy the show...trust me, I know."

I eased back and smiled at her. All words escaped me. I took some steps out and stopped. I don't know why, but I did.

Molly was standing there. She blew me a kiss and started singing.

"I'm just a little girl lost in the moment," she walked on and sang, *"I'm so scared but I don't show it. I can't figure it out. It's bringing me down I know...I've got to let it go..."* she turned back to me and bellowed, *"AND JUST ENJOY THE SHOW!"*

CHAPTER TWENTY-SEVEN

SO MUCH FOR THAT ENGAGEMENT; SHE'S BACK!

APRIL 2010
FISCAL END

The following week, Mike Fritton left an envelope on my desk with four tickets to a Tampa Bay Lighting game. The note on it read: "Friday April 2, 7:30 start – Club Section – Enjoy, Mike."

I tilted my head back in my chair and stared at the ceiling. Shit, that's next Friday. I had planned to have the family over to begin setting up the house that weekend. I texted Marie: "I got the tickets for the Lightning - Ranger game. It's next Friday."

She responded immediately: "We're coming for the weekend. How much of the list did you get done?"

I fell back to my desk and typed three responses before settling on: "I'm working on it." I hit send and braced myself. Within a few seconds, I frantically spun my chair to grab my laptop bag. The vision of stuffing the list in there two months prior hit me like a train. How did I neglect this? As I pulled it out, two pictures of Wendy and me, that I had to stash quickly, fell out. In an attempt to ease my remorseful state, I threw the pictures on the desk and smoothed the paper out beside them. That didn't help.

Within seconds of staring at the crinkled mess, Marie texted me: "What the hell are you doing over there? The move is only three months away."

I winced and glanced at the pictures, sighed, and rubbed my eyes. I forced my thoughts on to acknowledge that this would be an opportune time to get my life back on track. After that revelation, the dapper, Carmine Vito, (my only male key account manager) stuck his head in to say hi. During the few minutes of small talk my thoughts raced on. After he left, I packed up and made my way to the new house. With Wendy's engagement and my family on the way, I deluded myself into thinking that this splendid life in suburbia would miraculously refocus my mindset.

Twenty-five minutes later, while cursing the traffic on I-75, I merged left at my exit and came to a stop at the light at Bruce B. Downs Boulevard. I checked my emails. The first one was from Wendy. She didn't text me like before the engagement. She emailed me. I thought that was very professional. But then I read it. She wanted me to ride her market with her before a winery audit that she was told she wasn't going to be affected by. At least she didn't text me.

I took another left and cleared my head by admiring the gorgeous oaks lining the street to the entrance of our sweet new stomping ground. As I pulled up to the community gate, I noticed a cute little girl waving at me on her bicycle. I waved back.

As I drove on, I passed three happy couples: jogging, planting flowers, and washing their car. All fairly insignificant things, yet nothing Marie and I would ever do together. It triggered that reoccurring message a marriage counselor behest on us years before, the one that Marie didn't agree with her analysis. I then passed a neighbor laughing while loading sleeping bags into an SUV as my thoughts raced on.

There were many things that the marriage counselor broke down during those searing sessions, but the one that hit me, at this moment, was the importance of couples going to sleep together. Maybe it was the happy husband loading up the fucking sleeping bags in his car. She stated this was critical to a healthy relationship, and when she found out we rarely ever did this, she spoke to us individually with dire concern. Nothing was resolved. All of the issues festered over this time period to the point that stubbornness, pride, anger, hurt, and bitterness prevented effective marriage communication. To me, we unconsciously traded a healthy relationship for a comfortable lifestyle.

But let me back up a second.

One of the reasons this escalated to this point was that back when we had gone to counseling it was mainly for another special friendship of mine, which ultimately caused me to agree with Marie and chalk up her findings as being inaccurate; and the ones that weren't, were my fault. Ten years later, I could no longer deny there was more to this. The therapist, even back then, stated she was curious as to how I hadn't moved on. Honestly it was even more than divorce not being an option. It was that I truly believed I could fix it even though the therapist disagreed. "Larry, Marie has to agree with my evaluation first. She doesn't." In fact in my last private session, the therapist informed me that I would eventually meet a person who I would gravitate to without even realizing it, until it was too late, which now sadly seemed the case.

By the time I pulled into the garage, I was officially bothered by it all. Feeling peeved, I hopped out of the car and opened the door to our beautiful house and just stood there. Well, it was pretty. There was that. But as I stood in the family room, I felt as empty as the house was. I wandered into the bedroom, flipped off my shoes and collapsed on the three-thousand-dollar bed we had just bought. Well, it was comfy.

I sat up, took my tie off and threw it into my closet like a child while struggling mightily. After I made a sandwich I went to compile the daily program updates from my managers. I opened my laptop and saw two more emails from Wendy. I read them and rubbed my eyes thinking about my chat with Molly. I had a burning desire to reach out to her. So I lunged for my BlackBerry. Thankfully right then I received a text.

It was Bud Fox: "We're getting plowed out of our minds Thursday. I can't wait."

The night before he had convinced me that the issues with his team were finally resolved so I invited him to stay with me around two meetings we had scheduled after the close of the Cosmopolitan Brands fiscal.

Just days later, after a couple of really blurry nights with Fox, the company reported the fiscal 2010 final results. Despite the lingering economic challenges and the realignment of their distributor network, the outlook was positive.

With our performance deemed a success, The Rabbi began relying on me more to not only make up for the areas that weren't, but to expound on the accomplishments we achieved in an attempt to further assist them.

The culture I instilled hadn't changed. I insisted everyone be positive, passionate and have fun. The message to make a difference each and every day constantly resonated, but it was my weekly challenges that ultimately drove my management team to consistently overachieve. By this point, they were used to competing against each other and collectively against the state with a mindset to win without excuses. With each new task, the ardent team expected to be motivated in ways that would amuse and amaze.

The next day at the office, it was the amusement part of my latest team initiative that broke Wendy's "engagement" silence. She responded to the email right after I sent it and followed it up with her first text in days: "Hello, it's me."

I couldn't help but smile even though I was feeling increasingly unsettled. The reality of this was mortifying and oh-so alluring. I had the out, but simply couldn't take it. Molly was correct. I replied to the email, not the text, and then I needed a moment to regroup. As I sat at my desk, I had a clear vision of her and her rosy cheeks and felt enraptured. But then Mama Bear growled, discomforted.

"Did you see your girl's response?" she said sneeringly.

My eyes grew wide. I sat in silence. My hand crumpled a sheet of paper I didn't want to crumple. She yelled into my office that she was going to the bathroom. Probably to throw-up. That's when I jumped up out of my chair and did some push-ups. I don't know why other than nervous energy. I felt like a sixteen-year-old boy, but that's been established, and nothing had changed, so let's move on. Shortly after that, four more managers chimed in with texts. The last one read: "Check your email. Your Princess of Darkness is back in black and craving her Dark Knight."

Mama Bear came back in. "Did she call?" She snickered.

"Who?" I was ready for some more push-ups.

"Oh, Larry stop. Your princess...hahaha!"

I acted as if I hadn't heard her.

Literally seconds after that, the office line rang. Mama Bear let out a guffaw. "So much for that engagement; she's back!"

I felt anxiety that I hadn't felt before. "Tell her I'm at lunch," I pleaded peevishly. I ran out from around my desk like a child going to recess with no idea how to get there.

Mama Bear jumped at the opportunity to step in and answered, "Larry Sola's office."

I stood there breathless.

"No, he's at lunch. Wendy?" My hands shot to my head as she carried on. "I didn't realize it was you. You sound different. It must be the engagement."

My hands slid from my head down to my face.

"Oh, really."

I couldn't even look at her facial expressions at this point. My eyes closed in disbelief.

"Larry? Oh I'm sorry. I thought you meant. Oh, never mind. Uh, huh, no I doubt he's coming back today."

Oh my God! What the hell is this lady saying? I was thoroughly panicked.

"Is there something I can help you with?" Mama Bear was eating this shit up. "No, it says it in the email. Do you want me to resend it to you? It's no problem, this way you'll have almost everything you need." She winked at me. "Oh. Uh, huh. Okay, I'll let him know. Bye."

Click.

Mama Bear fell over in her chair, bright red. The Rabbi called. I ran back in my office, but missed it.

Wendy sent another text: "I need to talk to you. And I hate your admin!"

I held my BlackBerry with one hand and my head with the other gazing at the wall.

Mama Bear regained her composure just long enough to softly say, "Larry, Larry, Larry, that girl is..." She hesitated seemingly rethinking her words, before adding her usual, "Mmm, mm, mmm, mm, mmm."

The space then fell into a breathless silence, one that was broken just seconds later by none other than Wendy's call, now to my BlackBerry. It was pure slapstick. Mama Bear turned away from me to mask the smile curling on her lips. I wanted to play it off, but I just froze, watching her turn two deeper shades of red before she went a dark purple. I sent Wendy to voicemail.

"Are you okay?" I asked her as she attempted to push herself off the wall.

She nodded, unable to speak. With her hand against the wall she watched the shit show take flight all over again.

"Okay, we need to settle down," my voice jumped and quivered. "The Rabbi is trying to get in touch with me." My heart was racing as I received another text.

It was Wendy again: "So you're at lunch? She (Mama Bear) said you weren't coming back? I wanted to meet up."

I wiped my brow. Our office door was thrust open and Tony lumbered in. "Sir Sola, that girl is addicted to you, like crack."

I put up my hand. "Tony, please."

He stood there and simply loomed. "Did you see her latest response to your email?"

I struggled to get air into my lungs. "No," I muttered. "I was emailing The Rabbi." I now felt the little short story I wrote in that email was something I should've refrained from releasing as I hustled around my desk suppressing an irritated exhalation.

Tony blurted out, "I love this email, sir; it's brilliant. I must say, sir, one of your best, for many reasons. You really should look into being a writer on the side."

Five minutes later, my BlackBerry rang. It was Bud Fox. I snatched it off my desk.

"Hey," I said.

"Listen to me, my Goddamn good man, that little girl of yours called me to see if I was at lunch with you." I was discomforted with his choice of words. "What's wrong with you?"

I remained silent and only pretended I had control over my emotions with this girl. My eyes slowly closed. "Fox, hold on." I took a deep breath. I felt a presence behind me and spun around to see Tony, eyes narrowed and lips curled in a sinister sneer. "Sir Sola, today you seem frazzled, sir. Is it her engagement?"

I put my hand up contemplatively. "Fox, I have to call you back." *Click.*

I looked at Tony. "No. Everything is good."

"How is she?" he asked taking another step toward me.

"She's happy."

His brow titled forward. "That she's back with you?"

"Tony, don't even joke like that."

"I'm not, sir; I'm only speaking from viewing her own actions and reading her words."

I inhaled sharply. "Well, please don't." I realized how insane that sounded.

As his obnoxious snicker filled the space again, she texted me, sending a chill down my spine: "I'm going to lunch with Jessie. It's probably best anyway."

I pushed passed Tony. I had no idea where I was going. Within seconds, I was in the hallway closing the door to the office, almost on my foot. I dialed her back while walking down the hall. It rang once. She answered, "Really?"

I smiled with a feeling difficult to describe. "Hey."

She screamed, "Are you fucking kidding?"

I told her to calm down and that I was still at the office and what had happened. She wasn't happy. She was actually enraged, and as she carried on I interrupted.

"Why do I get so turned on when you go ballistic?" I spoke softly as I passed Jerry Lakers.

She ignored me. "How many days were you going to go without calling me? I cannot believe—"

I interrupted. "Hold please." I smiled awkwardly at Jimmy "Sweet Cheeks" Johns, who passed me walking into Laker's office. I felt like a traveling circus.

"Larry," she snapped, "who's there?!"

I spun around and whispered, "Hold on...damn you woman."

I was within three strides of the door. I made sure no one was behind me and shouted, "I'm scared to admit how much I've missed you!"

"Really..." her voice rose erratically, "REALLY...then why haven't *you* called *me*?"

"I just did—"

"After I called you!"

Our dialogue was frantic. We were like two quarreling teenage lovers and as I passed The Wizard he winced. I flew out the door and descended the steps to the executive parking lot. She repeated the line: "Why haven't *you* called *me*?" I fell against my navi. Breathless I replied, "Wendy, you just got engaged."

"I told you not to get EMO. (Emotional) I can't deal with that right now." She paused. "I told you I am never giving the key back."

"I bet you don't even remember what cloud the door is in."

"Um, I do! Where are we meeting?"

"Damn." I was so turned on. "You are one Dark Princess."

"You love it." She let out a gentle laugh. "Seriously, where are we meeting?"

I paused as two people passed; one yelled over to see if I was okay. I waved while I believe I called him the wrong name. He gawked at me.

"Larry?" Wendy shouted.

"Will you calm down? The entire building is watching me."

She laughed harder. "Get out of there."

"I will. But you need to calm down." I sputtered as we were powerless to the emotions that had clearly taken hold of us.

I had to hang up. I was about to black out as she texted me: "Don't be late. You know you miss me!!!"

I tripped over the curb reading it.

I leapt back to my feet and raced up the steps and into the building. When I passed by Jerry Laker's office, he gave me his patented "I love your shit show" smile. I nodded and told him we would do lunch soon.

He yelled, "Looking forward to it!"

I strolled through the door to our office. Mama Bear didn't even look at me, but said, "Tell her I say hi."

I turned to her. But then I thought it was best I just keep moving. So I did.

Within thirty-five minutes, we were both tucked away in our booth at our favorite spot. Wendy's eyes were twinkling bright, but were abruptly dimmed as she came back from the bathroom with a new waitress at the table. She was young and cute and flirty. She glanced at Wendy and walked away. Her expression tickled me.

"You're a bald version of Tony Stark, from *Iron Man*."

"What?"

"You don't play by the rules. You're a party boy, a narcissist, and you attract twenty-year-old girls."

I couldn't argue with any of it, so I gazed at her vibrating cheeks. "Well then, Pepper." I paused for effect.

She glowed white hot and jumped up ever so slightly in the booth. "I guess you're the only one who can keep me in line, so shall we have our usual?"

She looked away and attempted to mask her smile. She couldn't. "No one can keep you in line, but I am your Pepper, and I'm the only person who knows how to handle you." She hesitated. A salty smile spread across her face. "They keep showing *Iron Man* on TNT because the new one is coming out next month. I watched it twice thinking of you."

I thought that was totally understandable. Any trace of normality that I forced myself to muster instantaneously evaporated. And this Tony/Pepper dynamic was like adding rocket fuel to an inferno. Ironically, it assisted our sales as well. I actually began referring to her as Pepper in our team emails, which of course provided the spark I needed to have everyone engaged in an important program just when we needed a jolt. It worked. But as far as this star-crossed love story went, it became so spectacular that even one of my more conservative managers followed up a classic email with a perfect summation: "If this were a movie, no one would believe it. Romeo and Juliet have nothing on you two. But that didn't end well. Tragic actually. Just saying."

CHAPTER TWENTY-EIGHT

THE PLOT THICKENS

APRIL 2010
NORTH TAMPA

Two weeks later I sat at a traffic light on the construction ridden Bruce B. Downs Boulevard, reading a cryptic text from a Tampa number that wasn't programmed in my BlackBerry. It read: "Geno Franc is moving on...good luck. You will now need it."

I reread it, confused, but as the traffic began to move, Wendy texted me. I was on my way to meet her for a very early edition of our beloved "Wine Time." Later that afternoon she planned on checking out a new wine set outside her territory in anticipation for an upcoming wine reset in hers, before heading up the street to her grandparents' house for dinner. I had a dinner meeting planned with Matt McMullen down the block from where I was meeting her.

As I pulled into the parking lot, I called the Tampa number that had texted me, but it went to an unnamed voicemail beep with a full mailbox. I wanted to make another call and changed the radio station. For some reason I didn't hit my next preset station. I hit scan. It shot up the dial and stopped. It was a talk show. The host spoke in a hypnotic tone. She held me captive just introducing a therapist, who then continued as my eyes squinted at the dial.

"When love takes control of two souls, it takes the lovers on a journey. The journey is the growth of love throughout its many progressive stages and often leaves them powerless."

She went on to mention a webpage that had this transcript. I unconsciously wrote it down and printed it out—as if I already knew

I was writing this story. I continued listening:

"...*True love cannot be stopped, denied, or set off course....*"

My mind raced back to something that Wendy brought up hearing the week before.

Out of the corner of my eye, I saw her. I smiled as she yelled out, "Get out of that navi. I think we can still order breakfast."

I laughed.

We sat down at just after eleven-thirty in the morning at a table in the middle of the restaurant. I told her about the radio talk show knowing she had a similar situation happen to her a week earlier. I thought it had to be the same broadcast as this was too weird even for our shit show. But on this day she just looked away before turning back to me with an odd glare.

"I'm having a difficult time keeping up with everything I have to purge these days," She said, her voice dull with a suddenly somber demeanor. "It really is too much."

She then told me she had no recollection of it. I thought she was joking. Within seconds I realized she wasn't and fell back baffled, because this was something that freaked her out.

She didn't flinch though.

I began cracking up. I just couldn't help it, and I'm not denying that it really was too much, but that was the point. What we shared for each other couldn't be stopped, denied, or set off course. I leaned in and said, "Wendy that was crazy. I just hit scan and then that? And you told me the same thing happened to you a week ago..." I paused as her eyes closed before I added, "you were freaked out!"

Her eyes opened but averted mine. "No. Purged. It's too much."

I then made the weird sound we made to each other when an unbelievable statement was made and all was good again.

Three hours later, with her whimsical stare on high, there was a waiter change. We then moved to a more romantic table by the fireplace, an area that wasn't seated. By this point they wanted to hide us as we had the attention of the entire staff, once again, who peered on in awe.

Thirty minutes after that she passed on taking the notes on the new wine set up the street. And then she canceled another grandparent's visit, which by this point of the story she would only state to justify the trip to North Tampa more easily, not that she didn't absolutely love them. It was just that she was on a journey that took control of her soul, which often left her powerless, and quick to purge it all.

It was then that I had another brilliant idea proving that point, yet again. I leaned to her like a little boy. "Pepper, you should be a part of our dinner meeting tonight," I said excitedly.

Her eyes popped forward. "With fucking Matt? Are you crazy?" She took a deep breath and blew it out before adding, "I'm stressing out just thinking about that."

I smirked. "I could fire you now if that would take the edge off."

Her head dropped to the table before she flipped up to me with sparkling eyes. "I'm going with you," she blurted out triumphantly, as if she'd just been awarded a ticket to this dinner and streamers and balloons were falling from the ceiling.

I whispered, "Pepper, can you wear the dress I got you? (a line from the movie) ...the one I got you for your birthday...the one without the back?"

She squealed, "Oh Tony, that's totally inappropriate." Her eyes darted to the waitress staring at us before she attempted to whisper, "And would blow Matt's mind." Her eyes opened wide to reinforce her point.

"Pepper, I think regardless of your attire tonight that will be inevitable."

She couldn't utter a word. Now bright red she took a bunch of drunken breaths before shouting, "I'm not going tonight because of you. I'm going because Matt misses me."

At this point I couldn't utter a word. I took a deep breath, "Oh yes, of course."

She jumped up flushed with her hands over her face as I laughed. "That's why I suggested it."

It was now right around four thirty. We had been at the restaurant for about five hours. It was at this point that I went to the bathroom. When I came out a waitress shot me the oddest smile. It was the waitress who had referred to Wendy as my wife when I went back for her notebook; she'd left the month before. I passed her pressing my index finger to my lips, said sshhh, and took a call from Dan Schultz as she let out a chortle.

"Hey, Dan," I answered.

"Hey," he said. "Are you meeting Matt in my area now?"

I glanced at my watch. "Well, for dinner, yes."

There was an awkward pause.

"I think he's in route to you," he said with concern. "Are you hitting any accounts?"

"No, just dinner."

"Did you want to meet for drinks beforehand?"

"Oh, well, Wendy's coming to the dinner too."

"Wendy?" he snapped, "Really? So you're with her now?"

"Yes."

"Does Matt know this? What is she doing in North Tampa?" He paused briefly. "Never mind." With a raised voice he added, "I see nothing, I hear nothing, and I know nothing."

"What?"

"Nothing."

"No, I have to tell him, but come join us."

"No. I'll uh, I'll talk to you tomorrow."

Click.

I called Matt but he was on the other line, probably with Dan Schultz. I texted him: "Wendy is joining us for dinner." I didn't hear anything back from him for twenty minutes. I'm sure he sent the message up the flag pole, while alerting the media.

As we got our check he texted me: "Mayor, you two are too much. Doesn't surprise me. I'll see you two shortly."

We met Matt at another restaurant down the street and were taken to a booth. I sat on one side and he and Wendy sat on the other. He began to go over a winery program, but quickly realized he should save that for another day. He ordered a bottle of Kim Crawford Sauvignon Blanc and went to the bathroom.

Wendy nailed my foot under the table. "Does this giant jackass realize we've moved on from Kim?" Her rosy cheeks grabbed at my loins...again.

"Don't move," I said softly. "Your cheeks are glowing perfectly in that light."

She gave me her head nod and hit me with her boot. As it rode up the inside of my leg, I closed them, pulled the fucking boot off and dropped it to the floor. She stuck her bare foot between my legs and tried to hit my nuts with her toes.

"Those are my nuts," I hissed as she gave me another lusty little head nod.

She giggled uncontrollably.

The sexual tension began to boil over. She pressed her barefoot against my package at the GrillSmith the week before and I didn't think I would make it out of the restaurant so I grabbed her foot between my legs and wouldn't let it go. You know, pay back. She let out this loud intoxicated chirp like a bird that got shocked. When Matt came back to the table he was mortified. He sat down nervously.

Wendy smiled amorously and tried to retrieve her boot.

His gaze swept the far end of the restaurant.

She then went to the bathroom.

Matt turned to me, worried. "Mayor, are you shitting me? She's in fucking heat. What was that?"

I held up my hand. "I had to scratch her foot…it itched."

He threw back his wine. "It itched? It was between your legs."

I casually turned away. "I know I had an itch too. Where are we going after this?"

"Mayor…this is so fucked up. It's only gotten worse." He shook his head and suddenly smiled. "Amazing. Let's go next door, to the World of Beer."

My gaze then swept the far end of the restaurant. "How about someplace else?"

"Let me guess, you and your Dark Princess burned that place to the ground and are scared to go back. I heard you two were touring Brandon. How did you get up here?"

"Matty, it's difficult to put into words where this journey has taken us." I took a drunken breath and added, "How about that cigar bar…in that plaza up the road?"

He laughed uncomfortably. "I know it. Okay. You're fucking amazing, Mayor."

We left that cigar bar an hour later. I received a text from one of Bud Fox's sales reps: "I realize it's late, but I need to talk to you in the morning. Things have not gotten any better."

I reread it as Matt yelled out, "Take the front, Wendy."

She lit up, opened the door, and jumped in next to me, elated.

I replied to the sales rep, and said I would call him first thing in the morning.

When we got back to my house, Matt had this smirk etched into his face that was a perfect combination of alcohol and wonderment. We toured my wine collection when my BlackBerry rang. It was Marie. Matt wasn't particularly bothered, grabbed it, and went upstairs to talk to her. I think he wanted to get away from us. Wendy's shocked gaze humored me as it dawned on me what had happened.

"Oh my God, he is getting even stranger," she said as we walked out to the patio.

I took a step forward and frowned at her, a lousy attempt at discouragement. "Wendy, cut the guy some slack. Our shit show is beyond ridiculous."

"I know. Shut up." She gave me an intoxicated version of her head nod and gazed into the quiet of the night. I stared at her until her eyes met mine.

"We just rearranged our schedules to spend twelve fucking hours together."

Her eyes closed and as she sucked in a breath we collectively, without a word spoken, decided to block that out.

Within the minute she walked passed me and leaned into me on her way to the bathroom. It was literally nothing more than a brush of my back and not even done deliberately. She was drunk. At that point I noticed Matt awkwardly spin around panicked to head back upstairs. It was that very moment that a version of what he thought he saw would also play into the end of this story.

But at that moment I was panicked, because he was still on the phone with Marie. I jumped up to tell her I'd call her in the morning. I came back down, but Matt remained upstairs. When he finally came down, he ran right into us playfully strolling out of the bedroom like two children. That was great, I thought, as I would soon find out we had completely blown his mind.

The next day Matt left early. It was right before I spoke to Fox's sales rep, who rambled on with the same issues that Lisa Fenna informed me of four months earlier. After twenty minutes of detailed instances, I ended the call irately and reached out to another one of his sales reps.

Fox texted me: "It's getting difficult to help you. You and your girl blew Matt's mind last night. Mama Bear just called me."

I reached out to Matt, infuriated. He answered. "Mayor, what a shit show last night."

"Did you call Mama Bear this morning?"

"What? No. I haven't said anything to anyone."

"She already told Fox that we blew your mind last night?"

"No. I mean I said we had dinner."

"I just asked you if you called her and you said no. I have to make a call."

Click.

Rubbing my bloodshot eyes, I called Fox and calmly stated what I had heard. But I was now growing increasingly irritated with all of this.

Fox cut me off. "Larry, is this about my text? Everyone knows you're not going to stop this thing with Wendy."

His statement was so incongruous, I blinked in disbelief. "Fox, stop." I took a deep breath and spoke in my calmest voice. "This is about you."

With visions of the post-it-note on the pictures dancing in my head, he said stubbornly, "Nah, this is because you two are in total denial of the fact you both fell for each other and I just brought it up."

I emanated a more forceful gravitas. "Fox, you have a responsibility, as a manager in my division, to lead a productive team, and you are not doing that."

He went silent.

I scowled at myself in the bathroom mirror now knowing he only bluffed his understanding of anything we'd discussed to appease me. I attempted to reason with him. "I will help you, but I need to identify what you get and what you do not. You are not getting through to these people."

Not surprisingly, he had only pointed out how successful "we" were. I calmed my anger and stood intently while realizing I should end the call and again micromanage him until the "Take the Beach Incentive" kickoff in May when he was going to be staying with me.

CHAPTER TWENTY-NINE

A MERMAID AND MIRROR SHOTS

MAY 11, 2010 (MORNING)
NORTH TAMPA

Two weeks later, my eyes opened slowly to the five-thirty alarm. It pierced through my aching head like an arrow. I punched it off, dropped out of bed and onto the floor where I had thrown my running shorts and shoes the night before. Today's hangover was even more harrowing than the previous mornings, but I craved the new jogger's high I had been achieving, so I pushed on through. As the door closed behind me, I realized that the first few strides could cause me to hurl, but I figured the fog was dense enough that none of my neighbors would see me if I did.

For a month or so I had been attempting to exercise with the sentiment that I had abused myself long enough. I was closing in on forty-three and even though I appeared to be fit, my liver was screaming, "Don't you dare open another bottle!"

But I did.

I had the pond roughly a mile away from our house in my sights. Sadly, that was today's goal. As it came into focus it had a more ominous pearl-gray fog unfurling over it. With sweat dripping out of my pores, and my heart racing out of my chest, I needed any excuse to stop. Thankfully, I heard that text ding, and it sounded so special. My eyes were full of sweat so I couldn't make out who it was, but it didn't matter. I was stopping to read a wrong number at this point.

As I wiped my eyes, I noticed it was one of Bud Fox's sales reps. I set my ass against an oak to read, four houses down from the pond.

But as I did, and gasped for air, I couldn't deny that this wasn't so good. It was another complaint, and I was pissed.

Minutes later, on the walk back to the house, I realized that ultimately nothing had changed. As I regained my faculties, and headed up my driveway, I texted him back that I would call him from the office. Just as I did, a voice cut through the calm of the morning from behind me.

"Hi."

I turned to see an attractive woman, slightly older than I, in a Volvo with her arm waving in the air.

"Good morning."

I squinted into the exquisite sunrise behind her.

"It's Larry, right?"

I nodded, but had no idea who she was. "Yes. Good morning." I took a few courteous steps back down the driveway.

"You'll love the smoothie recipe. Fitness guys like you always do."

My eyes popped forward. While trying my best to play the part, I graciously said, "Thank you."

The Darkness whispered, "You can't fucking jog a mile, sport, but she thinks you're a personal trainer. You're welcome."

She drove away, and I didn't even have a moment to think about it. Another complaint came in about Fox. This one included threats and intimidation. I read it, now fuming.

After blowing out a deep breath, I made my way into the house. I bristled with righteous indignation. Ironically, what actually kept me calm was the jogger high. It hit me and I felt great, more level-headed, although in need of water, so I made my way into the kitchen. I felt a chill from the air conditioning, pulled my wet shirt off, and threw back a bottle of Evian. Halfway through it, the doorbell rang.

Just as it did, it was like a light bulb went on in my head. It dawned on me that the Volvo lady was Catlin's mom, my new little Mermaid friend from down the street. She had recently graduated from college and was back with her parents who lived two cul-de-sacs over.

She jogged every morning, and on this particular day, she stopped by with an exercise routine that had a smoothie recipe on the back. She wanted me to try it. At this time, I was only drinking coffee, water, and of course wine. I approached the door with my water, threw my sweaty shirt toward the laundry room, and opened it.

"Hey, Catlin," I said as she tightened her ponytail.

She held a small piece of paper that looked like an index card and bawled, "Larry, you're glistening. How far did you run today?"

I glanced down abashedly, thinking that only females glistened, and babbled, "Oh, a ways around." I motioned my hand in a circle. "Whatcha got there?"

She pulled her leg back behind her, held by her ankle stretching. "You're going to love this." She let go of her foot. It hit the ground, and an enthusiastic smile spread across her youthful face as she handed the note to me.

Ironically, I met Catlin right after a "Wine Time" back in April. I was talking to Wendy on my BlackBerry in my driveway when I noticed a young lady on a bike going back and forth in my rearview mirror. Not giving it a second thought—because I was caught up in the drama of the call—I noticed her, full of fervor, riding into my driveway. She squeezed her little horn and came right up to my window.

"Wendy, let me call you back. Someone on a bike is coming up to my car," I said curiously.

"Whaa? I can't drive around my block again, I have to go in. Who is it?"

"A neighbor. I'll call you tomorrow."

Click.

This little spark plug came right up to it. "Hi," she bellowed. "I heard you're in the wine business and I had a quick question."

I turned to her and said, "I love your streamers. Did they come with the bike?"

She held them out from the handle bars and shouted, "Oh my God. Everyone says I'm too old for them, but I don't want to grow up!"

Oh shit, I thought. Here we go. Boy do I attract them.

She hopped off her cute little bike with streamers. "It's so funny that you do too." She reached out her hand. "I'm Catlin."

She could've passed for Molly the Mermaid's sister: strawberry blond hair, blue eyes, ponytail, twenty-three-years-old and a personal trainer. Well, she had the body of one, but wasn't exactly. She spotted me jogging one day with her mother, somehow aware my family hadn't moved in yet, and explained the importance of being pushed by a partner. What a sweet girl. So after some more small talk, I handed her a Paso Creek wine T-Shirt from my garage. She held it up to her sparkling smile.

The next day Wendy called me early to ask me who was on the bike. After I told her the story, there was a brief moment of silence.

"When she saw you jogging, were you wearing your shirt?"

I thought about it for a second and answered, "No."

There was another instant of dead air before she shouted, "That fucking child didn't want your wine expertise, you jackass. She wants to fuck you, you freak of nature. What are you gonna do, send her an MS next?"

Okay, I just realized it's probably best I back up for second to explain an "MS" and how these now tie into the story.

It was right around this same time, roughly a month before, when we were attempting to set Bud Fox up with Wendy's friend Lisa Lively. We all went to a Ray's game. We were partying hard in St. Pete when I instantly recognized this would not be a love connection, but interestingly, would add a slapstick slant to our shit show.

The night before the game, Fox was excited about meeting Lisa. Even though he was now twenty-seven, he did what many sixteen-year-old boys that have crushes on girls do. He sent her a bare chested selfie shot in front of his bathroom mirror.

Wendy texted the picture to me: "Can't believe your boy beat you to it?"

At first glance, I thought, what the hell is he doing? Then within literally seconds, okay, two seconds, I thought, how did I not do this first? Prideful of my protégé, I called him.

"Hey," he answered softly. "I sent Wendy a shirtless picture to send to Lisa—"

"I love it. I'm sending Wendy one of these every time I get out of the shower."

Okay, let me stop here. It's important to also mention that it was the disturbing bonding moments like this one that kept me close to Fox. It was something that was extremely difficult to admit, yet critical to note. That said, at this moment he had scored one of them and relished it.

"I fucking love it, my Goddamn good man," he screamed out ecstatically.

"This is awesome. Now I have poems, songs and these (MS's), my young protégé." I sounded like an even bigger imbecile.

And to put this in an even more disturbing light, even though I was nearly forty-three, this idiocy somehow worked as if I was much younger. What I mean is that it actually added a layer of intrigue to this titillating tale just when it seemed to call for one.

A perfect example of that brings us back to where we are in the story, a day Wendy and I were deliberately not planning on meeting due to another anxiety ridden meltdown the day before. Now I know you're probably saying we would've met anyway because there were so many other times we said we couldn't, or wouldn't, but did. And I agree. But I must add that these MS's ultimately kept the story racing at a slightly faster pace toward the cliff. It was actually Wendy who began referring to them as MS's. Okay. Where was I? Ah yes, in front of the bathroom mirror acting like a sixteen-year-old.

I stood in my towel, dripping wet, and snapped another shot for my special friend. I sent it to her with love and a caption: "A taste of Italy."

Before I was fully dressed, I received her reply: "I'm free after 1 (one o'clock). Let's try that Italian restaurant I told you about."

That was totally appropriate, I thought as I smirked.

But then I began to pout. You see, it's also important to note that I was also like a sixteen-year-old girl. I thought that the picture was one of my best and was upset there was no follow-up text praising it, which she actually never did. But for some reason today I pretended she did. So I texted her: "Pepper, did you get my MS?"

She immediately texted back: "The fact we're meeting today, after yesterday should tell you I did, you narcissistic freak of nature."

But that still wasn't good enough. So I again texted her: "?"

She replied: "Yes, your image is burned in my mind forever. Thank you for ruining my life!"

Ah, much better.

Now content, I adjusted my tie just right, hopped in my big ole navi and turned up Katy Perry's "Teenage Dream," fantasying about our romantic rendezvous in Italy.

CHAPTER THIRTY

A TASTE OF ITALY

MAY 11, 2010 (AFTERNOON)
BRANDON

Three hours later, I finished The Rabbi's tracker and felt good about the additional information he seemed to be only requesting from me. Interestingly, it was then, he began relying on me even more than he had before. After another email was sent, he called. He asked me if I was alone.

"Yes," I answered.

"So, Larry, listen." He hesitated. "So I appreciate everything and I'm going to be flying to Orlando in the coming weeks. I want you there. If everything plays out like I think it will, I'm going to need your help with that area too."

He informed me that I was the guy he wanted to run Orlando. I told him that I was ready.

"Okay, good," he said haltingly because someone walked into his office. "Larry, I'll speak to you on the call. Thanks."

Click.

I worked out the additional cases, which took me right up to the time for our conference call. When that ended, I flew up the steps to take some pay change forms to The Wizard. As I passed him in the hall he said, "Coach, just leave those on my desk."

"Will do," I replied gleefully.

As I strolled along, Wendy texted me: "Looking forward to seeing what you think about this I-TALIAN restaurant."

I grinned, walked out, and glanced to my left. I noticed the door to

Geno Franc's office was open. I figured I should pop in to see him. I hadn't heard from him since our last get-together.

First I stopped by his assistant's desk, to let her know I was there, but since she wasn't, I went on in. Right away, something didn't feel right. And since he wasn't there either I turned to walk out, but stopped when I noticed most of his personal stuff was gone. I thought that was strange, but continued on, suddenly with thoughts of that text from the unknown number. I just couldn't believe or refused to acknowledge he was clearly moving on, although no one was confirming it, except an unknown number.

As I continued on though I had thoughts of this Bud Fox dilemma and it was eating at me. I scooted back to my office and gathered all of the information and dialed him. I had another lengthy conversation about it, all while now making it perfectly clear that if he was unable to make the necessary adjustments, I would have to make a change. It was something he refused to acknowledge, and worth noting that I didn't document.

He again deflected everything and brought up Wendy as someone who was getting preferential treatment. That was not true. I used Wendy as an example of someone who clearly was close to me, but could separate our personal friendship and business. She took my criticism as her boss, something that I envisioned him doing. I again explained that it made her a stronger manager. His animosity toward her built.

Within seconds he snapped, "You're tougher on me than her."

I confirmed that wasn't the case, and explained why.

Frustration again mounted with the sudden thought of how much time I've spent on his shortcomings, as I said, "I laid everything out for you and you repeatedly say you get it, but you don't."

He became noticeably upset. "Larry, these fucking guys suck."

"Point proven," I said seriously.

"What?" he replied, clueless.

"You're deflecting everything, again. You said that about Lisa. She's gone. You attempted to trash (Andrew) Rawley, but they're successful. You tried to slam (Bobby) Blue, but he's successful. You have to look in the mirror, Bud, and until you do, you'll never change. Regardless of who spoon feeds you, this is up to you, but I will not leave you there threatening these guys. I let Lisa down."

"Fuck her. How about me? Your fucking guy."

There was silence. I left him there with his words, not that it helped. He couldn't grasp any of this. Everyone else was a success, except him. The latest accolades from The Rabbi made it worse. It wasn't his doing. It was my own. It was my mindset. I thought of him as my only blemish, something I had to correct. This became more about my ego at this point than even him. He wasn't ready for that position and I allowed it to happen. I had this vision of being a savior, and targeted dates I would spend with him as critical bonding time, to set him straight.

The "Take the Beach" incentive that Mike and Matt were kicking off at a restaurant was my next one. The problem was that Fox refused to admit any wrongdoing.

I still thought he was a good guy, so I discounted the lies and thought that they would end when I fixed him. It was clear that would take an exerted effort from everyone so I had another conversation with Mama Bear. I wanted to make sure she stopped assisting him beyond what she would do for everyone else. By this point, it was clear he used her as a crutch.

She stated she understood. After some more small talk she turned and walked out of my office seemingly bothered. I then packed up to meet Wendy.

Forty-five minutes later, I met her at this curious Italian "Mom and Pop" restaurant out in east Brandon. It was an interesting little place with a sultry, romantic feel. I entered and just stood there grinning. This afternoon's going up in flames, I thought. It was just that obvious.

Within seconds of that deliberation, a little man hustled up from the back. "Good afternoon, folks. Come, come," he said as he escorted us to our table.

We giggled like children and wove around another table playfully bumping each other. He stopped at one and said, "Good?" We nodded.

I sat down, and pushed my chair in inadvertently glancing across at her. I couldn't look away. I marveled at her eyes as they were quite possibly even more elated than usual.

"Will you be having wine this afternoon?" the waiter asked.

"Yes," Wendy said enthusiastically as she excused herself to go to the bathroom.

My head tilted up to her. "Please hurry, dear." I smirked. "I miss you already."

Her eyes closed. "Dad. Stop."

I attempted to contain the grin inching across my face. The waiter dropped the wine list and raced off nervously as she came back toward me with that twinkle in her eyes.

I crossed my arms and ignored her.

She said softly, "Dad...are you gonna text me one of your poems?"

I turned away from her.

"Stop pouting," she said, amused.

With my arms still crossed I turned to her and said, "You know I hate when you do that, so you're not getting any poetry today...or my magnificent MS tomorrow morning."

With her smile spreading she spun around to walk out. I could already smell the smoke. But upon her return, one humorous conversation led to another one that she really struggled with; it was a carryover from the meltdown the day before. She had recently been on this overnight wine training in Orlando and had spent the late evening, and early morning, on the phone talking to me. Ironically, it was those conversations that lasted until two-thirty in the morning that would also be documented later in the story, as those storm clouds on the distant horizon grew darker and more ominous, fueled by this dark devotion.

But at this point we had no idea about that. Her recent escalated anxiety levels were only from the actual content of the conversations, although, at this moment, I was only consumed with her cheeks. The temptation to gently tilt her head to the side and suck on them was overwhelming me. Okay, never mind that. That's too disturbing. Where was I? Ah yes, she began rehashing the problem. So, not thinking at this point that it would be this major production, and still craving her cheeks, I made the mistake of heedlessly saying, "No big deal. We're not running off together. We just played house—again."

I mentioned "again" because she was now stressing that this sort of thing kept happening, while pretending she didn't know why. The reality was that after nine months of this wooing, she was on overload. She couldn't purge fast enough and the engagement made it all worse.

There was tension in her face. When it abruptly turned to anger I straightened up in the chair. "There is no explaining those conversations," she exclaimed full of mounting stress.

I felt it best not to enlighten her. So I just threw back my wine.

She turned back to me flushed. "Larry, newlyweds have those talks and—" She stopped mid-sentence, shaking her head while then making it seem as if I was the one who initiated the conversations.

"Wendy, you began those conversations—"

"Why do you think I'm so freaked out?!"

Wendy clenched her wine glass and took a healthy sip and then another. She mentally scrambled backwards. "I end calls by lying to Jessie to race off and call you…for hours…about that shit."

She looked away deep in thought, just as she did the day before. I felt as if I was in a rerun. She fell limp in her chair, at least for the moment.

I felt it was time to change the subject. "Pepper, *Iron Man 2* is out."

She lunged forward. "Jessie even knows something is up with that movie." She took another sip. "He asked why I kept watching the first one." She exhaled. "It's everything."

I searched for the waiter and said softly, "I think they turned the fucking air off."

I realized the bottle was nearly empty and quite possibly needed the rest more than she. But she pulled it towards her knowing what I was thinking. Her eyes closed and then rolled opened staring right at me. "What would you do if you were in Jessie's shoes?"

I looked away.

"Exactly." She blew out a big breath and said softly, "It scares me how much he blocks out. Larry, he knows. Obviously not much, but not much, with us, is too much."

I fidgeted in the chair as our eyes connected, feeling this devious smirk on my face.

She smiled mischievously and softly said, "You are Lucifer."

I put my wine down dramatically. Her head turned back to me. Her eyes were ablaze.

"I thought I was Peter Pan, ya silly goose."

Her hands shot over her uncontrollable smile. "Stop. I fucking hate you!"

"Take that back...or I'm locking you out of my sacred land."

"I have the key to the cloud door. Good luck with that!"

Grinning wide, she poured what little bit was left in the bottle into her glass and said, "It's been non-stop for nine months."

"You did take some time off after the engagement." I wondered why I just blurted that out, thinking she would erupt, but she didn't.

Her exasperation evaporated as she shouted, "It was barely a week."

I thought to say it felt like an eternity, but then rethought that. My brain was in a fog of love and lust and I couldn't think straight, neither could she. Her eyes teared up joyfully as she mentioned feeling buzzed and then she began to laugh deliriously.

Predictably, her mood lightened. I shook my head. She continued to go back and forth. "Those conversations, oh my God." She smiled even though they were the same conversations that caused her distress. "You're in your bed and I'm hiding all over the hotel."

I brought up something we discussed that tickled her just right.

"Oh my God, I couldn't talk to you in my room because of my roommate, so I was in that little waiting area. I remember that because that's where I was when you said that."

"I love it when your cheeks vibrate like that," I said.

She pushed them up with her hands. "How are my cheeks now?"

I smiled and had to look away.

"You better not have told Fox about that," she huffed before taking a sip of wine.

"He knows I love your cheeks, damn you woman."

She almost spit her wine out. "I'm talking about our conversations."

I leaned over the table. "I can't possibly explain that shit to anyone, well, except Molly—" I said, as she cut off.

"Who? The child from the corporate apartment? You freak!"

"Lower your voice, the entire restaurant hears you, and Molly's only a few years younger than you...and she predicted all of this."

She began breathing erratically so I casually excused myself to go to the bathroom. Within a few strides from where we were, I noticed an older couple eating with their red wine. The old man grinned eerily and motioned me closer.

"To love, young man," he raised his glass and motioned to the other side of the restaurant where we were. "It will always find a way."

My eyes widened at his forthrightness. There is no way this old man just said that. But then as his hand shook holding the fucking glass out in front of him, he said, "True love always does. Bathroom is to the right and straight down."

I thanked him, and took off.

Halfway down the hall, I saw the waiter and felt the urge to yell, "Tear the cork out of another bottle, please. This place is giving me the shakes." But thankfully, I didn't have too.

He saw me and said, "I'll bring another bottle right away, sir."

When I got back to the table, Wendy looked wistful. I sat down and I noticed the look in her eyes displayed the words of the song, "The Show."

Slow it down/Make it stop
Or else my heart is going to pop/Cause it's too much
Yeah it's a lot/To be something that I'm not
I'm a fool/Out of love
Cause I just can't get enough

And then she spoke it. "This is such a mess. It's too much. Why can't we just run off together? Why?" She smiled before frowning while rambling on. "I hate this. I was happy before you walked into my life and blew it up. I'm fucking serious, Larry." She hesitated.

Why did I go to the bathroom?

She continued. "You've made me question things I never wanted to, never thought I would have too. But I do."

I leaned in toward her and said, "And I don't?"

"We're so fucked up. We are, Larry. This is so unbelievable."

I began saying something I knew I would regret. I stopped and said, "I will figure out how to fix this."

"You're sick enough to think you can fix everything, even Bud Fox!" She took a breath and asked skeptically, "How can you?"

I felt it was time to have some fun because I had no answers to this. But interestingly, she knew that. By now, she knew my every move: how I thought, what I was going to say. So knowing she wasn't done with this, I took a brief time-out and said, "Would you like a taste of Italy, milady?" she violently cut me off, leaned forward and energetically bellowed, "I've switched to Spain."

Her eyes lit up like lightning strikes.

My smile frowned. My arms crossed. This was worse than calling me dad and she knew it. So I began to pout. She jumped up slightly in her chair overjoyed, and that's all that mattered to me. The pleasure of this relationship once again outweighed the pain.

"You know I hate when you do that."

I shrugged.

"Stop pouting, you freak." She stared at me. Her hands shot up over her scintillating smile. She became deliriously whimsical with watery eyes. "Your taste of Italy got me in this mess to begin with, you freak." Her rosy cheeks glowed.

"Will you stop calling me a freak? You sound like my wife."

"In Never Land, I am your wife, you freak. And saying it helps me deal with you." She leaned forward like a little girl as the waiter stuck his head in, thoroughly engrossed, before rapidly retreating.

"What's your plan?" she persisted and gave me her little head nod. I stared at her until she said, "Larry, you can't really walk on water. You do realize that? You can't."

I smirked believing I could as she leaned into my response anxiously. I was so desperate to snap myself out of this, I blurted out, "When Marie gets here, we're going to start doing things as couples. It will force us to transition this." I was never so fucking desperate to keep anyone in my life, regardless of the maddening circumstances that stood in our way, as I miraculously added, "It's that simple."

She fell over in her seat, with a momentary unsteadiness, visibly intoxicated, more so by my words than the wine. "Are you fucking kidding me right now?"

The waiter rushed over with an open bottle that I think they were drinking from in the kitchen. I stared at the guy as he poured it. But then I broke free of that and glanced back at her.

"No. Not in the least," I said. "It'll work. I promise. We can do this and we really have no choice because we can't stay away from each other, and for now, at least it's better than nothing."

I raised my glass, but she didn't. Instead she threw hers back, smiling thoughtfully. "You want to do this with them?" she said in a sedated tone. "Jessie and Marie...all of us...together...until?"

"Until one of them shoots us and puts us out of our misery."

She let out this intoxicated chirp that I had heard her make a few other times.

I added, "I'll figure that out. Besides, the wise old man I ran into said true love will always find a way."

Now exasperated, she slumped forward. "Whaa?"

"Nothing," I replied, realizing she couldn't handle the old man story.

We both smiled, confirming we collectively succumbed to being star-crossed lovers, who'd officially lost their fucking minds.

"We don't have a choice. We can do this," she said softly.

Even though she was convincing herself of this plan, the look on her face was as memorable as this afternoon was playing out to be. The problem was that we were now two bottles deep and still going strong into three. We were well on our way. Thirty minutes later, there was no one else in the restaurant and both waiters were gawking at us, thoroughly entertained.

One rushed out of the kitchen when he noticed me. He raised his glass of red. "You have us drinking. Cheers, my friend."

I nodded. Yes, I just paid for the bottle you two clowns drank half of. I merrily skipped on to the bathroom. When I returned, I called for another bottle.

"Can we cork what we don't finish, because there was no cork with the last one?" I said.

He nodded. "Sure, sure. But no, no, you will."

What? What the fuck was going on here?

Within an hour we succumbed to the inevitable: us.

We had seriously planned on seeing our movie, *Iron Man 2*, together, as Tony and Pepper. And Pepper was aflame.

"We can sneak wine in too." She shook a silly Styrofoam cup the waiter gave her, exuding such joy. And as my boyish grin curled on my face she leaned forward with a lusty smile, gently touching my fingers lingering on the bottom of my wine glass adding, "And we can have a little taste of Italy."

We laughed, looking away as our heads, in unison, came around and stopped at the same time. Our eyes locked as the visual of us tearing each other's clothes off in the back row and going at it came into clear focus upon the first scene with Tony and Pepper.

It was at this point, I began having recurring thoughts of Molly's message from the bar. Maybe this was fate crossing our paths, now bound to one another. There was truly nothing left to think. Her eyes displayed such a light that I couldn't help but smile, regardless of how wrong this was.

But amidst the pixie dust falling at a feverish rate, she took a bitter breath of reality. Her smile vanished. She was speechless just staring at a text. I knew it was from Jessie.

She fell back.

I wanted to scream out, "No," but this was reality and it just crashed our fantasy.

Instantly that older, more mature look I loathed covered her like tar. She smiled faintly but it didn't reach her eyes. My heart saddened. She sat in silence and stared at me as if her eyes were taking mental pictures that she knew she would have to lock away for a lifetime.

I wasn't only speechless at this point: I was breathless.

CHAPTER THIRTY – ONE

THE ASLYUM'S LIGHTS DIM

JUNE 4, 2010
THE TAMPA OFFICE

It was three blurry weeks later and I was in route to the office. The car in front of me slowed to yet another stop. A feeling of exasperation bore down on me courtesy of Bud Fox's incessant imbecility. This was the third day in a row he had run amok on the arduous morning commute that had officially begun to wear on me. With the traffic inching forward, I gazed into a puffy cloud pondering its resemblance to a clown. I took that as a sign and called him.

It rang four times when he answered, "What's up?" with his barking dog in the background.

With the words of the text bashing him, flashing in front of me, I said, "By now I figured you'd get that your people are quite anxious to expose you and your idiotic actions."

He sighed. "What?"

"You told your people I show up to meetings hung over?"

In a higher pitched tone he squealed, "No!"

"You blew off an important meeting hungover and told them I go to meetings that way all the time?"

He became defensive. "What? No, but you party hard—"

"You lied. And you just don't get it, yet you repeatedly have told me you do. When I was in your position, I gained the respect of my higher-ups for my achievements. You've only become a travesty while abusing these people. Work hard comes before play hard, Fox."

I paused and waited for a response, but none came. I sighed

deeply. "I cannot spend any more time on your insanity."

Click.

I was feeling high-strung. Not solely due to Bud Fox or the commute. This was the day the new changes to the state were being implemented. Geno Franc, the man responsible for bestowing a bright future tag on me, was moving on.

On Wednesday, June 2nd, 2010, the state was split in half consolidating the company's three divisions into two. This caused us to merge with the north, thus forcing Geno Franc to Miami as the general manager of another division.

So as the story goes, this would be his farewell meeting that, twenty-five minutes later, I was racing up the back stairway to catch. Inching in through the door to the meeting room, I pushed forward into the packed space. Two managers, who I hadn't seen in months, reached over to shake my hand.

"I hear you've been living the dream, Larry," one said softly with a guileful grin.

Not being a fan, I smiled subtly before I turned to the other who whispered eerily, "How do you feel now that Franc is gone?"

I anxiously buttoned the top button on my suit jacket. "He'll certainly be missed." I looked over the heads to the front of the room where the new, older VP-general manager was being introduced. The atmosphere of the room was instantaneously altered.

As he took the podium, the lights seemed to dim and an odd lump formed in my throat. In a weird way I felt like a boy who suddenly had his security blanket taken away. I stood paralyzed. The magnitude of what Franc had done for me hit me all at once. I wanted to again thank him. At the same time, I became tense thinking about all the warnings to stay close to him.

I took a subtle, yet deep breath and exhaled. My chin tilted down against my suit. Looking back up, I felt anxious, although without an inkling of the consequences that would ensue. To make matters worse, I had isolated my team so well that I never played the office politics game. I ignored the famous quote from Sun Tzu, "Keep your friends close, and your enemies closer."

Feeling uneasy, a recent conversation with Wendy caused a chill to go down my spine. She had called to tell me she was impressed with my latest speech to open our May sales meeting. That was the good news. The not so good news was that The Wizard seemed, again, to be troubled by it.

That was the reaction from many, although unbeknownst to me at this moment, it didn't matter anymore. You see in this place, at this time, regardless of noted success, or really anything else for that matter, The Wizard had the wand. As Franc exited the building, The Wizard turned Franc's plan for my career to dust with one wave of that wand from behind the curtain. Poof!

With my head firmly entrenched in the sand, I left the meeting room. I found it interesting to see the solace on certain faces walking out. I felt edgy. It was as if the good ole boy network raised their flag atop the building again along with their Bud Light bottles to rejoice a return to their glory days. And as I limped back downstairs, their good ole boy brigade rolled out to lunch with the pollution of their exhausts filling my office.

Just as I opened the door, it hit me. A few administrative assistants were huddled around Mama Bear ready to burn the place to the ground. Having little tolerance for today's mock lynching, I mustered enough of a smile to respectfully acknowledge their vexing vent while catching the fact they were again bashing one of The Wizard's top guys. What I gathered was that another complaint that was filed had just been expunged, curtsy of The Wizard's wand. Poof!

The excitable back and forth made my head spin. This was the first time I referred to the Tampa office as The Asylum. It came to me as I shook my head and moved on while one of them yelled, "And The Wizard thinks that buffoon is the best sales manager in the state."

With fleeting energy, I hobbled to my desk and collapsed in my chair. I heard whispering before everyone abruptly left. As the main door to our office closed, a curious Mama Bear scurried into mine. I guess some of what I was feeling must have found its way to my face, because she curiously asked, "Hey, are you okay?"

"Yes…I'm fine," I said unconvincingly.

Her head cocked slightly to the side and downward at me. "You're upset Franc is gone, aren't you?"

"Yes, I am. I wish I had more time with him."

She paused. "You think this place is fucked up, don't you?"

Slightly startled, I glanced up at her and shrugged. "Well, I work hard to keep us isolated from that, the negative energy."

"Larry, you have."

I sighed. "Yes, but you know what it really comes down to though," her eyes grew wide anticipating my next words, "a culture that deliberately smears the talented into the talentless to hide too many wrong hires they refuse to acknowledge." I stopped in mid-sentence shaking my head. "It breeds cancers. Yet as long as I've been here, it's been acceptable."

She took a step around the desk to level a frame on my wall. "Well, you've sheltered the team from that and created a positive environment that they enjoy. And I meant to tell you that I was impressed with your speech, very charismatic." She nodded, smiling softly. "You've really made a difference, Larry."

"Thank you," I said as my eyes rolled to hers. She was leaning in to me.

"And I wanted to thank you again for everything you've done for me, and the raise helped too."

Another manager wandered in, but did an about-face hurrying out.

She smiled, turning back to me and said, "What's going on with Fox?" Her eyes grew curious as the office line rang. She glanced over at my office phone to see who it was. "It's him," she snapped. "Do you want me to take it?"

I snatched it up as she ran out. "Why are you calling the office line?" I answered impetuously.

Startled, he hesitated before replying, "You never say that when Wendy calls it."

"Wendy always calls for me; you're bothering Lori. Why?"

"Wendy calls the office line to hide how many times she calls your BlackBerry."

"Fox, answer the question, why are you calling Lori?"

"I'm trying to get back in with you." He paused, exasperated, like a scorned lover. "And she was helping."

"You have a job to do and you're failing miserably. That's not how to do it."

He sat silently.

"I also just heard that your sporadic team meetings are recaps of our partying."

"I told them to stop calling you."

"Fox, you don't get it. You're lucky they have. I've prevented them from all going to HR." My voice rose. "To protect you. Do you understand how wrong that is?"

As the conversation persisted, it was clear that he didn't understand. Fox only knew he was again in trouble, scrambling to get back in with me; not to fix what was wrong, though. He craved the party, while wanting to stay close to his new girlfriend, who he ironically met when he was out with Wendy and me, although at the time we didn't realize it or meet her.

I rubbed my eyes red repeating myself. "Fox, do you realize how wrong that is?"

"Not as wrong as last week's debacle with those girls in the parking lot at the World of Beer."

His response caused me to cringe.

The Darkness celebrated as I hit a boiling point. "The night you left the garage door and front door to my house open—screaming out Lady Gaga?!"

"I thought you were going back out?"

"How do you think that looked when my neighbors went to work in the morning as wildlife was coming out of my house with wine bottles in the garden?"

"How it looked? You fucking jogged around that place for two months with a girl half your age and burned the neighborhood bar to the ground with your only female manager, who you knew fell in love with you months before she got engaged. How does that look?"

"Hey," I seethed. "This is about you!"

There was sudden silence, and if I had a gun, I might have shot myself. I fell back in my chair demanding his team meeting notes before hanging up. At this point, I should have realized he was capable of crucifying anyone, including me. I also should've realized there was no saving him.

But I didn't.

Ten minutes later, Wendy texted me: "Why is Fox blowing my phone up? I don't want to talk to him."

My eyes closed slowly in disbelief as I filled her in. She called me, panicked. I answered, "Hey."

"He deflects everything. Why do you continue to back him?" she replied brashly.

I took a deep breath and tried not to sound chronically frustrated, as I said, "I can't allow him to fail."

She laughed faintly and hollered, "He shaved his head because he idolizes you, and you thought that was normal? That's unbelievable, and so is thinking you can fix him."

"Please stop. Where are you? I need you."

"I was just going to suggest we meet at our new spot. I'm already in Citrus Park."

"Give me an hour."

"No, forty minutes and don't be late again."

Click.

Within seconds, Mama Bear blazed in to me. "What happened?" she asked even though she knew.

"In short, I allowed him to get too close to me thinking he could handle it all."

Her eyes grew wide. "Too close to you? How about Wendy?" She hesitated before she added, "Larry, he idolizes you. But what you have with her is way worse." She shook her head solemnly. "She can't go through with this wedding."

My annoyance had indeed been noted.

She rolled her eyes and turned to walk out before her head twisted back to me. "Hey, how's your wrist? I'm still so upset with Tony. He could've killed you."

She was referring to an injury I sustained at a team bowling event in May. After I had bowled a strike, I chest bumped Tony and he sent me flying through the air landing awkwardly on my wrist. They all thought I had broken it.

"It's healed amazingly well. Kind of freaky. But I'm good."

She gave a short, nervous laugh, peering at me eerily before I became uncomfortable and turned to read an email. It was from a manager in another division inquiring about a position. As I read on I realized the whispers that I was being promoted again began to spread. With a growing grin, I packed up to meet Wendy.

"Where are you going?" Mama Bear asked.

I froze in a moment of silence.

"Never mind, tell her I say hi."

I nodded and walked out.

Three hours later, Wendy and I were tucked away in a cozy booth at the Citrus Park BJs Brewhouse with the 2010 FIFA World Cup playing all around us.

"What are those giant horns? Vuvuzelas?" I asked Wendy, reading the word off the screen. With no reply, I glanced over at her. She seemed to be stressing over the bill. "What's wrong?" I said, as she took a deep breath rather anxiously.

"I don't want her (Mama Bear) seeing my expenses," she replied. "I don't trust that lady and I don't know why you allow her to do yours. We submit the same exact restaurants."

I took a sip of water and said, "It's fine. She's fine. No one looks at that shit."

"She does. And she's not fine, Larry. She's a bomb ready to blow." I was fixated on those horns as Wendy shouted, "Hello?"

"Listen to that sound those things make. I want one."

She looked up at the television over my head and then back to me. "Grow up."

I smiled. "No."

She smiled before she made that sound we made to each other when something absurd was stated, and fell back in the booth, glowing. "Let's go shopping," she bellowed like an excited teenager.

Ten minutes later, we strolled into the Banana Republic next door like two kids wandering into a candy store. She proceeded to hold up clothes, and yell out to me, "Dad, do you like this one?"

The staff was captivated by us, peering as our follies forged on. But then Bud Fox called. I thought I could take the call quickly and not have this be an issue, so on the third ring, I answered, "Did you send your team meeting notes?"

I scooted around a rack of clothes with an eye on the door. "I'm doing it now."

Wendy held up some cute little top and screamed out, "Dad, how's this one?"

My eyes closed slowly. She hadn't realized I'd taken the call. I threw the BlackBerry in my pocket thinking I'd hung up. But I hadn't; I'd put him on speaker.

As she shouted out again, glowing with my favorite whimsical stare, I heard Fox say, "Did Wendy just call you Dad?" My eyes popped forward as he shouted, "Larry!"

I tripped over this display block, landing up against a rack of clothes. I jumped up, grabbed the thing out of my pocket, and snapped, "What?" I turned to shut her up, but she was walking back in the dressing room, clueless to it all.

"Are you wasted at a mall with her?" His infamous hissing cackle kicked in. "Y-o-u are a fucking legend—"

"Fox, email the notes."

He squeezed his dig in. "Hey, did you see the email from Fritton? We're leading the state again. He would be even more amazed if he found out you were pulling this shit off wasted—with his fucking recruit who has spent her entire engagement dating you. Money doesn't sleep."

"Email the notes, please."

"I fucking love it!"

Click.

CHAPTER THIRTY – TWO

THE POLITICS THAT I REFUSED TO PLAY

JUNE 2010
THE ASYLUM

The following Wednesday, The Rabbi informed me that I would be taking over Orlando along with Tampa in a director role, and was finalizing the details. This remained a move he didn't want anyone knowing about, although many were aware.

On Thursday, Tony lumbered into my office wanting to chat about it. "You got a minute, Sir Sola?" I motioned him to have a seat as he then plopped in a chair in front of my desk. "Sir, I heard you're not interviewing anyone without a degree."

With my patience already waning I said, "Interviewing for what?"

"For your current position. Word has it you're again moving on."

I put up my hand, not wanting to drag this out. "If I were, I'd be looking for the most qualified person who is the best fit for the culture we have in place."

"Sir, that's great news and you know I play racket ball with The Wizard."

My eyebrow rose in bewilderment. He proceeded to carry on about the long-standing politics of The Asylum while making it clear The Wizard had the final word. As he continued to speak in circles, I received a text from Mindy Amour. I placed my BlackBerry down as Tony's bullshit became unbearable.

"...and well, even though I'm tight with The Wizard, I was concerned because I heard that you're promoting your friend Dan

Schultz."

I laughed. "He's a top candidate because of his abilities, not because we are friends. I can assure you that I do not do that."

"Sir, that's not true. Bud Fox, sir. You put him in a position he shouldn't have been promoted to. And look how that's turned out."

Although he had a point, he also knew the truth about Fox. I was disturbed by his response. "Tony, you know who I wanted for that position, but the other side wouldn't allow it. But for time's sake, okay, ultimately I did. And for the record, that will never happen again."

"Good to hear, sir."

He got up to walk out.

"But Tony, I thought Fox was your friend?" I said. "Why would you say that about a friend even if it were true?"

He turned to me. "Sir Sola, it's a dog-eat-dog world, sir." He explained this in all seriousness as I peered at him, puzzled.

"It doesn't have to be, Tony."

"In this place, it most certainly does."

I shook my head. "It doesn't have to be."

"Sir, I love the fact that you live in fantasy land, while achieving so much success. It's refreshing. Us mere mortals can't do that. It's a dog-eat-dog world for us humans, sir."

I sat back astonished as he walked out.

On the last Tuesday of June, The Rabbi informed me he had worked out the details to have me over both Orlando and Tampa with a director title. The importance of understanding the implications of my fourth promotion in five years came with intriguing subplots that were almost unimaginable to comprehend.

The very next day, I received an email from the new GM. It was my first one from him, and he seemed sincere, appreciative, and curious about the sustained level of success we had achieved. But as I read on, my office line rang, interrupting me. It was The Wizard.

"Hey, Coach," I answered.

"Coach, do you have a minute for me? I need to speak to you in my office."

"Sure. I'll be right up."

"Thanks."

Click.

I walked up thinking he was going to address the email that our newly appointed and impressed GM sent me, wanting to share my success. But he didn't, silly me. No, his motive for this impromptu gathering was to push one of his own into my old position. As I sat down, he casually asked me who my replacement would be.

Without hesitation, I said, "Dan Schultz."

There was an awkward moment of silence. He seemed discomforted. "Schultz? Really?" I sat there baffled at his reaction. His eyeglasses were low on his nose as he peered at me. "He hasn't even been here a year yet. How about Tony?"

I fell back as if I took a bullet. Adjusting myself in the chair I said, "Tony is not a right fit for this position."

He then fell back in his chair as if I fired a shot back at him. He leaned back up and blinked. "Tony's strong and he's been with us for years."

"I don't believe in promoting someone just because of tenure. I think that's why we have so many problems."

"Problems? What problems are you referring to?"

I felt lightheaded and baffled by his words. He gawked at me clueless to the reality of this as I only moved on. "Tony is not who I am looking for, for many reasons."

His menacing eyes surveyed the room before coming back around to me. A bad feeling consumed me. "You really think Schultz is like you?" he asked.

"No. But he has the qualities I am looking for to lead the group."

The Wizard glanced at his BlackBerry. "I need to take this," he said irritably.

I nodded dismissing my premonition as nothing more than worthless paranoia. I certainly shouldn't have. This was disturbing. Within minutes, it was obvious that he had informed Tony of our chat because he withdrew from officially interviewing for the position. But that didn't mean he wasn't busy weaving his web. By the time I made it back down to my office, I heard he and Fox were going to a Tampa Bay Ray's game together. A series of events were triggered that would begin to change everything.

At five thirty, I had a planned meeting with the Tampa key account managers and Mindy Amour at a trendy wine bar in downtown Tampa. Just as I was pulling out of the parking lot afterwards, Fox called. The premise of the call seemed to be to find out if I was with Wendy, as Tony sat next to him, breathless for more dirt. This further infuriated me as he didn't mention his sales tracker that every other manager completed. After a minute of probing he said, "Hey, you know I don't give a shit if you're with her."

"Fox, stop the bullshit. I'm still waiting for your display pictures and tracker."

"I'm sorry. I have them, but I'm having problems with my laptop."

"Again? What do you do on that thing? I don't want to know. Get them in."

Click.

The next day a manager in a different division ran into me in the hall. "I know it's not officially announced, but congratulations," he said quietly. He extended his hand as we walked down the hall passing The Wizard. He waited a few seconds and whispered, "Shit, you'll never be a good ole boy, but even The Wizard has to be proud of your run. You're killing it, really great job."

I thanked him, although irked he wasn't impressed. Not only that, but I never heard another word about the new GM's email request either. He copied in The Wizard when he replied to me. It was then I thanked him and let him know I'd be happy to help out, but it again appeared that The Wizard waved his wand because I never received a correspondence from the new GM again.

The next day I was preoccupied with two reports that had deadlines fast approaching. I sent one report and then spent twenty minutes being briefed that Tony was maliciously stirring the pot.

Later that afternoon, that trusted confidant came in to see me. The look on his face caused me to smile nervously before I said, "I don't like that look."

He took a deep breath and exhaled. "Tony is all of a sudden hellbent on destroying you. What happened?" I laughed and then informed him The Wizard thought Tony was promotable. His eyes popped forward in his head. "He wanted you to promote Tony?"

"Yes."

"So that's why he's telling everyone your partying is out of control, along with the shit with, what's her name?" He fell back.

"Wow, oh yeah and he's sending your team emails on too. They are floating all over the company."

I smirked and nodded. "Yes, somehow our new GM was forwarded one."

"How do you know that?" he asked inching forward full of curiosity.

I pulled a copy of the email out. "He told me he loved it," I said.

His eyes grew wide reading the new GM's response. "That's awesome," he said smiling. "Everyone loves reading your shit." He chuckled. "But did you ever think someone, disgruntled, can twist them into something negative?"

I compressed my lips and shook my head gravely. "No. The emails work."

And just like that, he began giving a remarkably detailed explanation of how Tony had manipulated things in the past. I glanced at my watch. "You know that's the reason he was dumped on you. (TJ) Faggalo didn't want him. (Danny) Koppeli didn't want him. He burned them both."

I nodded. "I know. It'll all be fine."

He walked out. "Just don't forget me when you're running this place." He hesitated, turning back to me adding, "Hey when is your family moving over?"

My eyes rolled up to his. "Ten days."

He just stood there before uttering softly, "How's that going to work with what's her name?" He paused as my stare caused him to nervously clear his throat. "Talk to you later."

Ten days later my family moved in. The very next day Wendy and I met when she planned on beginning her "two-week hiatus" from me to catch up on her wedding plans. Two weeks later the only thing that had changed was that I was officially appointed my new Sales Director title.

CHAPTER THIRTY - THREE

A DIRECTOR AND HIS DARKNESS

JULY 30, 2010
THE MORNING

On that morning my eyes opened slowly to the sound of a drawer slamming. I thought I was dreaming until I blinked at Marie's silhouette against the bathroom light. She held up my jogging shorts. "These will not be left in the bathtub anymore." She walked back to the bed. Her voice softened. "And happy birthday."

I thanked her as she jumped back under the covers and scooted over to me with a suspicious expression. Her head came over mine. I was unsure if she was going to head butt me or kiss me; it really was a coin toss. So I braced myself. I looked in her eyes and could tell that this ever-increasing drama with Wendy would be questioned thoroughly at any moment. It was all on the tip of her tongue, but she didn't utter a word. In spite of being on the verge of a panic attack, I noticed her cheeks were vibrating, which obviously overrode all of that, even though it meant she was ticking like a bomb. I was so drawn to those things, although under the circumstances, I derived it best to ignore that impulse, which left me with no viable options. So I whined pathetically.

"Marie, please stop. Just leave me alone."

Her face instantly lit up the dark room, humored. "You're such a little boy." She hovered over me like an excitable teenager. Those cheeks were still calling my name. Her eyes narrowed and her hand formed a fist. She shook it at me before kissing me, clearly torn.

At this point I was exhausted. "Can I say something?"

She smiled blissfully, breathless for my antics to amuse her. I continued in a soft yet serious tone, "Marie, this is typically my Zen time. Each moment is filled with a profound peace and clarity that's charged with magic. It's infinitely precious. So please don't ruin it."

She gasped for air. "Are you fucking kidding me?" She paused and took a deep breath and cachinnated. "Oh my God, your little fantasy world is so about to change."

I stared at her seriously and said, "It's Never Land, Marie, and it's real."

She began taking in erratic breathes before I slid to the side of the bed to get the hell out of there. She gave the sheet that somehow ended up under me, a yank and I flew onto the floor.

"How's that for peace and clarity charged with magic, Peter Pan?"

It was Friday, July 30th, 2010, my birthday. I turned forty-three on the day my promotion letter finally went out. I was officially appointed our division's Sales Director title over both the Orlando and Tampa markets. With the coffee brewing, I read a bunch of congratulatory emails on my BlackBerry before pouring my first cup.

I grabbed my Tinkerbelle mug and took a sip while moving on to two texts. I got caught up replying to them and bypassed my morning jog. I meandered outside with my coffee. Soft sunlight seeped through the palms in the preserve as I sat down at our patio table and read the reply. I was preoccupied with the numbness that had begun to eat at me.

I opened my laptop to a nearly perfect backdrop on a memorable day, and wondered why I wasn't ecstatic. The birds were chirping in unison. The sunlight splashed against the trees and made it look like a pretty painting. But The Darkness taunted me. "You knew this would happen, sport. I even warned you she was no Mermaid. I told you she was your Wendy. Hahaha!"

I forced my thoughts on.

A minute later, discomforted, I closed my laptop. I stared blankly out into the preserve. I felt conflicted. Part of that was certainly due to Geno Franc moving on and The Wizard's wand waving exploits, and even the embroilment with Tony Trappelleti and Bud Fox. But I could no longer deny where this thing with Wendy went. I picked up my Tinkerbelle mug and took another sip deluding myself into thinking I would miraculously receive a sign that this could eventually normalize.

And just then I got one. Unfortunately though, it was a precursor with flashing lights that it could never normalize. Sitting there discomforted, a song that I hadn't heard in a couple of weeks cut through the peacefulness of the break of day. I thought I was hearing things, but I wasn't. It was Taylor Swift's "Today Was a Fairytale" and it was getting louder. I inched up to the edge of my chair because it was coming out of a vehicle that had pulled into the neighbor's driveway.

Intrigued, I wandered out into the backyard to see the pool guy. He ambled between the houses as his eyebrow rose and froze. He peered at me as I stood there holding my Tinkerbelle mug wearing only my comfy pajama pants. "Is that too loud?" he asked me gesturing toward his truck.

"No," I said. "I like the song."

He nodded oddly, took a few strides, stopped and turned back to me. I smiled absently. My mind had raced off to a recent "Wine Time" with my "special friend" that the song instantly brought me back to.

It was two weeks before, when Wendy's return flight back to reality encountered a little turbulence, again. I jumped off the high curb and into the parking lot joking with her. Her laughter abruptly ceased. I glanced behind me. She was still on the sidewalk. Her demeanor rapidly changed before my eyes.

"What's wrong, Wendy?" She stood motionless. I took some curious steps back to her and she leaned into me. Her lips were so close I could feel her smile flat lining.

"I hate this," she whispered dolefully. "I told you I can't handle these back to back 'Wine Times' with you anymore." She took a breath and exhaled. "I can't." She paused and gazed at me before turning to the side with watery eyes. In a chafed voice she said, "I had too much wine. Why did we get that last bottle?"

I had to do something drastic because I was getting dizzy listening to her. Not to mention, I loathed looking at her in these woebegone states. It was all too much so I decided to put my magical glasses on. You know, those eyeglasses you do with your hands when you flip them upside down. So I made the circles for the eyeglasses with my index fingers touching my thumbs and flipped my hands over my eyes. I stood there for a brief moment. "Don't mind me. It's just that I don't like to see you unhappy so I'm putting on my magical glasses." I paused for effect. "They turn frowns upside down."

Her eyes closed slowly.

My voice rose. "Let me try this again. They don't seem to be working today."

As they reopened, her eyes had that light. She shot back, "Are you kidding me?" Her hands shot over her beaming bright red face.

"Oh see, much better. I told you they are magical, ya silly goose."

Her smile couldn't be contained behind her hands, suddenly in deep thought. The pixie dust began to fall on her. "I can still do this." Her head shot up to me. "Twice a week."

I realized I wasn't the only talented one in the relationship. This girl was amazing.

And then she confirmed her strategy. "Maybe once, and I'll be fine." She took a deep breath. That damn imaginary curtain had slowly begun to fall just minutes prior and shot back up as the outdoor patio bar speakers went on. "Today Was a Fairytale" blared out, and the look on her face was, well priceless.

And that was that.

The pool guy shook me out of that delightfully disturbing vision as he walked by. I jumped up with a silly smirk and made my way inside, aflutter. I roamed around our handsome home with only a true reprieve to how I felt when I reached my kids' rooms. It was only then a genuine smile spread across my face. They were sleeping. When I walked out, my mind raced again.

I stopped in my sports memorabilia room because that room of bullshit always cheered me up. But today it caused me to actually smile sadly. Now everything hit me. But as I read another text, I realized all of the neat shit that was hanging on the walls was part of the game. The one that for so long I had to win, and did. But that was no longer. The days of chasing bad business bonuses fueled by greed were behind me. In a sense, Gordon Gekko was dead.

The reality was that the program I had run was producing good solid business, great camaraderie, and a sales force that wanted to make a difference each and every day. Although with all of the communication highlighting our success, it was an email from another sales rep who had struggled in other divisions that was the most meaningful to me. He was sincerely appreciative for what he acknowledged was the best overall experience of his career.

I stood in front of my Derik Jeter autographed jersey and pondered it all until I received a text about a deal I challenged one of my managers to go get two nights prior. I felt compelled to push his buttons and it worked. What he accomplished was quite the feat. I was proud. This was good business. He was pumped and so was I. My mind was temporarily rid of the angst.

Twenty-five minutes later, I pulled out of our driveway in route to pick up pictures from one of our team's cameras. I felt energized. My BlackBerry suddenly rang. I thought it was The Rabbi, so I snatched it from the cup holder. I was startled when I saw it was Marie. I answered and asked her if I forgot something, but she ignored me and got to her point.

"So, what time are your little girlfriend and this poor guy, I mean her fiancé, coming out tonight?"

"Please stop."

"Why? It's true."

"She's calling me this morning."

"Oh, I know. She calls you every morning."

I took a deep breath. "Six. I told her six," I muttered as I received a text. "I'll call you later."

"Bye."

Click.

Just as I hung up, I noticed it wasn't the news I was waiting for. It was Bud Fox wishing me a happy birthday. He was still desperate to get back in my life. As the issues with his team worsened, he continued to inquire about having Marie meet his new girlfriend. Having no patience for him, I deleted it. I was preoccupied with solidifying the extra cases for the overall goal.

After picking up the pictures, I made my way into the office and pushed some more buttons. After three excitable calls, those cases were confirmed. I pulled into my parking space and received a text from Bobby Blue. He informed me he was done with Fox and would never help him again. I didn't even want to know. I rubbed my eyes and raced up the steps into The Asylum to email The Rabbi the news. He replied back immediately and was very appreciative. He let me know he would be calling soon.

I grabbed my Evian and then remembered the pictures. Interestingly, they came from one of our disposable cameras that had mysteriously disappeared and reappeared on my desk the week before. At the time, I didn't think there was any correlation to why Wendy insisted I destroy the camera before she wished it good riddance, while under the impression it was lost. I had thought she was overreacting, but I was wrong.

The first picture was of Tony, with his arm around me, happy as could be. Of course, this was taken back in May before I informed The Wizard he was not the person I was looking for to lead my team. Alas, his attitude adjustment and constant bashing of me ever since had me antsy to hang it in the middle of the picture board and watch him squirm. The next one was of Mike Fritton and me laughing at the bowling event, where I'd sprained my wrist. This also was one I happily hung up. It epitomized what I had envisioned the picture board to be: a focal point to display our admirable team camaraderie and winning spirit.

But as I flipped to the next one, The Darkness howled, "Just split the fucking board in half, camaraderie on one side and scandal on the other."

My eyes popped forward at the picture of Wendy and me glowing scandalously. The night came back to me. At the time, I had convinced myself this night wasn't all that bad. It's kind of pathetic how off I was. She was leaning into me, looking ridiculously cozy, as we both looked to be stabbed in the ass by Cupid. Nothing can shake you out of something you chose to block out like a picture can.

I swallowed hard and flipped to the next one. I thought one shameful shot wouldn't be too bad, but then I froze, stared, and quickly changed my thought process to two. She was facing me with her hand pulling my front pocket and her forehead resting on my chest, with Bud Fox and two random wine tasters in the background. We were at a wine tasting event in St. Pete Beach. I had no idea who took it and no recollection of this at all. I blew out a deep breath, quite unsettled.

The third picture was of our table at dinner that night. My arm was awkwardly positioned under it. I couldn't tell it was resting on her inner thigh until I went to the next picture, which was from another angle. And with this shot, part of the night rushed back over me.

My hand slowly went to my head. I became angered with myself, but also with the individual who was clearly sending me a message. I treated all of my people extremely well. The sudden thought of one of them holding these pictures over my head was disturbing. And then it got worse. I had a vision of Tony playing paparazzi with two other cameras. A shiver went down my spine. That fucking cocksucker took it.

I received another text from Fox as I visualized that post-it-note aware that he was spinning desperately out of control. A sordid act like this was right up his alley. I was on an emotional rollercoaster and became infuriated with myself for allowing this to happen. I leaned back. Maddening scenarios raced through my head. I was desperate for help at this point with only The Darkness sitting across from me, hissing, "If you're too much of a pussy to hang them up, just destroy them. But seriously, what the hell did you think you looked like with this girl?"

That dark voice haunted me. These pictures were the first I thought I had to get rid of since the one of us from her birthday. I became anxious. Why wasn't I more discreet? I realized it was because I continually convinced myself I had nothing to hide, which suddenly seemed ridiculous.

There were other pictures in a rubber band in my draw that I hadn't hung up, but these were different. They made me realize what we looked like together, off in our own little world. My eyes shifted to the clock. I had time. I tore them up and placed them in a sheet of paper from my notepad. I balled it up and tossed it in my trash. But within seconds, that damn dark voice in my head shook me out of the chair. "That giant cancer that runs amok in this place will sniff that shit right out of the trash. Are you stupid?"

I was clearly a bit punchy. I popped up to grab it and took the wad through the empty hall to the bathroom to dispose of it. I stormed back with my heart beating through my shirt. With each step I was more irate with myself. It now had me very stressed out. People use the term "stress" loosely. At this moment I wasn't. The reaction to my stimuli being threatened, challenged, or overwhelmed was not taken lightly. My eyes closed as I sat down.

Mama Bear came in. "Good morning, birthday boy," she bellowed as the office line rang. It was The Rabbi calling to ask me if The Wizard had set a time for our conference call to discuss the specifics of my new role and promotion.

Within a minute of small talk, The Rabbi seemed concerned he hadn't heard from him. He inquired if I had.

"No, I haven't," I said. "It's actually been weeks since I have."

There was a moment of silence. "Okay, so." He paused briefly. "So, he'll be in touch. He knows the letter went out. Just make sure you're available all day."

I cleared my throat and replied, "I will be."

Click.

Twenty minutes later, my office line rang again. I heard Mama Bear shout, "It's your little girl."

I spun my chair around anxious to answer, "Hey."

I only heard her exhale before she seethed, "I hate her."

I moved her along. "Are you guys good for tonight?"

Mama Bear made an unusual sound, it was one she had been making for weeks now.

"Yes," Wendy replied, overwrought. "I just can't believe we're attempting this."

"It'll be fine. We'll have fun."

She paused for a brief moment and took a deep breath. "Jessie and I will be out at six. How's Marie?"

I reached for my Evian. "She's good. I'm sure she's loading her gun now."

"Larry, I will cancel right now if you don't stop your shit."

"It would be so unfortunate if you lost your sense of humor at this late stage of our show." I glanced over at the remaining pictures and almost made the mistake of informing her that I found the "dreaded May" camera. I didn't, thankfully, but I started too. "I saw those pictures. I'm thinking of getting rid of the ones with the rubber band in my drawer." Since I already had uttered the words "those pictures"

I didn't know what else to say.

"I'll bet Tony took that camera from May…"

"We have enough on our plate. Let's focus on tonight, please."

She exhaled. "I can't sleep again and this is giving me an ulcer."

I shrugged. "Can I say something?"

"Oh, God. Whaa? No."

"I don't like your tone today. It's very doomy and gloomy and it's my birthday. I'm thirty-seven."

"I know it's your birthday, you freak. And you're forty-three."

"How could you not wish me a happy birthday?" I bit my inner cheek and tried not to laugh. "And I even invited you to my birthday party."

A moment of eerie silence was broken by another deep exhale. "I can't do this. I was happy and normal before you poisoned me in your fantasy land."

"Wendy." I deliberately hesitated. I could visualize her bracing herself. "You know the name of my sacred land and please use it."

She seemed delirious as she rambled on that this plan we had laid out would limit her to seeing me only once a week.

"Please, don't say that. It sounds like you're giving the key back and plan on using a visitor's day pass. I thought you'd always be my 'Wendy' with your own key to my sacred Never Land." It was then some of the pixie dust that didn't wash off her shirt from the week before hit her hard.

"You know I will be, and I never said I was giving the key back. But Marie scares the shit out of me. So this better work."

I fell back, tickled by this girl in a way that was scaring the shit out of me, for too long now. But I did my best to play it off. "It will, everything will be great. We'll have fun. I'll talk to you later."

Click.

I leaned back in my chair. Mama Bear wandered in. "Was that plans for tonight?" She smiled suspiciously.

"Yes, I'm having Wendy and her fiancé out to meet Marie." I grinned until she collapsed in the chair in front of me. "Are you okay?" I asked as I let out a nervous laugh.

She gawked at me, speechless, and pulled herself forward. "You're doing what?" Her hands went to her head. She was seriously distraught over this. I expected her to have a raised eyebrow or a slight twitch or some shit, but not the reaction she had. "Larry, please tell me you're kidding? Your family just moved in and it's your birthday."

I slumped back in my chair with wide eyes and thought maybe I should've just told her I was having a pizza party with the kids. But she wasn't done.

"What the hell are you thinking?"

Uh oh. Is this plan that blatantly ridiculous? Okay, never mind that. "I'm trying to fix this."

"Larry, there is no fixing what you have with her..." She stopped in mid-sentence because the office line rang.

I turned to see it was The Wizard. "I need to take this," I said.

She staggered out.

I answered, "Hey, Coach."

"Let's do this at four-thirty."

I couldn't believe he set this meeting for four-thirty on a Friday, on my birthday. "I'll see you then," I said.

Click.

An hour later, Wendy called to check in.

"Hey, remember Marie has no idea you've been to the house--"

"Um, hello? Do you think Jessie does? Are you fucking kidding me?"

Again tickled by her ways, I felt the urge to have some fun. "Okay, so what you do when we tour the house, you have to be like, 'Oh wow.' And not just in the room you achieved you're memorable moment of pixie glee."

She almost came through the phone. "Aaahh! Shut your mouth. I will shoot you. That did not happen, I purged it!" She took a deep breath and sputtered, "I should've never called."

Click.

Roughly six hours later, I was off to see The Wizard. One would think he waited as long as he could before finally acknowledging this, which he did. But at this point, I just wanted to get it over with. And as I ran up to him, Mama Bear, full of sarcasm, wished me good luck. Not with The Wizard, but with my incredulous birthday party gathering of my very special little lady friend, her fiancé, and Marie.

Wow, that did sound slightly fucked up. She banked on everything ending horrifically, which was something that would be obvious to me that next Monday. More on that shortly. For this moment, I refused to allow her morbid thoughts to cast a shadow on my ludicrous plan. I sat down in The Wizard's office and thought happy thoughts.

But that was short lived.

He opened his mouth and, with icy coldness, said, "I had no idea you were getting Orlando as well."

I twitched, speechless. He wasted no time dialing up The Rabbi. Within a few minutes, The Rabbi walked him though the specifics of me taking over the Tampa and Orlando markets, which included the East Coast counties, along with Sarasota.

To say The Wizard didn't seem thrilled to even be there, never mind listen to this grandiose plan, which further accelerated my career, was an understatement. The most interesting part of this was that even though my program achieved more than any other, he not only refused to acknowledge it, which was difficult in its own right, but now took a shot at it, and on the day I was being officially promoted. With each passing accolade The Wizard would wince, but when The Rabbi continued on with how positive this move would be for the company, he rudely interrupted.

"I really don't even know what he does," he seethed with disdain.

The Rabbi went silent. The statement was so absurd that all he could do was pretend it wasn't uttered and move on, which he did. But that was it for me. I couldn't help but have a complete loss of respect for him. This was nothing I ever wanted to feel, and the reason I refused to believe this for too long. I really wanted to like this guy, but it had just been too much, and so difficult to remain calm. But thankfully I did, although so many thoughts hit me.

My forced smile frowned when he concluded by having the audacity to ask me, again, who I was promoting to take my place. I casually confirmed my choice hadn't changed. "Dan Schultz is my choice and the best person for the job."

He took another call. I left his office and quickly exited The Asylum, in desperate need of fresh air.

CHAPTER THIRTY - FOUR

MY BIRTHDAY PARTY

JULY 30, 2010
THE NIGHT

I hopped in my Navi and turned up Jason Derulo's, "In My Head" as I texted Wendy: "I'm heading out now."

Seconds later, she replied: "I'm catching a buzz now."

I laughed visualizing her throwing back a bottle while hiding behind the dresses in her closet. Luckily, I had this black comedy to get my mind off The Wizard. Driving along I went over my insane plan of miraculously fixing our predicament by doing things as couples. But then I quickly came up with a plan B: drink heavily.

An hour later, plan B was coming into focus. I was admiring the brilliant clarity of my pale yellow glass of Nobilo Sauvignon Blanc sitting in front of me. I lifted it to my nose and as the intense aromas of pineapple and passion fruit hit me, the doorbell rang. It was Wendy and Jessie, right on time. I took a sip and placed it down before picking it back up and polishing it off. That infamous imaginary curtain rose as I opened the door to greet my special guests. I knew our first task would be to act as if Wendy hadn't been to the house before.

Marie was still getting ready as we quickly toured it. On a side-note, as we went through the rooms, I couldn't help but notice how nicely the house was coming together. But that was probably an observation for another day. I introduced them to Lauren and Jerry in the playroom. After a minute of Jessie chatting with them, I noticed Lauren staring at Wendy and felt it was time to move on.

"Okay kids, have fun," I interrupted, realizing this nice guy would talk to anyone. Heading back down the steps I thought, so far so good. Nothing had spontaneously caught fire and no shots were fired.

Three minutes later, Marie came out to greet them. I raced off for another bottle and prayed she didn't jam Wendy in the microwave and hit the high button. I flew back in to see her sitting safely on a bar stool. Whew! Although Wendy refused to even look in my direction she was laughing, probably after popping a pill, as Jessie was now chatting with Marie, who was attempting to put some frozen pizza things on a tray, which she ended up burning. But that didn't matter, with the new bottle came new cheer. Well, until we had...sorry, I had a slight problem. I had to lie down on the couch, due to the fact I was about to blackout with some hospital/needle story being told. It is an unfortunate phobia that I have and one that Wendy was very aware of.

So as Marie and Wendy were completely unfazed, the conversation persisted with Jessie gazing over at me on the couch, confused. His expression was of disbelief. He continued to stare at Wendy, who didn't flinch. By this point, she was used to all my special needs and as his perplexing glances to her went unacknowledged, he was left sitting there dumbfounded, which made it all priceless.

Within the hour though, certain conversations had Marie bringing up instances that I had shared with her about the few times the three of us—Wendy, Jessie, and I—had hung out. It was at this point I realized Wendy was right. Jessie blocked out what he couldn't deal with. After a few odd glances from her to me, I felt it best to open another bottle. That one went down quickly. We then ended up inviting them to our Mexican retreat in January. That would've been special.

It was time for another bottle.

An hour after that though, we came to a moment that could've needed an explanation, but miraculously it was barely picked up on. Well, to be truthful, it was deliberately passed on, but the important part was that it was all still good. It happened when we (Wendy and I) made the weird sound that we made when a situation in a story was either odd or just downright unbelievable. You could hear crickets as we both stared at each other with that look of oops screaming across our faces. Fortunately, there was the unspoken word from both Jessie and Marie to please, for the love of anything sane in this universe, just continue.

And continue I did.

But when the next bottle was torn open I caught Marie staring at me with something I missed. Wendy had said something, with a bit too much glow, and we began slipping up. That's when I realized we were now on borrowed time. Our dark devotion was just sitting to the side like the elephant in the room that everyone was aware of but no one would acknowledge. I knew we were minutes away from someone tripping over the bitch and bloodying a nose.

Since I was the most intoxicated, I figured it was just best that I take myself out of the running and call it a night. But that wasn't before I had to turn away, giggling, at the reality that Wendy and I ended up with Jessie and Marie; two of the sweetest human beings on the planet. Then I had another thought, but that one was too much. I smirked and moved along to the bedroom, now giggling deliriously. It was like everything just hit me all at once. The seven or whatever bottles of wine, no lunch or even dinner for that matter, the promotion, The Wizard, and the fact that I just turned forty-three and still felt sixteen. Well, never mind the last part.

But now, they all moved to the bedroom with me, kind of scary, but true. My head shot up as the laughter hit a fever pitch. Oh that's a great picture, I thought, staring at Marie and Wendy standing next to each other, giddy and making fun of me. I whined, "Leave me alone." What? I couldn't make it obvious I was gawking.

Minutes later, Marie began glancing over at Wendy. I was all too familiar with that look, from both of them. Marie was still laughing, but she was intently studying Wendy, who had now begun to really bubble over, causing Marie to shut it all down. She hit the lights and shot out to the patio with her. I didn't know about that interrogation until the next day though. More on that shortly; at this moment, I was consumed with a presence in the bed. Abruptly, I turned to notice Jessie was lying there next to me.

I tried to scream help because I thought maybe he took a knife from the kitchen and this was his little plan, but then I realized he too was wasted and giggling. I was oh-so relieved, while I mumbled for him to go crash in the guest room because lying in bed with another guy was another one of my phobias. I just didn't realize it until that moment when my world abruptly went dark.

Goodnight.

Even though the night was a success, Saturday was a bit taxing. I was watching a report that President Obama was pulling our troops out of Iraq when Marie sent her message, which was cut and dry: Wendy and I were way too close for her liking. And it was time for her to run down the six hundred and fifty-six subtle reasons why she drew this conclusion. Apparently she didn't get that I was busy watching this special news bulletin.

"Marie, the President is pulling our troops out of Iraq and I want to see this. Can you hold that thought?"

She turned to me and said, "I've held it long enough."

My eyes shot open as I turned to the kitchen frantically. I noticed she polished off a bottle, was about to burn another pizza, and was ready to rumble. I then panicked...and fell over.

"Marie," I whined, "please come and feel my head...I'm not well."

"Larry," she seethed, "I'm fully aware you're not well."

I took a breath and pushed myself back up on the couch and pretended I had a moment to strategize my next move.

But I didn't.

She continued, "I did everything in my power not to laugh out loud at her. The script she recited to me totally contradicted what Jessie said earlier in the evening, and she didn't realize it. She didn't hear a word he said. You both are two pees of the same demented pod." She let out this guffaw, which caused me to pop up awkwardly, while searching for a safe-haven.

"Are you aware she hasn't done a thing for their wedding?"

I hid in the wine closet.

Her onslaught continued, "Of course you are, she's with you. And I've lost my appetite for Acropolis, or anywhere else you've taken her." Her voice seemed to be getting closer.

I closed the door.

"And what does she do when Jessie asks to go to a restaurant that the two of you spent three hours in...looking like husband and wife?"

"What...I'm choosing a bottle...for you...and I can't multitask...hold please..."

"You better stop the shenanigans and come back from Never Land with answers to this mess you made...little boy."

CHAPTER THIRTY - FIVE

A SUDDEN SUMMER CHILL

AUGUST 2010
THE ASYLUM

Early that Monday, Wendy called me while I was jogging. I crashed against a tree out of breath as her name flashed on my screen. "Hey," I answered breathing heavily.

"Are you jogging?"

"No, I'm dying."

"So what did Marie say?"

"She thinks what you recited on the patio was a script that was a bit ridiculous."

"Oh, God. I was smoking with her; she freaked me out."

As the conversation persisted I could tell her anxiety levels were rapidly rising. But I had a busy week and another call coming in. I had a project due for The Rabbi and three meetings, one with the on premise group, before I flew out to Miami for a presentation that included members of the CWUS Florida team.

"Hey, I have to take this."

"Wait—"

"It's The Rabbi, about this week."

Click.

She immediately sent me a text: "When can we meet? You have a busy week."

After the call I sent her a reply: "I'll call you this afternoon. We'll figure it out."

I pulled into the office an hour later. Within minutes I realized our usually warm and inviting office felt a sudden chill. When Mama Bear realized there was no horror story of a tragic ending to the night, her mood changed, drastically. It officially became my next problem; but I guess that would be an understatement because what transpired had those ominous storm clouds swirling viciously. I sat at my desk working on the project when Tony walked into the office. And not in his typical fashion. I didn't know he was there until I came out of my office to see him whispering something to Mama Bear. I grabbed a wine rebate from a box that I needed for this report and walked back to my desk.

A couple of minutes later, he set his laptop up at the table just outside my door. I asked him how everything was going. He stated that everything was fine. I asked him where he found our camera.

His eyes grew wide and his head turned up to mine. "I didn't find any camera. I was going to ask you why we stopped taking pictures. I thought that picture board was a great idea. It made everyone smile as they came in." He paused. "But I guess times change. We're now no different than the rest of the company, with the changes and all."

I made sure I caught his eye. "Nothing's changed, Tony."

"Do you really think Schultz is like you? Not everyone is happy, sir."

I cringed. It was the same comment The Wizard made. "Our camaraderie will not change Tony, but I am curious to know where you found our lost camera."

He looked away. "I told you it wasn't me."

"No?"

"No, I have no idea. The last time I saw it was the afternoon of that wild meeting when you opened all of those bottles of wine."

I remained calm peering over at him. "The meeting you stated coming to my division was the best move of your career?" I paused for his reaction. I walked out and pointed at the picture that captured us gleefully celebrating it all.

He remained silent.

I took two steps back to him. "Was it after that wild meeting?"

He glanced over at the board with wide eyes. "Yes."

"We had two bottles of wine and there were six people who stayed."

He smiled awkwardly. "Oh, it always seems like more with you…"

At this instant there was little doubt in my mind that it was Tony who took the camera and placed it back when he felt the time was right to send his message.

In the dark hours of that morning I received another call from a sales rep under Bud Fox. He informed me that Fox had been threatening him to take the pictures for the "Take the Beach" incentive. Each manager was responsible for turning in their wine display pictures for the incentive, and I asked why they hadn't while informing him they were the only team that didn't.

"Larry, that's his job. It's his incentive and he's in Tampa."

As he rambled on, it seemed they had all been harboring ill-will for not only Fox, but now the company as well. He brought up the call with The Wizard wondering, how a vice president could simply blow them off after hearing their complaints.

I interrupted as calmly as I could. "I understand your frustration. But The Wizard's conference call was almost a year ago. This is my fault."

"Larry, you gave him an opportunity and he shit all over you. This is his fault."

I was now slightly confused.

I sighed. "But he's my responsibility."

His tone softened. "Listen, you should know that he is telling everyone he's not going anywhere. He claims he has enough dirt on you with that girl to have you fired." He paused and sighed. I fell back speechless. "It's his girlfriend who is feeding him this bullshit." He hesitated briefly. "I think all of this goes back to what she said weeks ago."

I explained to him that I had only met her once and didn't know her. He was shocked as Fox made it seem that we all hung out. I informed him that I don't hang out with him anymore.

"I had no idea," he said, stunned, before adding, "You should know his girl seems to be a control freak. A strange girl for sure, but dangerous and she's too young to know better."

In the moment of silence that followed, I again realized how much time this madness was taking up and became further unsettled. "Okay, listen. Dan Schultz will be over soon. I need you guys not to get caught up listening to Fox's stories. Please just focus on your jobs."

He sputtered, "Yeah…yeah…sure, Larry. Will do."

Click.

CHAPTER THIRTY - SIX

GEKKO RETURNS WITH VENGEANCE

EARLY SEPTEMBER 2010
THE ASYLUM

At one o'clock, on Wednesday, September 8th, I received a text from Wendy that she was held up at an account. I had pulled into the parking lot of another client's, where we were supposed to meet. Before I could respond, The Rabbi called to inform me of a two o'clock conference call. After texting her that I couldn't wait, I left. I passed our old South Tampa wine bar, "Cork." It had changed names twice and appeared to have lost some of its mysticism. I slowed to stop at a light and answered a call about a situation with an on premise key account manager. Afterward, I called Mindy Amour to discuss it.

In spite of these distractions, I took a slight detour to pick up a stained shirt that was left out of my last pick-up from my old dry cleaner on Harbour Island. It had been sitting there for months before my favorite little lady there found it and left me a message to pick it up. But that was back in May. A new voice left me another message that they were going to get rid of it if I didn't pick it up this week.

I swung over from South Tampa. Minutes later, I hung up with Mindy and slowed down in front of Jackson's Bar going over a speed bump. I smiled. I felt a bit nostalgic. The memorable moments from the past year rushed over me, as I pulled around to the corporate apartment. I was unable to deny the fact that I was desperate to turn back the clock.

Without consciously thinking about it, I pulled over in the traffic circle where Wendy used to pick me up at. It was hard to believe a year had passed. In a sense though, it felt like three; so much had happened. I stared at the top of the circle and visualized her zipping around in her little white car, smiling widely with her eyes as she picked me up. Suddenly tickled, I recalled the day Wendy had her seat heater on low, warming my ass for two hours, as we popped in and out of accounts before we realized it was on. It was ironically something that she had to share with Mama Bear. They carried on for minutes about this because I was taking a piss at every stop and they thought that was hilarious. But those days were long gone, and so was my old dry cleaner lady friend. She had passed away in June. I took a deep breath, a bit emotional. She was always so cheerful, and loved when I came in. I stood there for a moment before I hung my shirt up in the navi. I couldn't help but smile visualizing the "Wine Time" episode that caused the stain.

I pulled out as another call came in. I noticed it was Wendy. "Hey," I answered.

"I am not reporting to anyone but you," she snapped.

I chuckled. "Wendy, I can't exactly tell your new boss not to call you."

"I'm not dealing with Dan Schultz right now. Where are you?"

I took a deep breath and exhaled. "On my way back to the office. I texted you. I have a call with The Rabbi."

"When are we meeting?" She sounded like a little girl who didn't get her way. "It's our national holiday. Really, we can't not meet on our favorite holiday."

"Swing by the office later and I'll cork something."

"No." She hesitated. "Not with your admin there. There is no way."

"I can't go out that late. I got home an hour later than I said I would last Thursday."

"You need to figure this out...I did."

"You are one Dark Princess, but Marie refuses to block out everything that Jessie does." I paused as Wendy went silent. Within seconds Mindy was calling. "Hey, it's Mindy, let me call you back."

She quickly fired back. "How often do you speak to her?"

"She texted me at eleven-thirty the other night bragging about her

Red Sox while bashing my Yankees. I'll call you back."

I clicked over, but Mindy had hung up. I was okay with that. Consumed with my surroundings, I couldn't deny that the days when I began this adventure, a year before, were extraordinary; and not to sound corny, but also magical. It seemed Wendy was reminiscing as well. She texted me: "I want to go to the Greeks. We haven't been there in so long and Chops misses us."

As I drove out, I passed the parking garage to the corporate apartment. I hoped to see Molly the Mermaid's Jeep, but a Volvo was in her spot. I passed their corner room and noticed an even younger woman, who I didn't recognize, on their balcony. Shit, they must have moved out. I couldn't stop thinking about that night she first spotted me, locked out, with all my shit in dry cleaner wrap, and then the day with the song, and then the chance meeting at the bar. It seemed so perfectly scripted, so surreal, and so special. Now everything was very different.

Fifteen minutes later, I pulled into the office. I ran up the steps and into The Asylum. As I opened the second door, Wendy texted: "Hello, you were calling me back. Are we going to the Greeks?"

Since I was heading in to take the call, I didn't text her back. After the conference call, I asked Mama Bear for all the pictures of the wine displays for the "Take the Beach" incentive. I still had none from Bud Fox.

Since Dan Schultz was transitioning into my old position, he had suggested it was best that he handle Fox with somewhat of an understanding regarding the strenuous situation I no longer had time to deal with. Of course, no one knew that Fox was still attempting to get back in with me.

The next day I had to finalize the "Take the Beach" sales incentive and pass on the winners to Mike Fritton. This particular incentive was slated for St. Pete Beach. To qualify for the trip, as mentioned, each district manager had to submit pictures of their team's wine displays along with their achieved case goal. I would always give my team an earlier due date to submit the documentation for these programs. This would give me time to view everyone's achievements, while being able to retake any mistake shots, before sending them off to our friends at CWUS.

Well, I did that again for this incentive. Up to this point I had received almost every manager's complete account list of pictures to qualify, with only one manager, Bud Fox, not sending any. I then received another call. I found out that Fox had been in Tampa with his girlfriend the past two long weekends. They all stated he would leave his area midday on Wednesday to return that following Sunday night. I hung up with his sales rep, and was furious. I called Fox.

"What's up?" he said anxiously.

"Your complete set of pictures is due tomorrow morning." I paused, seething. "If they are not in for my viewing, you do not go. Do not fucking test me."

Click.

Did I mention Gordon Gekko was dead? Well, that was quite possibly bad information.

The next day, I walked into our office sporting my favorite old "Gekko the Great" tie. I noticed Mama Bear seemed uptight. She immediately slid a paper over, to cover another one on her desk. She appeared edgy. She seemed to be hiding something.

I stopped and asked her what was wrong. The tension built. She was shaking and knew she had a better chance at winning the lottery than I had of not completely losing my temper and raising the roof. As I stated before, she thought Fox was attractive, and she liked him. He knew he could play her like a violin, which he did--again.

When I noticed his store numbers on her computer monitor, I realized she once again was putting all of this together for him. Everything seemed to be in slow motion at this point. Well, until I did become enraged and raise the roof, amongst other things. Tears swelled up in her eyes. I knew he was probably at his house sleeping off his long weekend. Realizing I was a tad bit intense, I took a breath unable to fathom how she blatantly went against my direction for him yet again.

"Lori, what did I tell you? I specifically told you not to do anything out of the ordinary for him and you do this, behind my back? Again? You're not helping him, you're hurting him and he continues to use you."

She couldn't even speak. So I sat down in the chair by our manager's table. She continued to tremble. My phone rang. It was one of Fox's reps calling me. I answered, "Yes."

"Laaa, this fucking cocksucker Fox was in Tampa for four days again and now rolls back over here cursing us out to take all these pictures for his fucking beach trip."

She could hear the conversation and as those words came out of his mouth, Mama Bear was terrified for him. The look on my face meant bad news for Bud. I stormed into my office. She raced away to warn him and Dan Schultz.

I grabbed my Evian, took a swig, and dialed Fox. He didn't answer. I knew he was on the other line with Mama Bear. My temper was something I struggled with, and this guy was now pushing me in ways I could not comprehend. I dialed him again and it went to voice mail. Within the minute Dan Schultz called.

"Dan, I have to call you back."

"Hey hold—"

Click.

I could tell Schultz had heard how this had the potential to be a repeat of the Central Park scene in the movie Wall Street and was panicked. I slammed the phone down and dialed Fox again. I envisioned myself shouting at a dim monkey dangling from the broken branch of a diseased tree. I lashed out at him.

"Your actions are deplorable. I fucking gave you everything. I protected you from every rep you ever had. They all wanted to file complaints against you. I was the one who didn't allow them to. Me! Your last two bosses screamed not to promote you because all you do is lie. I gave you the chance you wanted. You told me repeatedly you understood me. You told me you were the only fucking guy who had my back. You lied over and over, and now you're telling your people you have shit on me? This is how you repay me, you fucking monkey?!"

I had completely snapped. All of the mounting tension erupted like a volcano. But he didn't care. It didn't even register with him. His own words would soon prove that. I shut his drivel down, seething. "You are a complete failure as a manager, and you've deliberately used my admin against my wishes to do your job because you knew she would. You've been thrown out of numerous accounts for lying and now you spent three months lying about where you are because you refuse to get your hands dirty in a store to help them. They call me every day updating me about your lies and threats. An easy task, to be awarded a weekend at the beach, and you fuck that up too?!"

He had the audacity to actually cut me off and say, "I'm fucking going on that trip."

"What did you just say? Are you fucking kidding me right now?!" I took a breath and exhaled. "You're not going on this trip. You are the only failure in my program and I will not allow this to continue."

I slammed my office phone down in disgust. Schultz called my BlackBerry.

I answered, "He's not going. And this is not up for negotiation." I fell back in my chair, into dead silence before I heard him sigh and then reply in a soft tone, "Can I talk to him?"

"Dan, listen. It's impossible for me to explain how close this fucking imbecile has gotten to me and where this thing has gone. I'm embarrassed to even have you brought in the loop on this madness, not that you'd ever believe it. But I will not allow him to lie and threaten my people again. I won't."

"Listen, I know more than you think, and I agree he's all that and more, and it is incredible, but I also know what you've done for me and for this division, and I can only ask that you allow me to handle him, in order to protect you."

In the moment of silence that followed I took another deep breath. "Take him. But he's not going to be awarded this (Take the Beach) incentive."

Click.

CHAPTER THRITY - SEVEN

TAKE THE BEACH
AND LEAVE MY SANITY

MID-SEPTEMBER 2010
THE DAYS AROUND THE TRIP

It was nine o'clock on Friday, September 17th, but it already felt like noon. My elbows rested on my desk and my hands framed my head as my patience waned. I never enjoyed solving cryptic texts, and now had two to crack while completing a task for The Rabbi. My office line rang. It was Wendy, but Mama Bear didn't yell out, "It's your little girl." She only made that disturbing sound she had been making as it continued to ring. So I grabbed it. "Hey."

"I'm going to reach out to Marie to see what she's wearing tonight," Wendy said cheerfully.

"What?" I replied, stupefied.

"For tonight...for the (Take the Beach incentive) weekend," she paused briefly. "What's wrong?"

"I don't know. Do you remember I told you about the warnings from Fox's people? About his girl?" I paused to read my screen. "Hey, let me call you back."

"Whaa?"

"Wendy, I'll call you back."

Click.

Another text flashed up. I read it: "Fox has lost his mind!" My eyes narrowed at the rest of it: "Your boy is totally depressed because he's not going on that beach trip. He says you had planned on partying with him at the resort, but now he knows you're done with him. He's telling everyone he's taking you out. Getting you fired. It's his crazy girl."

Each sentence was more incomprehensible than the last, and one text contradicted the next, leaving me with a feeling of vertigo. The harsh reality was that in just a matter of days, the drama that had unfolded with this "Take the Beach" incentive trip would've eclipsed even the wackiest reality television show you could ever imagine.

The premise of this unfortunate unrest had Bud Fox in such a desperate depressed state that he was now moving forward with a scheme to "take me out"—and not to dinner—to tarnish my name and destroy my career. Even though those were his exact spoken words, this was a plot that was supposedly orchestrated by the girlfriend. Now if we stopped there, this would be quite incredible. But we can't, because it was Fox who amazingly boasted about this insanity to his own people, who loathed him, and would call me to rat him out in any way they could. But he did it anyway.

So when the next sales rep called me, (just minutes later) he stated that Fox told him he was kept from the trip because his girlfriend was going to approach my wife about me hitting her ass. Stunned, I asked him to repeat himself. He did, and in a serious tone. I fell back in my chair and could not ever remember my spirit being so deflated. I sat tattered, only wanting to get off the phone and throw up. But it got worse. The next call brought me back to a disturbing ride back to my car the morning after I met this individual: the "crazy girlfriend."

It was just after eleven o'clock in the morning on Saturday, July 3rd, nearly three months prior. Bud Fox drove me back to my car and interrupted ten minutes of small talk after he read a text that he glanced at twice before turning to me to say, "You know that you goosed my girl?"

I asked him what he meant as he reread the text with a confused look on his face.

"I think you hit her ass getting up," he sputtered.

My head tilted to him. "Are you being serious right now?"

"Yeah," he said. "You were wasted and fell into her when you got up. You and your little girl (Wendy) were on your third bottle when we showed up."

I shook my head, not at all comprehending his words, and said,

"You were two hours late. But what are you talking about hitting her ass?"

"It was when we went to the other restaurant. I didn't see it though," he babbled.

Right after he mentioned this to me I asked to speak to her. He texted her back and nervously stated she was sleeping and would call me later. That never happened. I never heard about this again, until now.

I called Wendy to tell her. She made that ridiculous sound we made to each other when a topic was farfetched or completely absurd. But after I brought her up to speed on the rest of it, she lost it.

"Wait...what? I don't understand? This makes no sense?" she muttered.

"I'm telling you, Fox's reps just told me this. I even asked him to repeat himself."

"I told you that girl was fucking crazy back then. And I'm stressing about tonight and I can't deal with Fox's insanity." She took a deep breath. "You cannot trust these people."

"I don't."

"You trust everyone. And his sick man-crush on you has never been normal." She laughed. "And I'm starting to think Fox's people are as screwed up as he is. There is no way that happened—"

"Let me call you back."

Click.

I took a call from The Rabbi and agreed that quite possibly his people were trying too hard to have him removed because this was nuts. But herein lies my other problem. This was not the trip for me to suddenly decide to put this flunky in time out.

This was our first big trip and they wanted to acknowledge us as the number one team in the state, with everyone in attendance. Not to mention the fact that I was very aware these things were all he cared about. I knew he probably spent half the time he was in Tampa shopping for a new bathing suit and flip-flops, and I'm sure he only went home to pack his floats up with all intentions to be the first one at the tiki bar, hence his now desperate and delusional state now. So as you can imagine, it obviously didn't end there.

I glanced at the clock and rubbed my eyes. Forty minutes after those calls, I received another one. "Hello," I said.

"Hey," his rep whispered.

I asked him why he was whispering as my eyes blinked with dubiety.

"I'm still here, but Fox is saying you kept him away from this trip because of that girl, the one you're close with? And Larry, he's going after you."

"Excuse me?" I laughed. "I just heard it was because I hit his girl's ass."

"What? Larry I'm being serious—"

"So was I..."

"Fox said Wendy convinced you to keep him away because his girlfriend threatened to tell her fiancé and your wife that you're having an affair."

I heaved a long sigh. "This is incredible. I'll call Fox."

Click.

I hung up, thinking Wendy was right. There was just no way this was happening. My phone rang again, gifting me a giggle. It was Matt calling to inform me that The Wizard's bucket of Bud Light was in route to the resort to be delivered to his suite for the weekend. I hung up laughing gently. But within minutes of that reprieve, I received word that Mama Bear suddenly decided to pull out of the weekend. Of course, she claimed that she couldn't afford a dog sitter while proceeding to tell others that she wasn't going because the resort was destined to go up in flames. Why, you ask? Well, of course, because she was convinced that Wendy and I would spontaneously combust in some star-crossed lover's tragic tale. Quite possibly after we tore each other's clothes off in front of our significant others, who then shot us dead, as Tony snapped pictures with my deposable camera, while The Wizard lurked in the shadows grinning with glee, as he pulled his forty-sixth Bud Light out of the bottomless bucket the CWUS boys bought him, all while Mama Bear loaded Bud Fox's "crazy" girlfriend's gun, taking aim at our entangled naked corpses from the roof of the resort next door, screaming:

"They're not dead; they're just pretending to be. In five minutes they'll both disappear in a ball of pixie dust and reappear down the street in some bar's back booth, sharing a bottle, gazing in each other's eyes, before fucking each other's brains out. Stand back, Tony...and Matt. I'm going to end this nightmare once and for all."

By three o'clock that afternoon, Dan Schultz had developed a sudden allergic reaction to this event due to the above-mentioned scenario, which was whispered in his ear by Mama Bear. This caused him to play sick.

"I'm not feeling well," he said.

My eyes closed as my hands shot to my head again. But let's back up a second. The ironic part was that Schultz had observed enough on his own to make a judgment call on the matter. What I'm trying to say is that he was an intelligent guy who certainly didn't need Mama Bear's dramatic Romeo and Juliet ending sold to him, which unfortunately did alter his decision to attend this event. I say this confidently because he actually went on record twice with statements that were light and humorous about our dark devotion, and something that had me believe he understood it as an unfortunate situation without becoming irrational.

His last comment, proving my point, came at a winery supplier dinner at the Council Oaks Steakhouse in the Tampa Hard Rock. The supplier had flown in from one of the smaller wineries to tour our area and was ecstatic. We recapped the day with a lovely evening that had a positive and pleasurable atmosphere, as our entire world did at that time, not too long before this.

Thirty minutes into the delightful dinner, the supplier had been on the topic of wineries and had asked someone who their favorite Italian winery was. Well, after that individual answered, Schultz slowly turned his head to Wendy and said, with a shit-eating grin, "So Wendy." He paused just long enough for her to wince. "Who is your favorite Italian?"

Everyone's eyes at the table popped forward in their heads before rolling to her, and then to me and back to her, before staring straight ahead.

It was actually a classic scene, but anyway, amidst the harmless shits and giggles, it was clear he was aware of our unique dynamic. But more importantly, he was clearly joking about it. We had a fun night without crazy talk and then proceeded to the parking lot to go home without incident.

But that was overridden by the all-knowing Mama Bear. So as the story goes, Schultz missed the "Take the Beach" weekend where we were hailed the best in team the state. He should've been there.

Five days later, after a district manager meeting, on the afternoon of Wednesday, September 22nd, Bud Fox was seen talking to Tony in the warehouse. It was an intense conversation. The premise was that Tony convinced him to go to The Wizard and file a complaint against me. Fifteen minutes after that he was witnessed having a conversation in the parking lot of The Asylum on his cell phone. He was visibly upset. As the conversation persisted, a trustworthy individual confirmed that they heard him being screamed at by a female. Five minutes later, two witnesses spotted him heading up to the executive offices. I answered one of the two calls on the situation.

"Larry, he's walking up to the executive offices."

"What?"

"He's heading up to see The Wizard."

"Stay there for a few minutes and call me back when you see him come out."

"Sure, Larry."

"Thanks."

Click.

Ten minutes later, he was seen walking back down the executive stairway and heading to the Human Resources office, which confirmed the calls stating The Wizard made him file a formal complaint against me for being excluded from the "Take the Beach" incentive. The complaint was immediately passed on to the lead investigator for the state, as The Wizard hid behind his curtain and reached for his wand.

I fell back in my chair as a wave of self-pity hit me. I wished more than anything that I could turn back the clock. I regretted my actions during the TJ Faggalo draft and wanted to go back to that afternoon a year before and knock the egotistical smirk off my face, thinking I could fix anything including Bud Fox.

CHAPTER THIRTY - EIGHT

MAMA BEAR HOLDS COURT

EARLY OCTOBER 2010
THE ASYLUM

I wasn't exactly feeling benevolent on the following Monday. I deleted a voice mail from a counterpart seeking my assistance, and scrambled to find a phone number I never thought I'd need. I hadn't been myself, but realized I couldn't allow the distractions to alter our production. So I soldiered on and reached out to our state investigator, Chris Lyin. I felt it would behoove me to discuss this matter expeditiously, but was unaware of the curious angle he had already taken at the start of this so-called investigation.

The first time I laid eyes on him was a year earlier, when I was questioned during another company investigation. The rash flashback that hit me wasn't pleasant. It was of him screeching to a halt during his questioning to ask, "Why aren't you nervous? Everyone I question is."

My mouth parted slightly. A moment of awkward silence left me marveling at the power trip this guy was on. "Why would I be?"

He peered at me but didn't utter a response. I was baffled that a lead investigator would ask such a question.

Right after that I came in contact with someone who compared Mr. Lyin to a kid who was bullied on the school playground and was now fixated on getting even with anyone who reminded him of his scarred past. I wasn't sure how true that was, but I wasn't all that concerned either. I honestly never thought I'd deal with him again. And although I had that wrong, I believed that anyone would've immediately seen this for the desperate act it was and would have handled it accordingly. But I was wrong again. Mr. Lyin remained silent during the fifteen-minute call. He said he would be in touch, but never asked for any of the names or numbers to confirm what Bud Fox's team told me. I hung up and drove on, miffed.

Ten minutes later, I became riled when I found out that Fox had already put the victim hat (that he wore so well) on, and limped in to this guy with his slant to "take me out." Apparently, this guy saw himself in the weeping Fox, who then swore revenge.

I called Fox to speak to him directly. The call went to his voicemail. I would later find out Mr. Lyin told him not to have any communication with me whatsoever. Five minutes after that, I pulled into the parking lot of The Asylum and called Wendy. I filled her in.

She remained silent until she finally couldn't take it anymore, and muttered, "This is the most ridiculous thing I've ever heard. And he told his team this and then they called you?"

"Yes."

"Larry, I seriously want to scream. There is no way."

This conversation went on for five agonizing minutes before I received another call. I sat in my navi parked in front of The Asylum. I told Wendy I'd call her back and clicked over to talk to Dan Schutlz. He sounded stressed and informed me that he and Mama Bear needed to speak with me urgently.

"I'll be right there." I wondered what could possibly be next.

Unbeknownst to me, Mama Bear went against my wishes again and now had her new boyfriend fix Bud Fox's fried laptop, which of course was against company policy. This was the third time Fox was warned not to go to these sites, but of course, he did anyway. So once again he kept this from me and the IT department, and reached out to Mama Bear for help.

At this point in the story one would think Mama Bear would kindly or unkindly tell this moron she couldn't get involved, and possibly remind him that he'd caused enough trouble. But she didn't. She yet again embraced the fool and told him she would have her new boyfriend fix it without the company or me knowing. But with so much totally unimaginable shit unfolding at that moment, it's best we just keep moving.

Now mind you, the only reason she informed me of this was because she suddenly had to. Why you ask? Well, because Fox brought his girlfriend with him to drop the laptop off. And apparently the "crazy" couldn't wait to meet her and share some of her stories over tea, which brings us to this critical information Mama Bear felt the need to brief me on.

I walked into the office and they both had dire looks on their faces. Schultz scurried over and closed the door behind me. Mama Bear then proceeded to bring me up to speed on the Bud Fox laptop debacle, because now she obviously had too. I sat back, disgusted with her, but remained calm.

What I found the most amazing was that she really didn't even seem to get how astray she was for continuing to help him. But we can't slow down there either because this led to how she met Fox's "crazy" girlfriend, which was the premise of this powwow.

Although I was aware that this lady did sincerely like me and was appreciative for everything I'd done for her, I couldn't deny the darker thoughts I had, questioning how she came into my world. The vision of her playing this damsel in distress with her sweet southern accent in tow, begging me (the idiot egomaniac who truly thought he was a superhero) to save her, also seemed to be scripted. As I was fading fast, I noticed her hands go up in the air.

With that, she abruptly shook me out of that disquieting reflection with dramatic flair. "Larry, that girl is fucking crazy, and I'm very concerned.

"Lori...concerned about what?"

"She got out of the car shouting at me that you are something special."

"I met this girl one time, three months ago, and she has no idea who I am." I paused and calmly said, "And what did Fox say?"

"Not a word. He just followed her. He barely said anything the entire time."

"How can he listen to this girl and not say anything?" I rubbed my eyes. "How long were they there?"

"Not long, but what you're missing is that she's crazy."

"No, I got that," I muttered, leaning over and eyeing the ground.

But it didn't end there. Mama Bear was friendly with Schultz, who was obviously now in place as my new Tampa sales manager. I felt I did a good enough job on my own to paint my version of a bad boy without filling his head with her craziness. But she was in rare form and after informing me of how she thought this girl was certifiable, she threw out this inappropriate touch as being no big deal.

I shook my head and began to chuckle. I turned to Schultz and said softly, "That is not the bad boy I am, Daniel."

I couldn't resist, but I don't think he got my humor. His head slumped and she carried on like this was just the way I was with women. She was speaking as if she witnessed this and it was all part of my fun time.

I cringed. "Lori, who are you talking about? When have I ever touched someone inappropriately or said it was okay to do so? Close talkers freak me out. Are you kidding me?"

Schultz's head twisted nervously toward her as she said, "This was not a company event so there's nothing to worry about."

I looked at her. "What?" As if she hadn't heard me, I added, "I do not condone touching anyone in any way and I'm not concerned. This is totally absurd." I felt like I was losing consciousness again.

"Larry, but she is crazy," Mama repeated.

"I can't control that. But I have been warned about Fox pulling this bullshit for years. It's my fault for not listening to them all." I took a breath and exhaled. "He can't do the job and that's why I can't have you interfere with this anymore. You don't seem to understand. This guy has abused these people for a year, and I can't let it continue."

"Larry, he's safe now," she said, and she was right.

You see, since The Wizard had Bud Fox file this complaint, he didn't have to worry about any of his glaring issues as a manager. He was safe, at least for the time being, an untouchable if you will. It was the most unimaginable series of events, which would only happen in The Asylum. And Mama knew it. She had clearly been a part of too much in this place, and as I sat back and shook my head in frustration, I said, "This would never happen if Geno Franc was still in Tampa."

She interestingly had no response. I had already been distancing myself from her and realized that would continue. I wanted to like this lady but she now simply made me uncomfortable. And that was before I thought her mad slant could possibly affect this investigation. But she somehow did.

It wasn't until I was outside The Asylum that I relaxed enough to digest the rest of it. At that point Wendy texted: "Call me." I took a deep breath and did. Within the first minute of explaining this meeting to her, she became angered. By now, she couldn't stand Mama Bear and certainly didn't trust her.

As the conversation persisted, there were things Wendy said that made me think about how Mama Bear had viewed the other men she had worked for. And as those stories were outlandish too, it was now obvious, and important to note, that she actually enjoyed working for men who had promising careers of power. My mind raced on until I heard Wendy yell, "Larry?!"

"Yes..."

"I told you that lady has no idea who you really are. She compared you to Charlie on 'Two and a Half Men.' That lady is nuts! She doesn't even know you play or even like sports." She took a breath and added, "Or that you would black out in almost every ridiculous situation she has placed you in."

"Wendy, please stop. I'm in a fragile state right now."

"I am so upset with you. How many times have I warned you about her?"

This was the last thing I needed at that moment. And then Mindy called.

"Hey I have to take this. It's Mindy."

"Wait—whaa—"

Click.

We were dealing with an on premise problem when Mindy informed me The Rabbi shut her down for a trip to Tampa. Within a minute of the conversation, Wendy called back. I thought something had to have happened. "Mindy, let me call you back." I clicked over to Wendy. "What's wrong?"

"Schultz just called me."

My eyes closed. "He's your boss now, Wendy. That will be happening from time to time. I have enough problems right now. Please take his calls."

"I do, just not right now. What did Mindy want?"

"I didn't talk to her long enough to find out. I thought you crashed, so I told her I'd call her back. Oh, she did say The Rabbi doesn't want her to come up now."

"Um, shocking."

"Why?"

"Oh, I don't know, with all this shit going down, don't you think word has spread about your ways?"

"Take that back or I'm locking you out of Never Land."

"Good luck. I have my own key." She giggled. "Seriously, you have to admit it's unbelievable what you do to females. He's probably nervous." She laughed and added, "So what's the deal with the game?"

"Andrew Rawley's coming with us."

"I'm sure Matt knows you're taking me, and put us on the opposite side of the stadium."

"He does, and he did."

There was an awkward pause before she said, "I spoke to Lisa. She's going to meet us after in St. Pete."

"Lisa Lively? Our Lisa?"

"My Lisa. Do not start your shit, you freak." She paused. "My merch is calling. I'll call you back."

"Okay."

Click.

Three hours later, I met my family at the Greeks in North Tampa. Marie cooled off on her ban of all the bars and restaurants that I had shared a magical moment at with Wendy. That was quite possibly because we quickly ran out of other options; but anyway, the good news was that by October everyone had acclimated nicely to the Tampa area and was happy. I believe this would have been a perfect fit for everyone, if the storm clouds weren't viciously swirling.

By this point, even on a good day, this thing with Wendy radiated drama. Case in point was the "Take the Beach" weekend. Overall it went off smoothly, although there were moments that had Marie (and others) realizing the obvious, and refusing to block it out. She abruptly interrupted another conversation about it at dinner to make her point.

"Oh, Larry, stop. You two were on your best behavior and were still ridiculous. The girl started the weekend by running around the rest of your group to stand right up against you for that team picture. I threw up in my mouth. And the fact that she does it in front of me and Jessie, literally glowing, proves she's so far gone she can't even help herself. You do realize that's why Jessie pulled her aside and cursed her out. Even The Wizard couldn't look away."

I attempted to change the subject. "So are we going to EPCOT this weekend or not?"

"Really? You don't want to discuss the next night when Jessie went to the bathroom and she ran to you at the bar? I watched the entire thing through the window. Every head turned counting down the seconds before she was by your side. And she didn't disappoint."

I winced. "I didn't even see her."

"Sure, you did. You smiled wide after you leaned in and whispered in her ear as she lit up. You're both sick." She paused, and as I squirmed she added, "That's when Matt left. It was clear then he'd seen that show in reruns. It's no wonder he made other plans the entire time."

"Okay," I said reaching for my flag, the one you wave in the air to surrender.

"I can only imagine what you two look like alone. It makes me ill to think about it."

"Okay..." my eyes grew wide, "I get it."

She peered at me. "But neither one of you can stop it."

Marie was right.

The next day Wendy and I gleefully rolled into St. Pete for a Ray's playoff game against the Texas Rangers. We looked like two kids strolling up to the Trop escorted by our chaperone, Andrew Rawely. Although he was one of my closer friends from the early days, many had joked that he was the only person left who would've gone with us.

Anyway, after we had a grand old time at the game drinking our asses off, we met her friend, Lisa Lively, for dinner. And herein lies the next problem. Wendy and I had again exceeded our allotted time limit to be with each other the week before and were now doing something that was taboo. We let the afternoon party bleed into the night, and bled it did.

It was only natural that Andrew joined the committee that deemed it necessary to naturally comment on our dark devotion. He had a few curious smiles throughout the day and as the alcohol continued to flow, he uttered his first words on that subject before dinner.

We were standing at an outdoor table waiting for them to set it up when Wendy strolled off to make a call. He first discretely insinuated that she must have an entirely separate group of friends that had never met me. I uncomfortably confirmed they did. But I knew it wouldn't end there after I noticed his inquisitive grin.

When Wendy walked off to the bathroom, Andrew leaned in to me, swaying a bit intoxicated. "It's a unique chemistry." He made a gesture toward her strolling on and sported a silly smile. "You two together are certainly a show."

Glancing back at him I felt I had to have some fun. "Why, today wasn't too bad?"

"Noooo." He slurred sarcastically in a high-pitch tone and then lowered his voice. "But now I know why Matt sat on the other side of the stadium."

"Okay, don't repeat that," I said staring out at the beautiful harbor.

He laughed. "It's all good. But I have to ask one thing."

"You've already exceeded your limit."

He sputtered, "No—no...seriously, how has she been reporting to Schultz?"

"She doesn't."

As he chuckled uncontrollably, Lisa came over to inform us the table was ready.

I texted Wendy: "Make sure you don't sit next to me."

She texted back: "Why?"

"Just don't."

Two minutes later, she came back and peered at us from across the table. "Whaa?" she said as she sat down.

"I missed you," I mouthed.

Andrew caught it and then crumbled to the side and fell into his chair.

She texted me: "Whaa is going on?"

"Nothing. Andrew's fucked up."

"I am too," she texted back.

It was during the dinner, as the wine continued to flow, that we texted each other like two teens in heat. Lost in our own little world again, the sexual tension was on the verge of actually being painful. Obviously, by this moment in the story, it was more than anything just physical, which made it all even worse.

Halfway through dinner her head rose to me with a different look. Her smile disappeared from her face, but not from her eyes. She gave me her little head nod, (which I loved) to check my BlackBerry. I pulled it off the table and put it on my lap to read her text: "I can't keep denying my feelings for you. I'll do whatever you want. I can't take it anymore."

I glanced over at her and her eyes were ablaze.

She had used almost those same exact words a year before while following it up with: "Don't look at me like that. You feel the same way I do and you know it's true."

I fell back in the chair. My gaze shifted away as the message from Molly at that bar hit me dead on. To add insult to injury, the moon was high over the glistening water and the romantic atmosphere fueled the flames. Her eyes had such a light and were wide open to her soul as she sat there staring into mine. She looked so happy as she then texted me glowing: "I told you I can't do back to backs with you anymore. This is your fault!"

It was unfortunate enough that we got into this predicament and I didn't expect anyone to have sympathy for us, but I didn't think this conversation would be documented and included in this investigation, along with a picture.

After dinner we went barhopping. Andrew was now thoroughly fascinated and had his camera out as the flash from it was constant. Interestingly, the pictures of us jumping in the air together in an alley next to one of the bars didn't make it into Mr. Lyin's highlight reel, but one of Lisa, Wendy, and I on a couch at a club did.

My gaze met Wendy's after exiting the club. The night was over but for the first time in the fifteen hours we'd been together, her eyes displayed sorrow, almost pain. I turned away uneasily as she then walked up next to me.

"Are you okay?"

Wendy hesitated for an instant before nodding, "Yes, I'm fine. Why?"

"Because your eyes are saying you're not."

We walked on to Andrew's car in silence.

CHAPTER THIRTY - NINE

MR. LYIN'S SO CALLED INVESTIGATION

MID - OCTOBER 2010
THE FIRST MEETING

It was the next day, actually only hours later, when I woke up moving gingerly out of the bedroom and halfway through the family room before the entire room began spinning. I toppled to the couch and took a deep breath and blew it out as I pushed myself up at the same time. Andrew sluggishly came down the stairs heading out.

His bloodshot eyes and shit-eating grin said it all as we shuffled over to the front door together. Exchanging nods he passed through the doorway muttering softly, "What a show; thanks for the invite."

I let out gentle laugh—thinking if you only knew—as I closed the door behind him. Suddenly feeling nauseas I threw my hands up on the doorframe and held on tight. How ugly would this be if I blew chunks all over the foyer?

Marie stormed up behind me. "Look at you!"

I shot up straight and blurted back, "I just need water."

"You just need to grow up."

The tension suddenly overrode my nausea as she then barked, "You better not throw up in my foyer."

I winced as her fiery wrath closed in on me.

"So you took her to a playoff game and then to dinner and then out barhopping after your antics with her last week and the week before."

I turned to her. "She's one of my managers." I was still drunk.

Her eyes narrowed with fury. "You're fucking kidding me. First off, she's now under Dan Schultz...which I'm sure is the joke of that office—"

My hands rose to my head in agony. "Marie...please stop."

"Why, the truth hurts? That girl was never your manager because you flew her off on one of your wine induced Never Land trips right after you met her...isn't that what Bud Fox said that night last spring at dinner?"

"He doesn't know!"

"Oh bullshit! Everyone knows about you two."

Not having a clue what to do at this point, I took an obnoxiously deep breath in and moaned it out.

She hissed, "Cut your shit, little boy. You better come back to the real world because I'm done."

"I know. I'm trying."

She added, "Trying, to do what? Score your own reality show?"

I tilted my head up to the ceiling with hands over my eyes and let out another moan before I said, "Marie, please stop. I can't see."

By this point, even in my stupor I realized her indignation was cut and dry as she continued to berate me. I couldn't take it anymore and stumbled forward. "Marie...shit...step to the side...I'm moving!"

She jumped back. "Are you kidding?" She stopped in mid-sentence with her lips slightly parted as I stumbled passed her and into the wall. She then said softly, "I have three children." Her voice rose. "Do you have any idea what time you came home?"

I had no idea as I bounced off the wall and into the kitchen. It was then I threw the refrigerator door open and lunged for a bottle of Evian. "Late," I sputtered. "I'm sorry."

She shook her head at me and as I downed the water, she added, "You're a forty-three-year-old sales director; my husband...not hers, and the father of our two children, who acts like a child."

I interrupted in an attempt to humor her. "The Evian tastes weird...something is wrong...help me..." I stared at her hopelessly and held the bottle up for her to taste.

Her head shot away from me smiling, before she hissed, "Help you?" She paused as her hands went over her face before she added, "I'll kick your little ass into that preserve." Her arm extended pointing to the preserve behind our house before she snapped, "Your taste buds are shot, you freak!"

I grabbed another bottle when the awkward silence was broken by the ding of a text to my BlackBerry.

Marie shouted, "IT'S WENDY!" She went to grab it.

I snatched it off the counter falling back against the refrigerator.

"This is so unfuckingbelieveable," she seethed grabbing it and staring at a blank screen bewildered. "How did you delete it that quickly?" she added in awe as she threw it back to me in the throes of this tete-a-tete.

"Just hold on for a second," I replied as my hands went up in the air as if I was surrendering. "Please. You're making me crazy."

My heart was racing and beads of sweat formed on my forehead as she shouted, "I'm making you crazy?" She froze as the sound of another text came in from her. It was then that she began to sway, standing there, seemingly disoriented. "No one would believe this," she said in a soft tone regaining her composure and adding, "You two are seriously a match made in hell."

Thankfully my BlackBerry rang. Glancing down at it, I noticed The Rabbi's number and staggered outside to our patio to take the call. Collapsing in the chair, the heat of the morning felt like tar coating me. I wiped my sweaty forehead, and as The Rabbi rambled on, I suddenly struggled to breathe as the alcohol drained out of me.

Within the minute, the call concluded, but I remained there with the birds chirping, staring out into the preserve, feeling numb, and not only due to the alcohol drain. Even though I didn't take this complaint filed by Bud Fox seriously, today was the day I was going to inform Marie about it. But because of my day-night double header with Wendy, I didn't.

But let me stop here for a second. The fact that I didn't tell my wife about this investigation because I was now ironically avoiding answering any more questions about Wendy was extraordinarily detrimental to what happens next.

You see, Bud Fox was Marie's personal trainer before he came to work for me. She knew things about him that I never wanted to know; but a critical side-note nevertheless. Simply stated, she would've certainly reached out to Mr. Lyin and insisted that I call Geno Franc as the investigation absurdly advanced without any explanation.

This first meeting with Mr. Lyin took place at the same hotel where our East Coast Wine Show for the 2010 holiday season was taking place that night. As I pulled into the parking lot, I noticed him getting out of his car. He had a serious demeanor and seemed to be the same uptight guy I recalled from the year before.

After a cordial greeting in the lobby we proceeded up to a conference room while avoiding anyone setting up for the wine tasting. As we sat down at a large round table off to the side, Mr. Lyin pulled his notepad out of his briefcase and informed me that Dan Schultz would be dealing with Bud Fox.

"I don't want you to have any communication with Bud Fox. He's technically no longer under you, so this shouldn't be a problem."

As the questioning began, Mr. Lyin informed me he had already spoken to numerous individuals who were all very credible. I thought that was strange, as if he was implying he typically does not. The red flags rose above his head. But it was as he continued, that I found out none of these "very credible" persons were Bud Fox's team members. At this point I was slightly confused, yet still optimistic I would soon be enlightened. But that feeling faded rapidly.

Mr. Lyin had opened the meeting with a vague explanation of this complaint. The premise revolved around what he identified as a fifty-five-minute timeframe in a restaurant that wasn't a company event, where Bud Fox claimed my touching his girlfriend on the lower back was the reason he was excluded from the "Take the Beach" incentive.

This night in question happened over three months prior without any complaint filed.

Aside from Wendy, who was with me at the first restaurant, it was just Fox and I. That said, to kick this party off, Mr. Lyin began with statements from four different people who were not company employees.

He only mentioned two of them, one being Fox's girlfriend, in the final report, while having to do so because no other complaint was actually filed. In other words, he had to bridge the gap of insanity when this suddenly shifted to an investigation about Wendy and I. But before we get into that, Mr. Lyin ran through this night, which caused a rush of stories Fox had concocted in the past to hit me like a rogue wave. The similarities were comical.

As Mr. Lyin carried on, a curious smile spread across my face. But that didn't help me either. I only realized it when Mr. Lyin stopped abruptly while saying sternly, "I need you to take this seriously."

I nodded but couldn't help but to stare back at him with dubiety. I asked him how he can possibly know who these people were or what their motives would be for speaking to him. With his head down, he hastened to explain they were—again—all credible.

"Have any of these people stated this girl is touched or crazy?" I asked in a serious tone.

He shook his head. "No."

"That's interesting. I've only heard she is."

"I haven't heard that."

After a few minutes of setting this up, my head slumped forward as my eyebrow arched astonished. "This was three months ago. Why did they wait three months to file this?"

He flipped a page stating he would inform me of the reason why shortly.

I took a downward peek at my wristwatch thinking this should've already wrapped. As he continued his questioning I couldn't deny the terrible feeling I had about this guy, while thinking it was impossible to not see what Fox was doing. My arrogance turned appalling, which didn't help either, nor did my reaction to his next statement.

"I had to travel out of state to question this individual," he said averting my eyes.

"You traveled to another state, but you haven't had a conversation with Fox's team?"

With a scowl, he continued to read on. It supposedly was Fox's girlfriend's best friend who was there that night that Mr. Lyin flew off to meet.

Miffed, I sat and listened to him thinking I should call down to the tasting for a bottle to be sent up because this quickly became paradoxical.

After interestingly breezing over this "touch" I was warned about, he moved on questioning me about losing my temper on Fox in the restaurant. Mr. Lyin stated this was witnessed by this individual he flew off to meet.

I interrupted. "What is the actual complaint?"

With a darker scowl, he then only answered a question with another question. "Have you lost your temper with him?"

"I've had many heated conversations with Bud Fox. He's been a nightmare that I should've handled a long time ago, but what is this about?"

As he continued on, I interrupted irked, "Excuse me. I thought that I excluded Bud Fox from this weekend because I was nervous that his girlfriend would approach my wife on the trip about an inappropriate touch?" I paused taking a breath and added, "I take that very seriously and have never been accused of such a thing."

He looked up at me. "I never said an inappropriate touch." He flipped back a page in his notes. "You told me that you didn't recall that."

"That is correct, but if I didn't, and Fox didn't, and this person you flew off to meet didn't and not one person in a packed restaurant did, what are we talking about here?"

"Please, let me get through this."

I asked him if this was a sexual harassment case.

"No, it is not," he huffed, as he seemed antsy to move on.

So it was at this moment that I wanted to make myself perfectly clear. "Mr. Lyin, Bud Fox missed this incentive because he blew off three different deadlines to turn in his pictures. He failed miserably at his job and has abused his people and—"

"This is about one incentive, the 'Take the Beach' incentive."

I nodded and then continued. "He went against my wishes on this one incentive and got my administrative assistant involved in his shortcomings, which he had also done numerous times before. He left his territory, lied about it, and cursed his people out."

He held up his hand. "I have not received any complaints about that."

"They call me...everyday. That is why I need you to call them."

"Why didn't they file a complaint?"

"Because I protected him!"

"You are not permitted to do that."

"I now realize the mistakes I made with this individual. I wanted to fix him. He was my friend and I really thought I could get through to him. I was wrong. But his people have been crying out for a year. I had one girl quit the company because of him and I can't allow this to continue."

"Let me remind you, you are not to have any communication with Bud Fox."

This is something else that Fox knew would happen once he filed any type of complaint. Exasperated I said, "Don't you see what he is doing? He even told his people that. You need to speak to them."

"I will. But Lori Erstatz (Mama Bear) and others have stated something different."

"Hold on. My administrative assistant?" I snapped baffled.

"Yes."

"She had nothing to do with this night in question or his people's complaints." My hands rose to my head slowly interrupting the awkward moment of silence. "So you now know she was upset trying to enter Fox's pictures to beat the last deadline."

"No, she did not state that."

My elbows fell on the table as my hands went back to my head.

He looked over at me and then read another page from his notes. "Bud stated he confronted you about touching his girlfriend."

"Confronted me? No, that is not true."

"He said he did."

After a vexing moment I muttered, "He never confronted me. It was the very next day when Fox took me back to my car that he casually said anything about this and he never brought it up again. He knows I don't do that." I took a deep breath. "But I still asked to speak to his girlfriend personally."

"And what happened?"

"Fox told me she was sleeping. He then said she would call me later that afternoon. She never called me and he never brought it up again. That is the true story."

"Why didn't you bring it back up to him?"

"I do not grab ass and have never been accused of such nonsense, and Fox knows that."

He wrote nothing down and had no response. He only checked his notes before moving on. "Would you say that you intimidate people?"

"Intimidate people?"

"Yes, that is the reason they never filed a complaint back then. They were scared."

My angered gaze hit him. "You are being played by a pathetic person who does nothing but lie."

He fell back with wide eyes. "I will remind you not to go near or talk to Bud Fox."

My temper flared up. I crossed my hands suddenly irritable.

"Many people stated you are often intense when the team falls behind in programs?"

I blinked in disbelief. "Is this a joke?"

"No, and again, I need you to take this seriously."

"My intensity comes from being passionate about what I do."

"So not deliberately, but you are."

A sigh was my answer.

"Did a member of your team go on this incentive who didn't qualify for it?" He verified his name, "Chris Masters?"

I turned the corners of my mouth down. "This is nuts." Then I said, "No. Chris Masters is a solid manager who communicated with me while working diligently to achieve this incentive unlike Fox. I kept him out of it because he only lied, abused his people, and got my administrative assistant involved against my wishes."

He read from his notepad. "She had no problem helping him."

I leaned forward. "He uses her all the time and she had tears in her eyes when I walked back in the office. That's why I asked you before if she mentioned it. She also referred to his girlfriend as crazy, CRAZY numerous times."

He shook his head slowly and said, "She has not said anything like that to me."

I blew out a deep breath. "This all started when I noticed how upset she was because she was racing to finish his job against my wishes."

"She was only upset because of how intense you were. She was scared too."

My eyes closed. "Wow, did she tell you that?" He had no response as I added, "I explained to her very calmly weeks before that Fox was leaning on her in ways no one else did. He used her. He had done it all year. He knew she found him attractive and would help him, and I warned her it was making it worse. She said she understood but then continued to help him."

He checked his notes seemingly to confirm what she had said, as I continued. "I don't understand how you have traveled to faraway lands to speak to individuals who are not even company employees, but refuse to speak to his team who all warned me this would happen and why. If you don't want to talk to them, at least check his texts to me. Then, you will clearly see the truth to all of this."

His head rose and he said, "I am. But Bud Fox wants nothing to do with you."

I let out a gentle laugh. "Mr. Lyin, with all due respect, you have no idea what you're saying. Please check this guy's texts to me. And buckle up, because you will fall over reading them." His eyes grew wide as he stared at me with a look of disdain before I added, "The only thing that matters to Bud Fox is protecting his ass and getting back into my world. And yes, I realize what that sounds like, but again, that is the truth. And I know he stormed out to the parking lot to call his girlfriend the day this complaint was filed after the other disgruntled manager under me convinced him to file a complaint against me."

His eyebrow rose as he sputtered, "How?"

"I was called with a play by play. Two people close to me watched him the entire time, overheard his girlfriend cursing him out, and then watched him walk up to the executive offices. This all came after a conversation he had with Tony Trappelleti in the warehouse. It was there he deliberately lied to him by telling Fox I was going to fire him—"

Mr. Lyin interrupted by changing the subject.

"Is it true that he repeatedly asked you to take them to dinner to make this right?"

I rubbed my eyes. "To make what right? He begged me to have them over so the girlfriend could meet Marie. My wife can't stand him, knows his character flaws, and would never allow it."

It was interesting how rapidly Mr. Lyin moved on after that statement, while changing the course of the investigation. "Was Wendy Darlington with you in a back booth of another restaurant on the day you met Bud Fox and his girlfriend?" He asked as I frowned and rubbed my forehead.

Sitting back I said, "Yes, I stated that earlier."

"You were there for hours while consuming numerous bottles of wine?"

"Yes. Fox texted me to wait because he was running late—"

"When they walked up to you, you two were observed to be looking very much like a couple. Would you agree?"

"Because we're comfortable with each other."

"No, because you looked and acted very much like a couple."

"I guess anyone can say that walking up to two people sitting at a table."

"No. Did she recently get engaged?" He paused, peering at me eerily.

"Yes."

"It has been reported that you two are extremely close."

"We are. I consider her a close friend."

His eyes narrowed at me. "A friend?"

The room heated rapidly. "Yes, and I'm going to ask again, what is this meeting about?"

"Did she ever say that she wasn't going on that "Take the Beach" incentive trip because she was nervous Bud Fox's girlfriend would approach her fiancé about the two of you having an affair?"

I glanced up at the ceiling as my arms crossed. "No."

"You are telling me she never said that to you?"

I leaned slightly over the table. "Correct."

"Did she ever text you that you shouldn't allow him to go because of her concern?"

"I told you Wendy thought she was crazy."

He then informed me that he had proof she did in fact state that and it was confirmed by another conversation which was overheard by a "credible witness." He went on to say that this individual also stated we would "secretly" meet every afternoon for our "Wine Time" ritual. I shook my head. He repeated himself.

"Do you secretly meet her?"

"No. We enjoy each other's company, and that is not a secret."

He seemed increasingly irritated and asked if I gave her preferential treatment.

I said emphatically, "There is no manager under me that I'm tougher on than her. The only person in my division that had received preferential treatment was Bud Fox. That is why I could no longer allow it to continue. I blamed myself for letting this individual take advantage of my program, which is the best in the state."

"That is not being disputed. Please, focus on what is."

I paused briefly before adding, "I allowed this to happen thinking I could fix him. I am guilty of allowing my ego to interfere with the fact this individual is not capable of doing the job."

He took what felt like a minute to write on multiple pages before looking up at me seemingly frustrated. He then informed me that aside from my business success, which was not being questioned, what I was telling him was the exact opposite of what the credible witnesses had stated about Wendy and I.

"Would you say that Wendy has been known to lie about how close the two of you are?"

"Is this about Fox missing an incentive or Wendy Darlington, because I'm confused?"

He pressed on. "She has often downplayed how close the two of you are while also informing members of your team, her colleagues, that she was meeting her fiancé when in fact she met you."

"I'm not sure how someone would be able to comment on that."

He sat up straight. "On two occasions you told Bud Fox she was with you not knowing she had told the team she was meeting her fiancé. Bud Fox has stated that for months this has infuriated you..." he paused as his gaze met mine and added, "but Wendy continues to do it."

I blew out a breath of frustration.

"You have also been spotted, looking very much like a couple, in and around Tampa. You are a Sales Director of two of the largest cities in the state, and one who I have never seen so many people take such an interest in keeping tabs on. Believe me when I tell you, everyone is watching you and who you are with." I adjusted myself in the chair uncomfortably as he continued. "Were you recently at a lunch meeting with your managers when one of them let Wendy sit next to you?"

I cringed. "Excuse me?"

He looked down and flipped a page to his notepad and read from it. "She refused to sit in the only chair left when another manager of yours, who was sitting next to you, moved so she could sit next to you. She smiled and sat down and everyone laughed. Do you recall that?"

Increasingly unsettled I said, "No, but how does this pertain to this complaint?"

He wrote for a few seconds before looking back up at me. "It has been stated by numerous members of your team that she seemed very distant at a recent meeting with a supplier until you walked in."

"How would I know what she looked like before I walked in?"

He only read on. "Three members of your team said you stole the show, their words, with a humorous line that had nothing to do with the meeting. They also stated her mood brightened noticeably when you entered the room and that she was actually beaming after your one-liner."

"Someone used the word beaming...please pinch me—"

"I need you to take this seriously. Shortly after you left she informed the group she again had to meet her fiancé for a wedding appointment, but met you. This was confirmed by another manager in your division, who is currently under Dan Schultz. He witnessed both of your cars at a bar in Tampa."

I took a quick breath. "We have many meetings and I do like to pop in on the ones I don't run. And yes, it's possible she met me after she met her fiancé for their wedding appointment."

"The individual who spotted you on this day saw both of your cars thirty minutes after she left the meeting and then spotted you again hours later, still consuming wine." He flipped his page. "You two were on the bar's patio looking very much like a couple when he drove back by."

"And you don't think that is totally nuts and someone clearly with ulterior motives?"

"Lori has also stated this happens all the time."

I blinked and shook my head. "Do you check the people you question, because this is crazy?" I leaned in and said, "You should know now she is extremely envious of Wendy."

"Do you think that also might have something to do with you?"

"No."

He cleared his throat. "A conversation between you and Wendy Darlington was overheard, where you were extremely upset with her because she attempted to cover up how close you are when she met your wife."

"She met my wife months ago. How does this come up now?"

"Answer the question."

"Extremely upset? No."

His stare pierced through me. He placed his pen down. "Please understand I will have no problem taking out someone with bravado."

I fell back in the chair. First I couldn't believe anyone still used the word bravado, and then that a lead investigator would have sent that message in closing. I sat there for a moment in shock as he got up. He put his notepad away, and walked to the elevator. We rode down together, and when the door opened on my hotel room's floor, he said rather casually, "I'll be in touch."

CHAPTER FORTY

YES, I STILL CALL THEM MERMAIDS

MID-OCTOBER 2010
THE WINE TASTING THAT NIGHT

I called Schultz. He came up to my room with a couple of bottles of wine that were already opened from the tasting. He proceeded to pour two tall glasses.

I looked him in the eye and snapped, "The company is using Bud Fox."

He was speechless.

I stood at the window watching the sun fade fast on the horizon. My thoughts were racing back through it all. I pulled the curtain back. "Lyin knows his complaint is ridiculous. His people told me that Fox called them and told them The Wizard made him file this complaint against me. This isn't about Fox."

The look on Schultz's face was of utter shock. I walked back to him. He handed me the glass of wine and I took a long sip before continuing. "Lyin is gathering information about Wendy and I."

He dropped to the edge of the bed, letting out a sigh. I explained everything to him, including Mr. Lyin's closing line. Thirty minutes later, I could tell he was deep in thought. Schultz brought up a night after a meeting in the office.

"Your connection with her was obvious to me back in December," he said.

I took a much longer sip.

He gazed at me with an odd smile. "Knowing her, I was shocked." He took a breath and continued, "A few of us were in your office when she ran in to see you. It was the way you looked at each other. You didn't flinch, though. You thought her reaction to you was normal."

With a sigh, I rubbed my eyes, and then threw back what was left in my glass.

His eyes grew wide. "Everyone took notice. Do you remember Tony stealing your line?"

"Which one?"

"The eyes never lie. I agreed, but also realized why so many people were talking."

I sat down and then stood back up.

Schultz continued, "Do you remember the night we met at the Stonewood bar months after that? She strolled in with her fiancé and grandparents after spending the day with you."

I sat back down.

"The eyes never lie. Larry, it's true. They don't."

He filled his glass and turned to me. "You have to distance yourself from her…it's that obvious…"

I stared off at the wall. I wanted to say so much, but I couldn't. My blood began to boil. This was so out of control that I began to ramble. "She loves her fiancé…and I'm fixing my marriage…I'm fixing everything. It's all going to be fine." I forced myself into a defensive posture.

Schultz was speechless for an instant as he lifted his wine glass to his lips in awe. The awkward moment of silence was broken by a deep sigh. "Larry, that might be the case…but it doesn't appear to be…to anyone. This isn't something you can just fix with a charismatic speech or an entertaining email. Did you ever think you've been playing by a different set of rules than the rest of us because of the success you've had, the promotions? You've had quite a ride."

I glanced at the last seconds of the sunrise. "My program is a success. I refuse to have this affect us…and we will continue to win."

"I don't think anyone doubts that part."

"Well, Lyin knows Fox's complaint is totally absurd—"

Schultz interrupted. "But it's what you stated, with concern that has me worried."

I hid my emotions. "But that's not the complaint," I barked. I took a deep breath to calm down and added, "I'm sure Lyin will call me tomorrow to wrap this bullshit up."

Just then, I read an email on my BlackBerry. The Rabbi praised me on another program. I embraced this latest "success" and used it to override it all; including the fact I was devastated by the one guy I helped the most. I blocked out everything Schultz said because it truly scared the shit out of me. I had to. I was nervous.

I turned back to him. "What burns me the most is that I protected Fox from every single sales rep under him wanting to file a complaint against him." I lunged for the bottle and erratically topped my glass off and took a sip.

The alcohol would become a worst case scenario as the night unfolded. Schultz only chimed in to support, but I could tell he was taken aback. He then shared a story about himself while revisiting his dire concern; this relationship with Wendy.

I walked into the bathroom.

Cautious and circumspect, Schultz was a perfect foil to my occasionally impetuous temperament. He grabbed the wine bottle and said, "Listen, you don't have to go to this tasting tonight. I'll take care of everything. Why don't you just relax…lay low."

I threw back the rest of my glass. "No, I'm going," I said as I placed it down on the bathroom counter. I splashed some water on my face and stared at myself as The Darkness appeared in the mirror, hissing, "Fuck these people, sport. Normal rules don't apply to you. Your boss just boasted about you again. Go down there and let loose. You deserve it!"

Ten minutes later we were at the tasting and I was immediately hit with a glass of some special wine maker's reserve that I downed, having no clue who was acting as if they were my best friend. I continued on as it seemed everyone in the room patted me on the back, as if I was a superhero. That didn't help either. Before I made it halfway around, I envisioned my cape flowing behind me. As the event wound down, my eyes connected with an attractive brunette. And she noticed my cape. And well, made the perfect Mermaid for the evening. The Darkness celebrated. She was a winery supplier who I recognized but didn't know. As the party moved outside to the tiki bar, she swam out. Schultz attempted to reel me in. But I couldn't hear him scream my name.

The Darkness howled with delight.

I wandered to the other side of the tiki bar when I noticed The Wizard. He was standing off to the side alone, so I went over to voice my displeasure with today's proceedings. I could tell he wanted nothing to do with this conversation, his eyes were shifty. Within two minutes he held up his hand and said, "I knew I would need a drink for this. Hold on, I'll be right back."

He came back and passed me and then turned around and said, "Just lie!"

I stared at him, "What?" I said in bewilderment.

He repeated himself, "Just lie." He took a step back looking over his shoulder.

I was at such a loss for words; I had no idea how to even continue. I didn't. He took another step back as if sending me a message: this conversation was over.

Stunned, I heaved a conflicted sigh and strolled away. Paranoia set in. Was he attempting to set me up? I couldn't put into words how disturbing this was. I never mentioned a word about this conversation to Mr. Lyin. I thought I had to have The Wizard's back. I also thought this would be over in days.

I had both wrong.

Minutes later I was handed a shot. I threw it back and he yelled, "So...Laaaa when's the next promotion?" over Eminen's "Love the Way You Lie."

I shrugged and quickly moved on.

I then followed the wooden walkway that went down to the beach and responded to three texts. As I finished I stood there realizing this was the same sand I sat on when my career with this company had begun. I laughed recalling Jen the Mermaid—I meant a wine taster named Jen—hopping on my back as we made a dramatic exit from the officer's club tasting event eleven years before. The vision of us sitting just up the beach from where I was standing, suddenly shifted my thoughts to Wendy. And then to Mr. Lyin's questioning, which left me in need of another glass of wine.

I walked over for that glass as Kesha's "Your Love Is My Drug" blared out of the tiki bar speakers. As the salt air breezed over the dune, I heard my name and turned to see Jen Bogel. She was one of Andrew Rawely's new recruits. We smiled at each other. It then dawned on me there were as many new faces as old when she came over to say hello. Within a minute of small talk I noticed The Wizard peering on from the shadows while being interrupted by another slap on the back. The conversations began to blur as I inched up in the line to the bar. Just seconds after that a female's voice whispered salty words in my left ear; at the same time The Darkness sneered in my right. "She's been watching you since you gavotted around the tasting room. She fucking loved it...she'll get your mind off Wendy for the evening."

My eyes glanced to down and to my right into the sultry eyes of the brunette. She had that look in her eyes and I was in desperate need of a brief diversion to it all. We exchanged smiles as her statement fueled my ego. But it didn't end there. Swept up in the moment, and drunk enough to think nothing of this, I strolled off to a side table with her to have some fun.

Stand back, idiot's delight coming through!

Although this was nothing but shits and giggles, every eye was glued on us, thinking I was going to bend her over behind the sea grapes. Thirty minutes later, amidst more laughter and lust, we moved over to the pool. Schultz was about to go into cardiac arrest.

Twenty minutes later I was coming out of the bathroom when another voice whispered, "I heard about the (CWUS) dinner in Ft. Lauderdale." I turned and saw an old colleague. After some small talk he said, "I heard there was some drama at that dinner. Johnny Promise (my old boss) was there...right?"

"Yes, Promise was there, but no drama that I was aware of."

He put his arm around me, reeking of cigarette smoke. "So if this girl, tonight, screams out that she's going to end up in your bed," he sneered, "you won't think that's drama either?"

The room began to spin.

He backed up and pointed at me. "I heard it was an instant classic. I love you, dude!"

I suddenly remembered why I never liked this guy.

He took a few strides and turned. "Oh and...congrats on the

promotion."

I nodded.

I stumbled back outside. I was holding my BlackBerry and it rang. It was another old colleague who was watching me from the walkway above the tiki bar. With a feeling of vultures circling, I answered, "It's been a long time—"

"Turn around. I'm up on the walkway."

I turned, and he was waving like a child.

"Watch that beer. You're spilling it on the poor people below you," I replied.

"This shit brings me back to that tasting six or seven years ago." My eyes closed in disbelief as he continued, "Everyone was wasted and that little taster screamed out that she'd only do tastings for you in front of the competition that was paying her. Do you remember...she was wearing your jacket with the sleeves rolled up?"

Schultz's plea to stay in the fucking room was now flashing in front of me. I walked away from the speaker. "Yup...that was a mess. How have you been?"

"Good man, hey listen, the real reason I'm calling is to give you a heads up. The Wizard just asked Steve Tucher (an area manager) about your new Mermaid." He paused and added, "I still remember you calling them Mermaids...I'm sure you probably still do—"

"No, that was a long time ago. Fucking Mermaid, come on; I'm a forty-three-year-old Sales Director. I don't do that anymore." I hesitated, turned to him, and smiled. "Just kidding. Of course, I do. Hey, thanks for the heads up."

"Sure, Larry. Let's catch up. I miss hanging out. Oh, and congrats on the last promotion...I can't keep up. Just remember me when you're running the place."

I blew out a frustrated breath. "Thanks again."

Click.

Thirty minutes later, my world began to spin, badly. It was then my name was screamed out, again. I stumbled to a stop and twisted to the side, blinking into focus my old friend and manager, best known as The Cowboy. We were both wasted. He waved a cocktail at me, and spilled the shit all over the pool deck. "I need a bed, Cowboy," I slurred, as we both stumbled to the elevator with small talk. Minutes after that I collapsed on the bed, alone. Not that anyone believed that either, but it was the truth. Six hours later the sun was blazing through the window I had left the curtains open to. My eyes fluttered open. I woke up wishing I hadn't. My BlackBerry had a text from Wendy and Schultz. I called him first.

He answered, "How are you feeling, dear?"

"Fucked. What's the damage?" I moaned in a raspy voice.

"Well…no one could look away, especially The Wizard."

"Was it that bad?"

He answered after a long moment of silence. "Who is she?"

I lunged for my Evian and replied, "A supplier. That was the first time I met her."

"You didn't know her?"

I fell off the bed attempting to put the Evian back on the nightstand. "No."

"This was the reason I wanted you to stay in the room."

"I know. I was an idiot and angry and drunk and now hungover. I'll call you back."

Click

I went to take a shower when Wendy left a frantic message: "Chris Lyin wants to meet with me. What is going on? I need to talk to you!" She now knew she was going to be questioned about our closeness.

I called her back. She answered on the second ring.

"What is going on with Fox's complaint?"

"I don't know, but don't worry. I'm going to call The Rabbi and let him know."

"Let him know what? That Bud Fox is in love with you and can't live without you, your admin is totally nuts and wants me dead, and then you're going to attempt to explain us?"

"Wendy, calm down. I'm hung the fuck over and nauseous."

"How could you get wasted while being investigated?" She paused and gasped. "Oh my God. Please tell me there was no female."

I collapsed back on the bed as the room spun viciously.

Her voice rose and turned scary. "I can hear you breathing. What happened?!"

"I think I'm having a heart attack, because you're scaring me."

"You are not having a heart attack, you fucking freak. What the hell happened?"

"Shush, it's all coming back to me. The girl whispered some stuff in my ear. I was waiting for wine. I was in a fragile state because of the questioning about us."

"What questioning about us? Are you still drunk?"

"Yes."

She heaved a deeper sigh. "I cannot be questioned about...us...with my wedding five months away —"

Unable to handle her haranguing I cut her off. "NO! No...no, listen don't worry, but I have to hurl and I'll call you back...I'm fixing everything. It's all fine."

Click.

CHAPTER FORTY - ONE

MAMA'S MADDENING CALL

LATE OCTOBER 2010
NEW TAMPA LITTLE LEAGUE FIELDS

One week later, I was sitting on the edge of the couch against the window in our family room scrolling through my emails, when our daughter, Lauren, walked by.

"Hey daddy-o!" she said, as I glanced up and smiled proudly.

As I watched her cross the room, my gaze caught Marie. She was sitting on the couch across from me and looked radiant in the soft sunlight seeping through the palms in the preserve. She was watching Jersey Shore, a reality show, and laughing out loud at Snookie, one of the characters.

Seconds later, I was interrupted by Lauren's shout. "Mom, I need the other book for my assignment. Where is it?"

Just then, for the first time in too long, I caught myself admiring my wife's beauty. I was excited and full of trepidation at the same time. There was no doubt I was fighting the emotional ties that bound me to Wendy. I was desperate for any relief to it, but I knew I would have to first explain the investigation. I took deep breath. For just an instant I saw a flash of Marie's old smile, and sat up. But then her expression changed instantly. She took a quick double take at me after noticing the bottle of Evian in my hand.

"No wine again?" Her stare burned into me.

"No, I'm cutting back." Apparently, I was shooting her my lusty puppy dog glare. She got up to help Lauren, and turned back to me. Her hands shot to her waist.

"If you think that pathetic stare is going to get you anywhere near that box..." Her eyes rolled downward. "Think again."

"No, no...well...hold on...I really want to talk to you..."

Her hand that was holding the remote turned red, as she said, "Whack off, little boy...whack off!"

I whined, "Sex is the one thing we do well together. We can start there and—" I paused as her eyes almost popped out of her head, and tried again. "No, seriously. I wanted to talk...and did you know Italian males can get cancer if they don't have a release—" It was then the remote came at me, rather recklessly, and with intent to injure. After snatching it out of the air, inches from my head, I placed it on the coffee table as she continued on. Feeling a bit jittery, I went back to my emails...moaning. Within minutes she walked out to the patio.

It was then I had the brilliant idea to send her one of my MS's. I picked a good one and fired it off. I inched up and twisted to peek out the window at her. She picked up her iPhone and stared at it. She took a deep breath and then began talking to herself. I inched to the edge of the couch. It appeared she was typing her reply. Within seconds that was confirmed when her text hit my BlackBerry: "GROW UP! High school boys send these to their girlfriends, you freak of nature!"

I fell back on the couch and began to pout. A minute later I went to get more water, contemplating switching to wine, when I noticed her staring at her iPhone. I snuck up to the door and noticed she was staring at my MS, talking to herself, again. Seconds after that I was back on the couch and received another text: "Come out and talk to me and maybe you'll get lucky, little boy!"

Shit it worked. I jumped up and raced out.

She was glowing, like the old days. I made her laugh, she told me my dick had shrunk, I got her some wine, she again told me my dick had shrunk, as if I hadn't heard her, and pouted the first time; she laughed even harder, hysterically actually, the fucking birds were chirping, and lust was in the air. Then Wendy texted and the record skipped. I reread the text, "Can you talk?" in disbelief.

"I can't fucking believe this." I said softly.

"I can," Marie replied.

My head slowly tilted up at her. I didn't mean to say that out loud. She stood up, and smiled facetiously. "Work—work—work!"

Which for some reason was her jerk off word.

"Please don't do that—" I pleaded as she took a step forward.

"And if I find out you send Wendy your freak of nature shots I will hurt you."

My arms crossed as I huffed. "How sick do you think I am?!"

She breathed slowly and deeply through her nose like a bull about to charge.

I put up my hands. "Can I say something?"

"NO! ...What?" she muttered bracing herself.

"They are not called freak of nature shots...they are mirror shots. MS's! Please stay current."

"Is that what Wendy calls them?" Her voice rose to a scream, "You sick...FREAK OF NATURE!"

With my hands over my ears she looked away masking her smile before taking a deep breath and blowing it out. She twitched and turned back to me with her hands over her face under her spooky death stare.

My arms crossed as I said softly, "Please leave me alone; you're scaring me."

"Scaring you?" She turned away again, now giddy, before turning back while pretending to hiss, "Just understand I will hurt you!"

"I'm a lover, not a fighter, Marie...think happy thoughts—"

Bang.

The door slammed shut and she screamed something really bad, walking on.

Sadly, I actually viewed this as a small victory because at least she was humored. Unfortunately, it was only another missed opportunity to explain the investigation, aside from everything else.

I then texted Wendy back that I couldn't talk when Chris Lyin emailed me. My sorry plight worsened. I gazed out into the preserve contemplating the latest development in the investigation having solely to do with Wendy.

In short, even though all of the questioning in my second meeting with Mr. Lyin revolved around her, she had been expeditiously excluded from the investigation after her one interview, due to her amorous disposition. Regardless of her feelings for me, this was totally absurd. It was also clear he was much more comfortable manipulating the wicked world of our star-crossed love story than uttering another word about Bud Fox or his foiled trip to the beach.

Strangely, as if the rest of this wasn't, I was sitting at my desk the next day looking for a folder when I pulled open a drawer to find a picture of Wendy and I from her birthday. It was one I never hung on the board. I simply couldn't. It summed up that night all too well.

A night, which was a turning point in the story, and one that was about to play into the investigation as the snapshot of us looking oh-so lovey-dovey had me fighting for a breath.

My mind wandered through so much at that instant, like the fact that we looked like this, nearly a year before. My elbows hit the desk as my hands rose to my head when an email flashed up. My eyes rolled over to it. It was a date and time for my third meeting with Mr. Lyin. It was then that this increasing paranoia set in. I actually visualized someone deliberately placing the picture there. I typically didn't have thoughts like this. I sat back up increasingly piqued. The fact that everything I had put in place to fuel our success was now being affected, rasped my nerves.

I allowed these people into my world. They all had the time of their careers, and then had the audacity to take a dump and leave without flushing. They polluted my sacred land with their bullshit.

My anxiety turned to anger.

I snatched the picture up. Within seconds, Mama slammed her desk drawer as if she knew I was staring at it. I went to tear it up but couldn't because we looked so damn adorable. But then the Mama Bear growled and I ripped it into tiny pieces.

Ironically, just then, I received two texts from Wendy: "I'm wearing the stripes."

The damn shirt she wore when she felt the need to taunt me.

"Can you meet me?"

I fell back in my chair and then noticed I missed a text from her earlier. It was all too much as I then began giggling deliriously.

With my hands on my head leaning over the shredded mess, it worsened. Attempting to regain my composure I sent her back a rare, humorless response to express my displeasure with her taunting me: "Where and when?"

She immediately read into my cold reply and called on the office line.

After the first ring, Mama Bear growled again with that indescribable scary grunt noise she had been making whenever Wendy called. I gasped for air and lunged for the phone. "Hey," I said softly.

"I can't deal with you being EMO (emotional) today, and I'm pulling through a Starbucks so you better not hang up...I have to order."

I completely lost it.

Click.

Every time Wendy would drive through a Starbucks I would hang up and she knew it. It actually became a running joke.

She called me back laughing and screaming. "I told you not to do that today—"

I interrupted. "Do you remember that picture of us," I said in a low serious tone, "the one I couldn't hang from your birthday?"

"Do not ruin my good mood!"

Mama Bear made an even louder and scarier growl/grunt noise, this time coming from the core of her belly.

My eyes shot open, wide.

Like a little boy flirting too loud in class, I whispered, "Let me text you; I can't talk."

Humored, she didn't hear me, and shouted, "I texted you earlier and you never responded, and then that?"

I glanced at our torn up picture before I read her morning message: "I worked out early because of WW (Wine Wednesday)."

I began chuckling uncontrollably. After regaining my composure I informed her that Mama Bear made the sound.

"How is that explainable?" she asked. "Have you told that weirdo Lyin about it?"

"No, I haven't, because it's about as explainable as we are. Where are we meeting?"

"You're ruining my good mood." She stopped suddenly. And as my eyes slowly closed, she added, "It's a beautiful day. Let's sit on our patio."

I took a deep breath and softly said, "Old or new?"

Right after those words came out of my mouth, the office door slammed shut.

"Old...and what the hell is wrong with you?"

I didn't respond because I was busy peeking out of my office.

"HELLO? STOP POUTING, OLD!" Wendy yelled.

I pulled the BlackBerry back up. "Calm down, woman. You know I can't multitask. Mama just stormed out (it was at this point of the story I would often only refer to Mama Bear as Mama)."

"She's your Mama, not mine," she replied. "And stop making her laugh on your emails. Why do you still copy her in? Schultz hates it when you chime in at all, never mind include her."

"Well, I can't stand it when you deliberately wear your stripes. You know I'm like a sixteen-year-old Italian boy."

"You love it; stop pouting. Let's go to our old GrillSmith, and hurry up."

I collapsed in my chair thinking of how many times we took refuge in that place, away from the resentment and hostility of our dark devotion. I began chuckling, again. "See you in twenty."

Click.

Two days later, I was heading to the New Tampa Little League fields to watch Jerry's practice when I received a frantic, yet cryptic call from Mama Bear. I pulled into a spot, hopped out of my navi, and waved at my son so he knew I was there. Marie dropped him off to take Lauren to her volleyball game. Right after Jerry smiled and waved back, Mama Bear informed me she received a call from a blocked number with a threatening message for her to start telling the truth in the investigation. I stood there in disbelief, grotesquely uncomfortable.

It was a Friday, just after five o'clock, and my fuse was shorter than normal. She chafed my nerves so badly, that I had to walk over to the next field fiery, listening to her rant. The supposed urgency was because she was convinced the call came from Fox's girlfriend. Confused, I asked her if she was implying she didn't tell the truth during her questioning so far in the investigation. I never received a direct answer. All she was doing was perpetuating the frenzied state she was in because of the girlfriend's instabilities. And it's important to note she still hadn't passed on her adamant view of how crazy she was to Mr. Lyin. As I continued to listen to her, I suddenly doubted everything she said.

After five minutes, I couldn't endure any more of it. Her prattle, about how touched this girl was, seemed so contrived that I had to explain, once again, she was insignificant. She disagreed. I quickly asked her why. She then caught herself and spoke in circles. She seemed to be hiding so much.

"Larry she is crazy," she repeated erratically. "And this message was from someone who wants me to come clean."

"Come clean with what? No other complaint has been filed, and you had nothing to do with the one that was. You weren't even there. I have no idea why this is still an ongoing investigation."

"Larry, there is more than that—"

I cut her off, but I shouldn't have, because if I hadn't lost my cool, she would have said too much. "Lori, if this girl did call you, what can she think you can contribute to this?"

She then rambled on about Wendy, and the fact the girlfriend witnessed us together in the first restaurant. I wanted to question so much that I had heard her push forward in this investigation but knew I couldn't trust her. I fell against the chain link backstop; the disquiet didn't ease. The statements she made were identical to what I was questioned on in the second meeting with Mr. Lyin.

After I hung up, it took me a few minutes to calm down as her role in all of this came sharply into focus. She was the person Wendy had warned me about numerous times before. Restless, I called her. By the fourth ring I didn't think she was going to answer. It was too late. But then she did.

"Hey, Jessie's at the store, but he'll be right back."

I took a deep breath listening to her while shaking my head.

"Is everything all right?"

"No. Listen, she (Mama Bear) has lost it. This investigation is now solely focused on us and there are things that I never planned on telling you, but now have to. I need your help—"

She interrupted excitedly. "My wedding is four-and-a-half months away. I can't deal with this. I can't! And I only told Jessie I was being questioned." She paused as my eyes closed before she babbled, "I can't believe he hasn't even asked about it."

Her words hit me the wrong way as I abruptly snapped. "Wendy, he's not going to ask because he refuses to go there." I had to calm down so I took another deep breath before I continued, "This guy's not stupid."

"I know Larry. He fucking blocks it all out. That's what makes me nervous—"

"He's not going there or he would've already. I'm the one who is fucked—not you!"

Those words would soon come back to haunt me, but at this moment she sighed deeply. "What is that lady (Mama Bear) doing? How is she allowed to play into this when she had nothing to do with any of it? I can't deal."

I turned back to the ball field looking for Jerry, wanting to slam my BlackBerry into the ground. I felt like the wind was knocked out of me and just wanted to hang up when she said, "Larry? I'm sorry…but I can't deal with this…"

Nearly out of breath I sputtered, "You won't have to." I rubbed my eyes. "And don't ask me why, because you can't handle the reason, but I know Lyin won't call you back. I called you now in need of help and I shouldn't have." I paused waiting for her response but she had none. My mind wandered away before my son called my name. "Wendy, I'll call you back. Jerry's walking my way."

"NO!" she snapped viciously before softly saying, "He (Jessie) just pulled in."

Click.

CHAPTER FORTY - TWO

THE STORM CLOUDS START TO SWIRL

NOVEMBER 2010
THE ASYLUM

Nothing tangible had changed in the office, but still the atmosphere was almost completely unrecognizable that Monday. But on that morning, in my mind, I was more concerned with what I thought was a far more pressing issue: a decline in our numbers. That said the idea of even further distancing myself from Mama Bear seemed to be appealing in theory, as a call from Mike Fritton about Wendy's future had the dim light bulb in my head flickering.

As mentioned earlier, Wendy—a Cosmopolitan Wine (CWUS) recruit—was temporarily placed at our distributor to gain experience before eventually going to work for CWUS, just as Matt did in the spring of 2010. The timeframe for this was actually first talked about a couple of months before, as Mike ran a few scenarios by me. For the first time though, during this call, the outline of her remaining in a role close to me was not spoken of, and a departure date to leave me (no pun intended) was now sooner; in early 2011, rather than later that summer.

After I swiftly set aside the notion that news of this investigation, which she now co-starred in, had spread like wildfire up a dried out mountainside doused in gasoline. I couldn't help but become consumed with a delightfully disturbing thought, one that had Mama ecstatic with Wendy's departure, as Wendy then exited the loathsome Asylum with her middle finger waving out her window. She sped away before texting me: "I hate that lady. Where are we celebrating my great escape?"

Furthermore, as my menacing musing persisted, I convinced myself that I now had this clairvoyant power because I had called five of Wendy's texts upon the sound of them hitting my BlackBerry. And just like that I did it again. "That's Wendy," I said softly as my eyes shifted from reading an email to lunging like a child antsy to confirm my new found talent while adding, "Yup, six for six!"

Okay, I just realized it's now best that I get on to my point. You see, up until this moment I hadn't been hit in the head with our communication history, while being knocked the fuck out. This turned out to be a critical turning point in the next meeting with Mr. Lyin because it was truly unimaginable. And as he bundled that data up, I only pondered the mysticism of our unique connection, while pretending it granted me this fictitious power, as I wielded it once again with her next text.

Ding!

"Yup, I feel it, that's her," I said as I finally pulled it in to actually read the last two I hadn't.

Text #1: "HELLO!!! Are we meeting this afternoon???"

Text #2: "I need to know now because J (Jessie) just asked me to work out later and I have to respond U-DING!!"

I then shamefully texted my wife that I had a late meeting so I could race off and meet Wendy as Mama Bear snuck away to drop her duffle bag of defamation off on Mr. Lyin's lap. This was all courtesy of Friday's call as the dark clouds violently swirled over my head. And just minutes later, it was as if a bolt of lightning came out of them, crashing down directly in front of me.

It was during a numbers call with Dan Schultz when he made a couple of off the cuff comments that Wendy still reported to me, while then asking me to pass her goals along to her when I would see her. Suddenly, realizing he wasn't kidding, I sent her a quick text: "Make sure you answer Schultz's calls, U-DING! He's calling you after he hangs up with me."

Just as I hung up with him, she replied: "I will, U-GJA! (You Giant Jackass). But why did he leave me a voicemail that he's riding my market next week? Didn't you tell him you were?"

Thankfully I received a call. Unfortunately it provided little relief to Wendy's. It was Mindy Amour telling me that she wouldn't be able to make the Orlando holiday dinner, as another lightning strike seemed to have crashed down behind me, before yet another did beside me, as Wendy then called in on the office line.

I snatched it up. "Why are you still calling on the office line? You're lucky Mama isn't here."

There was a brief moment of silence before she replied excitably, "Really? This is so ridiculous...that lady should be shot."

I could then tell she was receiving a call as I heard the beep. "Oh God, it's Mike Fritton. Why is he calling me?" I leaned back in my chair, tickled by how hilarious (in a demented way) this was. She casually added, "I'll call him back." She paused before bellowing, "HELLO?"

I was speechless for a moment before I let out a gentle laugh and said, "Yes, Wendy?" That was simply all I could muster as I wiped the sick smile off my face.

She sighed. "You need to call Schultz and tell him you're riding with me next week because he thinks he is."

My head tilted up to the ceiling as I replied, "I think Mike and Dan are. And I wasn't invited."

"NO! Why?"

"Really? Well, where should I begin?" I fell back to my desk.

"Shut up," she snapped. I could tell she was getting another call. She shouted, "Oh my God. Now Schultz is calling me."

I shot up nervously as my chair hit the credenza behind me shaking the fifty bottles of wine I had jammed in it. "When was his voicemail from? You told me you were taking his calls."

With the bottles rattling, she screamed, "I texted I will. I didn't take his last one." My eyes closed again as she added, "We need to talk about this."

I collapsed in the chair. "Wendy, answer his call."
Click.

Not ten seconds later Wendy texted: "I missed his call and I hate it when you don't warn me about this shit. Are we meeting later?"

Incredibly I texted her back: "Yes, of course, ya silly goose!"

An hour later, Mama snuck back in. She didn't say a word though. And as she settled in at her desk, I read another email that I wasn't copied on that she had sent three other Tampa managers. As I glanced at the top of it, I found it interesting that Schultz wasn't copied in either. The email was forwarded to me by two of his managers and one of them wrote: "Mama now thinks she's you. Should I tell her she has the wrong dates for the crew drive? This is hilarious."

I lunged for my BlackBerry while deleting Wendy's reply to my reply, and texted Schultz: "Do you realize Mama is answering your people's emails with the wrong information?"

Two minutes later he texted: "I do and I'm handling it. I'll call you in ten minutes."

I placed the BlackBerry down as both my hands rose to my head. What the hell is this lady doing? I had spoken to her before about this. I rubbed my eyes while getting up from my chair. I shook my head as I marched toward the door to the main part of the office.

As I popped my head through the doorway, she turned to me, and I said sternly, "I am to be copied in on all emails that go out to the team, as are the sales managers." I hesitated before adding, "And all questions are to be sent to the sales managers to answer. It is not your job to answer those questions. Are we clear?"

She just stared at me and nervously nodded.

My expression was impassive but I imagined my hands around her throat shaking her violently so I turned to walk back to my desk.

To my detriment, I kept all of this from The Rabbi. I just felt they were my problems and I should handle them. And that probably was the case, especially for something such as this, but he still needed to be much more in the loop of what I was dealing with, like Friday's call. This was obviously another mistake I made as all he saw was the success, without an inkling to the rest.

And there was more.

Nearly a year before, Mama had repeatedly insisted she do my expenses. At the time, with everything seemingly extraordinary, I considered it, but didn't commit. But then on one hectic afternoon she casually said, "You have the call in ten minutes and then have to finish the goals and then have the meeting with Mike Fritton at four and your expenses are due. I can do them for you. It's not a problem."

It was at that point I looked up at her and replied, "Okay, sounds good, thanks."

Yes, I yet again raced passed the flashing red lights and warning bells, this time allowing her access to way too much information. Although I did have reservations about passing this task to her, I never could've imagined she would do what she did. In short, she had passed information on in the investigation about the night in question—even though she wasn't there—while neglecting to inform Mr. Lyin that she did my expenses. With that he also listed falsifying company expense accounts as another reason for termination, which we'll revisit shortly.

An hour later I had a curious conversation with one of the managers from another division who had just spoken to one of Mama Bear's old bosses. After some small talk he was quick to confirm he was in fact her boss because, thinking he was, he brought her name up, as he did others; but she was the only name he had no response to. A dark thought consumed me. It was one of a similar conversation that I had when I met with another one of her old bosses in Orlando.

This could've been purely coincidental, although it certainly seemed odd. My mind couldn't stop zeroing in on it all as the sky darkened even further when Wendy called me back. She now seemed distant and agitated confirming that Jessie had passed on our January trip to Mexico, something we discussed twice before as another lightning bolt seemed to crash down.

"I know," I said, slightly miffed and increasingly irritated. "Didn't we talk about this?"

"We did, but we were guessing why. It's because of the wedding...he's not upset with anything. He's fine."

She sold me, as cool as a cucumber.

Three hours later we met up for our "Wine Time."

The first topic of conversation was about the Rib Fest weekend we all attended together. She was still hung up on Jessie approaching me to have that what-the-fuck-is-going-on-with-you-and-my-fiancé chat.

I reminded her that I quickly moved on, but a fierce and thoughtful expression appeared on her face. She voiced her displeasure that I ended up alone with him.

"Wendy, you left me there with him?"

"I left with Marie and was freaking out about sitting with her at the bar."

I fell back in the booth, glaring at her suspiciously. "Well, I had thoughts of jumping off the fucking balcony—so we're even."

She gripped her glass. "I didn't know he was staying."

"You didn't notice he wasn't with you, in the hall or elevator?"

"No, I told you I was freaking out." She took a quick sip and blinked, as if her mind was racing back through it all, before she said, "God, I knew he was going to do that."

Displeasure flickered across her face. She carried on, as I nodded, too fascinated to interrupt her. Not to mention she actually looked quite sexy in this state and was turning me on. But then she ruined it, by again, rewriting the details of more than I could handle. I impatiently flagged the waiter down for the check.

But that wasn't the end of it.

Forty minutes later, all spent on another distressful call driving home—fifteen of it parked at the Lowe's a mile from my house—she interrupted me, frantic. "Jessie just saw me pass the house."

"What?" I thought you stopped driving around the block while talking to me."

"What am I supposed to do?" she shouted out.

"Not continue to drive around the fucking block until he wanders out into the street praying you run him over because he can't take it anymore."

"Shut your mouth! I'm going to tell him that I'm talking to Schultz about my goals."

"Oh, wow...yeah he'll believe that, and when you actually see your goals you will be crying, so that's perfect."

"I can't believe this."

"Of course not. It's all connected to the same reality you choose to rewrite—"

"Shut up. Shit...he's in the driveway."

Click.

Two days later, with only darker clouds swirling around us, we met up on "Wine Wednesday" as her rewrites continued. On this day though, they became intolerable. It began with two different topics that came up in the investigation only to shift into what really irked her: the sensitive subject matter she texted me the night of the baseball game.

I could taste blood on my tongue from biting down on it; she had no idea I was grilled on this during the investigation. I fell back astonished and increasingly irritated as she vehemently pressed on. Finally I interrupted her.

"I much preferred it when you just blocked out what you can't deal with."

Her eyes darted to the side. It was as if it wasn't her. "What?"

"You're scaring me with these rewrites." I narrowed my eyes, as her gaze averted mine with a poignant expression.

"I know I texted you, but I was only kidding about what I said to you—"

"Wendy, stop. Please stop. Forget the fact your communication to me has been documented by the company for the past fourteen months, this is me...me you're talking to." Into the dead air, I added, "I'm sorry, don't worry about it. Let's just change the subject."

She inhaled sharply and snapped, "No, just tell me! I can't remember—"

"Wendy, you can't remember because you can't handle the reality of this and I can no longer deal with you rewriting everything having to do with us. The content of your texts matched the message your sparkling eyes were screaming out that night, and for the past fucking year, so please, save the bullshit because I'm in too deep to continue to listen to it!"

There was silence.

Her head tilted oddly to the side with a combined expression of anger and sadness. "Well, you're not leaving Marie...and I'm not leaving Jessie." She paused tensely and glared. "That's why I rewrite...us," her voice rose, "because I have to," her stare intensified, "sometimes I can't deal with what I've texted you...so shut the fuck up...because I'm in too deep to continue to listen to you whine about how I fucking handle it!"

I began to pout...wishing we had more wine.

She then shifted subtly in the booth. She had a look of intolerable pain. It was that look, deep in her eyes, that caused me to turn away. I was desperate to snap her out of it. And just at that moment, I was again gifted a humorous out to hide behind.

My head turned and as my eyes scanned the space I smiled, "I spy with my little eye something blue."

I peeked at her. She twitched taking in ragged breaths as her eyes slowly closed. She began mumbling under her breath. Her hands were over her face.

I leaned forward over the table. "Psst, Wendy...hello in there? You have to open your eyes to play this game. I spy with my little eye something blue."

Her hands dropped to her lap. Her eyes shot open and for a fleeting instant every bit of tension in the fine muscles of her face vanished as she smiled. But she became suddenly choked up, her voice barely audible. "This has been such an unbelievable mess for so long..." she paused and her watery eyed gaze rolled into mine.

I had nothing.

We were fucked, plain and simple, and my world was imploding because of it all.

I paid and we walked out to our cars with only a cold goodbye.

As I pulled out, I noticed she turned the wrong way. Within the minute she called me. I answered, "Are you okay?"

"I turned the wrong way because of you," she said quietly.

Again, Molly's words from the night I ran into her at that bar hit me dead on.

I shook free of them and asked, "Are you good now?"

The call ended.

I pulled up to a red light staring at a spectacular sunset with swirling storm clouds all around it. Darkness framed the rays shooting out of the setting sun. As I went to take a picture, my eyes caught a car racing up from behind in my rearview mirror. I adjusted myself for a better look and noticed it was Wendy. It seemed as if she went through a red light. I peered on, as my BlackBerry rang again. Guess who? I dropped the damn thing attempting to answer it a bit jittery, yet thoroughly enthralled. She came to an abrupt stop besides me at that light.

A smile formed on her face so I answered, "Hi there." (An inside joke that always tickled her) She turned her head away fighting a smile, but pensive. When she turned back to me her eyes were actually sparkling. It was then I couldn't utter a word. Her eyes said it all. She was back. She leaned over her passenger seat, her voice breathless with astonishment, "I just ran a red light to end up next to you." Her eyes were ablaze. "Why is this happening?" Her voice rose. "WHY?"

I gripped the wheel tightly compressing my lips with my inner voice screaming, "Just shut up and smile."

I did.

She turned straight forward into the sunset. "Oh my God, look at that beautiful sunset." She turned back to me. "And there's a storm coming."

We both stared off into it before turning back toward one another as the light turned green.

Still on the phone, simply because we refused to hang up, we drove our separate ways under the swirling storm clouds bearing down on us.

CHAPTER FORTY - THREE

WENDY'S WINE TIME WORRY

NOVEMBER 2010
THE MORNING OF THE THIRD MEETING

Eight hours later, I woke up edgy and with more of a hangover from our conversation than the wine, so I decided to pass on my morning run. With all intentions of hydrating, I sat up to get out of bed, only to be held captive by an email. I collected my abated thoughts and ended up with my foot tucked under my leg for an extended moment which caused it to go to sleep. After I replied to the email I hastily leapt out of bed. It dawned on me that something was wrong, right before I hit the dresser with a thud.

"What the hell did you do?" Marie huffed as her head rose from her pillow.

"I got out of the bed dizzy and my foot was asleep." I stood precariously and stared into her brown eyes as they bore through me from the large mirror.

"What?" she snapped. "Dizzy? You're hungover...and put a shirt on you freak of nature."

"Sorry for waking you," I stuttered. I sensed a bit of leftover hostility from the night before. My eyes shifted to her jewelry on the dresser. I felt her scowl etch into me and took that as my cue to exit. I frantically hopped to the door, breathed heavily, and shut it behind me as tiny dizzy dots clouded my vision. I blinked a few times to shake them, but then my equilibrium went out. Marie screamed rudeness into her pillow, while I held onto the door for dear life and banged the feeling back into my foot.

I felt it behooved me to hobble toward the kitchen regardless of the fact that the room was now spinning. That was before I received a text from one of Bud Fox's salesmen. I took a deep breath before I pulled the insanity up to my bloodshot eyes: "Last night your boy told us he missed hanging out with you." I rubbed my eyes and read on.

I moaned before I received another text from one of Fox's all-stars asking me why I didn't respond to the text from the day before. It was a long winded message informing me how Fox was telling anyone who would listen that The Wizard made him file the complaint against me, which was something I had already heard. It also stated that he now had nothing to do with it because the focus of the investigation had shifted to Wendy. I didn't respond. I collapsed on the far couch, slightly closer to the kitchen. I wanted to scream.

It took me three minutes to actually calm down enough to push myself up and shuffle to the counter. I had a vision of head butting Mr. Lyin to the floor, then pulling him up, looking him in his eyes, and screaming, "Are you fucking kidding me with this bullshit?!"

I turned the television on and tore the cap off a small Evian bottle, which I promptly drained. I glanced back at the text, nauseous and in need of more water. I lunged for another bottle. I felt little relief though. A cloud of despair rose from my brainstem in anticipation of a third meeting with Mr. Lyin.

Discomforted, I fought down the negativity that steadily eroded my positive mindset. All of the magnificent mistakes I had made, largely public, came into focus. As I stood there, tangled in this turmoil, a smile emerged with an impromptu awareness of a memorable "Wine Time" with Wendy. It was strange how detailed situations were coming back to me.

It was weeks before, right after my second meeting with Mr. Lyin, and ironically, one of the last times we met that didn't have her rewriting something. It was just the old us, with her new concern. We were sitting cozily in a booth far away from the real world when she first felt compelled to confirm the rash stupidity I displayed by appointing someone to be my administrative assistant after only three brief conversations. And even though she wasn't there, she was dead on. They were chats heavily infused with a "flip of the switch" southern accent that had her acting as if she were a damsel in distress. Although Wendy knew Mama Bear had issues with her former boss, as she had claimed, she swore the lady played my ego perfectly, which she did. I immediately felt obligated to save her because, well, I thought I was a superhero.

"Larry, you're not a superhero. You cannot save people," Wendy said with a smile.

"You know I am," I fired back as if we were two kids on the swings in a schoolyard. "I'm Iron Man," I boasted proudly.

Her eyes opened wide to her soul, and craved more.

"And I have a wildly conflicted special little lady friend named Wendy 'Pepper' Darlington." Inspired by her expression of adoration, I leaned in and whispered, "And she's crazy about me."

She blissfully bounced in the booth, buzzed. Her elbows hit the table and her hands shot over her painted pink cheeks. It was perfect. She sat behind her nearly empty wine glass and sighed fervidly. Her hand fell to the side of it before she lifted it to her lips and tilted her head back to empty it. The pixie dust began to fall.

Wendy placed the glass down and gasped. "Order another bottle."

Her eyes had that "second star to the right" light as she stated that she was heading to the bathroom and would explain why I couldn't save anyone when she got back. I nodded and took a deep breath, fixated on her, as she excitedly slid out of the booth like a little girl. I counted to three and smiled as she amorously peeked back at me, almost exactly on cue.

Minutes later, she came back with that whimsical stare I had long been addicted to and jumped into the booth with purpose. "Okay. Once again, you're Tony Stark, not Iron Man," she explained rather sincerely adding, "We've gone over this."

She looked away to keep her composure because I did that upside eyeglass thing with my hands while saying, "I see."

She lunged for her freshly filled glass and giddily pleaded, "Stop it. I'm trying to have a serious conversation." She pushed the new bottle, which was rudely dropped out of our line of sight, and I stared at her for a brief moment. "Don't look at me like a lost little boy," she pleaded, enslaved in the moment. "You know that shit doesn't work with me."

Her eyes held me spellbound and spoke volumes, more so than her words. By now we were both beaming quite brightly. The unique energy we exuded was something I had been questioned about during the investigation which she then brought up.

"This is all because you had a heterosexual male fall in love with you and you're still joking about it."

"Do you have the sniffles? You sound a little nasally—"

"This is playing out eerily close to the actual movie, Wall Street. The only difference is that your Bud Fox is getting away with taking you down with the most ludicrous complaint ever recorded in the history of that nuthouse."

"Please refer to it as The Asylum, where pathological liars are considered credible and welcomed into investigations with open arms, while a wicked Wizard waves his wand over it all from his bath of Bud Light."

She rubbed her temples and began breathing erratically. "Twenty years from now, when I'm your age," she paused and gave me her nod. I glared at her disapprovingly before she continued. "No one will believe this shit show—" She stopped mid-thought pondering it.

So I said, "Which part? The part that has a beer-swilling good ole boy disguised as an executive sending an imbecile to file an idiotic complaint in an attempt to ruin a guy who was slated to be on the company's fast track to the top?" My finger rose in the air. I took a sip of wine. "Or the part that has the other idiot (me) stupid enough to think his jaw-dropping romance with his star-crossed lover, Pepper, wouldn't be used against him by some totally fucked up individuals?"

Her head dropped to the table and she let out a distressful moan before she put her hair up in a ponytail.

"Both," she snapped. She topped her glass off gleefully.

"Maybe you should slow down." I said, pointing at the new bottle, which was almost done. "I promised my liver we'd only polish off three this afternoon."

"Shut up. I have to tell you something serious and I don't know how you're going to take it. And you know I can't not be your Pepper, so stop pouting." She turned her head and beamed as her facial expression became intense. She stared across the restaurant. "They're changing shifts." My head turned and she lowered her voice. "Oh

God," she said eyeing our new waitress.

"I don't like your tone."

"If you weren't a freak I wouldn't have to use that tone."

"You're sounding more and more like Marie. Stop calling me a freak."

She inhaled sharply and held it for a moment. "You jog around a cul-de-sac until you're hit with another idea for a poem and then you walk back in, take a shower, and strut out in a towel proceeding to snap a mirror shot of yourself, smiling before you text both to me. You are a freak!"

I whispered, "You love my poetry and magnificent mirror-shots."

The waiter surprised us by clearing his throat as he walked up.

Our heads twisted toward him.

Our stick-in-the-mud waiter quickly introduced a new, young, and attractive waitress to us and hauled ass. Accustomed to many shift changes, we didn't even flinch as she held out the new bottle. I nodded pleasantly as she opened it and destroyed the cork with a smile. She began to wipe the cork debris off the table.

"Well done," I said with a smirk.

She tilted her head, amused.

I glanced back up at her. "And if I still had taste buds, I'm sure I would think this was delightful. Thank you."

Wendy shot me a warning glare and gripped her BlackBerry, which was ringing. "It's Schlutz," she said. She slid out of the booth frantically.

"Pepper, please keep in mind Schultz gets nervous when you're plowed out of your mind before four."

She twisted softly saying, "Shut up, Tony." She answered, "Hey Dan."

As she hurried out the waitress smiled wide, thoroughly engrossed. I smirked, "I hope you didn't take the un-fun bus into work like your buddy."

She laughed. "No, I always take the fun bus and I can't stand him."

I smiled. "Good. Don't you think Iron Man should have a cape?"

She let out this guffaw. The manager turned to us from across the restaurant.

"We were having a very serious discussion about superheroes and I was—"

"I love Iron Man," she said in a raised tone.

I smiled.

She jumped into the booth grinning deviously as I watched her speechless. "You guys were in last week and she was chasing you in the parking lot trying to grab something. It was hilarious."

Oh fuck, I thought, but said, "Ah, yes. She missed spin class that day and I had the new schedule."

A smile spun on her face. "You two have so much fun together. Is that your w-i-f-e?"

"Nah, that's Pepper. She's my...assistant."

Her lips parted slightly and she fell back. "Oh my God. Like Pepper in the movie? I heard her call you Tony."

"Yes. We're not at all well."

A smile exploded across her pretty face. "Hey, I'm not well, either. I get it," she said. "What business are you in?"

"Wine."

"I love wine—"

The manger startled us and motioned to her other tables with a stern look. She slid out of the booth. "I'll be back, Tony," she whispered glancing back at me.

Wendy sent me a text: "What are you doing?"

"I'm ogling her. Please hold."

"Are you kidding? She's a few years older than Lauren."

"I want one."

"No."

As I typed a rebuttal, she jumped back in the booth startling me.

She stared at me thoughtfully and became emotional. I fell back in the booth. Her eyes slowly closed. As they reopened she spoke softly, "You know, I had no plans of ever meeting someone like you. Never mind having you as my boss." She turned away. "And I'm nervous about this investigation."

My smile flatlined.

Her temperament had completely changed. "First off, I hate it when you keep shit from me and I know you are with this bullshit investigation." She looked away. "You really do have a rare talent and

Geno knew it." She turned her head to the side and took a deep breath. "But he's gone and The Wizard is scared of it. Of you. You know how he looked at you during your last meeting speech?" She sighed deeply. "Not to mention you make too much money, you don't adhere well to rules, you party too hard, and you send bare chested pictures of yourself like you're sixteen—"

I held up my hand. "I'm feeling a bit bloated, please don't bring up my mirror shots today."

She took a deep breath but remained serious. "Along with your poems and songs, all sent to me on your company BlackBerry for that weirdo Chris Lyin to see." She took another deep breath. "And then, of course, there's us...and what I've texted you."

Her hand began to tremble as she reached for her wine glass. "I had a dream they pulled me away from you again, out of your division, and Fritton had to pull strings." Distraught, she looked away. "I need you to take a break from being you. Please, just until this is over."

I adjusted myself uncomfortably in the booth like a little boy and had to unclench my jaw to answer. "What do you mean?" I swirled my wine nervously.

"We were out. It was late in the afternoon last February. The Rabbi kept calling you for extra cases." She paused and took a sip of wine. "And you got them as usual. But it was on that night I realized how we won so often, how you motivate, and why Geno relocated you to Tampa. We were wasted and you ended up going home to press everyone's buttons, perfectly writing that shit show short story. It was brilliant and dangerous and I loved it. As I read it, I realized the material you used came to you as we sat together that day. Larry, it's not normal how your mind works." Her hands went to her head as she gushed. "But you had to keep pushing it. Winning is no longer enough."

I leaned in. "Wendy," I said softly. "It's all going to be okay."

She turned away. "Larry this makes no sense." She took a deep breath. Her eyes pierced me. "You had to bring these fucked up people further into your imaginary wonderland, even though Bud Fox was so far down your rabbit hole he didn't know what was real or make-believe." She looked away with watery eyes. "Never mind working your subliminal messages to me in the team incentives, while copying in a divorced admin only because she loved it all too."

Her worried expression pained. "I don't want to burst your bubble, but half the people that kiss your ass are haters. And they were fucked up right next to us the entire time, full of envy and deceit and issues." Her eyes squinted with anger and her words left her lips at a frantic rate. "And issues that you don't even get, Larry. You just don't." She took a deep breath as she fell back. "But you still think that you are the exception to the rules and that you can save them all." Her head turned away before her eyes stared into mine. She barely whispered, "But you're not a superhero, Larry, and fairy tales don't always come true, and these are not trustworthy individuals. And I'm scared."

I heard my daughter's voice from behind me. "Hey, dad."

I was shaken out of that vision by Lauren who walked into the kitchen.

I took a deep breath and smiled, unable to utter a word. I felt uneasy, rubbing my eyes I went to take a shower.

CHAPTER FORTY - FOUR

THE THIRD MEETING

NOVEMBER 2010
EXECUTIVE CONFERENCE ROOM

Two hours later I walked into the executive conference room and noticed Mr. Lyin placing his bag down gently as if a bomb was in it. He moved to the desk and dropped down into a chair. It was evident we were both over each other as the tension caused the cool space to heat rapidly.

I leaned forward and glanced at my BlackBerry as I received a text. It was from Wendy: "Call me when you get out."

Falling back, I sighed while then enduring minutes of painstaking questioning about her. Interestingly, Mr. Lyin mixed his inquires up during this third meeting as the minutes that followed were full of distorted propaganda; lies that were more hurtful than anything else. I interrupted prideful of being respected across the board regardless of any "party boy" label.

"Once again, I have a folder of emails from people who respect me for what I've accomplished for years and wish to be a part of my program. I have a loyal team that has stated numerous times over the last fourteen months that this has been the best experience of their careers, including the individuals who have now blatantly lied because of their own circumstances."

He flipped a page to his notes. "None of your career achievements are being questioned."

Suddenly I felt indignant. My eyes closed for a fleeting instant and I could feel the tension in the fine muscles of my face. My emotions began to swing with The Wizard's words resonating in my head: "Just lie."

And with each tick of the clock, it became apparent that Mama Bear had met with Mr. Lyin after her call to me as the questioning shifted to her unique issues. It was that obvious. Everything he addressed was tied to Wendy, but now in different, petty ways. I stared at him exhaling gustily.

To put this in perspective, ninety-five percent of what was discussed in this third meeting never made it into his final report. What little did make it in was done deceitfully, while altered greatly from the reality of the actual conversation.

A perfect example of that was his next find. Of the countless emails Wendy and I had communicated on, he singled out one that turned into two in his final report, about Wendy needing more wood trim for her team's holiday tables. To begin with he didn't believe me that we bought and built these displays ourselves. After I walked him through it all he then still amazingly moved on to his point. His investigative prowess uncovered the "slang" definition of "trim" was a woman regarded as a sex object. It was at that point the room felt as if it were lacking air. I took a shallow breath, thinking I had to have misunderstood him.

With a ragged gasp of pure astonishment, I emphatically stated that in no way did I view her in that regard. And even though our interpretations of the "slang" definition were different, he spun the fact that I acknowledged knowing what it meant in the final report. He stated that I deliberately violated the company technology policy by using the company's communication system to send inappropriate messages—now two—of a sexual nature. Of course, at this point, he never said anything about that. He only led me to believe that he understood that I thought he was out of his fucking mind while moving on rashly.

I blinked at him in bewilderment as he blazed on. But as he did, it hit me that Mama Bear was concealing the fact that her boyfriend fixed Bud Fox's company laptop because he actually did violate the company technology policy by going to unauthorized sites. As I bit my tongue aware of both, the nervous dissension amplified before it all worsened, as Mr. Lyin brought up the deleted files for the incentive. This was something that she came to me about after her boyfriend informed her how he could permanently delete them from the company server. To protect her, I only informed him that I did not instruct her to destroy anything. That was it. Unfortunately, she used that Friday call to go back to Mr. Lyin to tell him I instructed her to delete the files, as was The Asylum way.

"Just lie."

He then flipped a page to his notes and asked me if we—Marie and I—in fact, did invite Wendy and Jessie to Mexico for our January vacation. I nodded confirming that we had.

He squinted at me in disbelief. "You and your wife invited Wendy and her fiancé on your vacation?" he asked again seemingly breathless for my confirmation.

"Yes, we have a villa down by Playa Del Carmen and enjoy their company," I said. He probably thought we were swingers because his mind seemed to be racing through much that he didn't mention. I added, "We also spent a recent weekend together at Rib Fest." I couldn't resist at this point. He gently cleared his throat, although he remained speechless. After awkwardly flipping pages to his notepad he glimpsed at the last one with twitchy eyes. He appeared dazed and confused.

The next topic moved back to something Mama Bear had stated. It was a picture on the board of Wendy, her friend Lisa, and me at a night club. It was from the night of the baseball game with Andrew Rawley. Lisa was leaning into me with her arm across my crotch and her hand resting on my knee. This too left me in need of smelling salts, but interestingly was something he viewed as proof that I was a partying playboy. He hesitated before reading from his notes. "Lori told me you took them down to only hide them during this investigation."

My blood began to boil. "That's pretty funny because it was her who had the issue. The truth is that I have years' worth of pictures in frames by promotion. You were in my office. I love taking pictures. I use some of them in those frames. But it was Lori who made the fuss about that one, and any others with Wendy." My voice rose as my temper flared. I leaned forward. "And you saw the frames in my office. I went over all of this in our last meeting."

His head nervously popped up. "I need you to calm down."

"It's funny how you never asked me about the one where Lori's cozy up next to me. But I guess since she had no problem with that one...or the one where her hand was in my back pocket." I paused grabbing my BlackBerry. "Would you like to see the picture...with her hand in my back pocket? My wife still has it. I could have her text it to me. This is nuts...and you know it."

"I'm questioning four pictures with Wendy along with the picture we just spoke about that didn't make the last promotion frame. Where did they go?"

"The frame I'm working on is not complete, and not all of them make the frame."

"Would your decision to put them in be based on how people would perceive the picture?"

I fought for another breath. "Of course. Not all the pictures are right for the frame. The picture board is simply there to display a successful program while being cognizant of the fact we can achieve that goal and actually enjoy the experience. Something we used to do."

He peered at me before writing on multiple pages. "Do you see how they can be perceived?"

I sat up straight and said, "Before Bud Fox missed this incentive and Tony Trappelleti didn't get promoted and this lady wasn't growling every time Wendy Darlington called the office line, that picture board was something everyone viewed as being special. There was never a problem before this. It instilled a feeling of camaraderie and enhanced the overall experience. That is a fact. That's the reason I have a folder of emails from people who want to join my program. It is a success and we have fun—"

"Do you think other sales directors do that?"

"No, my program is unique. So are the results I produce, which you choose to ignore."

"I'm not questioning that."

"You should be, because this is a productive program and none of this was an issue before these three loons became disgruntled. That, sir, is the truth, which you refuse to acknowledge."

His eyes popped forward, again disturbed by what he perceived to be arrogance, but at this point, it wasn't. He scrambled to find anything he could to throw back at me. Within seconds he asked, "Do you feel it's appropriate to have pictures where Wendy is seen wearing your tie and in positions with you, a sales director, that would be viewed as inappropriate?"

I loosened my tie with too many dark thoughts. "No."

He slumped to the side slightly as if experiencing muscle spasms. "Did you refuse to take down a picture of Wendy wearing your tie because you liked it? You stated that picture is not coming down, because she looks adorable."

I rubbed my eyes realizing this was all Mama Bear, and said, "Yes. But I didn't think it was inappropriate."

His expression tightened, as his gaze sharpened. He immediately brought up statements passed on from Wendy's birthday night, along with the picture of the two of us that I had just found, while reminding me about his findings.

I took in a jagged breath. "I told you we were close and that picture was never on the board."

He flipped the page and changed the subject. "You were at a lunch meeting with your team when you and Wendy were seen drinking from each other's wine glasses."

"No, I had a sip from hers."

"It was brought to my attention that you have a phobia about drinking from someone else's glass, yet you did from hers?"

I sat back. "I feel like I'm in a Twi-light Zone episode—"

He interrupted. "It was after another lunch meeting that you both stated you were going your separate ways before secretly meeting down the street. Do you recall this?"

"I go out with her all the time. I told you numerous times it's no secret."

"But she has repeatedly stated otherwise? It is very apparent she feels she has to lie about the two of you. She knows she did. She couldn't deny it."

I sat speechless.

He shifted topics to one I'd never heard before, which made no sense whatsoever, having to do with my wife being "extremely jealous" of Mama Bear.

"Not only is that absurd, but it doesn't pertain to anything you're talking about, and actually would be a contradiction to all of this questioning about Wendy. And you think this lady is credible? Have you even done a background check on her to find out why she has had so many bosses?" I stood.

His eyes went wide as he again sat speechless.

I could tell he realized he'd made a mistake.

I added, "That lady was wasted, out of her mind, the one night we took her to a concert, where my wife warned me that she was trouble because of the bullshit that came spewing out of her mouth. Lori thinks she knows things that she doesn't. I downplayed everything because back then everything was great. My wife laughed at her and I let it go. I like Lori and I always wanted the best for her, but this creepy dark agenda you're concocting here is disturbing. And I will be getting a lawyer."

My temper took hold of me. I went back, stupid enough to fight this insanity. That was the worst mistake I could've made. I should've kept walking and retained a lawyer right then. But I was burning up. "If this lady has truly said these things," I seethed, "which I pray she didn't—"

"She did," he said sternly.

"Then I blame you for believing her—"

He stood up. "I need you to calm down."

"You can't have any idea about what goes on in this place to continue doing this to me unless this is a set-up."

"I need you to sit down and calm down."

"There is a reason that I have separated myself and my team from certain individuals in this place and it starts at the top. When Geno Franc left, the lights went dim." I leaned across the table. "I told you I was no angel, and I'm not. And I told you I was too close to this girl. I am. And I told you we hang out all the time. We Do. But there are good, sane people who all know me very well and you haven't questioned any of them."

He quickly flipped a page in his notepad. "I'm curious as to how you would explain the communication we have documented between you and Wendy Darlington?"

I lost all oxygen at once, as if the wind were knocked out of me. It was as if he was waiting for the right moment to silence me. And he'd just gotten it. I sat there anxiously, now hit with something that was so inconceivable there was simply nothing I could say to explain it without sinking deeper. I knew he already had proof about the sensitive subject matter she texted me. I faded in and out. But worse, in his mind, I was guilty of playing with her heart. I shut down as he went through it all. Minutes later he flipped the page of his notepad.

He hesitated as if he was reloading his gun.

The tension built.

My heart raced.

Then he slowly looked up at me and pulled the trigger. "You told Bud Fox you had trouble taking off Wendy's bra at your house. Do you recall saying that?"

I couldn't catch my breath to even utter a word and I knew exactly what he was talking about. Although this was months before, I did share information with Fox. It was at a time when he simply couldn't believe we weren't having intercourse; no one could. No one did. But back then he was my boy and I was an idiot. And after a long-winded drunken debate, I shouted, "Fox, I'm not telling you things didn't get out of hand, but Wendy isn't the girl Tony and others are making her out to be. She's a good person. Honestly that's another reason this has gone where it has. So believe me when I tell you we have not had sex. I even got a sign when I pulled the string on her pants and it knotted."

What I told Mr. Lyin was that I didn't say it, because technically, I didn't. He stated "bra," not pants. See? I shouldn't joke though, because this was a grave mistake and this along with the communication records were the nails in my coffin.

He thought I was an arrogant, partying, playboy only looking to play on with a girl who he had documented feelings for me; a worst case scenario. Right at that moment, I should've come clean with my feelings for her while explaining the bra/pants situation. But I didn't, and it made everything else look true, including the next topic, which was another blatant lie, as this all became unfathomable.

Mr. Lyin looked up from his notes and said, "A supplier went on record as stating he witnessed Wendy straddling you on a chaise lounge at your house before your family moved to Tampa."

"That is a lie. We were on the patio late, but I don't even have chaise lounges."

"Who would just make that up?"

"Well, aside from the fact that three others have repeatedly done just that…"

"Go on," he said.

"I had heard this before—"

"If you heard it before why didn't you address it then?"

"I did. And when I asked the supplier about it, he, Matt McMullen, told me he never said it. The truth is that Tony, Matt, and Lori have huddled behind a closed door talking shit for well over a year. And even though he'd seen some things I wished he hadn't, it doesn't make it right to just make something up."

That was the truth but all I could see was Matt's facial expression on her birthday. I sank further in the quicksand of it all as Mr. Lyin pressed on.

"What was Wendy doing at your house late at night?"

"We were all partying together."

"Why were you entertaining a supplier with a direct report by your side?"

"As I stated in the last meeting they knew each other from their last company. The three of us would hang out back in the fall of 2009, back when everything was quite great."

"Were you partying with her beforehand?"

"We had lunch."

"I'm guessing in your world that means bottles of wine were consumed and you decided to continue the fun because you could." He paused; I nodded. He took a deep breath and grimaced. "And you're still insisting the supplier just made that up?"

"Yes. I can't explain why, and again, the supplier (Matt) denied saying it."

Months after this, (the last time I spoke to him) I had informed Matt of everything that was passed forward in this investigation that came from him. He denied saying any of it while only concluding that everyone knew we were too close.

When I informed Mr. Lyin that I was friendly with Matt, his tone immediately changed. "Larry, just to let you know, I can't interview any suppliers."

I crumbled back over the table. "Well then what are you telling me?" I snapped. "Bud Fox interviewed him and passed this on?"

"No, most of what came from the supplier was brought to my attention by Lori." My eyes closed and my head slumped as he added, "Some of this goes back to statements the supplier made to her in the fall of 2009 and early 2010."

He nervously distanced himself from the supplier commentary as it was against company policy to speak with them on matters such as this. Furthermore, it was obvious he wasn't going to say a word about that until I informed him we were friends.

He abruptly ended the meeting.

I knew I wouldn't be able to sit in our office after this so I left The Asylum, fuming. My mind raced through it all as I descended the steps to the executive parking lot. I hopped in my navi and sped off. Typically I would call Wendy, but because I was keeping this from her I didn't.

Twenty minutes later she called me. She began the conversation asking how everything went, hoping it would be over. I only informed her it was not. She was quiet at first, but seemed to have more dire news she wished to share as my mind wandered with thoughts of how I had protected Mama Bear, now eating at me. Why did I ever trust her? I was distant to the conversation when Wendy finally asked me if I was okay. I told her I was, but the fact I didn't elaborate on much of anything clued her in that I was sheltering her from it all.

And since the conversation on my end was limited she went onto the purpose of her call. When she first brought it up she wasn't at all emotional. In her normal voice she said, "Jessie confronted me about my feelings for you over the Thanksgiving weekend in Connecticut."

I sat silently with too much emotion tearing through me. I was overwhelmed.

As she carried on, I faded in and out of the details of it all. I sighed deeply, fast approaching the Lowe's down the street from my house, and pulled in. How many times did I end up finishing conversations with her here?

Finally with a shaky voice she said, "I didn't know what to say, so just ran out, crying." She sighed. "Right after you told me he wouldn't ask about us, he has, in so many different ways. Larry, it's just so weird."

I lowered my window in need of fresh air and softly said, "Wendy, I only said that because you told me he never questioned much of anything. It was crazy. Think about the last fourteen months—"

"I can't!" she barked. "I'm getting married in three months. I have to go."

Click.

CHAPTER FORTY - FIVE

DINNER WITH DRAMA AND A HUMOROUS NIGHTCAP

DECEMBER 2010
THE ORLANDO HOLIDAY DINNER

In the days that followed, I painstakingly went through the motions. I had never been this emotional in my entire life, and it didn't feel good. Plus, I hadn't heard a word from Mr. Lyin. As I pulled into the executive parking lot, The Wizard acted as if he hadn't seen me pulling out. I drove into my spot and frantically searched for an email on my BlackBerry. I came across one from Wendy to Schultz, and quickly realized she was only copying me in because she wanted to talk.

The last time we had spoken was the emotional call after my third meeting with Mr. Lyin, three days earlier. I exchanged my BlackBerry for my security card and raced up the steps to The Asylum swiping it to get in.

As I threw the door open, my mind was on the email that I had to send The Rabbi. I marched down the hall to our office, collecting my thoughts, as I passed Mama Bear sitting at her desk.

"I emailed you the confirmation for your hotel in Orlando," she said anxiously, with a scowl and a nod.

"Thank you," I replied, walking on.

And just then, I received a text from Wendy ending the lengthy, for us anyway, three-day radio silence.

"We're going to be in Orlando tonight; stop pouting."

I rubbed my eyes and dropped my bag at my desk. I collapsed in my chair, with dark thoughts ripping through my mind. I had to stay focused on the task though. I began typing the email to The Rabbi. Before I could finish, Mama Bear asked me when I would be heading over to the Orlando office for the meeting beforehand.

"Around one o'clock. Where is that final tracker?" My voice was impatient.

"I'm sending it now."

Just then, Schultz texted: "Do you really think it's a good idea to plan an after-dinner party with the new team while this investigation is still on-going? I know how these can go."

Not wavering and realizing Matt briefed him, I hit the keys to reply: "Yes. I'm not making any more adjustments because of these people. I can't stand this bullshit and refuse to have them affect my program."

Within seconds, he called.

I answered, "Hey."

"You do realize Wendy is in Orlando tonight," Schultz replied.

"Yes, she has another one of those wine training courses with some test—"

"And she's staying at the same hotel as you."

"What?" I hadn't realized she was going to be at the same hotel.

"Matt's losing it right now. He just found out and thinks it was all planned—"

"Hey, let me call you back," I interrupted, wanting to find out what was going on.

Click.

I texted Wendy and asked her where she was staying. She immediately replied.

"EEW! Really? I haven't spoken to you in three days and that's how you respond to me? Um, NO."

I spun my chair around, amused (as usual) by her ways, and grabbed a few bottles from my office wine stash. After I sent another email, I took a deep breath, and blew it out as my heart began to race. I stood up, placed my laptop in the bag, zipped it up, and left.

"I have to take care of a couple of things before the meeting," I said to Mama Bear as I passed her on my way out. "And remember I'm staying on the east coast this weekend, so I'll see you on

Wednesday."

Her eyes popped forward in her head. "Oh, right. Well, be careful and have fun. But be careful!"

I bit my tongue and nodded briskly, hoping the ceiling would collapse on her.

I raced out of The Asylum, flew down the steps, and jumped into my navi just as Wendy texted me again.

"HELLO? WHAA HAPPENED TO YOU?"

I began laughing deliriously.

As I attempted to regain my composure, I jumped up in my seat, scared shitless, when someone knocked on my window. It was a manager from another division.

He kept walking, but shouted back, "Every time I see you, you're laughing out loud. You truly are living the dream!"

I nodded, but suddenly felt nauseous.

I started my car, and called her as I was pulling out. On the second ring she answered.

"Really? I hate it when you're EMO!" (Emotional)

I readjusted the BlackBerry in my hand. "You make me EMO," I snapped back.

"You make me EMO. I hate it when you do this shit."

I took a right turn and sped away from The Asylum. "Wait, seriously, did you know where I was staying tonight?" I asked contemplatively.

She laughed. "Not until an hour ago. Can you believe this?"

"No—yes—actually—Yes, I can." I sighed.

"Um, you knew I couldn't handle that conversation. (She was referring to the last time we spoke after the third meeting with Lyin) And then you don't call me back, you just start pouting?"

"How did you know I was pouting?"

"REALLY?!"

I didn't want to tell her about the investigation so I said, "You love it and wouldn't want it any other way."

She sighed. "I was seriously upset and needed you to call me back."

I had another call coming in. "Hey, it's The Rabbi. I'll see you for dinner tonight." I deliberately waited for her reaction.

"W-h-a-t—Matt will shit! Are you kidding me?"

"No." I heard her chuckle delightfully as I added, "I need you."

Click.

Five hours later, my meeting with the Orlando team ended. I said hello to Keith Aden, who ran their off-premise division, and then stood in the parking lot. The sun was falling fast, but was warm on my face. I felt relieved—a refreshing change as opposed to The Asylum. Not having to waste any time pulling the imaginary knives out of my back, I made great time to the hotel. On my way, the Orlando key account manager called. She had finalized dinner plans and wanted to go over the details. Everything seemed to be going smoothly, until Matt called.

We had planned on meeting for a drink beforehand, but after some small talk, I could tell he had something he wanted to tell me. Sure enough, before we hung up, he informed me he was only paying for the Orlando team at dinner. I could tell he thought this was all planned. The truth was that the wine training had been set for two months, and Mama Bear would've never, knowingly, put me anywhere near Wendy—never mind at the same hotel. But there was no way Matt was going to believe that, and I couldn't blame him.

"Mayor, I'm not paying for any Tampa managers who are here for the training. Their dinner is next week," Matt said in a serious tone.

"Matt, if anyone from my team is here, they got an invite. If you don't want to pay, don't pay. This conversation is over. I'll see you in a few minutes."

Click.

Twenty minutes later we opened a bottle of Mondavi Cabernet Sauvignon Reserve. The deep, engaging aromas of cassis and blackberries wove harmoniously with dried herbs, and violet-floral. Matt lifted his glass to clink mine.

"Cheers, Mayor. It's always a show…"

I took a sip. The wine flowed elegantly into a long, lingering finish. The bottle was delightful, although Matt had this patch to the side of his eye that was freaking me out.

An hour later, after enjoying that in my room, we made our way to the restaurant.

My Orlando key account manager was late, but the rest of the group had made their way back to the table that had been reserved for us as an undeniable buzz was building.

I noticed Matt. The patch over his eye was still freaking me out, along with his nervous smile. The look on his face was almost of disbelief anticipating the imaginary curtain to rise.

The stage was set as my key account manager finally arrived. I smirked at Wendy who had looked at me slightly agog before turning to walk to the table. The key account manager walked up to introduce herself enthusiastically.

"Well, finally. It's great to meet you Larry; I'm sorry I'm late," she said reaching out her hand to shake mine.

"Yes, and no problem, Amy; I'm sorry it's taken so long," I replied as I then thanked her for setting up the dinner.

Within a minute of small talk we made our way over to the rest of the group. As she sat down next to me at the far end of the table, a comical scene ensued as twelve others filed in around me pushing Wendy further away. It looked like a game of musical chairs. The look on her face was priceless. Matt had orchestrated a planned seating arrangement that had her as far away from me as possible without being at another table.

With a distinct look of displeasure on her face, Matt ordered a bottle of Diseno Malbec to appease her, as he grinned teasingly seemingly taking a mental picture of the table. Within minutes the bottle was in front of her and she was taking her first long sips. As she promptly proceeded to down it, the buzz of small talk grew louder.

The key account manager seemed to be a nice young lady. I had spoken to her numerous times on the phone, but this was the first time I had actually met her. She filled me in on her territory and then shifted gears to sports and other unrelated topics before Wendy's fuse ignited. It was something Matt knew would happen, and it was just a matter of when.

There seemed to be a countdown clock just behind her, one that coincided with the wine left in her bottle. And within minutes, the clock hit zero, the bottle was empty, and the bomb went BOOM! Wendy tore into her so obnoxiously, that the entire table and wait staff took note. When asked about it later, I resold it as a compelling back and forth discussion between the two ladies, but the reality was that because Wendy was so repugnant, the key account manager changed her plans.

Within seconds of this she leaned into me and whispered, "I know you'll have fun tonight. It was a pleasure to finally meet you. I have to go though."

I turned to her, surprised by her comment. "I thought you were coming with us?"

"I was, but no. I have to go. You guys will have fun." My eyes rolled over at Wendy disapprovingly.

She loved it.

As I got up to walk her out, Wendy shot me her little sinister head nod. On my way back, I went to take a piss and ran into one of the young Orlando managers. He had this silly smile etched across his face and had no idea it was me who walked in.

"Enjoying yourself?" I asked, as his eyes popped forward, taken aback while spraying beyond the urinal.

"Yeah, Larry...this is great," he said. "And I have to say, we're very excited to be working under you. I love your style." He zipped up and walked by me touching my jacket, without washing his hands. I almost blacked out. "Nice jacket," he added.

I then wanted to burn it. I managed to nod and thank him, rushing to the sink as the door closed behind him.

When I got back to the table, Wendy's gaze immediately connected with mine. She was sitting in front of her empty bottle holding her BlackBerry up making a gesture for me to check mine. I did and realized I had missed her text.

"Could she sit any closer? Um, no. Bye."

I glanced back at her unable to contain my grin, aware she didn't want the night to end. I noticed Matt shaking his head as I winked at him before he huddled with two other managers.

As things wrapped up, the overall vibe in the room was electric and I could tell Matt was concerned. He told one of the managers to take Wendy back to the hotel.

I lifted my BlackBerry up to read her text: "Matt is trying to get me to go back to the hotel."

That wasn't my plan. I walked over to them and cut through the muffled chatter and snapped. "No!"

The other manager who was about to pull her out froze.

I protested instantly, "You're coming with us."

There was dead silence with a bunch of looks of wonderment.

"Team bonding," I concluded. "And you all need to compare notes."

Wendy lit up as Matt grimaced. I made a hand gesture to his patch and shook my head. He pulled me aside and snarled, "Mayor, she's already really buzzed and caused a scene." He paused turning back to her before he twisted back to me pleading, "And they have their exams early in the morning. She should go back to the hotel."

"One drink, no worries," I replied, patting him on the back as he just smiled.

Two hours later, the night had, indeed, turned out to be a special team-bonding event that everyone thoroughly enjoyed. Nothing crazy, just good camaraderie, although as the night drew to a close, I looked over at Wendy and said, "How did we end up at a table with a fucking candle tucked away in a corner?"

She smiled amorously. "Seriously…stop."

I smirked anticipating her to make the weird sound we made to each other when a statement was so unbelievable. She did, as two of the Orlando managers awkwardly fixated on something over our heads. We laughed gently as this would be a prelude to a humorous nightcap.

When we all arrived back at the hotel, which was enormous, with ten different wings, Wendy and I walked one way while unbeknownst to us everyone else walked the other way. Nothing spoken about, we were just going to our rooms. As we merrily strolled on, playfully bumping into each other, in our own little world, I heard a voice from behind us,

"Enjoy your night, you two!"

I spun around and nodded at them. We were all alone.

Our gaze rolled to each other.

"Where's your room?" I asked her.

She smiled broadly and named the same wing I was in as The Darkness's howl echoed throughout the suddenly enchanting space with delight.

Oh fuck!

Schultz's warning snuck up from behind me. I flicked it away though and turned back to Wendy, and as our eyes reconnected, they displayed a lustful light. With each step we took, it seemed as if our hotel wing had mood lighting; like it was on a dimmer switch that slowly turned into darkness.

"How are we the only ones in this wing?" Wendy laughed rather boisterously.

"Because we belong in the hedonism wing U-DING!"

It seemed to be getting darker. To make matters worse, we approached the elevator and no one was around, while the other side of the hotel was bustlingly with activity.

"After you, Milady."

Her smile exploded across her face and I wanted to tear her clothes off on the ride up. Thankfully it was a short one.

As the doors opened, we meandered down the long hall giddy as we got to her room. I knew I had to keep moving. And I did. I was so proud of myself, as if it actually mattered at this point, which it certainly didn't. But that aside, the only reason it had gone so smoothly was because she had no plans to call it a night.

As she opened her door, she said in a low voice, "Room 3428!"

I blinked at her. It was then it dawned on me that was my room. She had asked me earlier. Wendy's smile spun as the door slammed. I stood there for a moment before moving on.

Twelve minutes and thirty six seconds later, there was a soft knock on my door. I leaped out of the bed and raced to the door.

The Darkness celebrated. Bursting with excitement and trying to compose myself, I skidded to a stop at it, wearing only my jeans. I gripped the knob and thrust it open without even looking through the peephole.

Whoosh!

And there she was, in her cute little pajamas with her hair pulled up in a ponytail, just the way I loved it—imagine that! I kicked any morals I had left into the hall and slammed the door. She pushed passed me, with those rosy cheeks aflutter and that damn whimsical stare grabbing at my loins; she held me captive.

It was all way too much. I couldn't dwell on it though. Just then, I felt moisture on my chin. "I'm fucking drooling?" I frantically wiped my mouth and followed her well-scented cuteness like a dog in heat.

She stopped in front of the bathroom. I peered at her, confused, as she was making this weird face gesturing toward the shower.

"Don't look at me like that." She blushed now bright red. "It's that time of the month."

"What?" I said softly, with a baffled expression that matched my cluelessness to female situations such as this.

"I don't like the way you just looked at me," she bawled.

My head fell forward awkwardly. "W-h-at?" I sputtered now trying to digest this.

She laughed nervously, spouting, "Shut up, little boy. I have my period!"

"W-h-a-t..." My hands shot to my head. "Did you come here to taunt me? I'm surprised you're not wearing your stripes."

Her head turned to the side as her hands shot over her bright red face.

Breathing in and out rapidly, I was now only focused on catching my breath to have a little fun and she knew it.

"Fourteen months of this." I gasped, and lunged for the Do Not Disturb sign that hit my bare foot, adding insult to injury. "Fourteen fucking months of these meant to be moments, and now we end up at the same hotel, in the same fucking wing, alone, and you come to me bleeding? You know my phobias!"

Her smile couldn't be contained. She turned to my sink and began examining my aloe and face creams, which made it all worse...or better, depending on how you view this silly foolishness.

I put my hands on my head, attempting to send her off smiling. "Please, take your ponytail down," I said in an exaggerated tone. "You know what those damn things do to me."

Instantly she tightened it. "Grow-up."

"No!"

"YES!"

Smiling widely, she sashayed by me to open the door. My body twisted to follow her. She shifted the lock around the door so it wouldn't close all the way. Then she came back into the room prancing by me and flaunting her kittenish bliss.

"My equilibrium is going. What the hell are you doing?" I said in jest as she again lit up.

And like the many sexually charged frustrating moments we had shared before, I released sexual tension by reciting obscene lines that she always got a kick out of.

"I will spin you around and take you deep." I took a moment to search my memory because I went blank to the rest of the bawdy balderdash. But then the light bulb went on and I added, "And leave you in a puddle of potion, breathing in a bag, woman."

"Like you can leave me? Really." she spurted with her hands over her face relishing the obscene outbursts. I took a sip of Evian as she squealed, "Oh my God, put your shirt on."

"No, I will mount you with my nine inch I-TALIAN nail, woman!"

She fell back into the area by the bathroom heedlessly hitting the sink as I realized I should wrap it up because I was running out of material.

I lunged for the Do Not Disturb sign, waved it at her, and then pointed at the door.

She pushed herself off the sink and cried out, "Who fucking brings aloe on a trip with them, you freak of nature." She couldn't utter another word.

I waved the Do Not Disturb sign at her, and as her head rose, I pointed at my aloe shouting, "I'm using this thing, on that door, and rubbing that aloe all over you before I launch you across the room."

I thought she was hyperventilating. With all of her remaining strength she thrust herself forward and stumbled by me, threw the door open, and was gone.

Two minutes later, as I was watching Lady Antebellum' s "Need You Now" video, two of her texts hit my BlackBerry. I dove across the bed to snatch it off my nightstand to read them. The last one was: "Omg! I'm starting to think you are PP! (Peter Pan) GN. (Good night)"

I replied: "GN, Wendy."

With a goofy grin I dropped it on the nightstand and turned off the light.

Six hours later, my eyes slowly opened to the same soft knock on that same damn door. I pushed myself up ready for a re-run of last night's episode. I stumbled over to open the door and, sure enough, it was her. Fortunately, she was fully dressed with her little roller suitcase in tow, ready to take her test. No words were spoken. None were necessary. She just stared up at me as her eyes relayed everything her lips couldn't speak. I stood there, overwhelmed, I couldn't utter a word.

She turned her head to the side and walked away. I counted to three, and, almost exactly on cue, she turned to me and smiled.

I slowly closed the door, having no idea that that would be the last time I would see her as an employee of the company.

CHAPTER FORTY - SIX

HEADING EAST

DECEMBER 3, 2010

I fell back asleep until I heard a text hit my BlackBerry. I pulled it up to my squinty eyes and read it. It was Mindy Amour, informing me The Rabbi had neglected to copy me on an email that the morning conference call was moved up an hour. As I opened my laptop; she sent another text forewarning me that I was the only director who hadn't sent back the required information. Even wasted or hungover, I would never have allowed that to happen. As I thought about it, something seemed suspicious.

Rubbing my eyes redder than they already were, I quickly realized I didn't have an email about the information required. I frantically texted Mindy.

She replied: "WTF????"

She sent me a copy of the email and I compiled the necessary information and sent it back. Now slightly irritated, I tried calling The Rabbi, but it went to voicemail.

Thirty minutes later, the call began and all the directors were on it, along with Mindy. Within the first minute, I realized I was being targeted on every little thing imaginable. After it ended, Mindy sent another text wondering what happened because she knew that was a first.

"What was that? When did YOU, of all people, piss in his Cheerios?"

She was referring to The Rabbi.

I exhaled and replied, "I have no idea. You know that's never happened."

"NO, SHIT," she fired back.

Smiling at her spunk, I restively collapsed on the bed, swallowing hard. I tried to make light of it all, but The Darkness was there to turn the light off. In the corner of my eye, I noticed an email flash up. Now, in this heightened state of paranoia, I lunged for my laptop and pulled it closer. My heart raced when I saw it was from Mr. Lyin. He had sent me a time for the final meeting. It was set for December 8th in the Tampa office.

As I read it again, I noticed The Rabbi was copied. He had never mentioned a word to me about it, and he hadn't been copied on any of the other meetings. I tried to reach out to The Rabbi, but again it went to his voicemail. I had to convince myself I was overreacting, although this paranoia was wearing me down.

Since there is no rest for the wicked, I pushed myself up and headed out. On the ride back east, I mapped out half of the cases I had promised The Rabbi, but then stopped. "Fuck him!"

The Darkness chimed in on cue. "That bugged-eyed fuck should learn to appreciate what you've done over the last year. Let's see how he squirms when he's squeezing cases out of someone who doesn't view all this bullshit as a game they have to win. Hahaha. He'll be kissing your sick ass soon enough."

The truth of the matter was that he had been appreciative—to some degree at least, up until today. His reaction to me on this day was nothing I'd ever experienced before. Fidgeting in my seat, driving east, I couldn't deny the industry was changing rapidly either. This didn't help. Neither did my excessive pay, or this investigation happening at a time every winery and distributor was cutting back. Spacing out with that troubling thought, I turned on the radio and merged onto I-95 south turning up Eminem's "Not Afraid." It was then I missed a call from my old friend Bobby Blue. I lowered the music and listened to the voicemail. His voice was distressed: "Please tell me that fucking scumbag Fox didn't do what I just heard he did. Wait till your Cowboy hears; he'll load a gun and kill him. Call me...we'll laugh about this one over a bottle."

In that very instant, as emotional as I was, I was still appalled that I allowed this to happen. And then I was getting another call.

I pulled my BlackBerry back and noticed it was Schultz. I took a deep breath trying to regain my own composure to speak, and answered. Schultz began the conversation focused on the numbers email I had sent him before leaving the hotel. I calmed my emotions as best as possible, but within minutes, I realized he had another message as they swung again. He brought up Wendy and my ego, all in an attempt to protect me. As he continued I finally had to set the record straight.

"Dan, this thing with her has nothing to do with my ego," I said calmly. I took a breath and added, "Believe me, I wish it did."

There was an awkward moment of silence that was broken by him clacking his tongue before he said seriously, "I'm starting to see that and I'm guessing you were attempting to avoid her after the third meeting with Lyin, when she copied you on that email to me."

"We both try…but it never seems to work…"

He cleared his throat. "I know I've said it before, but I have to say it again. I know what you did for me. And I'm sure this will all work out but I thought it would be over by now and it's not."

"Thanks, Dan, it'll be over on Wednesday. But I'll see you on Monday. And don't forget we have that dinner with Dave Turkot on Tuesday."

"Of course." He paused, perhaps noticing my voice was strained. "Hey, are you okay? You don't sound okay."

"Yes. I'm fine," I lied.

"All right. I'll email you the numbers this afternoon."

"Thanks."

Click.

CHAPTER FORTY - SEVEN

HOME ALONE

DECEMBER 4, 2010

Twenty-eight hours later, I was sitting alone by our fire pit after I snatched a bottle from our east coast home's wine cooler. I had planned on spending the weekend there to check on the house, but thought it made more sense to go from Orlando straight to the east coast for the meeting I had on Monday, and then the dinner with my old friend, Dave Turkot, on Tuesday.

Just as I opened the bottle I had selected—Wild Horse Cheval Sauvage Pinot Noir—I heard the ding of a text. Thinking it was Marie, I put the cork down and picked up my BlackBerry, but noticed it was Dave Turkot. I turned back to quickly grab the bottle and poured a glass. The earthy and herbal aromas pleased my senses as a smile spread across my face: "Shady, (my nickname when I began my career with this company was Slim Shady) we are a go for Tuesday! WE HAVE LIFT-OFF! We will down some good wine, my friend!"

With a scarce smile spreading, I enthusiastically replied: "Dirty Turk, you have no idea how much I've missed you!"

As I took my first sip of the earthy goodness, relishing the lengthy finish, he shot back: "Shady, you are fucking living the dream, my man. I just want to have a taste of your good life. See you Tuesday."

My eyes closed slowly as my woe returned with a vengeance, causing me to get up and wander around the fire. Halfway around it I wondered what I was doing. My eyes rolled to the dark clouds infiltrating the sky as I jumped back in the chair. A cold front was coming in. For minutes, I adjusted, unable to get comfortable. I then fixated on the raging fire that I fueled like a child without supervision by dumping the tiki torch shit all over it. My head slumped. I had no idea why, it just did.

Then as I stared to the pebbles beneath me, I noticed a cork as The Darkness howled. I reached below the chair and grabbed it noticing it was charred. Anguish settled over me. I realized it was the cork from the bottle of Opus we opened to celebrate my monumental move to Tampa.

I didn't even want to touch it. My thoughts raced back to what felt like a lifetime ago, back when I was well on my way to being king of the world. The vision of Bud Fox throwing it into the fire along with the words I ironically spoke hit me with a hauntingly cool wind that came out of nowhere.

I quipped, "Fox, that's taboo. Get that out of there! It's bad luck to burn a cork from a celebratory bottle. Everyone knows that."

As laugher echoed above the flames, they all knew I'd just made that shit up to see my boy—now hard to believe he was ever my boy—sticking something in the raging fire to try and get it out. Little did I know it would haunt me fifteen months later as if it were true.

It instantly became a surreal, grim blur in my mind. I sat there for what seemed to be a minute only distracted by a somber rain that suddenly fell. But when I pushed myself up I checked my wristwatch: twenty minutes had passed, and the vision of all the people celebrating with me disappeared. And I was cold and alone.

CHAPTER FORTY - EIGHT

"FUCK!"

DECEMBER 5, 2010

Twelve hours later I was full of worry and consternation. I breathed out a long, slow breath, but only a small amount of anxiety. The dream from the night before was on my mind. Typically, I didn't remember my dreams. But these were vivid and concise accounts that brought me back to my father's concerns early on in my career. Attempting to avoid any salt in my gaping wounds, I ignored the correlation and then checked my emails. But that didn't help.

It was then I realized I'd only received one from an Orlando manager thanking me for the dinner and a great time. And the fact that they'd all checked in by this point as having a memorable night wasn't even any consolation to the reality that I hadn't heard from The Rabbi.

I thought about calling him, but I knew if I got his voicemail again I wouldn't make it to Monday. Then I went to text Wendy but stopped. I realized she was living her other life over the weekend and instead, I just stuck my head in the sand. Blocking out the fact that something was awry seemed to be a brilliant plan. But that didn't even work, as the thoughts of being moved into another division then consumed me.

Rubbing my eyes, I quickly dismissed my thoughts. I worked out that it made no sense, especially with my pay package. I thought I was losing it. My mind raced through so many scenarios, but none of them were as dire as the reality of what was already signed off on: the death of my auspicious career.

Within minutes I began walking around our home. It was almost exactly as we'd left it, since we'd bought all new furniture in Tampa. Some of the pictures were still there too, mainly the old ones when the kids were babies. That helped my downtrodden spirit.

But then I heard my BlackBerry ring. Grabbing it, I saw it was Marie. The conversation began with her super excited about what she was buying the kids for Christmas and then went into plans for our January trip to Mexico. And as the dollar signs danced in my head, I became agitated as my anxiety levels escalated.

"Is all that necessary?" I said.

"What is wrong with you lately? Yes, it is. Goodbye, Larry."

I waited for her to hang up, but since she didn't, I said, "I'm sorry…it's just that we've spent a fortune." I paused before adding, "And I have a lot on my mind."

"Yeah, well, I wouldn't know!"

Click.

I felt the same disorientation that I had the day before, only now multiplied exponentially. I collapsed on the couch in the family room and turned on the television. Flipping through the channels, I found out Russia won the bid to host the 2018 World Cup, and the House of Representatives passed the Child Nutrition Bill implementing improvements to the health of the foods available for children. But then, I watched a report on the rising unemployment levels and noticed that Tampa was one of the highest cities in the country at over eleven percent.

I turned off the television.

I fell back and heard a text hit my BlackBerry. It was Schultz: "I don't know how you put up with Fox as long as you did. This guy really is something else."

I lied down on the couch without responding. I began harboring anger.

My eyes opened shortly after they'd closed; suddenly overwhelmed by the thought of keeping all of this from my wife. She knew nothing because of Wendy, well, because of me not wanting to answer any more questions about her. My mind raced back to the baseball game, and then to so many varying circumstances that caused my emotions to again swing widely. I couldn't stop rehashing it. It then worsened with a text from Marie: "I'm on Facebook and a picture was posted from one of Jessie's friends. It's a picture of them out. He's next to Wendy, but she looks like her mind is elsewhere. I hope you haven't seen her this past week."

All at once a terrible dark cloud descended on me.

"F-u-c-k!" I said softly, staring at the ceiling.

There was no doubt reading the same texts from Marie over and over wore me down. I couldn't answer any of it. I was pissed. That's right, I actually had the audacity to be angry at her for calling me out on something that would end my promising career and alter our life forever. Never mind everything else that a spouse would be beyond livid about. But I was.

I was hurting so badly and couldn't even admit why. It was at this point, a million "what ifs" hit me, along with why didn't I have the drive to fix my marriage when I said I would? The truth was that I was done trying to fit a square peg into a round hole, while constantly wanting to scream, as I had thoughts of running to Wendy.

So I just ran to Wendy.

But as my emotions took hold of me, I felt there was no way I could just throw the towel in on my marriage. But then another recent conversation leveled me where Marie refused to acknowledge we were on two totally different pages, while again blaming it all on this thing with Wendy. After I reminded her about our little visit with the marriage counselor she shouted, "That was ten years ago, Larry, enough!"

I exhaled heavily. "That's my point, Marie, and we're still dealing with those unresolved issues…you can blame whoever you want, but at some point you have to look in the mirror."

We again ended on two separate pages, miles from each other.

So I again screamed, "Fuck!"

With that came more thoughts invading my head. One that kept hitting me was that I was only pretending I wasn't lying to Marie, which made it worse. So I justified it (again) by saying to myself, "Well, she knows we're close. I was upfront with that." But then I suddenly had a vision of Mr. Lyin gawking at me in disbelief (again) so I (again) shouted, "Fuck!"

And since Marie was now pissed off she decided to stick a hot iron up my ass by sending me another text: "Maybe you should reach out to your special friend to see if she's all right. She actually seems sad in this picture that flashed up...oh wait, that's right, you have to wait until Monday because she continues to hide it all when she's with Jessie living her other life. Like what I'm scrolling through now on Facebook!"

My arm went limp as I dropped the BlackBerry on the couch next to me. I was exhausted and just wanted to go to sleep. Within the minute though I winced with the sound of another text as her onslaught continued: "And the fact you haven't responded to my first text tells me you did see her, which would explain the way she appears in these pictures. When does it end?"

I pounded my fist onto the coffee table and screamed to let out some of the anger. Falling back onto the couch I let out a hard breath, and screamed even louder, "FUCK!"

CHAPTER FORTY - NINE

CAN I BLAME THIS MESS ON THE GIRL WHO FIRST CALLED ME PETER PAN?

DECEMBER 6, 2010
DREAMSTATE: JULY 1990

Her eyes had that undeniable light as her friend sashayed over to me with a shot. I continued to watch her over the petite brunette's shoulder until she stopped in front of me. My gaze shifted to hers.

"I'm Jill," she said guardedly. "This is from..." she inelegantly pointed behind her, "my friend Katie."

I glanced back over to her blond accomplice who was now beaming while smiling at her as the high held me captive. It was the same sensation I scored that afternoon as my play time with Mrs. Silverstein and her daughter incited another signature on the dotted line for my company's moving services.

But during the evening version of this high I suddenly saw my father over Jill's shoulder. Taken aback I blinked and he was gone. I thanked her graciously for the delivery of the shot and her eyes warmed to me. As I threw it back she informed me that it would send me to Never Land. There were times, I thought, that meant to be moments were magical. This was one of them. I was suddenly enthralled.

Giggling like a little girl, she threw her hands up as to stop me from thinking she was nuts. "I'm sorry, we just watched Peter Pan with her stepsister. She's seven and loves Wendy." She hesitated briefly as I smiled. Peering into my eyes with a touch of sarcasm she added, "So you're a nice bad boy. Great! Enjoy your trip to Never

Land."

I grinned mischievously. "I'm sure I will. It was very nice meeting you."

"Likewise," she said, walking back to her friend.

With her departure, my imagination took flight, as I now viewed the blond as one of the Mermaids in the movie, playfully splashing water on me from Mermaid Lagoon. Her eyes followed me over to a high-top table to the side of the bar. It was at that table where my buddies, oddly from all different times of my life to this point, were vacating. One said, "Larry, you coming?"

I didn't answer though. Instead I credulously asked, "Have you ever received a high when a girl stares at you and their eyes open up straight into their souls?"

They all froze, speechless.

After an awkward moment, two of them, in unison, muttered, "No."

One remained silent while only squinting at me eerily. The last bellowed, "Larry, it's called 'fuck me eyes!'"

I shook my head. "No...no—"

"Yes...yes! She fucked your little boy-band-ass with her eyes, no offense. So are you coming with us?"

"No. There's a Mermaid that craves a play date," I replied as he gawked at me.

"What?" His head fell forward as his eyebrow arched. "What the fuck did you just say?"

"The blond in the corner," I replied.

He turned and said, "Jesus. She's staring at you, dude! Mermaid, huh...that's fucking good. Like a code for the sexy, scary bitches you want to fuck, right?"

"No, no...like the cute ones in the Disney version of Peter Pan."

His eyes closed, and as they reopened he hissed, "Larry...Jesus, no. That's totally fucking gay. And I hate to tell you, but that Mermaid's boyfriend is the bartender. Try again." He stopped suddenly before adding, "So I'm guessing now you'll be coming with us?"

"No. The eyes never lie. I want to meet her."

Laughter filled the space around me as I saw my father again. I rubbed my eyes and he was gone. They moved in to mess up my perfectly teased Rick Springfield hair before strolling onto the stage for the next band's performance. It was then I walked back to the line for the bar and noticed my Mermaid swimming over. I took a step forward as I heard a female's voice ask the guy behind me to cut the line. I knew it was her as I ignored the brush against my back pocket.

Within seconds, I felt a tug as she yelled, "You look like that guy on TV."

I turned to her. She was glowing. "Thanks very much for the shot. I'm Larry."

Her hands hit her waist dramatically as she snapped sarcastically, "You mean you're not Charles in Charge?"

I stared into her deep blue eyes as they opened up to her soul and innocently replied, "No, ya silly goose."

Her mouth dropped open before she bawled, "SILLY GOOSE?" She flipped her hair, full of intrigue, and took two steps right up to me. "Seriously, who says that?"

I only smiled. She beamed brightly before she looked away, putting her hair up in a ponytail. I waited an instant and leaned forward to whisper, "I like your ponytail."

Her head crashed against my chest as if she just took a bullet before she slowly lifted it and backed away from me, mock-fanning herself. Her eyes narrowed to mine as she said, "You're not a player. You're fucking Peter Pan." Her hands came together with a single clap, seemingly ecstatic with this risible revelation as she came back into me, whispering, "Are you going to take me to Never Land now, ya silly goose?"

My eyes snapped open. It took me a second to realize I was dreaming as I then flipped my soaking wet pillow over. With my heart racing, I pushed myself out of bed to change into a dry T-shirt, cognizant of the fact that this night was special.

Excluding the visions of my father, and the fact that my buddies were from all different times of my life, this dream was almost dead on to a noteworthy night out early in my career. Obviously, one that began my Mermaid/Never Land references, without any thought of what adding my Wendy would do to this frenzied fantasy twenty years later.

Suddenly overwrought, now wise to the ramifications of such an addition, I actually attempted to blame this girl's gift trip to Never Land as the reason I ended up in this mess. But that only lasted seconds as my father's worriment about the way I achieved my early career accomplishments began to haunt me.

Four hours later I poured my first cup of coffee unable to escape it all; not only the highs that drove me, but my father's concerns that I was able to rely more on pixie dust than any actual expertise to achieve a monetary windfall. It was all incredible, but critical, to where I was now twenty years later.

Falling back restless, I had a vision of dominos falling into each other as all of this was surely connected to the forewarned dangers that I had repeatedly neglected. The wrong doing that I tucked under the twenty-year-old blanket of my stellar success; something that would soon be yanked off me exposing the fault line that I'd built my promising career on, had opened to become a mile wide cliff...one that I was about to race off of, because by this point, I truly believed I could fly...to my sacred Never Land...with my Wendy.

Rubbing my eyes anxiously I heard the ding of a text hit my BlackBerry. I pushed myself up to grab it off the counter. It was Wendy. I took a deep breath and read it: "I didn't sleep all weekend and I'm blocking Thursday night out of my mind forever. When are you back in Tampa?"

I collapsed back in the chair, distraught, but still unaware that I had already become a casualty to the wild desire we shared for each other that simply ran too deep.

CHAPTER FIFTY

THE LAST SUPPER

DECEMBER 7, 2010

I eased out of bed Tuesday morning sluggishly. I was hit with another text. Wendy was relentless in her efforts to push forward her revisions of Thursday night. The four texts she sent before eight o' clock were follow-ups to our lengthy Monday afternoon call. The tension mounted when she swore we had texted each other to meet in my room. My astringent response compelled her to then call.

With a nearly out of breath voice I answered, "I'm in no mood for this, Wendy."

All I heard was the wind blowing before her vexing reply. "You're in no mood? I had to leave the house before I was even ready because I couldn't take it anymore. I have been driving around since seven not even knowing where I'm going. I haven't slept all weekend. And I didn't just show up to your hotel room in my pajamas announcing I had my period."

I should've hung up, but I didn't.

I clenched the BlackBerry tightly, my eyes widened, mouth dropped open, and I said, "We never texted each other about you coming to my room and we never discussed having wine in my room."

She replied hastily, "I have no idea how I got there then."

"You asked for my room number at the bar, repeated it in the hall outside your room, and showed up in your fucking pajamas."

Her breathing became erratic. "And I just told you I had my period?"

"Do you really want to continue this?"

"Yes!"

"After you stood in front of my bathroom—"

She interrupted, "I was looking at your fucking aloe on the sink."

"That was after. Before that, you made a gesture towards the shower, became panicked by my reaction…and informed me you had your period."

She became defensive. "Seriously, stop. I did not go there to fuck you in the shower."

"Wendy, I'm only telling you what you did do. When you left I figured it was to get the scrabble game you left in your room…but you never came back."

There was silence. No wind or anything, but then I heard her car door shut and her breathing heavily. "I can't believe this," she sputtered.

I sighed, "This investigation's been brutal, but your rewrites of everything having to do with us have made it worse."

Restive, she threw up her favorite recycled line. "Why is this happening?"

I was over that line too. "How can you possibly still ask that question?"

An eerie silence was broken by her exhale. "Because it keeps me sane."

Our affliction was interrupted by the beep of a call.

I checked my caller ID. It was Schultz. "I have to take this call. It's Schultz."

"No way," she barked, "call him back!"

"I can't, Wendy. I'm the one on trial for this."

Click.

I clicked over. "Hey."

I heard voices in the background before Schultz replied, "Are we still on for tonight?"

I collapsed on our couch. "Yes."

Wendy texted: "REALLY???? Call me back because that was so WRONG!"

My eyes closed after reading it as Schultz said, "I'm going to finish up with this idiot (Bud Fox) around three and head to you. We can open a bottle before dinner."

I sighed, "I'll be here."

"Are you all right?"

"I don't know," I said. "But I'll see you later."

Click.

An hour later, Wendy called me back, but I didn't answer. I was an emotional wreck. She didn't leave a message. Thirty minutes later she sent me a text: "I can't concentrate on anything. Thanks." Ten minutes after that, she sent another: "I'm going to work out. The anxiety is killing me."

I replied: "I'm sorry. I just need to have this investigation end. I'll be fine after Wednesday. I'll call you later." It was as if the storm had surrounded us with nowhere left to hide and lighting bolts crashing all around.

Seven hours later, as my anguish spread and heart ached, we met Turkot and his buddy at a little seafood restaurant on the river just up from my house. Little did I realize this would be my last supper, and how ironic having the most influential wine buyer of my early years with the company in attendance for the end of it? As my mind continued to race, darker thoughts had begun to consume me about the final meeting with Mr. Lyin. I attempted not to be distant, but it was difficult.

"You guys want to come back by the house? We can start the fire pit up and get into the good shit from my cellar." I was doing my best to snap out of it.

"Shady, we are in, my man!" Turkot replied as we headed out.

Twenty minutes later, I was walking around the house with Turkot. He again brought up that I was living the dream. My anxiety levels escalated. As we made our way down to the fire pit, I drifted in and out of the conversations struggling, with so much.

And as I stood there freezing, it had become apparent to everyone. "Shady," Turkot said, "you look like you have the weight of the world on your shoulders, relax and drink up. We'll get this fire going to warm you up."

Before they could, the night turned bitterly cold (for Florida) and the temperature seemed to be dropping by the minute. The forecast was for a low of thirty-one degrees, and within the hour, we'd run out of wood. Everyone panicked.

After a quick brainstorm, I remembered we had wooden pallets in this giant bush area between the houses. Our east coast home sat on a landscaped acre and those pallets were from a mulch delivery that summer. I just wasn't sure if they were still there. With my fingers crossed we found them.

Just before eleven o'clock, as the flames were now licking the starlit sky, Turkot lowered Pink's "Raise Your Glass" and raised his own full of Mondavi Reserve Cabernet Sauvignon for a toast. "To fucking Slim Shady, my dear friend, who is living the dream. Your future is bright, my man. I am proud of you."

In the crisp air that clouded with my breath, I could feel the tension tearing through me. His words struck like a fist to the gut. I swallowed hard as Schultz made eye contact with me. He now knew I was struggling mightily, and did his best to wrap it up. I held it together with my fake happy face and within minutes, the boys said their goodbyes. Staring at the empty bottle I then picked it up and tossed it into the fire. I felt I had to wipe my eyes, and as I heard their car start, I was relieved that I could go to sleep. I walked back up to the house under a moon that was shining bright, unable to see the light.

CHAPTER FIFTY - ONE

THE DARKNESS

DECEMBER 8, 2010

My eyes opened slowly to The Darkness that had crawled up beside me, hissing.

"Time to get up, buddy boy. You have to get back to Tampa now. The fat lady is about to sing in your honor."

Lying in bed, cold and apathetic, all I could do was watch the ceiling fan spin in the cool morning air. Schultz had left, but I lacked the energy to follow suit.

I should've turned the heat on.

I reached for the comforter to pull it up under my chin. I desperately searched for anything positive to inspire me out of the funk that bound me there. After nearly five minutes, I mustered enough energy to sluggishly scroll through my emails with The Darkness checking in again.

"You're not gonna see any emails from The Rabbi, sport."

It was right, and as I rolled over and dropped my BlackBerry on the pillow next to me, numbness set in. The idiotic gaffes I had made, and the lies contrived from them, left me reeling. And The Darkness knew it, and it taunted me.

It chimed in again.

"Living out your exorbitant little fairy tale, pretending it was nothing to hide wasn't your brightest move, sport. Oh how these violent delights have violent ends...hahahaha!"

Peevishly pondering it all, I lunged for the bottle of Evian on my nightstand, cursing out loud. "Where is that little bug-eyed motherfucker?"

I was referring to The Rabbi.

As I called him, one of the few conversations we had had on this investigation resonated in my head and casted further doubt on everything. It was all too bizarre as his phone went to voicemail. As I laid there, The Darkness whispered again, "You should wear your black suit today, sport."

Anxious, I leaped out of bed and aimlessly wandered to the other side of the house. I stood motionless, staring in the bathroom mirror. I realized I should've taken a long look in it way before now. After splashing cold water on my face, I walked into the bedroom where both Lauren and Jerry once had their cribs. Within seconds, the cherished memories consumed me.

All I could think about was how quickly these thirteen years had passed, and that I'd pay any price to hit the reset button on all of it. The thought of them never knowing I had worked for any other company caused me to fall back into the wall. I slid down it, to the floor. Before I could gather my thoughts, the phone rang. It was Dan Schultz. I slowly stood up and answered, "Hey."

It took him a couple of seconds before he asked, "You okay?"

"I don't know. What's up?"

"The Rabbi called."

With a great tension in my voice, I responded, "And?"

"He wants me back in Tampa right away."

"What?" I took a deep breath. "Does he know you're on the east coast?"

"Yes," he paused. "Larry…"

"What?"

"Something is wrong."

"What?"

"I don't know, but I don't have a good feeling about this."

The Darkness had found me again. "Knock, knock, can I come in? I would strongly advise you to pull your little Peter Pan hat over your eyes now, sport."

I was struggling for a breath as Schultz snapped, "…Larry?"

"I'm here. Dan, what the fuck is going on?"

"I think The Rabbi's flying to Tampa right now—"

"He didn't tell me that."

"Have you spoken to him?"

"No."

My response fell into an eerie dead silence.

"I'm calling him now," I spouted desperately. "Thanks."

Click.

I called him again, only to get his voicemail as The Darkness took another jab at me. "You had a great thing going for you right here in this cozy little home of yours. You were making real decent money. Shit, you could've lived happily ever after right here."

I stumbled out of the room and through the French doors, stepping out to the pool area in an attempt to clear my head with some fresh air. But The Darkness followed, relentlessly ridiculing me about my relationship with Wendy. "Everyone was in awe of that connection from the first day she placed an apple on your desk, yet you only downplayed it, knowing she wasn't just another Mermaid. You knew you had finally met your Wendy. You knew you were unable to stop those flights to your sacred Never Land. Well now, you'll both have to accept the fact that you are doomed, star-crossed lovers, pried apart by the most insane investigation in the history of *The Asylum*. And left in the ashes of what would've been an extraordinary career. Hahahaha!"

I became lightheaded and bent over to put my hands on my knees. The only thing that kept me from blacking out was the peacefulness surrounding me. Standing back up, I couldn't help but take in the tranquil landscape and how much I had missed it. Something I hadn't thought about for the year-and-a-half I had now been gone. And as The Darkness continued tormenting me, I walked down the steps and along the path to the fire pit. It was still smoldering. The empty bottle of Mondavi Reserve Cabernet I threw in it, leftover from my restless night, had rolled off to the side, charred and still burning.

Symbolic of my career.

I stood there, alone with my affliction, until a cool breeze sent a sudden chill over my half-naked body shaking me free of the anguish just long enough to make it back into the house. While taking a long hot shower, I could hear my BlackBerry ringing. I had missed calls from Schultz and Josh Mathews, my Orlando sales manager. Interestingly, he was looking to have me drop off the iPad he had won as part of an incentive, en route back to Tampa.

An hour later, I called him as I was heading out. "Hey, Josh," I said, attempting to sound chipper. "I got your message and I have your iPad."

"Hey, Larry," he replied. "That's great. Can you meet me on your way back?"

"Yes." But I had a strong suspicion that The Rabbi had warned him to get it, and quickly.

"Just tell me when and where, and I'll be there."

"Champions Gate Publix, in an hour and a half."

"Did you want to tour the store?" he asked, trying to be polite, but knew I wouldn't have time.

"No. I have to get back to Tampa."

"Okay, I'll be there."

The bleakness of the day was even apparent outside, with ominous clouds rolling in overhead, as the perfect storm bore down on me. My mindset had become desperate and fearful with The Darkness riding shotgun.

"Shall we reminisce on the ride back, sport? I was laughing about that call she made to you on this same ride back to Tampa. I realize there have been many, but this particular one tickled me. You were so happy. You looked like a little boy...who lost all control. That was a year ago...hahaha."

Desperate to settle my thoughts, I made a call, but it went to voicemail.

The Darkness continued, "...How about the night you two love birds just showed up at a bar, on a night you weren't supposed to meet, wearing matching stripped shirts...with the shooting star...how romantic was that shit...hahaha...just call her!"

I drifted into the left lane.

Succumbing to my despair, I went to call Wendy. But just as I did, she called me. I froze, staring at her name on the caller ID, before dropping it back in the cup holder. I was certainly jumpy, and then, instead of calling her back, I unconsciously turned on the radio.

The song playing was Lenka's "The Show." Words can't describe where I was at this moment.

I got off at the wrong exit.

Gripping the steering wheel, I spun around racing back on I-4. I was very aware I'd never heard it on the radio, and as a chill shot up my spine, The Darkness howled,

"I LOVE THAT SONG!"

I drifted into the left lane.

I had no control over my emotions. The shock turned to anger and then denial that this was happening.

I veered off at the Champions Gate exit.

With my thoughts dark in tow, I dumped the iPad off and raced on, as each mile marker I passed read like a countdown to Waterloo. I dialed The Rabbi. Once again, the call went to voicemail. He now was tainted, and unaware of the many layers to this; including The Wizard's maneuvers in the dark—behind the curtain, back at The Asylum.

I kept going over in my mind that I should've informed him of so much more. I just had no idea this could have ever escalated to this point. But even with that aside, it was the sudden vision I had of The Wizard's uncharacteristically quiet and disturbed demeanor—the one I first witnessed during Geno Franc's "grand plan for my future" meeting, right before the relocation—that caused to me realize I had been a naïve fool. By this point, though, it was as if I had to tilt my head back just to see, and the quicksand was almost covering me.

Pulling into the executive parking lot, a knot formed in my throat when I didn't see The Wizard's car. I swung into my spot and ripped the keys out of the ignition as The Darkness cried out, "Did you really think that guy would be anywhere near here for this?"

I jumped out, slammed my door, and flew up the steps into The Asylum. As I walked into the main part of the office, Mama Bear was unsettled as she only nervously muttered, "Hello." She barely looked up at me, and as I stared at her in passing, she feverishly hit the keyboard in front of her. Continuing into my office, I collapsed in my chair.

As I struggled through my emails, I realized I hadn't received the daily trackers or even heard from Mr. Lyin. I emailed him to confirm the time of the meeting and made a couple of calls to inquire if The

Rabbi had sent out the trackers, but both went to voicemail.

A pain shot up my back as I adjusted myself in the chair and glanced over at my stellar, nearly thirteen-year career with the company, one that I had proudly displayed by promotions in handsome frames on my wall. Within seconds of reflecting on all of it, I felt greatly pique.

Unable to deny how different everything felt since this investigation began, I just sat there. We typically had the busiest, and certainly most jovial, office in the building. Not now. Growing restless and fearful, I turned back to my wine cabinet, seriously entertaining thoughts of boxing it all up and running it out to my car. But just then, I received a text from Marie. She informed me about a Christmas present she'd found for Lauren. I read it twice as tears welled up in my eyes. We were certainly afforded a comfortable life from this career, and now it was evident that something would change; I just had no idea how drastically. I let out a deep sigh, unable to ignore the fact that everything I had created was crumbling around me.

I began second-guessing everything, with a vision of Gekko beating the shit out of Fox in Central Park. All the madness of this ever-changing investigation had drained me. And just then my gaze caught a picture on my credenza. I was with Wendy and Matt at the Greeks. We were all smiling wide. I could almost hear the laughter. Everything was so special at that very moment in time.

Deep in thought, I began sinking even further into this unknown depressed state; one that was beginning to scare me. I was a control freak who now had completely lost all control. As my hands went over my face, I exhaled deeply thinking that this was only supposed to be the first real step in that bright future plan. One, now, that only had minutes to live. And then there it was, Mr. Lyin had finally responded to my email.

The email: "We are in the executive conference room. Please come up now."

CHAPTER FIFTY - TWO

THE EXECUTION

DECEMBER 8, 2010
THE EXECUTIVE CONFERNCE ROOM

I clenched my pad of paper and began the trek up. My mouth was dry and I struggled to swallow, worn and lessened by the burden of grief. Halfway down the hall, I noticed one of the managers from another selling division coming toward me.

As he glanced up from something he was reading, he blurted out, "There he is, L-A-R-R-Y! When's the next promotion?"

I could only nod and shrug as he smiled, slapping my hand. Once I passed him, I realized this dispirited state had consumed me as I neglected to turn my frown upside down acknowledging my reflection in the window of the door.

I pulled it open and headed into the lobby, seeing the head of The Asylum's security team. He was standing somberly by the steps going up to the executive offices. I buried the pain, as the look on his face prevented me from uttering a word. Harried, I hurried by him as he bestowed me a respectful nod and sigh. Jittery, I ran up the steps with an edgy energy and swiped my security badge to get in.

It was dead quiet and vacated—another telltale sign I was walking into an ambush. I marched up to the executive conference room door. It was open. My heart was now racing. The first person I saw was The Rabbi. He stood up with a doleful look on his face.

"Hello, Gary," I said. "I didn't realize you were coming. I called you—" I stopped in mid-sentence as he only nodded slowly, speechless.

Next to him was Mr. Lyin. He was going through his notes. I asked them if they wanted any water before we began. They said no. I went into the kitchen, hit with an unwelcomed scent, and opened the refrigerator to find nothing but leftovers. There wasn't even one bottle of Evian. Now, uncomfortably struggling to swallow and with no water, I walked out, again reminded of how different everything had been since Geno Franc moved on.

As I reentered the conference room, I sat down across from the investigator. The Rabbi was at the end of the table, to my left. Pulling my chair in, it seemed as if everything was suddenly moving in slow motion. I sat tense, bracing myself for the words: Ready, aim, fire.

Mr. Lyin inclined his head and proceeded to pull loose pages out of a folder while reaching across the table to hand me my copy. He did the same for The Rabbi. The top, right-hand side of the cover page stated, MEMORANDUM. It had my name on it, the investigator's name, the date, and the title: Investigative Findings and Written Notice of Termination.

My heart was now beating through my shirt as I struggled to breathe and swallow. I read the words, but none of it sank in. For the first twenty seconds or so, I only saw his lips moving. Then it hit me. I felt a raging anger, but knew I had to keep it under control. The tension was stifling. And as the room heated, as if it were on fire, The Rabbi's eyes restlessly rolled away and shifted to the middle of the conference table. As he digested the words spoken by Mr. Lyin, his mannerisms were uneasy. Regardless of how this was sold to him, it immediately seemed as if he had buyer's remorse.

My eyes closed as my head slumped forward with so many conflicting thoughts racing through it. My breaths were erratic, quickly going in and out, as the text from Marie about Lauren's Christmas present hit me. I wanted to push the table right through the wall, with Mr. Lyin in between. This was just so fucking wrong. As I wiped my forehead with my sleeve, he stated that everything had already been signed off on by the state VP and general manager—a man I had never met.

He began reading the report, word for word. And if not for the raging fury burning inside me, I would have blacked out. First, I wanted to see if the original complaint, the one filed by Bud Fox, would be mentioned. I was tipped off by an employee, who had once dealt with black magic of these kinds of proceedings, that it would have to be included. His reasoning was, that no other complaint was actually filed. And, as bizarre as he thought it all was, he was correct.

The first words Mr. Lyin read were:

"On September 22nd, 2010, Bud Fox filed a complaint against you claiming that on July 2nd, 2010, while intoxicated, you slid your hand inside the jeans and underwear of his girlfriend, and touched her buttocks, on two occasions."

This was the dubious inquiry I had briefly been questioned on during the first interview; only now, it was brought back to life with a twist. It was now two touches into her underwear.

Fighting back my emotions, Mr. Lyin was aware his review of this report was not destined to uninterrupted cogitation. His eyes showed concern.

Within seconds, I had enough. "You're telling me this is a sexual harassment case now?" I yelled, totally blindsided.

Mr. Lyin, without hesitation, sternly responded. "This is not a sexual harassment case."

"How can you possibly say that and write this?" I hissed, as The Rabbi fell back in the chair.

Mr. Lyin's words continued to fall through the gaps of anything sane as he then read an elaborate confrontation between Bud Fox and me that never happened.

I furiously snapped, "That never happened."

It looked as if he was going to read on, but the words were so wrong he couldn't deny it. "You have to sign the last page," Mr. Lyin deadpanned.

My head rose to him as my eyebrow arched, envisioning my fist going through his face and out the backside of his head. I turned to The Rabbi, who glanced back to Mr. Lyin, and then both of them anxiously peered back at me. With a captive audience, I leaned forward, narrowing my eyes at Mr. Lyin, and seethed, "Are you out of your fucking mind? I'm not signing this."

The Rabbi's eyes bulged further out of his head, as Mr. Lyin then incredibly read on, "Bud Fox was eligible for a supplier trip—"

I slammed my hand down. "Bud Fox is an incompetent manager

and liar, who I protected when I shouldn't have." I took a deep breath and added, "I know for a fact The Wizard sent this imbecile down to file a complaint against me. And I'll bet everything I own he is fired within a year."

(Bud Fox was, in fact, fired within the year for lying.)

Mr. Lyin shot The Rabbi a look of puzzlement.

All of this was beyond inconceivable, but it didn't matter. Mr. Lyin's head tilted back down at his report, and with a cold, distraught stare, he warily flipped the page and continued reading. I turned to The Rabbi for help.

"There's more," he softly responded, with his hand in the air to me.

With his head down, Mr. Lyin plodded on, brows furrowed. "Because Bud confronted you about your conduct at the restaurant, and told you his girlfriend was going to confront your wife, you decided to exclude him from the supplier trip."

I fell forward over the table with my elbows hitting it and hands holding my head. "I told you the reason Fox was kept out of this incentive and it absolutely had nothing to do with the lies you wrote and are now reading."

His eyes scanned the sheet providing no relief to the tension tearing across his face.

"I told you exactly what Fox told me, how he told me, and when he said it. There was never a confrontation in any stretch of the imagination. And as far as my wife goes, he used to be her personal trainer." I paused, as a bird could've flown in this guy's mouth, as he sat there clueless to so much. "She would have laughed at you for even putting the word 'credible' in the same sentence as anything having to do with him. And that's the reason you never reached out to his team. You knew they would've burned The Asylum to the ground if they heard you referring to him as credible."

It was then as if he hit the reset button and everything he had stated prior was never read. This was one of the most amazing scenes I'd ever been a part of in my entire life. He looked like the bitter beer guy as he fought to reform his contorted face, muttering, "You were concerned about her confronting both your wife and Wendy's fiancé about your relationship."

I pushed myself up in the chair, stupefied. He swallowed uneasily, as I said, "I told you I don't know this girl. I told you I have only heard that she is, 'crazy' from both Wendy and my administrative assistant."

"She never stated that to me," he maintained, his glower intensifying.

"Then you need to call her up here, right now, because one of you is lying."

He rubbed the center of his forehead abhorrently ignoring me while flipping the page. Within the first sentence, I heard Tony's name.

"Wait, who?" I snapped, lurching over the table.

His weary eyes grew wide as he responded to my interruption.

"Everything we are going over was reported by the individuals listed in this report. Much of what they brought up to me was done voluntarily. They did so without me questioning them."

I slumped to the side, unable to fathom him admitting that again.

Mr. Lyin read on in a more assertive voice.

I then scanned the next paragraph. My voice rose, "How do you allow a disgruntled manager who recently did not receive a promotion from me, into an investigation he had nothing to do with by volunteering information that had no correlation to the original complaint? I'm having a difficult time just remaining upright in this chair, this is that insane!" I collapsed in the chair as The Rabbi tried interrupting me, but I wasn't done. "Gary, you don't have a clue." I screamed, slamming the table as his bulging eyes shot forward further in his head.

"The Wizard plays racquetball with Tony, and called me in his office, trying to coax me into promoting him over Dan Schultz, and I refused to do it. And then, mysteriously, my entire world changes? And, of course, The Wizard's nowhere near here. How many times did I hear you say none of this bullshit is hearsay, while swearing these people are credible? I'm the one who has maintained a clean record in this nut house with four promotions in five years—"

"What you're neglecting to acknowledge is your inappropriate relations with Wendy Darlington. The evidence is overwhelming, and quite honestly, like nothing I've ever seen before." He hesitated and looked up at me. "Your work resume was never in question, and I told you that numerous times."

"No, everything is in question. It's not just my bright future here, it's my entire career that I've worked twenty-one years with three companies, to achieve. And in each of these three companies, I fought to be amongst the most productive, and I was—" I took a deep breath, exhaled, and went on "—But the other two companies operated as functioning sales corporations, with sane people. This place operates like an Asylum, where cancers flourish and liars thrive. People live in the shadows with dirt on corrupt executives and are left there because of it regardless of the fact they haven't hit a fucking goal in ten years." I fell back in the chair struggling to breathe. "Only The Wizard knew what Franc's career plan for me was and he couldn't stand it...now he'll be able to say he didn't know anything about it—this is nauseating."

He continued on as I wiped my eyes. "It was stated by all three of them, that you had trouble taking off Wendy's bra."

I saw his lips moving, but didn't hear a word after that as I lunged for the report. After reading it myself, I inquired in absolute disbelief, "Now it's three of them?" I placed the report down. "How could I have had sexual relations with her if I couldn't get her fucking clothes off?"

It appeared as if he had lost his place, but he took a breath and continued, "It doesn't matter if you had sex with her or not, although the information I have collected strongly suggests that you have. You must understand, however, that it doesn't matter. This was clearly a relationship you carried on with her for well over a year."

I turned abruptly to The Rabbi. "Gary—"

Unfortunately, he appeared to be praying for Scotty to beam him up, and had no idea I even called to him. I turned back to Mr. Lyin.

He wasted no time pointing out the "romantic and close relationship policy," which is what they were sinking me with. The most comical part of this "supposed" policy was that we were more than guilty of that charge without all the fabricated nonsense smeared all over it. And, was it grounds for termination? No. But just as fast as I had that thought, and that this had become so out-of-this-world insane, it got worse.

I flipped to the back of the report and noticed he had manipulated the lies into infractions against several company policies. The infractions ran down two separate pages. Within the minute he started reading the first one. It was the deletion of the files for the incentive in question. In short, as explained in the third meeting, he included this as part of his report. He stated that I instructed my admin to do this, when, in fact, it was her who came to me with it all. That was the main reason she called Mr. Lyin back, while only saying to me it was a concern about Bud Fox's crazy girlfriend. What she did, I now realized, was blatantly lie to cover her own ass because her boyfriend at the time panicked that he had fixed Bud Fox's company laptop while informing her he could permanently delete the files.

I reread it, fading into the chair.

"Guilty of destroying evidence by instructing this lady to delete records related to this incentive trip."

I completely lost it. "It was her boyfriend's idea. There is no way she said that—"

"She did."

I began breathing in and out, furiously, muttering, "This truly is an Asylum—"

He squeezed the pages before quickly releasing them back down onto the table, and then changed the subject back to the relationship. "You are guilty of carrying on a relationship with Wendy Darlington for well over a year and—"

"This is nothing but a set-up." My voice rose with fury, "FUCK YOU!"

There was dead silence, except for the pounding of my aching heart.

He snatched the report off the table clearing his throat while mustering a stern voice. "In doing so, you also violated the company's discloser policy for romantic relationships."

My head slumped. "During all the hours of grilling me on her, why didn't you ever bring that policy up?"

He sat silently only staring down at the report.

I hit the table with the palm of my hands as he jumped backwards in his chair and I seethed, "You knew we didn't sign that bullshit and now my career is over because of it!"

I began to fade to black as Mr. Lyin said, "Your career is not over."

He was wrong, yet again. I reached out to Mr. Lyin in May of 2011 with proof. All I will say for this book is that he verified everything I informed him of, which I have neatly stored away, and pleaded me to allow him the opportunity to "make it right." What he seemed to be doing was buying time. He left the company eighteen days later.

At this moment though I literally went bye-bye for a few seconds before realizing I had to hold it together. If not, they would've thrown me off the fucking roof and then released a statement saying I slipped on a banana peel, flew off the side of the building, and died. So thankfully, I was gifted a jolt of adrenaline as he continued in a frenzied effort to wrap it up.

I turned to The Rabbi in silence with only dark thoughts. The absurdity of it all caused him to stand in utter shock as Mr. Lyin said, "In conclusion, you and Wendy Darlington have never signed the company relationship waiver."

I struggled to swallow and take a breath.

The room felt as it were closing in.

I blinked at The Rabbi, who displayed a look on his face I couldn't recall seeing.

His eyes darted from one side of the room to the other as he swallowed hard. "Larry, please…let's go…" He took steps toward me. "Please…" He looked frantically worried.

I leaned over the table, waved the termination report threateningly at Mr. Lyin, and said, "I will not be a happy haunt to the walls of *The Asylum*. That I promise you."

***

By five o'clock on December 8th, 2010, my stellar career was dead.

At eleven o'clock, Mama Bear sent Marie a message on Facebook: "I know you unfriended me. I know you felt you had to. I'm sorry for everything that has happened. Larry was so good to me. I'm so sorry for what has happened. I know it doesn't help. But I don't know what else to say."

And with that, *The Show* ended…exit, stage right…curtain lowered to a dark night with no sign of the second star to the right…

About the Author

After many early successes as a salesman, Lawrence H. Sola moved on to the wine industry in 1994. In 2009, he achieved the 'bright futures' label before being relocated to run a new sales division in Tampa, which inspired his novel, *The Show*. His prior publications include *Jeremy's Adventures: Miracle on Main Street*, a story about a boy who inspires a town to never give up on their dreams.

Purchase other Black Rose Writing titles at and use promo code PRINT to receive a 20% discount.

CPSIA information can be obtained at www.ICGtesting.com
Printed in the USA
BVOW08s0144180716

455925BV00001B/25/P